WHERE HAVE ALL THE BOYS GONE?

Jenny Colgan was born in 1972 in Ayrshire. After Edinburgh University, she worked for six years in the health service, moonlighting as a cartoonist and stand-up comic. She is the author of five previous bestselling novels: *Amanda's Wedding*, *Talking to Addison*, *Looking for Andrew McCarthy*, *Working Wonders* and *Do You Remember the First Time?* Jenny Colgan lives in London. For more information, visit her website at www.jennycolgan.com.

For automatic updates on Jenny Colgan, visit HarperCollins.co.uk and register for AuthorTracker.

Acclaim for *Do You Remember the First Time?*:

'Funny stuff.' *Heat*

'Snappy and wickedly entertaining.' *You*

'Full of laughs and lipgloss – brilliant.' *Company*

***Working Wonders*:**

'Funny, magical and moving, this is a rewarding read.' *Time Out*

'We laughed a lot.' *Heat*

'A delicious comedy. Will melt even the hardest of hearts.' *Red*

'Colgan's witty book perfectly captures the frustrations and petty vexations of office life.' *She*

'Hugely entertaining and very funny.' *Cosmopolitan*

'A funny, clever page-turner.' *Closer*

'Fans of *The Office* will love this witty tale.' *Woman's Own*

'A quirky tale of love, work and the meaning of life.' *Company*

'If you think David Brent causes mayhem in *The Office* wait till you see what town-planner Arthur and his team get up to in Jenny Colgan's comic romp.' *In Style*

***Looking for Andrew McCarthy*:**

'Colgan is on top form in this, her latest outrageous romp.' *Cosmopolitan*

'Jenny Colgan is one of the leaders of the pack and this, her third novel, will delight her legions of admirers. Fast-paced, funny, poignant and well-observed it reads as a pastiche of the movies she loved . . . If a time capsule were buried to capture the world at the turn of the 21st century, this would be a candidate for inclusion: her sense of time and place are that authentic.' *Daily Mail*

'*Looking for Andrew McCarthy* will strike a chord with anyone who did their growing up in the 80s. Wonderful, warm and resonant for anyone who ever wondered what happened to teenage dreams.' *Hello*

'*That's Life* meets *This Life*, with *Once in a Lifetime* thrown in, all talking heads, witty one-liners and angst-ridden relationships . . . Did I like this book? Well, d'uh! Do hedgehogs have quills? A pure belter of a novel.' *Glasgow Herald*

'Colgan's enjoyable new bestseller investigates the notion that having it all can sometimes mean having precisely nothing at all.'
Marie Claire

'Colgan's *Looking for Andrew McCarthy* is sharp, well-observed and hilarious.' *New Statesman*

'Colgan's got an ear for sarky dialogue and a humour that gives her more options . . . retro-irony, perfect for a conscientious objector's beach holiday.' *ID*

'Jenny Colgan delivers the goods with her new novel . . . absolutely brilliant! What really sets Jenny apart from most of her contemporaries is this: she is very, very funny, so much so that this book had me laughing out loud.' *Express*

'There's razor-sharp wit to this tale of romantic confusion.'
Cosmopolitan

***Amanda's Wedding*:**

'*Amanda's Wedding* is a scream.' *Elle*

'*Four Weddings and a Funeral* meets *Friends*.' *Tatler*

'Compulsively comical.' *Cosmopolitan*

'Funny and insightful.' *Mail on Sunday*

By the same author

Amanda's Wedding
Talking to Addison
Looking for Andrew McCarthy
Working Wonders
Do You Remember the First Time?

JENNY COLGAN

Where Have All the Boys Gone?

HarperCollins*Publishers*

This novel is entirely a work of fiction.
The names, characters and incidents portrayed in it are the work of the author's imagination. Any resemblance to actual persons, living or dead, events or localities is entirely coincidental.

HarperCollins*Publishers*
77–85 Fulham Palace Road,
Hammersmith, London W6 8JB

www.harpercollins.co.uk

This special overseas edition 2005
2

A catalogue record for this book is available from the British Library

ISBN 0 00 715900 5

Set in Sabon by Palimpsest Book Production Limited, Polmont, Stirlingshire

Printed and bound in Great Britain by Clays Ltd, St Ives plc

Acknowledgements

Thanks to Ali Gunn, Lynne Drew, Maxine Hitchcock, Fiona McIntosh, Amanda Ridout, Jane Harris, Martin Palmer, Lee Motley, Kelly Edgson-Wright and all at HarperCollins and Curtis Brown, plus Nick Marston, Tally Gardiner, Nick Sayers, Rachel Hore, Deborah Schneider.

Also: Mark Blakemore, PGA Professional (www.pgaprofessional.com); Wesley Moody; Sandra, Shappi, Susan, Karen, Katrina, Mueller, Roni, Dan, Mum & Dad, Robin, Dominic & Bron, Marina and Tom Holland for the Scrabble.

Special thanks to the EZcrew, who make me feel very lucky to be Jenny from the block – particularly Lisa, Chris, Maddie & Victoria for the 20–21st Feb.

For my beloved boys, Mr and Baby B.

Chapter One

There is a very small envelope of seduction time available between the stages 'just pissed enough' and 'disastrously over-pissed', and suddenly, Katie wasn't sure she was going to make it.

This man sitting in front of her wore little heels on his shoes, she remembered, swaying slightly. She'd noticed under the chippy, awkwardly tiny bar table in this stupid new bar called Square Root. OK, he was her first date in four months, and she had her best bra on, but still, she really ought to have paid more attention to the shoes . . . it was just, it had been a difficult week.

It had started on Sunday. Louise was still on her international bang-athon, leaving her and Olivia, who came around on Sundays to avoid getting inky fingerprints on her pristine white sofa, studiously reading the papers, watching *EastEnders* and ignoring the obvious sounds of sexual intercourse coming from the spare bedroom.

'How come Kat Slater is really fat and covered in slap and millions of men are in love with her?' Katie had asked.

There was a particularly vigorous grunting noise.

'Umm,' Olivia squeezed her eyes shut. 'For the same reason everyone's in love with Phil even though he looks like a barnyard animal. Drugs.'

'OK,' said Katie loudly, 'I UNDERSTAND.'

There was an endless tense moment next door as everything went quiet. The two girls looked at one another. There was a pause. Then the ritual banging started again.

'Jesus,' said Olivia. She looked at Katie. 'Couldn't you have bought a bigger flat?'

'In North London?' Katie nodded. 'Sure! I should have gone for the rooftop swimming pool. And the maid's quarters. I'm a complete idiot.'

'I'm just saying.' Olivia believed in karma and therefore probably did think having a tiny flat and a huge mortgage in Kentish Town was Katie's fault.

Katie loudly turned the page.

'Bloody hell!' she exploded.

'What? New revolutionary soundproofing spray just invented?'

'No.'

'New laws make it easier to expel noisy tenants?'

'No.'

'Sex makes you put on more weight than Atkins' diet?'

'Look,' said Katie, pointing at the paper.

Olivia squinted at it upside down.

'"Women Going Men Crazy,"' she read out loud. 'You really have to stop buying these women-hating papers.'

They both read the article rolling their eyes. It asserted that their generation of women was a clutch of uncontrollable pissed-up hose-monsters on the loose, terrorising the five nice remaining men in the world. The problem was, from the sounds next door, it was tricky to disagree.

'It says here that there're no men left and we're all going barking. Well, that would explain a lot,' said Olivia.

'If that's true, why is it him in there who's doing the barking?'

Suddenly there was a high-pitched wailing sound.

The two girls looked at each other.

'I'd start a round of applause,' said Olivia, 'if I'd heard even the tiniest little peep out of Lou.'

'Also, we want to pretend absolutely nothing just happened,' said Katie, turning back to her paper. 'It says we're all drunken slut-buckets.'

'Slut-buckets? Really?' said Olivia.

'Honestly, I haven't yet thought up a better way to cope with the modern London man,' said Katie sadly.

The door opened down the corridor, and the paper-thin walls shook slightly. The room they were in, Katie's living room, had a band of old kitchen on the far side. The estate agent had assured her this would make it wonderful for entertaining. In fact, it merely made sure that Katie never ever cooked fish.

Louise tiptoed in, ostentatiously yawning. She had great legs, which she ignored, and a big nose, which she fixated on.

'Ooh, just been asleep . . . thought I'd have a bit of a lie-in . . . tea . . . I think . . .'

The other two girls looked at her and waited.

'Sleepy sleepy sleepy . . .' continued Louise, trying to turn on the kettle in an overtly surreptitious manner.

'I heard about this girl once,' said Olivia. 'She told terrible lies and then one day she got run over by a car because she was such a terrible liar. Karma.'

'Yes. Her name was Chlamydia,' said Katie sternly. 'Chlamydia Liar.'

Louise rolled her eyes.

'OK. OK. I met someone.'

'Someone? Or something?'

She shot the two girls a look.

'I just had sex with a man. Which is more than you two have done for months.'

'I don't think I've seen a man for months,' said Olivia. 'What are they like?'

Louise shrugged.

'Umm . . . they have less hair than us in some bits. And more in other bits.'

'Like monkeys,' added Katie helpfully.

'What else?' Olivia was handling the kettle now, so it was filthy organic green tea in the offing.

'Umm, they have these kind of lever thingies,' said Louise.

'What do they do?' asked Katie.

'They go up and down,' said Louise, stirring in three sugars whilst Olivia gave her a disapproving look.

'The way they work is, in Soho, other men have a hole shaped like the lever,' said Olivia. 'The two bits fit together.'

Katie took her horrid tea and went back to the sitting-room area of the room.

'Ahh,' she said. 'Will we ever get to meet one of these remarkable specimens?'

Louise looked guilty.

'Uh, maybe not this one,' she said.

In Square Root, Terence – that was his name – was explaining how he'd dicked someone over at work in revenge for beating him on a deal. This was the date Katie had been looking forward to for weeks. She'd come to view it as the end of an intolerable dry spell, the way a prisoner views their parole date.

She took another sip of wine, feeling groggy. One shouldn't really place such high expectations on things.

Why was Terence wearing a Burberry cap that also said Von Dutch on the front? And what was underneath it?

'Fing is,' said Terence conclusively, 'I'm all for equal opportunities, and I don't care if it was a bird – she still had it coming to her.'

Then, on Tuesday morning, she'd run into Olivia on the Tube. It was an unseasonably hot day for early in the year, and everyone in the rush hour was miserable in woollies and heavy jackets. Katie was a master of the Tube; avoiding eye contact, walking past buskers and unfolding her *Metro* with a hearty flourish. She may not like London all the time, she often pondered, but by God, she *belonged*.

Olivia was Katie's boss and, behind the scenes, secret friend. It was a bit like having an office romance, with the result that at work she was a lot harder on Katie than she would have been otherwise. At least, that was Katie's hypothesis.

'I wouldn't have minded,' said Katie, swinging off the filthy Tube holds and wondering as usual if anyone ever washed them. They were squeezed together in a carriage full of women, jolting their way into Soho where they worked. 'But I did see him. He was even worse than he sounded.'

Olivia rolled her eyes. 'How could he not be? She practically dug a tunnel to get him out of there. Bald fat midget?'

'Fat beardy twat face.'

Katie shook her head. Poor old Louise had never been the same since Max left.

'Well, we were watching *EastEnders*. A world where people fancy Shane Ritchie is obviously a place where things have gone very very wrong for women.'

They looked around the carriage. The scent of perfume

was strong in the air. An elegant woman – one of those types that can pull off casually draped scarves – was skilfully applying lipstick despite the motion of the rickety old train. Three others stood buried in women's magazines and copies of *Metro*; a couple were hidden behind novels. On the seats were three men buried in newspapers, ferociously showing how post-feminist they were by not giving up their seats. A mixed group of backpackers stood at the end, but they existed in the parallel universe of travellers; Kiwis and Australians and South Africans and Poles and cheap nights in special bars and internet cafés and their own magazines. But the vast majority of the carriage was female. Dozens of them. Katie squinted. Had it always been like this? Was she only just noticing?

Olivia was rudely reading someone's paper over their shoulder. She nudged Katie suddenly.

'Look at that.'

'No! It's rude!'

The woman whose paper it was turned around and Katie got a dirty look. She felt hard done by and narrowed her eyes back. Had she been this aggressive before she moved to London?

'Look,' whispered Olivia this time, scarcely quieter.

Katie didn't get it, the paper was full of its usual rubbish. Olivia was trying to indicate a corner with her eyes, like someone in a coma. Eventually, with lots of grumpy snuffling from the woman to indicate that, though not the type to instigate physical violence, she certainly did not approve of the practice of newspaper stealing, even a free newspaper, and if she could move in the packed sardine tin she would, thank you, Katie saw it.

'Final census results for London' said the headline. 'According to the 2001 census, women outnumber men in the capital by 180,000.'

Olivia was wiggling her eyebrows madly. 'See?'

'See what?'

'What the papers are saying is *true*.'

'What do you mean?'

'Well, what do we say every time we walk into a bar?'

'It smells bad in here?'

'No.'

'We're getting too old for this?'

Olivia rolled her eyes. 'OK, besides that.'

'Where have all the men gone?'

'Bingo.'

'Well, that –' the woman holding the paper was no longer sniffing, but listening to them intently '– that's our proof. We're the L.O.S.T. generation of women.'

'The what?'

'London-On our Own-Single-Twentysomethings.'

'That doesn't sound so bad,' said Olivia.

'It's bad! It's bad! It says so in the paper.'

'Stop worrying about it! What kind of a feminist are you?'

'One that wants the right to decide if I want a bloke or not.'

'OK,' said Olivia. 'And . . . do you?'

'YES!' said Katie. 'And men can sense it. That's why I never meet any. I give off strange vibes.'

'Ssh now,' said Olivia.

'OK,' said Katie. They travelled on in silence for a while.

'You know Louise's fat beardy twat face didn't even call,' she said finally.

Olivia rolled her eyes. 'Probably staying in and washing his hairs.'

'There are NO MEN,' sighed Katie for what felt like the nine millionth time.

'Yeah,' said a voice near their ankles. They both looked down. An extremely short, sandy-haired man with a nose like a sun-dried tomato was addressing them both.

'What?' said Olivia, loftily.

'Yeah,' he said. 'You mean, there's no tall rich men.'

'No, we don't,' said Katie. 'Do we?'

'You're wearing a wedding ring,' said Olivia suspiciously.

'She's gorgeous,' said the little chap. 'And twenty-four.' He looked at them pointedly.

The woman who'd been holding the paper looked down too.

'You are right you know,' she said to the girls, her initial frostiness thawing. 'The paper says so. But I knew it anyway. Statistically, there are no men.'

An obviously gay man standing next to her raised an eyebrow and flared just one of his nostrils.

'You think that,' he said.

All three women rolled their eyes.

Another woman leaned over. This was unheard of in the Tube in rush hour; an actual conversation. This woman was tall, skinny and wearing lime green fishnets and what looked like a bin bag.

'I work in fashion,' she said.

'No kidding,' said Olivia.

'No men,' said the fashion woman.

'Publishing,' said the woman with the newspaper. 'No men.'

'Try being a nanny!' came a squeaky Scandinavian voice from the back. 'Only married creeps there!'

The little man looked smug and grabbed Katie's skirt.

'I've banged them all,' he whispered.

* * *

Katie hadn't minded so much at the time – after all, she had a date, the date she was now in the middle of. Terence had now embarked on a story about a fantastic deal he had made at work that had made everybody else look like idiots, except for him. This, it came to her in a moment of clarity, was why she was getting drunk. And she should leave quickly, just in case she tipped over the edge and suddenly started finding him inexplicably attractive.

She'd asked around the office, pretending it was research. Working in PR, as Katie and Olivia both did, you could pretend a lot of things were research.

'Well, what do you think?' she'd asked Miko in the office, who was trying to be sympathetic and maintain her perfect inch-long fingernails at the same time. 'Are there really no men?'

'Yeah,' said Miko lazily, peeling off a strip of old polish. Katie couldn't bear it when she did this. Katie herself was doing a wrinkle check in the cosmetic mirror Miko kept on her desk. She felt troubled.

'I mean,' said Miko, 'they're just spoilt for choice, aren't they?'

Katie thought about this for a second. 'You think . . . what, men are just too nonchalant with all the women around now?'

Miko shrugged. 'Well, look.' She indicated the trendy sloped glass wall which overlooked the lobby of their Covent Garden building. Katie looked down. It always made her feel slightly sick, as if she were going to fall in.

'Girl girl girl,' intoned Miko as people walked through the door. 'Fat bloke. Girl girl girl. Hairy-wristed bloke shagging that girl there. Married too. Girl girl girl.'

Katie sat back. 'So, what – you're saying the men all have two women each and there's still lots of girls left over?'

She thought back over the men working in their office. There were two. Fat Paul who did the books and smelled of egg sandwiches, of which he consumed copious amounts, leaving a trail of watercress wherever he went, and a small gremlin in the IT department who veered away from direct sunlight. Both had unexpectedly attractive wives who turned up stoically at the Christmas party knowing everyone was looking at them thinking, 'Really? Is he fantastic in bed?'

'Hi Lucca,' shouted Miko to the gorgeous, tawny-coloured Italian girl passing her desk, who worked in the marketing department. 'How did your blind date go?'

Lucca swung her heavy beige-blonde hair in a circle. 'I know why you call it "blind date" now,' she hissed.

Miko shrugged. 'Why?'

'Because I want to stab my eyes out with fork! Tell me, why does he think I am interested he meets Robert Kilroy-Silk?'

Katie and Miko both shrugged.

'Why he want tell me – before drink before dinner even that he is not ready for long-term relationship?'

'Would we be better off with Italian boys?' asked Katie sympathetically.

'No! Only if you be their mother always.'

Lucca made a wild emphatic gesture that indicated a general wrath towards the male species altogether and headed off to dish out more abuse to the coffee machine.

'Lucca's much more beautiful than me,' mused Katie sadly.

'Yes, she is,' said Miko.

'But still gets dickheads.'

'Who do you get then?' asked Miko.

* * *

Terence, clearly. He'd seemed all right when they'd met at that barbecue. OK, there'd been lots of other people there, and quite a lot of beer, but now . . . As if doing the opposite of reading her mind, Terence confidently placed a podgy hand on her knee. Inside, Katie recoiled.

'I just want you to know,' he said, boozily breathing in her face. 'I'm just in this for a bit of fun, yeah? Nothing too serious.'

Katie hadn't liked the way the conversation with Miko was going.

Really, what was wrong with her? True, Katie Watson would never win any international modelling competitions. She liked to watch documentaries where hatchet-faced women run up to lanky adolescent girls in the street, whisking them off to new modelling worlds of fun and rock stars in Milan and Tokyo, but she never kidded herself that was *her* destiny. Olivia said once this had happened to her, but although she certainly was lanky, Katie thought she might have been a) telling a fib (not out of character for Olivia), or b) been a victim of a misunderstanding concerning teenage prostitution.

Katie was, well, cute, she supposed. 'You're a cutie,' her ex-boyfriends had said. None of them had ever said, 'Katherine Watson, you are the most staggeringly beautiful thing I have ever seen in my life. I would kill for you. I would lie down and die for you. Your muddy-coloured eyes sparkle like moonbeams; your soft lips, though not in the Angelina Jolie class, are like peaches. Your wide hips are life in my hands and your slightly short stature I consider nothing but a delight.'

Still, it made her look younger than she was, that was something about having a pixie face and a pointed chin. Although she was definitely growing out of the age where she could wear pigtails to accentuate trying to be cute, which she supposed had benefits in no longer having men ask her how long her stockings were.

OK, on a level of perfectly scientific analysis, she was better looking than about sixty-five per cent of the people she had been to school with and, according to Friends Reunited, every single one of them now had kids. All of them. Even Magda with the Sellotape on her glasses and you couldn't tell if she was looking at you or not. Even Mary Tracey Frances McGoolie, who gave off BO like a blowtorch. And, up until now, Katie hadn't had a date for four months.

Four months, entirely chap-free. And if she was being strictly honest . . . she doodled about while her computer warmed up, still staring into the lobby . . . if she was going to be utterly honest, Clive hadn't really been the stuff of her dreams. In fact, if she was honest she'd only dated him to break her *previous* three-month date-free desert. That was why she hadn't minded so much that he had a skin condition behind his ears and scratched it all over his caesar salad.

Katie quickly sniffed under her armpits. OK, so it wasn't that.

'What are you doing?' asked Miko.

'Nothing!' said Katie. 'Checking my email.'

Miko looked under her own armpit.

'Have you got something new from IT they haven't told the rest of us about?'

'No.' Katie sighed. 'What's wrong with me Miko?'

Miko gave her a narrow look. 'Nothing,' she said.

'That sounded like hmm hmm BUT,' said Katie. 'You know, as in nothing . . . BUT; or I'm single . . . BUT.'

'But look at the facts,' said Miko.

'Ahh,' said Katie.

'We're in the middle of a crisis.'

'I wish people would stop saying that. What crisis?'

'The no-men crisis, you idiot.'

'Is that a real crisis?'

For the first time Katie noticed that Miko wore false eyelashes to go with her false nails. Was anything about her real? Was that Katie's problem – *too* real?

Miko stared at her.

'What?' asked Katie.

'You mean you really don't know there's a crisis?'

Miko patiently indicated the big glass lobby wall again. 'Girl. Girl. Baldie. Girl. Girl. Don't you get it?'

'There are no men?'

'Durr.'

'But that's just something people say. We say it every day.'

'Because it's true,' said Miko. 'Why do you think I bought these tits?'

'Maybe I should buy some tits,' said Katie absent-mindedly in the Square Root, hiccuping for good measure.

Terence's little toad eyes lit up. 'I think you look gorgeous,' he said hopefully. Katie couldn't believe she'd just said that out loud and, taking it as her own final warning, stood up. If his job was as brilliant as he'd been claiming for the last three hours, perhaps he wouldn't mind getting the drinks. She stumbled to the ladies.

On Tuesday night the girls had met up in the wine bar. All around them were lots of other girls having girls' nights out. A lot of white wine was being slugged. Shoes and voices were high. The only man in sight was the waiter.

'Oh God,' said Louise. 'Keep me out of sight of the waiter.'

'That waiter is the biggest slag in NW11,' said Olivia loudly. 'Oh. Sorry Louise.'

Louise was pink. 'I'd had too much white wine. They serve it in those enormous glasses.'

'And then a dog ate your homework,' said Katie. Really, she wanted to talk about work but it was really difficult with Olivia there. Recently, she'd felt as if, on some level, there was a tiny teeny-weeny possibility that doing PR for new food and drink products was . . . perhaps just the slightest bit . . . pointless? Not that there was necessarily anything wrong with anchovy pretzels and pink cola, it's just, that sometimes – like every morning on the Tube – she wished maybe she were doing something a little more useful.

'What was he like?' said Olivia to Louise, eyeing the dark-haired waiter preening himself in the bar mirror and deftly jamming two glasses down in the glass washer as if it were an incredibly cool thing to be doing.

'Perfunctory,' said Louise uncomfortably. 'He gave me the impression that, working here, it's part of his job description.'

'Ladies.'

He had materialised at their elbow. Louise was suddenly peering for something so deeply in her fake Birkin she looked like a horse with a feedbag.

'What's that thing we're meant to get because we're too cool for chardonnay now?' asked Olivia.

'Pinot Grigio,' said Katie. 'Tastes the same, more expensive.'

'Ah, the plastic Prada bag school of ordering,' said Olivia. 'One of those please.'

'Of course,' said the waiter. 'You all look very nice tonight.'

'Thank you,' said Louise from the nose up. 'Again.'

The waiter gave her a quizzical look which showed absolutely no signs of recognition whatsoever, and scooted off.

'Maybe you should rethink that whole "having unbelievably casual sex" thing,' said Olivia.

Louise grimaced. 'I'm getting over Max, OK, and having a great time. Really, really great. Plus, as I keep telling you, it's the law of averages. If there's only one perfect person out there for you, you've just got to get cracking. And never look back.'

'What if the one perfect person out there for you is a pig?' said Olivia dreamily. 'Or married to Jennifer Aniston?'

'What if they live in Laos?' said Louise. 'That's what bothers me. Or if they speak Tulag. Did you know that's the hardest language on earth to learn?'

The other girls stared at her as the waiter popped out the cork from the bottle with practised ease and poured them large glasses.

Louise looked sulky as all around them the women squawked and chattered, their slim legs and expensive shoes glinting in the flattering soft light reflecting off the beige leather chairs. Katie looked at Louise and worried about her. And herself.

'Goodnight Terence,' said Katie when she got back from the loo. She tried to be as nice as possible.

'£60!' Terence was saying. 'For this shit! Jesus!'

'Would you like me to go halves?' she asked.

He shrugged. 'If you like.'

Crossly, Katie put down half the money, noticing Terence counted out his share and didn't leave a tip.

She felt infinitely more sober once she hit the open air. She liked walking in the city at night. People and couples lurched, shouted or shuffled along, no one paying her the blindest bit of notice.

The familiar sounds of sirens and late-night misadventures echoed as she cut down past the Opera House, her heels clattering on the cobbles, leaving the heavy traffic behind her. A chap was weaving slightly by the side of the road, and she subconsciously hurried up a little bit.

''Ello darlin',' he shouted after her. 'You look nice.'

Probably only compared to him, a very drunk man attempting to take a piss on the street, but still, she appreciated the gesture.

She was wondering how low she could possibly plummet on her male-attention appreciation charts, when suddenly, out of nowhere the man was right in front of her. She jumped six feet in the air.

'Fuck!' she said. 'You gave me a fright.'

Her heart started to pound, hard, when she realised it wasn't the same man after all. She couldn't work out who this person was or how he had landed in front of her, but late on a Thursday night on a deserted street, it didn't feel good . . . Her eyes whipped around to the side, but the genial drunkard was gone.

'Ah,' said a soft voice with a slight accent. 'Yes. That can be what happens.'

He was tall and, with her heart banging furiously, Katie saw that he was dressed all in black, with a hat pulled down over his eyes. He was standing directly in front of the streetlight and she couldn't make out his face. Oh shit oh shit oh shit. This was not good. Man in black on deserted street – either there was Milk Tray involved or this was definitely the opposite of good. Her eyes flicked to the side to see where she could run to and she cursed her ridiculous heels.

'No,' warned the voice. 'Running. Don't do it. I have

a knife. Or a gun. Or something really bad. And you look like a nice person.'

Katie stared at him, frightened beyond belief.

'I – I am a nice person,' she said, her voice two octaves higher than normal. 'Can you let me go?'

'I can always tell,' said the man. 'I only go for nice people.'

Oh fuck oh fuck. She was going to get raped or killed or kidnapped or tortured. The worst, the most awful thing was happening. Oh God. She was in the middle of one of the most crowded cities in the world. Where the hell were all the people? Oh no. She was going to be left for dead in an alley. She wondered how they'd describe her in the papers.

'Show me your phone,' said the man gruffly. He took her by the arm – Katie flinched and started shaking like a foal – and led her to the dark side of the road. They could have been a couple talking.

Her phone. Of course. If she were an actress in *24* she would have thought to have done something useful with that. But she knew from her trembling fingers she'd have been incapable of pressing the tiny keys as she drew it out of her bag.

'This is a shit phone,' said the man, staring at the cheap little black handset.

'Yeah,' said Katie. Everyone kept telling her it was a shit phone. Maybe that would save her life – or make him kill her out of sheer disgust at her poor taste.

The man dropped it on the ground and crushed it under his boot. 'You should be more stylish,' he said. 'You should have a better phone.'

He carefully took her bag from her and started rummaging inside.

'And look at this mess. What a mess. How can you

ever find anything in here? It's full of tissues and lipsticks.'

'It's to deter muggers,' said Katie. She still couldn't get a look at his face, but for a murderous rapist, he didn't seem very interested in her. In fact, he was looking at her lipstick with more interest.

'You have a boyfriend?'

'*What?*'

'Yes, I think you have no boyfriend. You should ditch the orange lipstick. Orange, not good for you. Maybe why you have no boyfriend.'

'Are you going to make me up like your dead mother and rape me to death?' asked Katie in a panic.

It was dark, but she could catch the incredulous glint in his eye.

'No!' he laughed. 'I'm going to take,' he emptied out the coin section. 'Twenty-four pounds and nineteen pence. And these cards, for about half an hour. Don't worry. They'll give you the money back, so it'll be fine. Except for the twenty-four quid. Sorry about that.'

'Don't apologise,' said Katie, furious. 'Don't do it!'

'Yes,' said the man. 'No. I'm going to do it.'

He handed her back the bag.

'That's a messy bag. You should have a stylish bag. Don't you have anyone to look after you?'

'Shut up!'

'Nice girl like you. Should have a nice man to look after you. Buy you nice bags.'

He looked regretful. 'Well. Thanks. Have a safe trip home. Have you got a travel card?'

'Yes.'

'Good. OK. Be safe. Bye!'

Katie turned around to stare at him as he dived off, quick as a cat. Her heart couldn't quite take in what had happened and kept whumping away, and she suddenly found it difficult to get her breath. She leaned against the wall.

'Fuck,' she heaved.

The drunk man wobbled over.

'Hello darlin'!'

'Where the fuck were you?' she shrieked at him. 'I could have been killed!'

He straightened up and managed to focus for a second.

'Sorry love,' he slurred. 'I've already got a girlfriend.'

And he wobbled off.

'Don't worry love,' said the policeman.

Louise, who she'd called in from home, was hanging about worriedly.

'I mean, he didn't, like, touch you up or nothing, did he?'

Katie looked at him hard. Was this the new, softer, in-touch policing she kept hearing so much about?

'No,' she said calmly. She was feeling a lot less shaken up now than when she'd stumbled into the police station at Covent Garden. In fact, after a couple of cups of tea, she was actually feeling strangely embarrassed about the whole thing, as if she shouldn't have bothered troubling anyone for something as clearly unimportant as a non-rape/murder-related mugging. Outside a car alarm was blaring away, but nobody was paying it the least attention.

'He just jumped me, took all my stuff and scared me half to death.'

'Yeah,' said the policeman, as if he'd just been told one of his shoelaces was untied. 'That happens.'

'Go find him and put him in prison,' said Katie. 'Now, please.'

The policeman looked down at the blank sheet of paper

on his desk. 'It's just, we're not doing too well with the witness description.'

'Black hat pulled down over his face. Foreign accent.'

'Oh, him,' said the policeman. 'He shouldn't be any trouble at all.'

'Do you work late?' said Louise, batting her eyelashes.

'Louise, would you kindly shut it?' said Katie.

Louise shrugged. 'Sure, sure, just . . .'

'I work shifts,' said the policeman, bluntly appraising her. 'Often up late, know what I mean?'

Katie quickly spotted the wedding ring and raised her eyebrows.

'Do you . . . come and go in the night?' said Louise lasciviously.

'Actually, now I come to think about it, I hit my head on the pavement and now have concussion,' said Katie crossly.

'Depends if it's an emergency,' said the policeman over her head. 'You know . . . if you really really need me.'

Katie stood up from the dingy grey plastic chair. 'I don't suppose there's any chance of getting a lift home in a police car while it's going "nee naw nee naw" is there?'

'Maybe,' said the policeman, still looking at Louise. Louise coloured.

'I'll just take the form for my insurance, thanks.' Katie snatched the banda sheet away from him.

'There's no need to be like that,' he said. 'You've just described something that happens a thousand times a day in the West End and you've given us nothing to go on. We're really sorry.'

Katie harrumphed. 'Well, it shouldn't happen at all. Anything could have happened.'

'Yes, trust me, you're not the type. Can I offer you some victim support?'

'I'm not the type???'

'Shh,' said Louise. 'He probably just meant you don't look like a soft target. That's good, you know. You look like a proper Londoner, not a rube.' Louise brushed down her micromini thoughtfully.

Katie grimaced. 'I don't think that at all. I think I'm . . . I think I'm getting tired of this stupid city, you know.'

'Shh,' said Louise again. 'You don't mean that. You love London.'

'I thought I did,' said Katie. There was a car alarm going off here too, but she didn't think it was the same one. She wandered over to where Louise was making instant coffee from a tiny fun-sized jar. That was one of the disadvantages of her new flatmate; she wasn't quite the coffee purist Katie had learned to be – another important London skill. She picked up the jar.

'How on earth could this jar of coffee cost £2.39? It's scaled for a family of mice.'

'It was late,' said Louise. 'It was all I could get from the corner shop.'

Katie looked at the massive patch of damp over the kitchen wall. 'You know, I can't fix that patch of damp because every ten minutes someone new moves in next door and they won't share the cost so nobody knows what to do.'

'And you're lazy and disorganised,' said Louise. 'What's your point?'

'I don't know . . . I think maybe London is driving me nuts.'

'Just because of one lousy mugger? And one crappy

date? What about all the fantastic museums and parks we never go to?'

'OK, but that was just tonight. But London . . . it's so full of show-offs and loudmouths.'

'But we like those kinds of people.'

'I know – maybe that's the problem,' said Katie. She stared at the damp patch and tried again. 'It's just . . . everyone always wants to know what your job is. Why is that?'

'Because when you meet a lot of new people, you have to ask them something?' said Louise. 'If you live in a small village you don't need to say anything at all. Everybody already knows how overdue your library books are and how much money you make and whether or not your husband's having an affair with the goat from the next village. And whether so and so's daughter cheeked Mr Beadle at the bus stop. And who threw away the advertising leaflets in the big hedge.'

'You really hated Hertfordshire, didn't you Lou?' said Katie sympathetically, patting her knee.

'Well, London is what it is. I mean, so there's the rain and the buses and the clubs you can't get into and the Congestion Charge and the snotty shops and the way everything is always fifteen miles away and takes for ever and the way no one from the north, south-east or west ever sees anyone from anywhere except those places and despises the people that come from anywhere else. It's obsessed with trainers, cocktails, guest lists and whatever the fucking *Evening Standard* tells them to be obsessed with.'

'That's not sounding so good,' said Katie.

'But it's all we've got,' finished Louise. 'Don't you see? We don't have a huge amount of choice. It's this, or having people discuss everything you buy in the Spar.'

'The what?'

'The Spar,' Louise pouted. 'If you have no shop, you're a hamlet. If you have a Spar, you're a village. If you have a Fairfields, you're a town. Anyway, that's not the point . . .'

'And if you have a cathedral, you're a city! So that's how it works,' said Katie. 'I never knew that.'

'Well,' Louise pouted again.

'There's always the suburbs,' offered Katie.

'Do I look like I enjoy having my hair done and committing adultery?' sniffed Louise.

'Yes,' said Katie.

'That's not the point. The point is, that the city is *cool.*'

'Why?'

'Because it's urban, and hip, and . . . there's hip things going on, and . . .'

Katie sipped her coffee carefully. 'When's the last time you bought *Time Out*?'

'What? Why?'

'Just asking.'

'When's the last time I bought *Time Out*?' Louise looked as if she were trying to remember.

'You're scared of *Time Out*,' said Katie.

'I am not.'

'You are. You're scared of it. I remember. You moved here, read it for six months, never ever did any of the cool things it suggested that you do. Now you're scared of it because it reminds you that there's lots of things happening and all we ever do is go to work, go to the wine bar, and look for men.'

'So, what do you want? A pair of flashy wellies? Some chickens?'

'I don't know,' said Katie. 'But I do know I want a change.'

* * *

A week later, they were at a new, trendier, cocktail bar. Olivia and Louise were staring grumpily into their espresso martinis. Katie's head was hidden behind a paper.

'Press officer required for a children's hospital,' she read. 'See! I could do some good in the world.'

'Are you thinking about hot doctors?' asked Louise.

'With cool caring hands and a lovely bedside manner? No,' said Katie quickly.

'Make sure you ask them about the cool caring hands bit at the interview – there's a lot of girl doctors these days.'

Katie turned the page and sighed.

'Put the paper down,' said Olivia. 'You're not leaving, and that's the end of it. I need you. We've got the carbohydrate-free chip coming up. It tastes like shit, but the magic is, it *looks* like a chip.'

'Plus, we've got lots to do. You know, there's that new dating thing on at Vinopolis,' Louise said. 'We could go to that. You eat your dinner in the dark, and get to know people without seeing them.'

'You can tell if people are fat just from the way they sound,' said Olivia.

'No you can't!'

'Yes you can! And if they're drippy and wet.'

'You are an evil, prejudiced woman.'

'Hey, look at this,' said Katie.

She showed them the advert.

> Can you see the wood for the trees? Fairlish Forestry Commission is looking for a press officer with at least three years' experience in a related field. Knowledge of local wildlife/degree in zoology preferred.
> Contact: 1 Buhvain Grove, Fairlish IV74 9PB. Salary £24k

They gathered around to take a look at it. There was a long silence.

'Katie,' said Olivia gently. 'Put the paper down. You know your degree is in history of art and theatre studies.'

'It says "preferred",' said Katie.

Olivia sighed and jumped down inelegantly from the ridiculously high stools to join the queue for the ladies.

'Think, open spaces, fresh air . . .'

'You hate fresh air,' said Louise.

'Maybe I just don't know what it is . . .'

'Forestry Commission?' said Louise. 'Katie, all you know about is lipgloss and low-fat fudge.'

'That's related,' said Katie. 'We do lots of not-tested-on-animals stuff.'

'OK, question one,' said Louise. 'What is the local wildlife?'

'Badgers?'

'Well, I wouldn't know,' said Louise, 'because I haven't the faintest clue where Fairlish is. Do you?'

'You're being very negative,' said Katie. 'Is it so bad to want a change?'

'It is if they're only paying you 24k.'

'I think I'll head for home,' said Katie, folding up the paper in a suspiciously noisy flurry.

'Why?' Olivia, returned, sounded suspicious.

'Bit tired . . . no reason.'

'Are you going home to make up an imaginary CV?' whispered Louise as she got up to walk Katie to the Tube – she was still a little nervous late at night.

Katie didn't answer.

'You realise you'd put the lives of hundreds of innocent animals at risk?'

'What if Fairlish is actually in Liberia?' said Olivia.

'Lots of people read this paper, all over the world. You'll be sorry.'

'Well, I'm in PR,' said Katie. 'I'd put a brave face on it.'

Chapter Two

There were only three other people on the train. The rolling stock seemed to be pre-war, and big clouds of dust had risen from the seats when she put her bag down. One couple of old men were talking a language she didn't understand, didn't recognise from anywhere, despite her year travelling. It seemed to consist mostly of Bs and Vs and sounded as though they were singing.

It wasn't them that captured Katie's attention however; further down the carriage was a woman stroking the nose of what Katie had assumed to be a poodle. She had had to check herself to see if she was sleeping (it had been a *very* long journey) when she heard the poodle baa.

Katie turned her head and stared out of the window. She couldn't believe she had travelled so far and was still in the same country – well, on the same island. Instead of small mean houses and grey buildings filling her window, there were dramatic hills soaring steeply up on either side of the track. The hills were dark colours, greens and purples and blues. It looked cold and austere, with occasional shafts of sunlight breaking through and the occasional flash of something bouncing through the undergrowth – rabbits, probably.

Katie shifted uncomfortably. She still couldn't believe she'd applied for this job. It may as well be the rainforest out here. Olivia had thrown her hands in the air when she realised Katie had never even visited Scotland before.

'Not even once? To take some crappy show to the Edinburgh Festival? School trip to the Burrell Collection? Horrible school holiday where it rained all the time and you lost your Pacamac, your sandwich lunch and your virginity all on the same day?'

Katie looked at her curiously.

'Not that that ever happened to me. Or anyone I know,' continued Olivia quickly. 'But that's not the point. How can you have been to India and not to Scotland?'

'Have you been to Northern Ireland?'

'That's not the point either. And I'm not the one who's got an interview in a country I know nothing about. Which, by the way, you're not taking, as I need you on the margarita toothpaste account. Where are you going to change your money? Are these interview people going to sort out your working visa?'

Katie's eyes widened. 'I need a . . . ?'

Olivia put up her hands. 'Oh God. This is going to go horribly, horribly wrong and we, your faithful, lonely, overworked, underpaid London spinster friends are going to have to find time in our packed schedules to pick up the pieces when it's over. In about a month.'

She'd been right about the money though, Katie thought, feeling for her coat pocket. She didn't even know pound notes still existed.

The letter had been brief.

Dear Ms Watson,

You are invited to an interview at Fairlish Forestry Commission at 4.30 p.m. Tuesday April 20th. You will be picked up at the railway station. Travelling expenses may be claimed.

Yours faithfully,
Harry Barr

Katie had pored over this letter a hundred times, trying to read between the lines, of which there weren't many, admittedly. Was she expected to stay overnight (given the length of the journey, she couldn't really see any other way, barring a helicopter airlift)? Was she expected to find out lots of information on the commission by herself? She'd done as much crash-course research on national parks as she could manage, but she was very nervous that her obvious lack of experience would tumble out as soon as she opened her mouth. Then there was her Southern accent, which had made her few friends the four times she'd had to buy herself a connecting ticket on the journey so far.

She smoothed out her wrinkled Tara Jarmon interview suit. This was probably an enormous mistake too. She should have probably worn rubber overalls and a Barbour. No, forget probably – there was no place here for anything but wellingtons. Where was she anyway? The train had already stopped at lots of stations that appeared to be in the middle of nowhere – Dundonnell, Gairloch – which seemed to be nothing more than platforms, with miles of scenery around them.

The few people that were left on the train got off, including the woman with the sheep, until it was just Katie, her briefcase, a headful of terms like 'judicious pruning' and 'sustainable development' that she didn't understand, and a slowly mounting sense of panic.

The tiny train cut through a huge oversized valley and gradually slowed to a halt. There was one weather-beaten sign that said 'Fairlish – Fhearlis'. Shocked out of her reverie, Katie jumped to her feet and stumbled about, as if the train were going to carry on without her.

The station confirmed her worst fears. She did a 360-degree turn. Above the purple mountains, a black cloud was ominously moving across the sky, and there was no building at the station at all; it was simply a halt, a platform in the air.

'Bollocks,' said Katie out loud – there was no one to hear her, just some enormous birds circling silently in the air above.

There was a torn old timetable on the side of the platform, but she didn't have the energy to look at it. She felt tired, grubby from the journey, starving hungry, and as far away from London as she'd ever been in her life – certainly a lot further away than she had felt on her year off in Goa, which had been full of Brits, Kiwis, Aussies and South Africans. This place was full of nothing at all, and she didn't know what to do. For a second she let herself remember the wide-open spaces and hot colours of India. She'd felt so free there.

There was a rumbling noise above her. Katie looked up. The birds had fled. Instead, the cloud had hit the side of the mountain. A few spits turned into a deluge. Katie's blue peacoat, of which she'd been rather proud, was no match for it at all. Within thirty seconds it was soaked through.

'Shit!' she yelled, staring straight at the sky. This was the stupidest waste of a day's annual leave she'd ever had in her life, applying for this stupid job on a whim, just because she had been upset.

The rain showed no signs of letting up, as she stared

into the horizon, but she thought she saw something else move; a white dot, far in the distance. She stared at it hard, blinking away the water from her eyelashes. The white dot got bigger. Hugging her arms around herself, she stepped forward and squinted. The white dot resolved itself into a moving shape, then a car, then a Land-Rover. She kept her eyes on it as it bumped over the undergrowth towards her, windscreen wipers going furiously. After what seemed like ages, it finally drew up in front of the platform, and she slowly went down the wooden staircase to meet it.

The engine stopped and a man leaned over, opened the passenger door and beckoned her over. Katie wasn't sure what to do. This person could be anyone. On the other hand, he could be the person coming to pick her up. After all, how many murderous rapists would pass by a deserted local station in the rain on the off chance that there might be a nervous young city girl hanging around? On the other hand, maybe the whole advertisement had been a trick to get someone here. On the other hand, that was a lot of trouble to go to if you were an unhinged murderous rapist, down to the headed notepaper and everything. And that was a whole lot of hands anyway. This stupid mugging had upset everything.

Katie dropped her head and peered into the front of the car doubtfully.

'Get in,' said a voice crossly.

'Umm, who are you?'

'I'm the Duke of Buccleuch, who the hell do you think I am? I'm Harry Barr.'

He had a weird accent; he sounded a bit like Scottish people on the telly, but a bit Scandinavian too. She'd never met a Highlander before. He also sounded impatient and a bit pissed off.

'I'm Katie Watson,' she said, and, taking a deep breath, she slipped into the car.

'Is this all there is?' said Harry irritably. Tall and broad, he was dressed as if on his way to a Highland landwork fancy-dress party; checked shirt, cords, wellies and a Barbour jacket. A thick mane of unruly black hair was flopping over one eye. He reminded her of someone, but she couldn't put her finger on it.

'Well, I may not have a lot of experience in the field, but I'm very quick to learn,' said Katie, unhappily aware that the interview appeared to have begun.

'No, I mean – are you the only person?'

Katie glanced around. She didn't appreciate being spoken to like a naughty dog.

'Let me just check – yes.'

Harry Barr eyed her suspiciously. 'I invited ten people.'

'I killed and ate them,' said Katie, and regretted it immediately.

'What?'

'I mean, maybe they're just behind me. When's the next train?'

'Tuesday.'

Perhaps this was some sort of psychological chill-out interview, thought Katie. Oh God, what was he doing now? He was bent over to his feet and seemed to be searching for something. He was getting out his knife! Or his gun! They all had guns in the countryside!

'Here,' he said. He opened a tartan flask and poured her out a cup of what looked like extremely strong tea.

'Thank you,' said Katie, taken aback. They sat in silence for a moment, while she gratefully gulped the hot sweet tea.

'So you're the only one,' said Harry again.

'Guess I've got the job then,' said Katie cheerfully, trying to get the conversation going.

'I guess so,' said Harry. He didn't sound overjoyed about it.

Katie stared out into the pouring rain in disbelief. He couldn't be serious. Here she was, sitting in a stranger's car (a dirty car, that smelled of dog), after a crumpled, filthy, ten-hour journey, staring at the pissing rain in the middle of a godforsaken hellhole in the outer reaches of absolutely bloody nowhere, and he wasn't even going to ask her the equal opportunities question.

'I'll have to think it over,' she said.

Harry sighed. 'So I have to do this again.'

'Do what? You haven't done anything so far. I'm the one who travelled ten hours up here for a cup of tea.'

He rolled his eyes. 'You know the train back is in another five minutes.'

'Really?'

'Yes.'

'Well, I'd better get it then.'

Katie wondered if he would ask her to stay longer, find out a bit about her. After all she had travelled all this way . . .

'You should.'

Well! That was the last straw. She hadn't travelled all this way to be insulted by some Scotsman with a radish up his arse and the dress sense of Father Dougal MacGuire on a bank holiday.

'Nice meeting you,' she said, trying to make her voice drip with sarcasm.

She unlocked the door of the car. After all, she was already soaked through, so a bit more rain wasn't going to make any difference. Maybe she could spend the night in Inverness . . . she pictured herself wrapped up in a blanket in some cosy b. & b. after a long hot bath, sipping hot chocolate and watching *EastEnders*.

'You probably wouldn't have fitted in here anyway,' said Harry suddenly. Oddly, his voice sounded kind, and when she looked at him he was giving her an apologetic half-smile.

'Yes, I would have,' she said firmly. 'I'd have been great.'

Then she stepped out of the Land-Rover, misjudged the height of the car and landed with her new Russell and Bromley boots up to her shins in mud. For several seconds she and Harry regarded each other.

'I've got a tow rope in the back,' said Harry, finally.

'That *won't* be necessary,' said Katie, pulling her feet up with clumsy distaste. 'Goodb . . .' As she was speaking, she felt the rain stop suddenly, as if someone had pulled a switch. Without warning, a shaft of brilliant sunshine struck the car. Turning around, she saw a vast, full double-bowed rainbow leap from hill to hill. It was utterly awe-inspiring; completely different from the washed-out colours peeping behind grey buildings one rarely even glimpsed in London. She gaped.

'Wow,' she said.

Harry watched her for a moment. These daft city lassies really had no idea what they were doing. Still, at least she'd stopped acting all superior for ten seconds.

'That's amazing,' she said.

'There's your train,' he indicated the little red rolling carriages making their way down the glen. 'You don't want to miss it. There isn't another one until . . .'

'Tuesday. Yes. You told me.'

Still keeping her eye on the light show, she made a bedraggled figure limping towards the buffers, her damp cheap briefcase in her hand. Harry gunned the Land-Rover into reverse. Another wee media girl with bucolic fantasies. Best to nip it in the bud. But he was never going to get anyone to sort out this bloody mess. He looked at the business card she'd left him. LiWebber PR. God, he'd have to be desperate.

Chapter Three

'So you hated it and everything about it in every conceivable way. Well, glad that's over,' said Louise. Katie hadn't yet mentioned to Olivia she'd actually gone for an interview for the job.

'And I ruined a new pair of boots.'

'Invoice him.'

'That's not a bad idea. Although I'd rather invoice for the ten hours of my life it took me to get back. Mind you . . .'

'Mind you what?'

'Nothing,' said Katie. 'It was pretty, that's all. You could breathe. And do you know how many people in vests stopped me on the street to annoy me for charity while I was there?'

'How many?'

'None at all.'

Katie clicked her email thoughtfully. Oh God. Another one from Clara. As usual she would have to fight with herself over whether or not to let Louise see it.

Katie thought back to the days when Louise hadn't had

her knickers permanently on a Venetian blind. Max had been so affable. He and Lou had been joined at the hip for years, it seemed. He was beefy, amiable, liked *FHM* magazine and, secretly, Jordan, but was never much of a one for doing anything more than having a few beers with his mates, mostly surveyors like him and Louise, or old friends from college when they were all a lot more sporty and trim than they were now; sitting on the sofa and letting Louise make him pasta for supper.

Louise thought he was great and Katie and Olivia found him inoffensive, which, in the current climate, was saying quite a lot. Louise had moved in with him, and it had started to look like they would roll gently on this way for ever. Louise had begun happily to think of engagement rings, honeymoons, joint dinner services . . .

Then Katie's sister had come to stay at Katie's, back in the days when she had a spare room. Twenty-two and just out of college, Clara was an imp and always had been. There were very few photographs of her as a child that didn't show her either screaming or sticking her tongue out. She had bowled down from Manchester University with various colours in her hair, piercings and a tiny pair of combat trousers. She ate everything in the house, weighed seven stone and stayed out all night dancing and taking drugs in mysterious nightclubs. Katie felt like her mother.

'Well, my chakra therapist would say it serves you right for always being the good child,' Olivia had said harshly. 'If you'd misbehaved a bit more you'd both have balanced out a bit and she wouldn't get away with nicking all the hummus.'

'She's a free spirit,' said Katie uncomfortably. They'd been sitting in the kitchen trying to ignore the loud jungly banging music coming from the room next door, that had been playing nonstop for thirty-six hours, shattering the three days' peace they'd just had while Clara was at Glastonbury. (Her birth name was Clara; she made all her hippy friends call her Honeydew.)

'She's going to get you done for intent to supply,' said Louise, sniffing.

'What am I going to do, tell Mum on her?'

Their mother was living an extremely quiet life on her own in Blackburn – their dad had never been around very much except for the occasional Christmas pressie – and she was constantly amazed at her daughters' ability to do anything at all – cross the road, find a job, get a mortgage – never mind be exposed to any actual horrors of the modern world.

'Hey!' Clara bounced in. She was sun-kissed from a summer of music festivals and hanging around road protests, tiny in her tie-dyed dungarees, and appeared to be growing dreadlocks.

'Your hair smells,' said Katie. She had spent the summer writing long proposals to pitch for edible flowers. Unsuccessfully.

Clara pouted. 'You need to chill out. Would you like a massage?'

'No, of course I don't want a massage. I'm not that desperate for human contact that I'll let you stick your nails in my spine. I haven't forgotten the havoc you wreaked with my Barbies, thanks, never mind real humans.'

'How am I ever going to get my massage business started if you won't let me practise?'

'You're opening a "massage" business?' asked Olivia. 'Do you do extras?'

'She's got a degree in bioengineering. Of course she's not going to open a massage business,' said Katie. The four-year age gap was meant to disappear as you got older, but she'd seen no evidence for it yet.

'Well, there you go, maybe I haven't quite got my degree,' said Clara, poking her tongue out as usual. 'But that doesn't matter, because before I start the business, I'm going to India.'

Katie sighed looking back. She had been two years into her job then, working all hours, living on hardly any money. It was fun, of course, living the life of a young professional, meeting friends for drinks after work, feeling terribly grown-up and important, but she'd loved her six months travelling around India at the end of her degree. The sense of escaping; of doing something different . . . she'd loved living on coconuts and fresh air with young people from around the world. And now, here she was, jealous of her baby sister off to do the same thing. How could she feel nostalgic at twenty-nine? And really, what was she doing here anyway that was so great?

She supposed she could chuck it in any time she wanted to. People were always talking about it down here. They were off to open a vineyard in France, or start an adventure holiday business, or import silk. Nobody ever did. London seemed to exert some kind of mystical centrifugal force on everyone, that sucked all ambitions other than a corner office and a cottage in the country out of you as quickly as it sucked the money from your pockets.

Plus, look what the outcome had been. She'd thrown a party for Clara's leaving. It had been a really good night, actually, full of people (although some of them had dogs on bits of string). Clara spent the whole night holed up in a corner with Max, with whom she'd always had a cheeky, flirtatious relationship. Louise scarcely noticed. Max was furniture; part of her life, and Clara was the baby sister.

Max left his job and flew to India two days later. The one who got away.

And look at the mess you left behind you, Katie thought. If the whole world just did what they wanted all the time, the whole damn place would fall apart.

After assuring Louise through the tears and tequila haze which followed that he would immediately see sense and come back crawling with his tail between his legs, begging her (and, more pertinently, his employers), he hadn't. Actually, what made it much, much worse was that he decided he needed to rent the flat out to subsidise his new wacky lifestyle, and gave Louise notice to quit, which is how she'd ended up making loud noises in the tiny room Katie had once earmarked as a study.

Clara didn't seem to have a big problem with it. They were having fun, chilling, and 'finding themselves'. In fact, over the last six months, as Louise had careered further and further away from the home and hearth she'd thought she'd shared with Max, Max and Clara got more and more relaxed about how exactly they'd got together in the first place and were practically sharing an email address. No one knew when, or if, they were coming home. Louise was dealing with it through a twin approach of martinis and dating, tiger-pouncing any man that crossed her postcode. Max's name was best not mentioned, but sometimes – like now, when Katie got an email, it was difficult.

Hey Sis!

Clara still liked to use fonts to make her wacky and different, Katie noticed. It was like being shouted at by a Dickens novel.

> **HoWZIT? HOT in HERRE! Goa just amazing. Coconuts for twenty pence, xxxxx**
>
> **Max says Hi to everyone back home - we're missing you loads in London and the pouring rain! Not!**

It wasn't a nice feeling, being torn between a friend and a relative, particularly when you didn't even have the distraction of a love life of your own to worry about.

The problem was, it seemed to get harder to raise the subject with Louise, not easier.

At first, of course, when she'd moved in with Katie, she had gone horribly pale and thin, and started her maniacal sleeping around punctuated with 2 a.m. crying jags, side by side with an understanding that one in such a fit of dispossession had to be absolved from housework, keeping regular hours, or in fact much apart from corkscrew wielding and very long scented baths.

But, as time had passed, and everything (apart from the yo-yo knickers) had seemed to ease a little, Katie found it harder and harder to be in the middle. Her sister seemed happy, but Louise still seemed terribly sad, and Katie bringing the subject up just seemed to make things worse. In some way, Katie could see, Louise blamed her for her sister's behaviour. And whilst comprehensible, it was hardly fair. Being the only conduit between them didn't help either. Katie thought wistfully for a moment of Clara having fun. Of course she had fun, London fun, in expensive bars, with loud nights. Loud. Having fun in London tended to be loud. Everything in London was loud; the Tube, the traffic, the bars, the shouting of arrogant young careerists showing off. Sometimes Katie really felt like a bit of peace and quiet.

Living with Louise was just about bearable. Katie was trying to be a sympathetic friend. She really was. She didn't want to be one of those people who had you to stay in their house, then made little remarks about how to clean a grill pan and how different towels had different meanings, thus making Louise feel even worse than she was already. But she'd found it did very little to improve her general disposition towards the world.

Katie turned her attention to the pile of work on her desk. Today she was working on a new diet, which substituted chocolate-covered peanuts and cheese for every meal. Apparently once separately considered high-fat foods, it had been discovered that taken in combination and omitting all other food groups, it had a staggering effect on weight loss and had caught on like wildfire, and was called the CCPC plan, which looked really scientific and everything. Katie's job was to minimise the coronary or acne scare stories that popped up now and again. She was busy.

She wandered into a reverie for a second about what it would be like doing press for a Forestry Commission. Then she realised she didn't have the faintest idea. Maybe a lot of people stole the trees at Christmas time. No, hang on, that would be a matter for the police. Maybe they were trying to attract campers . . . to a forest in a remote part of Scotland? No, surely not. Only the intrepid would survive, she didn't want to be responsible for deaths by hypothermia . . . although . . . she looked at the latest CCPC files and sighed.

Miko bundled into the room, her lovely face looking furious. 'How much better-looking than you did we say I was again?'

'Fifty to a hundred times?'

'So he hasn't called, why?'

'Because you have a bad personality?'

'I scarcely think so.'

'Because you're frightening?'

'It's 2005. ALL women are frightening.'

She examined her blood-red talon nails carefully. 'Do you think these nails are a bit much?'

'Do you gorge nightly on human blood?'

'Look at me. I'm a size six. I gorge on NOTHING.'

'Well, we're back to the whole personality thing . . .'

'Olivia wants you,' said Miko, curtly.

'How are you? Keeping well I hope? What did you have for breakfast this morning?'

Oh no, Olivia was in 'I'm your boss now' mode.

Katie had eaten the last four chocolate digestives in the flat. 'Two bananas and a fruit smoothie,' she said.

Olivia's brow furrowed, but not very much. It looked suspiciously taut. 'Smoothie? You know there's dairy in smoothies.'

'A whole dairy?' asked Katie.

'Well, we can't be too careful. NOW.' She placed her arms on her desk in what was meant to be body-language-speak for 'Look at my wide stance! How approachable I am!' This wasn't good at all. 'Now, you won't believe this . . . it's just the funniest thing.'

Katie's ears pricked up. Was this going to be one of those kind of nettle-drinking sample things she got in her office that she was always stuffing down unsuspecting juniors, to check their vomiting reflexes?

'Yes?'

Olivia's office was full of crystals that made annoying tinkly noises whenever anyone moved even a finger, and scattered various colours in different parts of the room. Years after everyone else had moved on from Feng Shui, Olivia was still clinging on to it with the tips of her fingers.

'We have,' she said, opening her eyes very wide in the manner of a nursery teacher, 'a new client!'

'Great,' said Katie. 'Well done.' She hoped it was shampoo. Her hair had been all tired and gritty recently – not entirely unlike her mood. Plus, she'd plucked a grey one out in the mirror.

'And it's in a completely different field to our usual one!'

Now she had her attention. Ooh, maybe it was celebrities? She saw herself suddenly being one of those barky dog PRs who sit in rooms with celebrities and growl when cheeky journalists bring up their drugs hell/adultery.

'Yeah?'

'Yes. this is really going to put the LiWebber name on the map. It ticks all our boxes, does our bit for the environment, fills our charity requirements . . . oh, it's perfect really. Of course, you know I've always been very in tune with the environment . . . I'm not surprised they came to us really . . .'

'What is it, Olivia?'

Olivia spread out her hands in excitement. 'The Fairlish Forestry Commission! The one you saw in the paper!'

Katie took a step back, felt a chair behind her legs and collapsed onto it.

'. . . and, well, apparently, would you believe this, they couldn't find anyone to take on the job. So they called us.'

Katie looked up. Hang on. She would have taken the job. Well, possibly. That wasn't the point. The point was, that bloody Harry whatever his name was hadn't 'offered' her the job. That was the point. But she'd given him her card . . . and now presumably he was calling to see who else was available. But if she told Olivia she'd already been up for the job without telling her, Olivia would mince her innards. Crap!

'And, well, I spoke to Miko and she agreed with me that, well, you do seem to have been a little under the weather recently, with Louise and the mugging and everything.'

Under the weather? The weather has been FARTING on me, thought Katie savagely to herself.

'So we thought, maybe a bit of fresh air . . . change of scenery for a few months . . . go up there and sort them out . . . gorgeous scenery I've heard . . . take a few photos . . . get our charity bit in the annual report by next year and Bob's your uncle. What do you say? Fantastic, eh?'

'Well, I'm not sure the outdoors is quite . . . I mean, my hayfever gets quite bad.'

Olivia looked up, her face instantly less beatific. 'When I said "fantastic", Katherine, you understand I meant "pack".'

God, Katie hated 'boss mode'.

Chapter Four

'You can't leave me too,' said Louise, clinging to the toaster as if it were a life preserver (which, given her lack of cooking skills these days – all built up to cater for Max, all immediately abandoned – it was).

'Yes, that's what I'm doing,' said Katie. 'I've been planning this all along. Put the toaster down, I'm running a bath and no longer trust you.'

'Oh God,' said Louise, in a tone of voice that Katie recognised was gearing up to start on about the future course of her life, involving loneliness, misery, telly and gradually slipping into obesity brought on by sadness inspired TUC-biscuit blowouts. Louise put on a good face in public, but once they were back in the flat it was a different story.

'I'm having a bath,' said Katie heavily. 'I have a premonition it's going to be my last one for six months that isn't shared with goats or something.'

'Do you want to go?'

'Durr! No. It was just a stupid whim at the time. Which has come right around to bite me in the arse, because now, do I have a choice? No. Is everything going great guns for me here? Not, as it happens, necessarily.'

'Things aren't going that well for me either,' said Louise, sticking her finger in the Philadelphia.

'Really? I hadn't noticed.'

'Where is this place?'

'It's on a higher latitude than Moscow.'

'Is it pretty?'

'If you like that kind of thing.'

'What kind of thing?'

'Lambs. Fresh air. Stink. That kind of thing.'

'What kind of stink?'

'It might have been the fresh air. Or some cow thing.'

'Does it smell worse than the litter bins on Oxford Street on a hot day?'

'No. It's in Scotland, not the devil's anus.'

'It might be fun.'

'I've been there. It is not fun. It has no cable, no Joseph, no proper coffee, and everyone up there is horrible. I know I moan about the shallowness of London life, but I've kind of got used to these staples.'

'How many people did you meet?'

'Only one. But there's only about twelve people there anyway, so it's a reasonable statistical sample.'

Louise stirred her coffee thoughtfully. 'When do you have to leave?'

'Two weeks on Monday. I don't know if I'll have time to knit all the waterproofs I'll have to take.'

'What's the job involve?'

'Trees. Looking after trees. Apparently trees need a PR.'

'I thought they had Sting.'

'He's on tour. Anyway, he only cares about foreign trees.'

'That's bigo-tree.'

Katie looked at Louise. 'That's the first joke you've made in about three months.'

'That waiter was a joke.'

'You know, I wonder if you might just be recovering.'

'Huh. You know, I think it might be really interesting. It'd be great to get out of this cesspit for a while,' Louise said wistfully.

Katie suddenly had a great idea. 'Do you know how long it takes to drive up there?'

Louise shook her head.

'Me neither. Wanna come?'

Packing for three months in March was absolutely not easy. In London, the daffs were out in the public squares, and you could make it on a sunny afternoon with just a cardie. But according to www.middleofnowhere-weather.com, Fairlish still had six inches of snow and a wind-chill factor of minus ten.

Olivia was very grumpy that Louise was going too. She had found it very easy to get leave from her employers, who were still trying to work out if her behaviour at the Christmas party constituted sexual harassment.

'I can't believe you're leaving me alone here, desperately trying to ferret out the last good-looking, rich, kind, straight man in London,' Olivia wailed.

'You sent me on this stupid assignment!' said Katie.

'Yeah, but I didn't want you *both* to go.'

'I'll be back in a couple of days!' said Louise indignantly.

'But you're either a biscuit-strewn crumbling mess or under a waiter. You're no use at all!'

'Well, that's nice.'

'I'm just saying,' replied Olivia gruffly, 'good luck – I'll miss you.'

'Well, I'll miss you too,' said Katie. 'Along with electric lighting, central heating, comprehensible English,

Belgo, sushi, mojitos, movie theatres, wine bars, radio, fajitas . . .'

'I'll get the drinks in,' interrupted Olivia.

Katie's Fiat Punto fought a brave fight, but it still took them twelve full hours, much circling around and two full bouts of crying (one and a half Louise's, one half Katie's, who felt that red eyes and a crack in the voice wasn't quite as bad as Louise's full-on tantrum on the subject of unmarked B roads, leading to an extremely long diatribe on Max's inability to find his way anywhere which meant he was probably lost in the foothills of the Himalayas, which, Katie had thought, was exactly where she'd like to be right now, a thought she committed the profound error of voicing) to finally limp into Fairlish late that evening.

To Katie's horror, the Forestry Commission had politely turned down Olivia's offer to organise their accommodation and said they'd sort something out. Which in practice meant that rather than automatically booking the nicest hotel in the area and billing it to the client, Katie was somewhat at the mercy of . . . well, the fax she was clasping in her hand. It didn't say anything along the lines of 'Gleneagles'. It didn't say anything along the lines of 'hotel'. It said, '4 Water Lane. Do not arrive after 8 p.m.'.

It was 11.30 p.m. The last time they'd got out of the car, near Killiemuir, it had been so cold, Louise's sobs had frozen in her throat. It had hurt to breathe.

The darkness was almost complete. Louise was looking out of the window, failing to spot a single road sign, whining, 'I can't see a thing.'

Katie was trying her best to be patient, but it was like travelling all day with a six-year-old.

'Well, look harder. I'm just concentrating on trying not

to run over any more squirrels or rats or badgers or hedgehogs or deer, OK?'

'No need to get snitty,' said Louise. 'It's not my fault you forgot to pack the night-vision goggles.'

Without warning, the Fiat dropped into a huge puddle of freezing water. The girls both screamed. Katie somehow managed to push the car on through before it stalled, and they came to a shuddering halt. They looked at each other, neither wanting to get out in the cold.

'Where's the torch?' asked Louise, finally.

Katie looked at her soaking wet feet. 'Um, I didn't bring one.'

'What did your dad say about driving at night without a torch?'

'I don't have a dad.'

'Oh, yes, bring that up now we're trapped in a flood in the middle of nowhere.'

Gingerly, Katie opened the door. There was definitely water running under their feet. 'Bollocks,' she said.

Louise gasped sharply.

'What?'

'There's a light . . . over there.'

Sure enough, a tiny light could be seen bobbing up and down towards them.

'Do you think it's a rescue boat?'

'Uh, yeah,' said Katie, whose first thought had, in actual fact, been that it was aliens.

'Hellaooowww!' screeched Louise. 'Carn you come and help us, pleayse!'

'Could you sound a little less like the Duke of Edinburgh?' hissed Katie. 'Haven't you seen *An American Werewolf in London*?'

'Cooeee!' shouted Louise.

'What the MANKIN HELL . . .' a strident voice, closely

followed by the beam of a torch and an equally visible bosom, strode out of the darkness '. . . do you think you're doing?'

An imperious nose followed the bosom, along with an expression that looked far from the welcoming Scots of tradition, with two eyebrows that wouldn't have been entirely out of place on an old Labour minister.

Katie and Louise immediately splashed to attention.

The woman sized them up and down. 'And you are?'

'We're looking for number 4 Water Lane,' said Katie, in her best well-brought-up voice.

'D'you think this might be Water Lane?' said the woman, staring pointedly at their shoes.

'Is that a yes or a no?' replied Katie. Playing humorous word games with Attila the Bun would be all well and good if they weren't on the brink of hypothermia.

The woman sniffed in a manner that implied that yes, it obviously was, surely even to the educationally sub-rate specimens in front of her. 'You'll be the London girls then.'

Katie and Louise swapped glances.

'I thought it was quite clear that you were expected before 8.30?' she continued.

'It took us a while to get here. From London,' said Katie.

'Really? Is it far? Maybe you had to stop for cocktails and to buy some shoes on the way.'

If she hadn't been so very, very wet and very, very tired, Katie would simply have turned around and driven all the way back home.

Number 4 Water Lane was not, as the girls had fantasised for the last two hundred miles, a tartan-festooned haven of horseshoe antiques, a stag's head or two and a blazing open fire. It was an enormous house, shrouded in almost complete darkness, with creaks and peculiar noises emanating from different corners. It was freezing – 'heating and hot water 7–8. Breakfast 7–8' read the sign on the wall that Attila, whose name was in fact Mrs McClockerty, had pointed out, leading them to ponder the invention of time travel as she led them through endless gloomy corridors, pointing out a terrifyingly pristine, anti-macassared floral monstrosity called the 'residents' lounge'. They appeared to have been billeted in the old servants' quarters, directly under the eaves. Fortunately the lighting was terrible: Katie was sure there were cobwebs and God knew what else in the corners. The beds were single, and both mattresses and blankets were painfully thin.

'I need the toilet,' whimpered Louise from her bed after they'd put the light out.

'It's down the hall,' whispered back Katie.

'I'm too frightened.'

'Oh, for goodness' sake.'

'Katie?'

'Yes?'

'Are you sure we haven't been kidnapped by white slavers and sold into service?'

'Ssh!'

There was a short pause. 'Have you seen that film *The Others*?'

'NO!'

'*Gaslight*?'

'Goodnight Louise.'

'*Amityville*?'

'If you wet the bed, I'm telling Mrs McClockerty.'

There was a pause, then a rustle. Katie stiffened. Sure enough, the covers on her bed were being pulled back.

'Louise!'

'Please!'

'Well, no funny stuff, OK?'

'I would never fancy you even if I was gay,' said Louise loftily. 'I'd fancy that bird from *Location Location Location*.' And, despite her avowed terrors and full bladder, she immediately fell fast asleep.

Katie wriggled a little to try to get comfortable, but it was no use. Grateful for the warm body beside her, she lay staring into the dark as the clock ticked away until morning.

Getting up the next morning proved near impossible – the room was icy and so huge that getting to their clothes seemed an epic journey, never mind the arduous trek to the bathroom. Only by holding hands, closing their eyes and shouting 'bacon and eggs!' could they inch their way forwards into the frigid air.

Sadly, bacon and eggs weren't exactly forthcoming.

'It's continental breakfast,' announced Mrs McClockerty, as if what is delicious-freshly-made-in-a-patisserie-under-a-heartwarming-early-Mediterranean-sun was in any way a comparable experience to the dried-out pieces of toast studded on the tray before them while the wind audibly howled around the house.

'Two pieces only!' she barked.

There were three other people in the dining room, all men, sitting on their own.

'Perhaps it's a lonely murderers' convention,' suggested Louise, trying in vain to warm her hands on the coffee pot.

'It holds up Olivia's male–female ratio theory,' said Katie, inhaling her tea greedily. Before they'd left, Olivia had pointed out that seeing as the main industries in the region were farming, fishing, forestry and a large research centre down the road, they might be in with a bit of luck totty-wise. Although studying their fellow inmates, Katie wasn't entirely heartened by what was on offer. One of the men was dropping crumbs all over his *Aberdeen Evening Post*, another was unselfconsciously exploring the inside of his nose. At the far end, Mrs McClockerty was surveying the room in silence, making sure nobody took more than the requisite number of condiments.

'So, are we going home today?' asked Louise brightly. ''Course we are!'

Katie grimaced. 'I think I'm going to have to at least look at this job thing. Otherwise Livvy will have my farts for parts.'

'Surely not,' said Louise. 'She won't mind. This place is cruel and unusual.'

Outside, rain was throwing itself against the window as if it were trying to get their attention. Katie looked at her watch. Eight thirty.

'I'm going to have to go,' she said apologetically.

'OK, I'll get the car started,' said Louise.

'You're not coming!'

Louise looked taken aback. 'Of course I am.'

'Of course you're not. This is my job. I'm not walking in there like Jennifer Lopez with an entourage. They already hate me.'

'Do they know it's you?'

'What do you mean?'

'Do they know it's you? The person who already got turned down for the job?'

'I did *not* get turned down for the job! I . . . declined.'

'What? They offered it to you and you turned it down?'

'In a manner of speaking.'

'By default?'

'That's a manner of speaking.'

'Well, what am I going to do all day?'

'You should have thought of that,' said Katie sternly, 'before you started with the "Ooh, please can I come, boo hoo hoo, blah blah".'

Louise gave her a look.

'OK, everyone out!' said Mrs McClockerty. The men started shifting around, collecting his papers untidily together, in one case, and wiping his finger surreptitiously under the table in another.

Mrs McClockerty came and stood so her bosom loomed over their heads, blocking out all light. 'You must exit the premises until 6 o'clock. This isn't a hotel, you know.'

'It is a hotel!' said Katie.

'It's a boarding house,' said Mrs McClockerty, as if Katie had sworn at her. The girls waited for further elucidation as to what the difference was, but none was forthcoming. The bosom swayed towards the door and vanished into the endless bowels of the house.

'Can I hide under the seat of the car while you're at work?' asked Louise desperately.

'No! You have to go explore.'

There was a pause. 'Can I have the umbrella?' asked Louise.

'I forgot it,' said Katie in a very quiet voice.

'You forgot an umbrella when coming to the Highlands of Scotland?' said Louise in an even quieter voice.

'Yes,' said Katie.

Louise sat very still for a minute. Then she stood up, slowly. 'I will see you,' she announced, 'at 6 p.m.' Then she picked up her coat, still wet from the night before, and, with a great sense of purpose and wounded pride, walked out of the big old-fashioned door. Katie watched her go for a moment, feeling guilty, then feeling annoyed that she spent so much of her life feeling guilty.

Mrs McClockerty poked her head around the door and looked pointedly at the brass clock on the wall. It was 8.40. Katie jumped up, guiltily.

Chapter Five

Katie hadn't known what to expect of the town – she hadn't seen much of it from the tiny railway station. But on first impressions, Katie felt happier despite herself. The rain was easing off, and there was even a hint of sun in the air, trying hard to make itself felt behind a watery cloud. The town was tiny, built around a little harbour. The houses were brightly painted and picture-postcard cosy. The town looked like it should be hosting a perky children's television series, and, although the streets were deserted, Katie could imagine it thronged in the summer. The roads were narrow and cobbled, and a tiny church was perched on one of the hills above. The directions to the Forestry Commission indicated it was out of town, though, and so Katie reluctantly set off in the opposite direction, following the badly-faxed map.

The rain did stop, but the Punto was still having some trouble navigating the muddy roads through the thick woods. It was the first time Katie had ever driven somewhere where she could see the point of those ridiculous Land-Rover thingies, other than to transport skinny blonde women and their single children to the lycée whilst squashing cyclists in the London rush hour. Olivia, who usually cycled to work of course, always suggested that they use the bull-bars on the front of their vehicles to tie little posies of flowers to commemorate all the cyclists and pedestrians they'd killed that week whilst being too far off the ground to notice anyone and too busy doing their make-up to care.

Katie wondered how things were going to go with this Harry character. The best thing, she supposed, would be if nobody mentioned their previous encounter. After all, he had said she could have had the job if she wanted, hadn't he? Even if grudgingly so? Maybe he wouldn't recognise her? Surely he'd think all London girls looked the same anyway? Nervously, she smoothed down her plain black sweater and burgundy skirt. It would be fine. She would do the job and get home. Breathe fresh air. Eat . . . well, kippers and things, she supposed. She quickly put to the back of her mind how unhappy he would be when he found out he was paying consultancy rates rather than £24k a year.

Suddenly, she reached a clearing. As if out of nowhere, a building appeared amongst the trees. It consisted of a wood frame in a peculiar rhombus shape. The walls were sheer glass, rising diagonally outwards from the grassy forest floor. It looked exactly like what it was: the office of the forest. It was beautiful.

Katie got out of the now mud-encrusted car and took a deep breath. She could see two shadowy figures inside – presumably they could see her a lot better from the inside out. She squinted at the glass, trying to work out where the door was. She had a vision of herself walking straight into a wall and breaking her nose. Maybe she'd get sick leave and have to go straight home. And they'd give her a nose job on the NHS.

She spied the door and walked through it.

'Hello?' she said tentatively. There was no answer. She could hear voices, and stepped through the wood-panelled foyer.

'Hello?'

Inside the large clean open-plan room, with a picture perfect view, two men were poring over a single newspaper.

'Hello?'

'PRICKWOBBLING DICKO!' shouted one of the men suddenly. Katie recognised Harry's voice immediately.

The other man was heavier set and his voice much more accented. 'God, if only we had someone to deal with the bloody papers, like.'

'Ta dah!' exclaimed Katie.

Both the men whirled around, startled.

'Yes?' said Harry, his dark eyes flashing at her in a cross 'can I help you?' kind of a way.

She walked towards him, smiling confidently. 'Hello, I'm Katie Watson.'

Harry stopped and looked her up and down, clearly trying to place her from somewhere.

'Olivia at LiWebber sent me,' she said. 'For a temporary assignment.'

'Hello,' said the older man. 'I'm . . .'

'I remember you!' said Harry. 'You're the girl that came up on the train!'

'I have no idea what you're talking about.'

'I think I asked them to send me somebody else. I'm sure I did. Didn't I?'

Katie decided to ignore this, and shook hands with the other man.

'Derek Cameron,' he said. 'I'm the . . .' he coughed suddenly. 'Executive assistant. Which isn't like a secretary or anything. Nothing like it.'

'Derek, make us both a coffee, while I sort this out,' said Harry loftily.

'Sure thing, boss,' replied Derek, disappearing into the back.

'Well,' said Harry, sitting back in his armchair and eyeing her carefully. 'Uh, welcome.'

'Thank you,' said Katie. He stared at her again, then blinked. With his dark eyes and thick curly hair, Katie suddenly realised who he reminded her of – Gordon Brown. When he was younger and thinner. Much younger and much thinner, she thought. But there was the same brooding, distracted air and lack of speaking terms with combs.

'Find your way up all right from the big smoke?'

'Yes,' said Katie, 'although we're not staying in a very nice place.'

'Really?' he leaned over his desk, suddenly looking interested. 'What's wrong with it?'

Katie described at length the horrid food, scary demeanour and general grimness of the Water Lane guest-house. About halfway through, realising that Harry was still staring at her, she remembered suddenly that there were only about nine people living in the town and he must know all of them.

'. . . so, but, actually, apart from that, it's lovely, great and we're very happy,' she finished in a gush.

Harry was quiet.

'She's your mum, isn't she?'

'Not quite.'

'Gran?'

'Aunt, actually. Brought me up after my mum died.'

Uncharitably, Katie's first thought was, 'well, that explains a lot'. Her second was, 'how annoying, having that to throw in every time you wanted to win a conversation'.

Fortunately it was her third that actually came out of her mouth. 'I'm really, really sorry.'

'It was a long time ago,' said Harry. 'And she couldn't cook then either, to the best of my recollection.'

Katie stared at the floor, her face burning.

'Well, anyway,' said Harry finally. 'I find it's probably best to . . . buy your own sheets, stuff like that. There's a woman in town gives you a discount if you tell her where you're staying.'

'Thanks,' said Katie, thinking it best not to mention that the plans she and Louise had discussed that morning included moving out as soon as humanly possible, burning the place to the ground, then salting the land.

'So, what's my first assignment?'

Derek returned, bearing three cracked mugs bearing pictures of trees on the side. They said 'Don't commit TREEson, come see us this SEASON'.

These people need help, thought Katie.

'The prickwobbling dicko,' prompted Derek.

'Oh, yes,' said Harry. 'Iain Kinross. Iain Kinross of the *West Highland Times*. Yes, yes. Iain Kinross.'

'Our evil arch-nemesis,' added Derek helpfully.

Harry brandished the paper and threw it down on the desk. 'You have to sort him out.'

Katie picked up the paper.

'He's pursuing a vendetta against us,' said Harry gravely. The headline read 'Further Deciduous Cuts'. It meant nothing to Katie.

'He writes that we're killing all the trees.'

'Are you?'

'Yes,' said Harry. 'We start by weeding out the gay and disabled trees.'

'Don't listen to him,' said Derek.

'No,' said Katie, who'd come to this conclusion on her own.

'Yes!' said Harry indignantly. 'Wages paid by me, both of you. Now, you –' he pointed at Katie '– go into town. Introduce yourself to Kinross. Simper a bit, you know, do that girlie thing. Toss your hair a little.'

'I will not,' said Katie. 'I'm not a horse.'

Harry rolled his eyes. 'Just tell him you're new here and that you were kind of hoping he'd go easy on you until you've settled in.'

'That's not the kind of thing I've usually found works on journalists,' said Katie. 'Especially not evil ones.'

'Well, what's your great plan then, Miss Whoever-you-are?'

Katie didn't know, but given the atmosphere of outright hostility, she was on Iain Kinross's side pretty much already. 'Let me go and talk to him,' she said, trying to sound professional.

'Exactly. Bit of the old eyelash-fluttering. See, Derek, I told you a lassie would help things around here.'

'Of course, boss.'

'They're like Mr Burns and Smithers.'

Katie had run into Louise with comparative ease, given that there were only three streets in Fairlish, and only one person on any of them.

'Great,' said Louise. 'I'm starving. Let's cut our losses and run. We could be in Glasgow in five hours, and it rocks.'

'I don't think it's going to be that easy,' said Katie, looking around her. 'Do you know, Starbucks would clean up around here.'

'Who from? Mrs Miggin's pie shop?' Louise pointed to a little bakers-cum-teashop. It still had the original round glass panes in its tiny windows, and was painted pink. It looked cosy and welcoming, with condensation fogging up the glass. 'Why isn't it that easy? They can take the high road, and we'll take the low road, and we'll be shopping at LK Bennett's before them.'

The heavy bakery doors clanged as they walked in. The shop was hot, steamy and full of old men chattering away in a musical brogue. Everyone fell silent immediately. Katie and Louise were about the same height as most of them.

'Do you sell coffee?' Louise asked the friendly-looking red-haired chap behind the counter, which would have been fine if she hadn't felt the need to over-enunciate in a very posh-sounding way while making the international signal for coffee by shaking imaginary beans in her hand, and looking a bit of a Gareth Hunt in the process.

Alongside the chap there was a tallish, angular young girl, with a sulky expression and a face that was quite possibly rather beautiful, if it were not crowned by a ridiculous pie-crust, olde-world elasticated bonnet and a murderous expression.

'Aw, caawww-feee?' she said, shaking her hand in the same stupid gesture Louise had used. 'Ah dunno. Mr MacKenzie, dweez sell CAAWWW-FEEE?'

Mr MacKenzie looked at the two girls with some sympathy. 'Don't be stupid, Kelpie,' he said. 'Serve theys.'

Kelpie gave the all-purpose teenage tut and walked over to a silver pot in the corner, slopping out two measures of instant into polystyrene cups before adding half a pint of milk and two sugars to each without asking them.

'Anything else for you girls?' said Mr MacKenzie pleasantly. 'Macaroni pie?'

'Let me just check my Atkins list,' said Louise. Katie kicked her.

'Umm.'

Nothing in the case laid out in front of them looked in the least bit familiar. There were pale brown slabs of what might have been fudge, only harder, lots of circular pies with holes poked in the middle of them which seemed, on closer examination, to hold anything from rhubarb to mince. There were gigantic, mutant sausage rolls and what may or may not have been very flat Cornish pasties. But both girls were starving. Suddenly Katie's eyes alighted on the scones.

'Two . . . um, of those please.' She couldn't remember how to pronounce the word. Was it scawn or scoone?

'The macaroons?'

'No, um, the . . .'

'French cake?'

What on earth was a French cake?

'The scoones,' said Louise. Katie winced. There was a pause, then everyone in the shop started laughing.

'Of course,' said the man serving, who had a kind face. 'Would that be a roosin scoone or a choose scoone?'

Maybe not that kind.

Louise and Katie found a bench in a tiny sliver of public park overlooking the harbour. The boats were coming back in, even though it was only ten in the morning. They looked beautiful and timeless, their jaunty red and green painted hulls outlined against the dark blue water. Katie was throwing most of her (delicious) scone to the cawing seagulls.

'Now I've got to find some complete stranger and try and intimidate them.'

'Ah yes,' said Louise. 'A great change from your usual job. Of finding complete strangers and licking their arses until they buy something.'

'That is not what PR is about,' said Katie. 'Except in, you know, the specifics.'

Louise kicked her heels. 'What do you think people do around here for fun?'

'Torture the foreigners,' said Katie. She nodded her head towards the baker's. Kelpie was heading over their way with two cronies. She had shaken off her ridiculous pie-crust hat to reveal a thick head of wavy hair with four or five rainbow-hued colours streaked through it, and taken out a packet of cigarettes. Even from fifty feet away, it was clear that she was doing an impression of Katie and Louise.

'We're big news around these here parts,' said Katie. 'I think we'd better make ourselves scarce, before we get bullied by a pile of twelve-year-olds. I'm going to find this Iain Kinross character. Sounds like some anal old baldie geezer who sits in his bedsit writing angry letters to the *Daily Mail*. He'll be putty in my hands.'

The three girls had seen them now; Kelpie was pointing them out. They were screaming with laughter in an over-exaggerated way.

'Oh no you don't,' said Louise. 'Not without me. They'll flay me alive.'

'They're harmless,' said Katie as they both got up from the bench and started to back away.

'I don't care,' said Louise. 'Take me with you, please.'

'I can't!'

'Of course you can! Just say I'm your . . . PA.'

'I'm not paying you.'

'Oh my God, you're a true Scottish person already,' said Louise.

'I'd like a SSSCCCCOOOOOOOONNNNE,' came from the other side of the park, carried on the wind.

'OK,' said Katie. 'But you'd better keep your mouth shut.'

'A SSSCCCCOOOOOOOONNNNE!'

* * *

It took them a while to find the offices of the *West Highland Times*, situated up a tiny alleyway off the main street of old grey stone buildings, which hosted a post office, a fishmongers, a kind of broom handle/vacuum cleaner bits and bobs type of place, a Woolworths and sixteen shops selling pet rocks and commemorative teaspoons. They looked very quiet at this time of year.

The small oak door was set into a peculiar turret on the edge of a house made of a particularly windworn granite. It was studded with large dark bolts, and only a tiny brass plaque set low on the left-hand side identified it. There didn't appear to be a bell, so, taking the initiative, Katie bowed her head and crept up the spiral staircase. Louise, whispering crossly under her breath at the exercise involved, followed her.

A little old man with grey hair sat at the top in a small room with an open door leading into the main body of the building. Katie could glimpse computers, typewriters and masses of paper beyond, and hear the regular dins and telephone calls of a newsroom.

They were not greeted with a welcoming smile.

'Did ye's no knock?'

Louise screwed up her face. Was no one going to be friendly to them around here?

'Sorry?' said Katie politely. 'Hello there. I'm from the Forestry Commission. I'd like to see Iain Kinross please.'

'He's busy.'

'How do you know?' said Louise.

'Shut up Louise,' said Katie, and motioned to her friend to sit in a chair, awkwardly positioned around the curve of the wall.

'I'm sure he won't be too busy to see me,' said Katie. She'd dealt with tougher hacks than this. 'Could you tell him I've come from Harry Barr's office?'

'In that case, he's busy for ever,' said the man.

Katie heard a snort come from Louise. 'I've got for ever,' she said. 'I think I'll just stand here and wait until he comes out. Or in.'

'You cannae do that,' said the man. 'I'll . . . I'll call security.'

'Unless your security's name is Kelpie, you're not going to scare me with that,' said Katie. 'My name is Katie Watson and I've come from the Forestry Commission. Please just tell him I'm here.'

The man looked at her, then turned back to his computer. 'He's busy,' he muttered in the tone of somebody feeling they definitely weren't being paid enough to take this kind of abuse.

'Yes, busy slagging off my employer,' said Katie. 'Let me see him!'

'No!'

The door to the newsroom finally banged open.

'Archie, Archie, can ah no get a wee bit of peace and quiet in here?' said an amused-sounding voice. 'I'm never going to win my Pulitzer with this racket, am I?'

Katie looked up. The owner of the voice, with its gentle Highland burr, was tall with green eyes, untidy curly brown hair and a mouth that looked as though it was permanently teetering on the edge of a grin. He turned to face them.

'What can I do for you? Let me tell you, if it's for prize cattle, you're swing out o' luck.'

The man on the desk gave Katie a look which clearly read 'I am now going to hate you for ever.'

'I heifer feeling you're not going to like it,' said Katie, pushing past the now incandescently annoyed assistant.

The green-eyed man opened his arms in a gesture of

surrender. 'What about your friend?' he said, looking over at Louise. Louise flashed him a beaming smile.

'She'll be fine,' said Katie, storming into the room beyond. Then she stopped suddenly. What she'd imagined to be a full and busy newsroom was really quite small, about fifteen feet long. There were three desks, one empty, one containing another very old man talking quietly down the phone, and one clearly belonging to the man beside her. In the corner was an old-fashioned record player, playing, at full volume, a sound effects track of typing, telephoning, shouting . . .

'You're really not meant to be in here,' said the young man with a sigh.

Katie stared at the record player and back to him.

'It's for advertising,' he said apologetically. 'That goes through Mr Beaumont there, but not everyone has a telephone and some people like to pop in on market day and . . .'

'You want them to think there's a million people working here.'

'Working for the good of the town.' The man's green eyes danced mischievously. 'Well, you've scooped us. Unfortunately, I'm not sure the local paper will run it.'

Katie smiled and put out her hand. 'Well, I'd like to say your secret's safe with me . . .'

He took it and bowed low. 'Yes, bonny English maid?'

'But I'm afraid I've been sent here by Harry Barr.'

He dropped her hand as if it were a live snake. 'Och, you have not now.' He looked around as if for assistance.

'You have to be Iain Kinross.'

He rubbed the back of his neck. 'Um, no. That was him out on the front desk. Bit of a dour type.'

He paced across the room and sat down on the comfortable green leather swivel chair in front of his desk. He had an antiquated computer in front of him, and a rather more used-looking typewriter; small Stanley knives and tubes of paper glue littered the tabletop and floor, and piles of paper filled the shelves around his desk. He squinted at her, and pushed back a rogue lock of hair. 'You don't look like a rottweiler.'

'I'm the new forestry PR,' said Katie.

'Oh God,' said Iain, and, suddenly, he disappeared below his desk.

'Are you being sick?' ventured Katie, when he didn't reappear.

'No, uh no.' He emerged. 'There's a mouse in here somewhere. Thought I saw it in one of the coffee cups.'

'*One* of the coffee cups?' said Katie. 'How many do you have under there?'

'One,' he said quickly. 'You don't want a coffee do you?'

'I sooo don't.'

'Good. That's good. So, I suppose Harry has told you lots of horrible things about me?'

'No.'

His open face brightened. 'Really? That's good.'

'Just that you were a "prickwobbling dicko".'

It fell again. 'Oh.'

'And that he's not killing all the trees.'

At this, Iain leaned forward. 'Look. Are you a country girl?'

'Yes,' said Katie quickly. Well, she'd nearly gone camping on the Duke of Edinburgh's Award scheme once. It wasn't her fault that it had started raining and her mother had given in to her noisy and tremulous tantrum and let her stay at home and watch *Dr Who* and drink hot chocolate instead. Katie had picked up a thing or two from her canny younger sister.

'OK well, you should understand then. If they're going to cross-fertilise from the GM firs just because they're gaining on their EU dispensation, it's going to be no surprise to anyone when they start to lose the red and have yet another heron panic.' He snorted at the ludicrousness of Harry's position.

'Heroin? Really? Up here? Well, I suppose it is Scotland,' said Katie.

Iain stared at her suspiciously. 'OK, well, let's pretend I was explaining to you as if, for one minute, you weren't a country girl. Just for fun.'

Katie got her notebook out.

'I mean, if you keep planting one type of tree instead of lots of different types, you're going to have to understand why animals who like lots of mixed habitats might move on. Which then affects the environment and turns back on the plantations themselves.'

'That sounds terrible,' said Katie. It *did* sound terrible. Though she didn't know why.

'It *is*,' said Iain, pounding his fist on the desk, which made lots of suspicious-sounding clinking china noises. 'That's why you . . .'

'Katie,' said Katie.

'That's why you, Katie, have to help me. That man is *killing trees*.'

'Yes!' said Katie, fired up with zeal. 'Oh, hang on. No! I can't! I work for him.'

'This isnae about "me" or "him",' said Iain, gazing into her eyes. 'This is for the trees, Katie.'

She looked at him for a second, then the moment was broken by the low trill of a mobile phone. A nice masculine ring, she couldn't help thinking.

'Kinross. Yeah? Oh, cock. Right, right, OK.' He snapped it shut. 'I'm so sorry. I have to go. Some stupid sheep's just had octuplets and it'll probably make the front page. Drink tonight?'

The invitation was so direct, Katie didn't even see it coming and wasn't sure what it meant. Was it a date or a continuation of their business conversation? She shouldn't really be fraternising with the enemy, should she – even if he was hot? On the other hand, the alternative was huddling under two sheets in a hayloft with Louise, so she wasn't in a position to be picky.

'Um, OK. Where?'

Iain, who was now shrugging his way into a parka, laughed. 'Well, take your pick. There's the Rum and Thump or the Mermaid or . . . nope, that's it.'

'The Mermaid, please,' said Katie fervently. The name sounded a bit more appealing.

'Got a taste for the wild side have we? OK, see you at seven. Remember –' he indicated the audio-challenged room sternly '– tell no one. Or Mr Beaumont will be on you like a cougar.'

The aged Mr Beaumont declined to look up from his whispered conversation on the telephone. Or maybe he couldn't.

'A cougar,' warned Iain again. Then he was gone.

Katie trailed behind him weakly as he swept out of the turret. She could see Louise's plaintive face follow him down the stairway as she emerged. Louise raised her eyes expectantly.

'I have to go back to the office,' said Katie, officiously. In fact, she needed five minutes by herself to think.

'Well?' asked Louise as they exited the small building, pausing only to give the receptionist evils.

Katie was feeling slightly more understanding. 'Well what?'

'Well what what? Did you just see that guy?!'

'Iain?'

'Ooh, yes, *Iain*, of course. You know him so well now. Yes, how was *Iain*, your husband. *Iain*. Everyone likes *Iain*. *Iain* and Katie.'

'Shut up Louise,' said Katie, trying to swallow down a blush.

'Well spill then. Jeez, the first hot, non-psychotic male we've seen in months and now you're trying to pretend you're Joan of Arc.'

'Well, he seems all right,' conceded Katie. 'First person we've met so far that didn't hate us on sight anyway.'

'That's good,' said Louise. 'Definitely, that's a good sign.' She futilely pulled the collar of her Karen Millen coat up against the stiff breeze coming in from the sea. 'Christ. You'd have thought people would have realised it was *cold* up here.'

'They did,' said Katie as they looked out across the bay. 'That's why there's so few of them. You have to admit, it's pretty though.'

'The South of France is pretty,' mused Louise. 'I'm amazed it's never occurred to them to just go *there*.'

Katie turned back towards the car. 'Well, there's no parking problems.'

'Can I sit in your car all afternoon?'

'Yes. And by the way, Iain asked me out for a drink tonight.'

Louise squealed. 'You bitch! You cast-iron bitch!'

By a tremulous stroke of bad luck, around the cobbled corner at that exact moment came Kelpie and her two cronies. They stared at each other for a moment. Then hurried away in barely concealed hysterics.

'CAAARRRRSSSTTTTT AYRRRON BEEETCH!' echoed up and down the high street.

'I'm actually glad to know we've doubled the entertainment available in this town in such a short space of time,' said Katie, unlocking the car. 'We should sell tickets.'

'Well?' Harry barked, somewhat rudely. He seemed preoccupied, eating a large home-made sandwich. Derek was nowhere to be seen. Katie was starving and watched him munch away, salivating. Carelessly, he ripped off a piece of his sandwich and threw it on the floor. Before Katie had time to object, there was a lazy snapping sound. Leaning over the desk, Katie saw the most beautiful black Labrador stretched out at his feet.

'Ooh, lovely doggie,' said Katie, before she could help herself. Harry looked at her as if she'd just insulted his mother (which of course, she'd already managed earlier).

'Francis isn't a "doggie",' said Harry, spluttering crumbs. 'He's a working animal.'

Francis didn't look anything like a working animal, unless he was a member of a particularly strong trade union. He batted his long eyelashes at her twice, then fell asleep.

'Sorry,' said Katie. 'Does he bite?'

'Yes, that's the kind of work he does,' said Harry scathingly. 'He bites ditzy PR girls. Got his paws full around here.'

'You're a very hostile person,' said Katie. 'Is it the sandwich?'

For once, Harry looked nonplussed. He soon regained his sangfroid. 'What did Kinross say?'

'I think you may have something of an image problem,' said Katie.

'In English?'

'Um, he says . . .' she consulted her notebook urgently, 'that there's an issue with biodiversity, herons, food chain implications, blah blah blah . . . basically you're killing all the trees.'

'Typical!' said Harry furiously. 'I'm going to kill that little prick.'

'And we come back to the image problem.'

'OK,' said Harry. 'Now you see our problem. So, what are you going to do about that little shit?'

This was Katie's moment. She was usually pretty good at the client pitch of how they were going to find the USP and work it to their point of view, then extend that point of view throughout the nation. Although usually facing her across the table were excited haircare product manufacturers and the implication was that she could get it about that Jennifer Aniston used their gunk. She wasn't used to trying to convince a homicidal tree-hugger and his gently snoring dog.

'Well, first, I think we need to have a meeting. Have a frank and fearless exchange of views. Really get to grips with what the underlying misunderstandings are. Maybe over a nice lunch somewhere. Then . . .'

'Well, that's absolutely out of the question,' said Harry. 'Next.'

'There's nowhere to get a nice lunch?'

'Well, that too. But I hate that lying son of a bitch.'

'Why?'

Katie was excitedly picking over the possibilities in her head. There must be a girl involved, surely? Hearts broken? Ooh, maybe they were long-lost brothers? TWINS, bitter rivals, born on the same day, to grow up to strive over the heart and soul of the town, nay, the very Highlands themselves . . .

'That's none of your business,' said Harry, heading out of the door.

* * *

'He's such a grumpy bastard,' moaned Katie later, back at their digs.

'He really does sound like Gordon Brown. Are you sure he's not a bit romantic and rugged?'

Louise was putting make-up on, thus intruding on Katie's date by insinuation whilst pretending to be simply trying out new lipstick. She'd managed to find some candles with which to light their dank room, which, although flattering, was forcing them to apply lipstick in the style of Coco the Clown.

'No, retarded. He's clearly got some kind of big gay crush on Iain.'

'Haven't we all?' Louise circled some rouge on her cheeks.

'You're not coming, you know.'

'Just a quick drink. Please. I've seen the visitors' lounge here.'

'What's it like?'

Louise shuddered. 'There was an old man sitting in the corner watching *University Challenge*. He didn't look up when I walked in. I think he was dead and ossifying. Oh, and they can't get Channel Five.'

'Big whoop.'

'. . . or 4. And ITV is called Grampian and BBC2 is in foreign.'

'What do you mean it's in foreign?'

'I don't know, do I? It looks like *Postman Pat* and then they all go "*Grbbrrtggtthh tht ht ht th thvvvvv*".'

'Interesting. But still, no.'

'Do you love this guy?'

'*No!*'

'Do you love me?'

'That is Very Unfair.'

'You dragged me up here.'

'You forced yourself on me!'

'I did not! And . . .' Louise pouted her bottom lip in a way Katie recognised both from primary school (natural) and secondary (fake and put on for boys and suggestible male teachers alike). '. . . I'm going through a difficult time. I thought you of all people would understand, seeing as it's your sister that . . .'

Katie put her hands over her ears. 'La la la, not listening! OK. Well, maybe there'll be another man there for you to talk to.'

'Are you serious? Are you really considering trying to get off with someone you might have to work against for the next eight months? Wow, you're very brave.'

Katie hadn't looked at it this way at all. In fact, ever since Iain had grasped her hand in his, her insides had been on something of a repeater track, like a scrambled record, which went 'green eyes green eyes snog snog yum yikes snog snog green', repeated ad infinitum. It didn't really give her brain much room to process any other information. The practical consequences of the matter – that they were in a very small village, that he may well be married and that whatever the outcome she was almost certainly going to have to see him every day – had faded into the background of the insistent beat of her groin reminding her she hadn't had sex for five months.

She pretended to give it serious consideration. 'There are plenty of people who've slept with people they've worked with and it's turned out great,' she said decisively. 'Don't you think?'

Louise looked at her as if she was holding a dangerous animal. 'Umm . . .'

'Come on. What about . . .' Alas, all that flooded Katie's mind at that moment was the memory that Louise had met Max when she'd been briefly working at his office. Suddenly, she had a mental picture of her and Louise in fifty years' time, with her still treading on eggshells all the time. It was a sad fact that Clara's act had changed not only Katie and her relationship but Katie and Louise's too. 'Ouf,' she said.

'Come on,' said Louise, changing the subject. 'I hope you're not wearing your pulling knickers.'

'I didn't even *bring* my pulling knickers,' said Katie as they braced themselves against the wind outside the front door of Water Lane. 'I just brought my thermal knickers.'

'Maybe they find that sexy up here,' said Louise. 'Brrr.'

Chapter Six

One would have thought, given the size of the town, that it would be easy to find one of its two pubs, but after stumbling up and down cobbled stairways for fifteen minutes in a howling gale, they had to concede this would not in fact be the case. Louise shouting 'taxi', and standing in the road with her hand up very quickly ceased to be amusing too. At last, panting and red-cheeked, they collapsed down a narrow stairway near the harbour and spotted a tiny doorway with light and heat and smoke exuding from the tiny open window. It looked immeasurably welcoming, and a ceramic statue of a mermaid adorned the wall, the centrepiece of a mosaic of pretty shells.

'Ooh,' said Louise, excited.

Katie tentatively pushed open the door into the hubbub of warmth and heat. At first it was hard to get her bearings. The pub was crammed with people, but actually it was little more than a small room. There was a roaring fire at one end, surrounded by strange-looking bellows and brass implements, red velvet stools on the wooden floor around old pitted tables, a dartboard that looked positively dangerous in such a tiny space and an old-fashioned bar, with golden bar taps gleaming, and large optics clinging to the back wall. Furious fiddle and whistle music was playing.

There were people everywhere, on every available seat, leaning against the bar, hovering around the fire. A couple of dogs dozed blissfully under bar stools.

There wasn't a single woman there.

The room gradually fell silent as Katie and Louise hung by the door, taking it all in. There were tall men, short men, thin men, fat men. Rough-looking fishermen, with tattoos on their knuckles and salt in their hair. Intense-looking techie men with specs, rucksacked travellers. A couple of tweedy young bufton-tuftons at the bar who could have been (and were) the local laird having a pint with the local vet. Prosperous-looking farmers, furtive-looking labourers. Bald, ruddy country men, withered old men. Men everywhere.

Finally, after a long pause, Louise leaned over to Katie. 'Is this my surprise party? Or heaven?'

'Come in if you're coming then,' came a voice. 'Don't let the weather in noo.'

Somebody said something the girls couldn't make out, and there came a hearty guffaw from the back. Stiffening, Katie eventually took a small step forward.

Behind the bar was the most extraordinary gentleman. He was precisely the height of the bar itself, with three tufts of hair, one on either side and one on the middle of his head, and his cheeks were ruddy. He looked like a garden gnome.

Space cleared at the bar for them instantly, and Katie and Louise had the uncomfortable experience of settling themselves gracefully on stools whilst being eagerly watched by every single person in the room. Katie had scanned as many faces as she dared without looking as if she was up for trade, but there was no sign of Iain. Surely if he was there he would have leaped up immediately anyway. She smoothed down her skirt, wondering if perhaps her prized Kenzo Japanese-style skirt was pushing it a bit for in here. Everyone else's clothing appeared to have holes in it too, but not for fashionable reasons.

'What can I get you lassies?' asked the miniature barman. Katie had been going to order a vodka tonic, but didn't want to put the barman in a difficult position vis-à-vis reaching the optics.

'White wine please.'

'Same for me please,' said Louise.

'Ah, foreigners,' said the man, but not in an unfriendly way. He ducked behind the bar and started shifting through what sounded like many bottles and kegs. 'Now . . . wine, wine, wine. I know we had it in here somewhere.'

'I don't know whether to be over the moon or scared shit-free,' whispered Louise. 'It's like a cross between *The Box of Delights* and *The Accused*.'

'Sssh!' said Katie as the barman straightened up, beaming and holding up a sticky, dusty bottle of something so old its label had peeled off. It was less white wine than a kind of rusty yellow, and half empty, with a screw top. There was a crust around the top.

'That looks lovely,' said Katie politely.

'Is that Feather's sample bottle?' came a masculine voice behind them. 'Bloody been looking for that for months.'

The tiny publican's eyes widened. 'It is too, you know.'

A huge beefy hand reached over their heads and hit Louise on the ear.

'Oww,' said Louise. 'Sorry, I forgot I had an invisible head.'

'I've just stopped you drinking horse piss,' said the voice. 'I'd have thought you would have shown a bit more gratitude.'

The girls turned around on their stools. A tall, chunky man with a pink, florid face stood in front of them, in a ratty old tweed jacket.

'Really?' said Louise. 'Or is that the worst chat-up line ever invented?'

The man blinked twice, then smiled. 'It belongs to Fitz's mare. 'Course, you're more than welcome to find out through empirical testing. Lachlan, get us a couple of glasses.'

'Right away,' said Lachlan, and busied himself at the back of the bar.

'I don't want to come on like a health and safety inspector,' said Katie. 'But why are we being served horse piss in a bar? Is it like, a hazing ritual?'

'I'm sure Lachlan just forgot,' said the man. 'Or I forgot to pick it up.' He took the bottle and put it down by his briefcase, then held out his hand. Both the girls declined to shake it.

'Craig MacPhee. I'm the vet around here.'

'Yeah? Or are you just taking the piss?' said Louise. 'Ha aha aha.'

He smiled. 'Can I buy you a real drink?'

'Yes,' said Louise promptly.

'Thank you,' said Katie. The normal hubbub had restored itself to the pub, as the two women ordered vodka tonics (Lachlan had a little step behind the bar, so it wasn't difficult at all).

It was a quarter past eight, and still no sign of Iain. Katie sipped her drink as Louise pestered Craig as to whether there was more to vetting than horse piss and sticking your hands up a cow's bottom.

Finally, the little door pinged to announce another customer's arrival, and it was Iain, his collar turned up against the chill, his lovely green eyes roaming the room as he hung up his coat, to general murmurings of welcome.

'Lovely girls! You both came!' he said as he approached the bar, looking as if they were the most beautiful creatures he'd ever seen.

'Hey,' Katie said.

'I hope that's vodka or gin or something,' he said. 'I was going to warn you, this isn't much of a wine town. Don't know what you sophisticated London ladies drink.'

'Oh, any old horse piss does us,' said Louise.

'Hmm,' said Iain. 'Another?'

Katie realised about halfway through her third vodka and tonic that she was surreptitiously feeling guilty about something, but couldn't work out what it was until Iain leaned over closely. She could smell his aftershave (nice, something gentlemanly, like Penhaligon's, which was a huge relief. She didn't like those blokes who bathed in Egoïste) and felt a little faint. What was he going to whisper? She closed her eyes in anticipation.

'So, are you going to be my spy at the Commission?' he whispered quietly. 'Come on. It'll be fun.'

She cracked one eye open. 'Of course not!' she said. 'Anyway, spying's not fun. Look at David Shayler. He put on six stone in prison.'

'Yeah,' said Iain. 'But think of the noble cause.'

'You're a journalist! You don't have noble causes!'

'Perhaps I'm the exception.'

'I've known you five minutes and you're trying to bribe me with vodka to spy on my employer!'

'Oh yeah,' said Iain. 'I see. Yeah, I can imagine that,

viewed in a certain way, that could appear a tad suspicious. Another vodka?'

'Yes please. And anyway,' she said, feeling bold, 'maybe I just don't want to mix business with pleasure.'

His eyes sparkled at her. 'I'll drink to that.'

'I's sure there weren't this many steps on the way down,' said Louise, as they negotiated their way back to Water Lane.

'I's not cold any more,' said Katie, who was quite fired up by all the vodka and the unaccustomed male attention.

'Yezz,' said Louise. 'Good. I like it here.' She slipped in a puddle. 'I hate it here.'

'Come on.' Katie put her arm around her shoulders.

'That Iain is a veh veh veh veh handsome man,' said Louise, as they turned into the darkened driveway.

'He is,' said Katie. 'Deffo.'

A large bosom loomed at them out of the night.

'What time do you call this?' boomed the imperious voice of Mrs McClockerty.

Louise stumbled a little. 'I call it time to avoid the scary lady in the dark,' she hiccuped. 'Katie, there's a scary lady standing here in the dark. I'm frightened.'

'I'm sorry,' said Katie to Mrs McClockerty, crossing her fingers behind her back. 'She's never like this normally.'

'I should hope not. You're abominations.'

'We're abomiwhats?' said Louise, who suddenly looked as if she was squaring up for a fight.

'Nothing. Nobody,' said Katie. 'You're asleep and having a dream. I'm sorry. This won't happen again.'

Mrs McClockerty sniffed loudly. 'I'm docking one of your breakfast pieces. EACH,' she said, then stormed back indoors, slamming the door behind her. Half dragging Louise, Katie made her way around to the servants' entrance at the side, thinking of a few alternative uses for the now denied breakfast pieces on Mrs McClockerty, all of which would require the immediate application of a team of highly-trained surgeons.

'And there isn't one of those for hundreds of miles,' she thought viciously to herself. 'You'd have to make do with Craig the vet.'

It was with a heavy hangover and a rumbling stomach that Katie turned up to work the following morning, feeling slightly bad. She hadn't agreed to be a spy, but on the other hand, she'd always prided herself on being a professional, and dallying with the enemy, and his gorgeous green eyes, wasn't exactly professional. She meditated on this whilst trying to get to grips with the antediluvian computer which was so slow she was wondering if she'd missed the handle you had to turn on the back.

'What's up with you?' asked Harry, who had an office of his own, but seemed to spend most of his time in the open-plan section, discussing things with Derek, or out somewhere. 'You're looking at my sandwich like Francis does.'

'I am not,' said Katie, turning her glance to the screen.

'Are you hungry?'

'I'm a girl. We don't get hungry.'

'Is Auntie S not feeding you?'

'Auntie who?'

'Oh, Mrs McClockerty to you. Senga. S.'

'Actually, no, she isn't. We were only allowed one "piece" at breakfast this morning. Which means one slice of bread. I hope you're not paying too much to keep us in all this luxury.'

Harry laughed out loud. Katie suddenly saw that he had a lovely broad smile, with healthy-looking white teeth. It totally transformed his face when he laughed. It was something he didn't do much of.

'What did you do?'

'What do you mean, what did we do? Nothing. She's starving us.'

'I'm sorry, but Auntie S's One Piece Rule is extremely serious. She's harsh but fair.'

'Exactly the qualities one looks for in the hospitality industry,' said Katie. 'Anyway, it's not fair.'

'What did you do?' He was grinning now.

'*Nothing*. If you aren't allowed to go out and explore your local surroundings in a new environment . . .'

'Ahh,' said Harry annoyingly.

'What? "Ahh" what?'

'Scooshed?'

'*What*?'

'Were youse scooshed?'

'Do you mean *inebriated*?'

'I thought so. Don't go home scooshed, she hates it. Thinks the demon drink is the ruination of young ladies.'

'We know it is. That's the point.'

'Well then, you'll have to get used to only getting one piece.'

'Give me a sandwich.'

'And risk Auntie S's wrath? You must be joking. Come on, I'd better show you around.'

'Show me around where? I've seen the Woolworths.'

Harry shook his head. 'How many times did I promise myself I wasn't going to take on any daft city lassies . . .'

It quickly became evident that Francis usually sat up front in the Land-Rover and wasn't delighted at being usurped, so there was an unseemly tussle of Harry and a flurry of muddy paws before Francis dejectedly slunk into the back. The storms of the night before had abated, and although the breeze was still biting, the world looked washed clean and harshly fresh.

Instead of taking the bumpy cobbled road into town, the Land-Rover bumped around the back of the office and took off down a muddy track, straight into the heart of the forest. The trees closed off much of the morning light far quicker than Katie had expected.

'This is *coille mhòr*, the forest,' said Harry. 'Mostly coniferous trees, planted by us – that's why they're in such straight rows. They do a lot for the soil, and they're useful for lots of timber applications.'

'Christmas,' nodded Katie knowledgeably.

Harry looked at her. '. . . including the highly competitive forty-foot Christmas tree market.'

Katie squirmed. So, she hadn't quite got the sense of scale right.

'. . . they also provide a habitat for over two hundred species, including one of the last major outposts of red squirrels in the UK, plenty of deer – actually too many deer. There's always been deer in Scotland, but we kind of overdid the restocking.'

'Deer are lovely,' said Katie, peering to see if she could spot a fawn between the trees and thinking of Bambi. 'I'm glad there's lots of them.'

'Yes, that's right,' said Harry. 'Pretty animals are always the best. Actually, they're a pest. They clear miles of vegetation and make it difficult for the other animals to survive. Even other pretty ones, like rabbits. Oh no, Katie, how would you decide between them?'

'Deer,' said Katie decisively. 'Definitely. Unless there were otters involved.'

Harry closed his eyes in exasperation. 'You were really and truly the best your office could come up with to come and work here? Seriously, you're the cream?'

'I was joking,' said Katie defensively.

'Well, there's joking and there's ignorance.'

'I'm trying my best,' said Katie sulkily. 'I didn't ask for this job, OK?'

He turned on her suddenly. 'What on earth do you mean by that? You came up here for the interview. Then you came back. Why are you doing us all such a massive favour?'

'I did come up here, but then I met you and decided I didn't want the job! Then they sent me anyway! But if you want me to do anything for you, you've got to explain things to me and not give me evils all the time. I can write, I can place things, I can spin things and I can do my best to influence people to look on the best side of everything you do. If that offends your delicate country sensibilities, then tough. Don't hire a PR firm then, because that's what we do. And it's not my effing fault that we don't have a branch in Fairlish where we all study five years of pine tree bloody science! You're the one spending taxpayer's money, take some responsibility!'

Harry drove on in silence. Katie bit her lip. Bloody hell. Where had that come from? Oh God, what if he sent her home? Olivia would be fuming and actually she had quite started to enjoy herself. There was a reason why she didn't get the big jobs at the agencies and she knew it was her inability to keep her big mouth shut and let the client always be right. Bugger, bugger, bugger.

She reached a hand back in the Land-Rover and Francis licked it. Oh well. She scratched the fur under his chin and he rubbed his head on her wrist, making pleased noises.

Eventually, Harry sighed. 'My dog seems to like you,' he said. 'I don't, but he does.'

'Maybe you should put your dog in charge.'

'He hates responsibility.'

Katie took a deep breath. 'I'm really sorry,' she said. Her least favourite words in the world. 'If you want to let me go, I understand.'

Harry rubbed the back of his head and laughed. 'I think that's a bit of an overreaction, don't you? Plus, on that evidence, I think it might be a better punishment to keep you.'

Katie harrumphed.

'Do you think you could at least pretend to listen when I'm talking to you and try to keep down the sarcastic remarks?'

'Yes,' said Katie, biting her tongue.

They spent the rest of the day touring the forest in relative calm. Harry described the flora and fauna of each area, how they were important, how they undertook the husbandry and what the gamekeepers and tree surgeons did. Katie was amazed to find it was actually incredibly interesting, and also astonished by how many people Harry's office employed. She even managed to keep remarks about how much her mother wanted her to marry a doctor to herself.

'You never see any of the surgeons,' said Harry. 'They don't like being indoors. They start pacing, like panthers. Willie Mac spends more time sleeping in his bothy than he does in his house.'

'What's a bothy?'

'It's like a little hut in the woods. Not exactly five star, but it suits some. It's quiet.'

'The woods aren't quiet,' said Katie. 'Full of creaking

noises and scary rustlings. I mean, well, just general nature taking its course kind of stuff, of course,' she added, aware she was going to have to toughen up and get used to country ways quickly. 'Not scary at all.'

'Don't know about that,' said Harry. 'There used to be lots of boar here, and we're thinking of bringing them back. Wolves too. And adders.'

'Maybe I'll just stay in the car,' she answered, all resolve instantly evaporating.

Finally, when they were miles away from town and, it felt, any other living human being, Harry forded a stream in the Land-Rover, and brought them to a halt.

'Here,' he said.

The afternoon light was settling on the tops of the trees, which were just, here and there, beginning to show signs of green, distant promises of a spring still not quite making its presence felt. This wasn't a carefully managed forest, like the endless acres they had just driven through; it was natural and running wild. Roots snaked around each other, and the vegetation lay thickly rotting on the ground. Everywhere there were signs of life just flashing by out of reach; a quick streak of silver in the stream, a rustle in the undergrowth; a vanishing pair of sharp yellow eyes.

'Wow,' said Katie, stepping out. 'Where's the gingerbread house?'

She was glad she'd bought those stout boots at the outdoor shop in Soho (or the 'Big Outdoor Nerd's Shop' as she had called it until that first visit) before they left.

As she stepped forward, the dead leaves crunched underfoot.

'Shh shh!' said Harry, grabbing her arm and pointing. Rising out of the woods, outlined by the fading sun was a huge golden kestrel, rearing backwards. As if having seen them and found them wanting, it immediately twirled away and soared upwards towards the sun, lazily batted its giant wings twice, then disappeared into the far yonder. It was one of the most beautiful things Katie had ever seen.

'My goodness,' she said. In that way you do when something unexpected happens and you've had a really mad few days and are feeling a bit homesick and unfamiliar, she suddenly felt like crying. She choked it down hard. Fortunately, Harry hadn't noticed; he was striding forwards into the forest.

'I love it here,' he said. 'It's my favourite place in the whole . . . well, the whole world probably.' He smiled apologetically for his unaccustomed hyperbole.

'Hmm?' responded Katie, still not quite trusting herself to speak.

'Look at this,' said Harry, pointing out a thick tree stump, covered in vines, that was exactly the right height for a stool.

He put his fingers on the rings. 'See this ring here?'

Katie nodded.

'When Queen Victoria was alive, she used to come riding here. And this ring was made when Bonnie Prince Charlie was leading an army to London. Here, further in, Mary Queen of Scots was in Holyrood when this was still a sapling.'

Katie traced the lines with her fingers.

'This tree was over four hundred years old when she fell,' mused Harry. 'Sometimes I think they have more claim to the earth than we do.'

His face looked distant and brooding. Katie found it hard to stop staring at him, and felt the need to break the mood.

'Ah, but can they make pancakes?' she said suddenly.

He smiled. 'No. They can't make pancakes. They can't make wars either.'

They walked on to a glade covered in toadstools. Although still chilly, the late afternoon sun filtered through the trees in slices.

'My mother used to bring me here when I was small,' said Harry suddenly. 'I really did think fairies and elves lived here then. Sorry,' he apologised embarrassedly. 'That's stupid.'

'Of course it's not stupid,' said Katie. 'I still kind of believe it now.'

Harry gave a half-smile. 'Thanks.'

'No, I actually mean it,' protested Katie.

'You act that daft, I'm not surprised.'

'Don't talk about the fairies like that – they'll come and take your teeth.'

He shook his head. 'Anyway, this place is called *Gealach Coille*. It means, "Moon Forest" in Gaelic.'

'Oh!' said Katie.

'What?'

'The language. I just realised what Louise was watching on BBC2.'

'Well, I'm delighted for you. Anyway, this is one of our greatest concerns and, really, at the heart of why we're recruiting PR now. To strengthen our armoury, if you like.'

'What?'

'Can you keep a secret?'

'Of course,' said Katie, crossing her fingers. She'd learned her lesson about that one.

'This cannot get out, do you understand? The only people that know are me and Derek.'

Katie nodded solemnly.

'This is your job, do you understand? You can be as annoying as you like, but this is the really important stuff.'

'OK, OK.'

'So if you want to go back to London, you have to say now. Once I tell you this, you're committed to the end.'

Katie looked around her. Motes from the leaves floated in the beams of sunlight. There was a gentle rustle of breeze through the trees. The peaty earth gave off a rich, dank odour underneath her feet. Without thinking, she leaned her hand out and felt the stump, the lichen damp and the wood flaky underneath her fingers. It felt effortlessly strong, one of the anchors of the world that stretched far beneath the earth. Harry watched her, quiet for once. She wasn't always a stuck-up harridan, he supposed. When she kept her mouth shut for more than ten seconds, she was almost attractive.

Katie looked up, and seemed surprised to see Harry staring at her. He dropped his gaze immediately.

'Um, OK,' said Katie, who had indeed been a little taken aback by the intensity of his slightly craggy stare. He still looked like a young Gordon Brown, but there was a weird bit of her wondering if that was really such a bad thing. It surprised her so much she wasn't exactly expecting to say what she said next. 'OK. Yes, I'm ready. I'm staying.'

His face suddenly cracked into a grin that looked like the sun coming out.

'What?' said Katie crossly. 'Stop looking at me like that. What, you think I won't make it?'

'No,' said Harry, who was as flustered by his idiotic grin as she was. 'Don't know what I was thinking of.'

'Good. So, what's this big secret then?'

Harry took a deep breath as his thoughts instantly returned to more serious matters. 'Well, *Gealach Coille* isn't protected.'

'What do you mean? I thought all forests were protected?'

'Well. We're victims of our own success really. We've hit our quotas on replanting; on environmental impact, and, well, I already explained about the deer.'

'They can't pull this down!' said Katie, outraged suddenly. 'This has been here longer than anything, than any one of them!'

'Yes,' Harry agreed earnestly.

'And there's millions of animals living here.'

'Yes.'

'And the fairies would be furious.'

'Let's head back to the car,' said Harry.

'So what are they going to do with it?'

'Well, they can't knock it down completely – yet. But they can clear a great deal away and build . . . ahem,' Harry cleared his throat as if he couldn't quite bring himself to say the word.

'Yes?'

'Um, I believe they want to build a golf course of some kind.'

'They just want to chop everything down right here – for a golf course?'

Harry nodded.

'But that's just *stupid*. Plus, imagine, golfers everywhere. They'll all wear yellow sweaters and toast the Queen.'

'Quite,' said Harry. 'Although to be quite honest, I wouldn't care if it was a convent for sick children. I really don't want to lose this forest.'

He fondled Francis's ears, who had been too lazy to come for the walk and was firmly ensconced in the front seat, pretending to be asleep. Katie climbed around into the back without comment.

'And once they've got planning for that, they get it for anything. Petrol stations, Holiday Inns, a stupid airport or something.'

Katie sat in the back of the Land-Rover, looking out of the tarpaulin. Brilliant pink rays of sun were hitting the tops of the trees. They looked as though they were on fire.

'Well – and don't take this the wrong way, OK, I'm just playing devil's advocate . . .'

Harry's grunt indicated that he rarely thought of her as anything but.

'. . . but it's progress, isn't it? Isn't it what people want? Won't it bring a lot of money to the area? Isn't it a good thing?'

'Now that,' said Harry, stabbing the steering wheel with his finger, 'is exactly what I'd expect that prick from the newspaper to say.'

'I'm just *saying*,' said Katie.

'Every single part of this country is "developed",' growled Harry. 'They've concreted over all of the south, and now they're after us. And they won't be happy until they've squeezed every bit of profit out of the soil, and covered it all with golf courses and Starbucks and McDonalds. There's nothing wrong with our area. Bring outside money in and the same thing happens as it does everywhere else: people can't afford to buy houses in the towns they were born in and neighbour falls out with neighbour.'

'You know, you talk like someone a lot older than you are,' said Katie. 'But I see your point.'

'I just think,' said Harry, 'that they ought to leave just some of the country as it is. Just a tiny wee bit. Leave us alone. Give the damn country a little space to breathe.'

'So, why's it a secret?'

'Well,' said Harry, 'I was kind of hoping that we could fend them off and nobody in the town would find out. And that's your job.'

* * *

He drew the Land-Rover to a halt some way further on. They'd been sitting in silence for ages.

'There's one last place I want to show you,' he said, clambering down and disappearing into the trees. Katie could hear a whooshing noise as she headed after him.

'What?' she yelled. God, it was dark in here. She could just see a flash of Harry's coat ahead.

'Are you going to leave me out on the hillside for wolves?'

Harry turned around to face her. 'What kind of boss do you think I am . . . Actually, don't answer that.'

Behind her, Katie noticed Francis hopping down from his seat and following them into the woods. She threw Harry a dirty look, which he ignored and continued thrashing on.

After ten minutes of this, during which Katie was really beginning to regret the afternoon's rapprochement, the thick black coils of the trees suddenly beamed a canopy and she emerged blinking into the golden late-afternoon light. Ahead was a huge tumbling waterfall, crashing through shiny, moss-covered rocks, ending in a deep pool that meandered off into a river through the trees at the far side. This was obviously the source of the crashing noise Katie had heard coming through the woods.

'It's magnificent,' she smiled.

Harry nodded. 'I know. Come here – drink some of the water.'

Francis had already run up to the side of the pool and was lapping enthusiastically.

'It's got a dog's tongue in it,' complained Katie.

'Don't be a woose. You can drink from above it if you like.'

'Don't birds pee in it?'

'Do you pee in your sink?'

'No, although I've known some fellows that did.'

The water was the coldest, clearest, most refreshing Katie had ever tasted. It chilled her body right through to her stomach and was sweet and clean. She scooped it up with both hands and felt like throwing it over her face.

'Good?' asked Harry, watching her closely.

'They should bottle this stuff,' said Katie.

Harry rolled his eyes. 'They do. But this is nearer the source. It's best here.'

'It's wonderful,' said Katie, sitting on a rock and letting her fingers trail in the bubbling water. On the other side of the water were four large white birds sipping delicately. They seemed completely unafraid of them, and even Francis ignored them, preferring to drink his fill, then settling back for a quick nap.

'So,' said Katie finally, 'what is it you want me to do exactly?'

'Stop the golf course.'

'Oh, no, that much I've got. I mean, do you have a plan of action you want me to follow, or do you want me to take the initiative and handle it from scratch?'

'Hmm,' said Harry. He didn't look as though he was quite sure.

'OK,' said Katie. 'Well, there's a few ways we could go about it. We could confront them directly. Or we could chum up with the local MP and the planning board and try to stop them that way. Or we could aim for more direct action. It's going to need money for advertising, banners, campaign slogans – the more money we can get together, the louder the fuss can be. And if we can kick and shout and scream and get enough publicity together, well, that would probably be enough to make it not worth their while continuing.'

'OK,' nodded Harry seriously.

'OK what? What do you want me to do?'

Harry threw a small pebble into the water. 'You're absolutely sure you can't just have a quiet word with them and make them all go away?'

'Do I look like Mike Tyson?'

Harry shrugged.

'Shut up!'

Smiling, Harry expertly skimmed a stone across the water. Then his face grew serious again.

'A secret for now, OK?'

Chapter Seven

It was a difficult dilemma, but Katie had given it much thought and, fifteen minutes after she'd reached the boarding house, had decided to spill Harry's secret to Louise. Because she truly didn't know quite what to think, and Louise would give her some much needed impartiality. Plus, Louise really wouldn't care that much so she wouldn't be prejudiced one way or another. They were huddled in the teashop, which was open until seven, thus meaning if they were quick they had half a chance of getting something to eat for dinner that wasn't from the Spar and thus entirely composed of nuts, refined sugar, E129, FL98 and glucose extract. No Kelpie today: they'd checked. The steam rose from the tea urns and fogged up the small windows that faced the port. The lights from the boats gleamed in the darkening twilight. From the headland, a lighthouse glowed every few seconds, illuminating the bobbing boats, creaking and chattering to themselves up and down on the waves.

'God, he's quite right,' said Louise, tucking gratefully into a hearty helping of shepherd's pie. 'You don't want to change things around here. I walked six miles today, and only got rained on twice. I got asked out four times when I passed the research institute. Don't you think they're good statistics?'

Katie toyed with her shepherd's pie. She really wasn't feeling that hungry. 'But, I mean, just not telling anyone and keeping quiet about something that might completely change the community . . . that's not right, is it?'

'I thought it was part of your job to cover things up?'

'You're confusing us with Exxon Valdez. No, our job is to tell people things.'

'Or to sit on harmful information. Anyway, it hardly matters. It would be awful if this place got infested with tourists. It would change completely. Everyone would want Sky Digital and complain about not being able to get a mobile signal. Then they'd start putting masts up and, before you know it, Las Vegas.'

Katie stared at her. 'You know, Louise, I think you really are a country girl at heart.'

'Bollocks I am. I wouldn't know a cow if it pissed on my boots. Which, incidentally, one nearly did today.'

Katie noticed, however, that Louise hadn't said a single thing about going back to London. In fact, her cheeks were flushed pink from the unaccustomed exercise of walking everywhere. In London, she could barely make it as far as the corner shop without whining.

'Anyway,' said Louise, scooping the last of the carrots into her mouth. 'Gotta go. Got plans.'

'Under what circumstances do you have plans? You do not,' said Katie, outraged.

'Yes I do. I told Craig the Vet I might see him in the Mermaid. And Fergus. He's the tree surgeon.'

'He's not a real doctor you know,' said Katie, dismayed.

Louise tutted. 'I know that, stupid. Have you ever met a doctor with biceps the size of a melon?'

'No, and I'm not sure I'd trust one if I did.'

'Anyway, it's all very casual. Katie,' Louise leaned forwards, as if imparting some knowledge of great import. 'Did you know there are LOADS of guys here?'

'As far as I can tell, there are *only* guys here, Louise.'

Louise's eyes shone with the fervency of the true believer. 'I've just realised that this is where they've all been hiding! All the decent ones, I mean, not the slime-ball magnets I run into. All the hunky single men – they're here! Out making themselves even more hunky in the open air! It's so obvious when you think about it. This place has a disproportionate amount of men. I can't believe we missed it for so long!'

'We've been blind,' nodded Katie.

'Don't you just want to bring up everyone we know? Maybe we should start a travel company for single women.'

'I think Turkish waiters have already cornered that market, but go right ahead.'

Louise smiled and looked out of the window.

'We are rubbish feminists you and me, aren't we?' said Katie, playing with the saltcellar.

Louise sighed. 'Why can't I be a feminist and want a boyfriend at the same time?'

'I don't know,' said Katie. 'Honestly, I really don't.'

'Well then,' said Louise. 'Are you coming with me or not?'

Katie looked down at her untouched dinner. 'I don't think so, no.'

'Oh well – less competition for me,' said Louise. 'Hang on – that means *no competition at all*. Yippee!'

As Louise bounced out of the shop into the twilight, Katie smiled ruefully. So much for help over a delicate issue. She was still convinced Harry was wrong. Surely if they could rally the local people against any schemes to change their environment, that would work best. She recalled the anti-road protesters from a few years ago – all those filthy-looking chaps who lived in trees for months on end. But hadn't they failed and the roads had been built anyway? Oh, it was so . . .

'Now, what great thoughts are going on in that head?' came a friendly-sounding voice. 'You can't be puzzling out Mr MacKenzie's recipe for mince and tatties, that's for sure, because your dinner looks rum.'

Startled, Katie's head reared up, and she found herself staring straight into the green eyes of Iain Kinross.

'Huh . . . hi,' she stuttered. 'Imagine running into you again.'

'Hi,' he said. 'Sorry – you're from London, right?'

She nodded, taking a gulp of water.

'Yeah, well, you should know you bump into absolutely everyone you know in a village every day.'

She nodded.

'So it's not really that much of a coincidence.'

'OK. Doesn't that get a bit annoying, seeing everyone all the time?'

'It depends on who you see. Listen, are you hungry?'

Katie glanced meaningfully at her plate, and grinned at him. 'I'm actually eating right now. What do you think I'm doing here, in a restaurant, with a plate of food in front of me, and a knife and fork in my hands and, you know, a napkin and stuff?'

'Och, you haven't touched it!'

Katie realised that, having skipped lunch out in the Land-Rover with Harry, she was in fact hungry – just not hungry for badly mashed potatoes and stringy, cold mince.

'Well . . .'

'It's just . . . a friend of mine runs this little restaurant up country. And usually they're booked for months in advance, but they've just had a late cancellation. So Shuggie called me as man about town and asked if I'd like to go and eat there . . . They've been paid, but he doesn't want to see the food go to waste . . .'

'What kind of restaurant?' asked Katie, slightly suspicious.

'Its specialties are cold mince and tatties,' said Iain, a bit peevishly. 'Look, it's a nice place. Do you want to come or not? Craig says he's busy and on some kind of a promise.'

Katie weighed up the potential excitements of a night at Mrs McClockerty's, looked once more at her greasy plate and made a decision.

'Yes please,' she said.

For some reason (probably because she was influenced by Harry's evil mind control), she'd subconsciously expected Iain to have a sports car, but he didn't, of course. He had a nice little new Golf, tidy, like men's cars tend to be. Katie could have started a landfill in the Punto. She thought of his desk. Why were men's cars tidy and the rest of their lives such disasters?

Owls twittered in the woods as they headed out of town. Iain didn't talk, but concentrated on driving fast, and rather well in fact, around the sharp country corners of the roads, the hedgerows reaching out to featherbrush the windows. Katie felt strangely excited. Going out to a mysterious dinner in the middle of the country with a mysterious young gentleman . . . OK, Iain wasn't mysterious in the slightest, but somehow he looked different in the dying light, his eyes fixed on the road ahead. She glanced down at his left hand on the gear stick, dark hairs prickling out from under his leather watchstrap. Her own neck hair prickled in response and she found it hard to contain a grin.

'Where's this place then?'

Iain didn't look at her, but also grinned. 'How likely are you to have heard of it?'

'Is it Edinburgh?'

'No.'

'OK then, not at all.'

'It's on Mars,' said Iain.

Outside, a cloud of birds rose from the hedgerow and raced the car across the fields.

'I really have to stop getting into cars with strange men,' said Katie.

'God yeah – one of them might feed you for free,' replied Iain. 'I thought you PRs were meant to see the best side of everything.'

'That's a very common misconception,' said Katie, settling back in her seat. 'Are we there yet?'

Iain ignored her, leaned forwards and turned on the CD player. Instantly, a plaintive violin struck up, and a beautiful voice started singing about two lovers who were getting on great then suddenly both got drowned in a big river on a stormy night. It was unexpectedly involving, and Katie found herself sniffing as the car tore down a tiny twisting lane leading to the sea. The car came to a gentle halt on a gravel driveway in front of a small grey turreted house that looked austere, outlined against a darkening grey sea.

'Is this Skibo?' asked Katie curiously.

Iain rolled his eyes. '*No.*'

Her feet crunched on the gravel. There was only one other car – and they had been a good half hour driving there, and hadn't passed one town. She felt sorry for Iain's friend, probably putting all his life savings into this chilly house so he could run a stupid restaurant in the middle of nowhere. She shivered; it was absolutely freezing too.

'Quite a view, huh?' said Iain. A small vegetable garden ran down to a cliff then stopped abruptly. Beyond was nothing but sea and sky. It was sublime, like falling off the end of the world.

Katie nodded to stop her teeth from chattering. The wind was going right through her.

Iain noticed and smiled. 'God, you really are a softy southerner, aren't you?'

'It's nearly APRIL,' she said. 'Spring!'

'Och, you get snow up here until June.'

'June?'

He nodded.

'Can I borrow your car? I just have to quickly drive to Spain.'

'Well, you'd better have some dinner first – it's a long way.'

Inside, the walls were painted a dark, rich red and there was a blue tartan carpet. It shouldn't have worked, but somehow it did. There wasn't a reception, just an anteroom with a huge blazing fire that Katie stepped up to gratefully. A friendly-looking woman was standing there waiting for them, and she came up and kissed Iain on the cheek.

'Your lucky night, eh?'

'You can say that again, Margaret,' he said, smiling. 'But we'll pay for the wine, noo, OK?'

'Ah, you'll pay cost. He paid us already. We can't do it any other way.'

Katie didn't understand any of this, but liked the usage of the word 'wine'.

'Welcome to Auchterbeachdabhn,' said Margaret to

Katie. 'Tonight we're having hot smoked salmon with leeks and hollandaise, Angus beef fillet with smoked garlic broth, and iced raspberry cranachan with white chocolate sorbet and pistachio. All the vegetables from the garden of course. And today's bread is pumpkin.'

'My favourite,' Iain was saying hungrily, but Katie was staring past him into the dining room beyond. It was at the back – or, possibly, the front – of the house, a circular room that overlooked the water. It had windows looking out in five different directions that were currently showing a panoramic view of a quite spectacularly self-important sunset, shading itself down from deepest purple through fuchsia and on to a fiery yellow.

What was really catching Katie's eye though was the table, beautifully laid with crisp cream linen, gleaming silver and sparkling crystal. It was the only table in the room.

'What's going on?' she asked, interrupting Margaret and Iain, who were discussing the merits of spring versus summer vegetables.

Margaret looked at Iain. 'Did you no explain? The lassie will think you're abducting her.'

'I wanted it to be a surprise!'

And, as Margaret fetched them the best vodka tonic Katie had ever tasted, Iain explained. Margaret (and her husband, Shuggie, who was busy in the kitchen) ran a single-tabled restaurant. All the food was local, there was no choice in the catch of the day, they were famous the world over, earth-shatteringly expensive and booked up eighteen months in advance.

'Metropolitan enough for you?' he said at last.

Katie's eyes were round as saucers and she could hardly speak.

'Thank you!' she managed finally, as Margaret forced

tiny, exquisite salmony hors d'oeuvres on them. 'Oh my God, what a treat. What would you have done if I'd stuck to my mince and tatties?'

'Oh,' said Iain. 'I've got the Hilton sisters on the speed dial.'

The food was exquisite. The salmon was by far the best Katie had ever tasted, and the meat soft as silk. Katie wished she looked smarter, that she'd had some time to get ready, had even just put some more lippy on. Soft fiddle music was playing in the background, candles had been brought in to light the room as the sun went down. In fact, it was so unbelievably romantic, it was embarrassing. Both of them were quiet and slightly awkward, a million miles away from the easy banter they'd shared the night before. Katie knew exactly what Iain was thinking because she was thinking exactly the same herself. He was thinking this was a far too romantic place he'd brought her to, completely over the top, given it was only the third time they'd met. He might as well have covered his car in rose petals and started singing Lionel Ritchie songs.

This was in fact exactly what Iain was thinking. He was feeling, frankly, a bit of a dickhead, and was desperately hoping Katie didn't find out there was a bedroom upstairs. Not that he expected her to . . . oh Christ, this had seemed such a good idea when Shuggie had called him up. If she only knew how few women they saw up here . . . no, best not tell her that, that would sound even worse, like he was a sex pest waiting to pounce.

They both took a breath and murmured – yet again – how amazing this all was. Then they caught each other's eye and Katie saw the impish spark she'd noticed before.

'OK,' she said. 'I know you've been trying to keep this

a secret for a long time. And I know it's not going to be easy for you. But go on – you can propose now, I don't want to swallow the ring when they bring it in the ice cream.'

'Actually, I thought we'd have this dinner because I have to tell you . . . Darling, I've been sleeping with the nanny, and I want a divorce. Please don't make a scene now.'

She grinned and they finally started to relax. She told him about Mrs McClockerty's latest act of evil and he agreed vehemently, nodding through a mouthful of dauphinoise potatoes and red vinegar cabbage.

'The thing is,' said Katie, when she'd finished her diatribe, 'um, why does that woman keep looking in here? It's like being around at your mum's.'

Iain smiled. 'Margaret's the *waitress*, Katie. Just because it looks like a house doesn't mean she's my mother.'

'No.'

'Plus, she wants to measure you up against all the other women I bring here on a regular basis.'

'I *knew* it,' said Katie, and threw her napkin at him. 'You're the town Lothario.'

At this, Iain laughed for longer than was necessary or indeed polite.

'What?' said Katie, feeling uncomfortable. If he was gay and just being friendly, something was very very wrong with her gaydar. Maybe that was it – she'd been so long out of the game she'd lost the knack completely. She was going to turn into one of those old ladies who develop impossible pashes for the local vicar and make exhibitions of themselves.

'*What?*' she asked again, as Iain continued to laugh uncontrollably.

'Sorry,' said Iain. 'I started laughing, then realised that

it was embarrassing rather than funny but still couldn't stop somehow.'

'WHAT?'

'You do know about Fairlish, don't you?'

'I know it gets very damp in the evenings,' said Katie, eyes narrowing and wondering just what the hell was going on here.

'We're the town with the highest number of blokes in the UK. To women, I mean. The ratio's about 16:1 I think.'

'You're joking.'

'I'm not, I can assure you. We're statistically unique.'

And then it all suddenly clicked into place. Katie thought about how few women she'd actually come across so far in Fairlish. Barely none, although Mrs McClockerty had certainly made her presence felt. But practically everyone else, in every shop, pub or office, had been a chap. No wonder Derek liked to be called an executive assistant.

'How come?' she asked.

'Well, between the farms, the fishery, the port, the Forestry Commission, the technology centre outside Muchlan, the research institute, the helicopter base and those secret submarines in the loch nobody's supposed to know about, it's just mostly chaps working up here.'

'I met a young girl . . . Kelpie.'

'Ah, the head of the coven,' said Iain, tucking into his pudding. 'Friendly, was she?'

'She and her gang shouted at me in the street, if that's what you mean.'

He smiled. 'Side effect from living in this town. I believe they may be suffering from, er, high self-esteem.'

'I've never seen that in a woman before,' said Katie wonderingly. 'Well, they'll be suffering from a good crotch kicking if me and Louise get our hands on them,' realising this was an idle threat even as she was saying it.

'Rather you than me, that's for sure.'

'So why do you stay if there's such a dearth of women on offer?' asked Katie, between delectable mouthfuls. She'd thought she was too full for pudding, but now realised she wasn't, and actually whatever this crunchy raspberry stuff was, it was going down incredibly easily.

Iain shrugged. 'Grew up here. Like it. Run my own ship, that kind of stuff.'

'Don't you get lonely?'

He fixed her with an unambiguous look.

'Sometimes.'

It's so nice to be driven by a good driver, Katie was thinking muzzily, drifting off in the comfortable front seat of the car. She really shouldn't have accepted that delicious whisky liqueur Margaret had pressed on her . . . but it was rude to refuse really. Now, she was sure there was something she had thought about bringing up with Iain . . . something about trees, something really important . . . she felt her eyes droop as she caught a flash of a tail in the hedgerow.

Iain cut his eyes sideways from the road. She looked different when she was asleep; her snarky look disappeared completely.

Later, outside Mrs McClockerty's, he had to shake her gently to wake her up. She came to with an undignified snort.

'Oh God, was I dribbling?'

'No,' replied Iain slowly.

'Oh, thank God.'

'You muttered something about having sex with a goat though.'

Katie stretched her legs and got out of the car. Iain left the lights on to show the pathway to the house, and got out too. They both moved around to the front of the car, and stood, illuminated.

'Uh, thanks,' said Katie, rubbing her mouth nervously. 'Thank you for a lovely night.'

'Not at all,' said Iain. 'It was . . . um . . . any time. Well, not any time because it's always booked up, but thanks for not making me have dinner with Craig the Vet. He's nice, but he spits.' Aware that he was talking too much, he bit his lip.

'OK then,' said Katie, and looked at him. Caught in the car headlights, his green eyes flashed at her, nervous, but full of excitement and mischief. She stepped towards him, and then he, gently and carefully, checking her face to make sure what he was about to do was all right, took her face in his hands. In the next moment they were kissing.

It felt so good to be held again. Katie literally could have swooned. His mouth – soft and hard at the same time; his long body and strong arms holding her tightly against him made her giddy.

'Oh God,' he groaned, when they came up for air. 'Sorry, it's just . . . it's been a while. I mean . . .'

Katie smiled to herself and wondered what had happened to the self-contained character who had swept her off to dinner. Then she melted into him again.

'GAH!' came a voice from behind them. Instinctively, they leaped apart, though their hands found each other soon after.

'Sorry!' said Louise, lurching up the path. 'I meant to creep silently by and leave you some privacy, but then I accidentally shouted out "gah".'

'That's all right,' muttered Katie, embarrassed.

'Bloody hell, but I had a great night. You'd almost think the men here hadn't seen a woman in months.'

'Well . . .'

Iain looked at Katie and smiled. 'I think I'd better go,' he said, opening the car door. 'Mrs McClockerty might come out, and she does have a rather dampening effect on ardour.'

'And toast,' added Louise helpfully.

'Come on, let's go try and save tomorrow's pieces,' said Katie, putting her arm around her friend's shoulders as the car pulled away. 'By the way, did you tell Craig the Vet he was on a promise?'

'Yeah yeah yeah,' said Louise. 'Craig the Vet thinks he has the local sheep on a promise, horny old devil. Believe it or not, I don't particularly feel like sleeping with anyone at the moment.'

She stuck her tongue out at Katie's astonished look.

'*Far* too busy being the femme fatale of a generation.'

'Boy, am I glad we didn't waste money sending you into therapy,' whispered Katie as they crept up to their attic room.

Settling down to sleep, it felt almost comforting to hear the rain starting up, bouncing loudly off the old eaves.

Chapter Eight

Three days later, the rain finally stopped.

'Let's go for a walk,' said Louise to Katie after work.

Katie looked at her. 'What?' she said.

Louise looked embarrassed. 'You know . . . that thing you do where you put one foot in front of another and stuff.'

'You know this isn't one of those northern towns they've built a Harvey Nichols outpost in, right?' said Katie.

Louise nodded.

'How long have we known each other?' said Katie.

'Ten years?'

'Have we ever just gone for a walk?'

'There was that time we strolled past the lido trying to catch the lifeguard's eye.'

'I'm not sure that counts.'

'Well, no then.'

The two girls looked at each other.

'This better get me foxy-looking rosy cheeks,' grumbled Katie, lacing up her boots.

* * *

Louise had been out exploring the area – and the men – quite a lot, so had quite an appreciation of the local charms and was eager to sample them once more, whereas Katie had been stuck in a deadlock with Harry over how to go about the project for days now. Yesterday, she'd seen the planning report – the developers wanted a big golf course all right, plus a clubhouse, a bar, a hotel and a new road cutting straight through the forest that was, quote, 'wide enough for 4x4s'.

'Yuk,' she'd said.

'It's worse than yuk,' Harry had replied.

'What about getting the local MP onside?'

Harry had snorted. 'He'd sell his own grandmother for a lift in a Jaguar. I'm afraid,' Harry had continued, 'we're on our own.'

Katie had looked at him. 'You have to let me do my job, you know, the proper way. The noisy way.'

'Yes, yes.'

'We've got to get out there and start shouting our heads off.'

'Read the papers again,' Harry had answered. 'There must be a quieter way.'

Katie and Louise walked out past the boats on the shore and up onto the headland, following an old, ploughed-over track.

'You almost look like you're having a good time,' said Katie sternly, watching Louise swinging her arms enthusiastically.

Louise looked at her. 'I know,' she said, suddenly serious. She turned around, indicating the glorious view out to the Western Isles.

'This . . . I think this has been really . . . I think it's quite good for me up here. Given me room to think.'

Katie nodded silently. It had taken Louise a long time even to get to the point where she could talk about the Max situation, and Katie hadn't been convinced that she was making much progress back home, especially if her choice in one-night stands was anything to go by, yet here she seemed content, almost happy.

'I'm sorry,' Louise blurted out.

'What do you mean?'

Louise looked awkward. 'I think I . . . you know, kind of blamed you for what your sister did.'

'That's OK,' said Katie.

'No, I just . . . I've been a bit of a pain in the arse.'

'Oh, I don't know,' said Katie. 'It's been very entertaining watching you . . . no, I don't mean that. I mean, I'm sorry too. I really am. And I'm sorry there's not more I could have done.'

'You took me in,' said Louise, biting her lip. 'And I dragged a lot of pond life in my wake.'

'Don't worry about that,' said Katie. 'In fact, you gave me hope. That a sex life was still possible for the single London almost-thirtysomething female.'

Louise made a face, remembering some of her less desirable conquests. 'Well, that's over.' She looked around again at the amazing landscape. 'I think I'm getting better.'

Katie smiled at her. 'Must be something in the water.'

'Oy! YOUSE!'

Turning back from the headland, the girls were shocked to see a bent-over figure, carrying a stick, marching towards them.

'Get off!'

'Who's that?' said Katie.

Louise shrugged.

The figure waved his stick at them.

'Is he going to hit us with that stick?' asked Louise,

preparing to run. 'Maybe he's a crazed hermit and we're encroaching on his land.'

'He looks a bit doddery for whupping us,' said Katie, as the slightly feeble figure got closer. 'In fact, if he threatens violence, just kick his stick away. He'll probably go right over the cliff.'

'You're quite scary,' Louise said to Katie. 'HELLO?' she cried out to the figure.

The old man wobbled up to them. He was craggy, with white whiskers, and was wearing a tweed jacket that looked as though it had already been nibbled on by ten cows.

'You're on mah land,' he said, sternly.

Katie looked at Louise questioningly.

'We're on the cliff path!' said Louise. 'And we've got . . .' she grabbed the concept out of thin air, thinking of what she'd read in *Heat* about Madonna '. . . rambler's rights.'

The old man looked around. 'Och aye,' he said. 'Bugger.'

He stepped closer and looked them both up and down. 'Are you those two new lassies in town?'

Katie smiled widely to show willing in case he was more dangerous than he looked. 'Yes we are!' she said brightly.

'Here to sort out that poor Buchan boy,' said the man. 'Guid.'

He turned around as if to stomp off, then turned back. 'Aren't you comin' then?'

'Sorry,' said Louise. 'Who are you?'

He stared at them as if he'd never been asked this question before, and indeed he probably hadn't.

'Who am I?' he asked incredulously. Then he straightened up. 'Laird Kennedy,' he said. 'Now would you like a cup of tea?'

* * *

'I think this is the point where my marrying a laird and living in a castle fantasies are about to hit the wall,' said Louise as they followed the old man, who'd been joined by a mangy Labrador, down a narrow path through a hollow.

'On the other hand . . .' she said, stopping short as the view opened up ahead of them. It was less of a castle, more of a manor house, in grey brick, but silhouetted against the sea ahead, just around the curve of the coastline. It was magnificent. It had dozens of forbidding-looking windows on two floors, and wide steps leading up to the entrance.

As they drew closer, however, the building revealed itself to be in a desperate state of disrepair. Paint was peeling off the window ledges, and water was dripping down the eaves. Tiles were missing from the roof, and the big front door badly need repainting. Up close, in fact, the house looked quite scary, like something out of *Scooby Doo*.

'Come in,' said the Laird, taking them around the back and through a large kitchen with Formica units and an old-fashioned cooker that had undoubtedly seen better days. 'Sorry about the mess,' he added, looking around as if he was as surprised as they were. 'My housekeeping staff . . .' he trailed off for a moment. 'Well, anyway, they're all dead. Tea?'

Katie and Louise looked at each other, unsure whether to brave consuming anything in such a place. But then again, they ate at Mrs McClockerty's every morning.

'Sure,' said Louise.

'Just water for me,' said Katie, at the same instant.

Kennedy lowered his eyebrows at her. 'Nonsense. Have some tea.'

He ushered them through the door and started clattering

about looking for mugs. Katie caught a glimpse of a dusty cupboard almost entirely filled with cans of baked beans and spaghetti hoops.

The hall outside was absolutely massive, with a huge, not entirely safe-looking three-sided wooden staircase winding up to the second floor. A large grandfather clock stood solemnly next to the banisters.

'God, look at this place,' said Louise. 'Don't you think it would make just the most fabulous spa?'

'Have some respect,' said Katie. The tumbledown mansion made her oddly melancholy for some reason.

'I respect spas,' said Louise. 'Where do you think we're meant to go?'

There were several large oak doors leading off the hallway.

'Well, which one do you think is least likely to have the corpse behind it?' said Katie, not entirely joking. The only light coming in was from the windows upstairs, which, unsurprisingly, were none too clean.

Louise stepped bravely forward and pushed at the biggest, a large double door with an elaborate coving on top of it. It creaked.

'I've been on this ride at Alton Towers,' said Louise.

Katie crept up behind her and held on to her arm. Both of them were pretending not to be frightened.

'Better push it harder,' said Katie.

'You do it,' said Louise. 'Once upon a time there were two girls lost in the middle of nowhere who accepted a drink from a strange man . . . and they were never seen again.'

'Stop being daft,' said Katie nervously. She shoved at the door.

The door creaked even louder this time, and slowly opened. Both of them leaned in, wide-eyed.

The room that greeted them was huge, with a dirty wooden floor, filthy old chandeliers and windows, so mucky you could hardly see through them, running the full length of the room. There was no furniture in it at all.

'My God,' said Louise.

'It's a ballroom,' breathed Katie, completely enchanted.

'Just *think* what this would be worth in Kensington,' said Louise. 'Can you spell a gajillion dollars?'

But Katie was already walking into the huge room, bewitched. Although it was as dusty and abandoned as Miss Havisham's party, she could sense the past here; grand nights of dancing and flirtations; silk fans and punch and huge billowing skirts. She realised she was recreating various Jane Austen mini-series in her head, and the reality up in the remote Highlands was probably rather different, but she couldn't help live the fantasy just for a moment as she advanced further in, imagining herself filling a dance card, whatever that was, and doing curtseys. Or, she told herself sternly, slotting back on her business head, perhaps an ideal place to hold a fundraising event for the forest. Mind you, it looked like this house needed a benefit more than they did.

She felt herself drawn to the windows. Outside, the lawn was growing wild, although it looked like somebody was having a manful stab at it every now and then, with mixed results. Mist was curling in from the sea, entwining in the trees at the bottom of the garden. It was rather eerie. But hang on a minute, was that a croquet hoop?

'AAAAAAAAAAAAAAHHHHHHHHHHHHHHH!' she screamed.

'What is it!' Louise dropped her handbag and rushed over.

'A face! A face at the window!' yelped Katie, her heart thumping so hard it was difficult to catch her breath. Louise looked up. Through the filthy windows it was just possible to make out a very shocked-looking face.

'LAIRD KENNEDY!' squealed Louise, although he was already at the door.

'What on earth was that noise?' said the Laird. 'I thought I had a pig in labour.'

Swallowing hard, Louise stepped towards the window, holding Katie's hand. Katie was shaking violently – and the face had disappeared.

'He's gone!' said Katie.

'Well, that's that settled then,' said the Laird. 'Tea? In the sitting room I think – it's a bit draughty in here.'

'But . . . there was a man . . . a man . . .'

'Och, there's people up around about all the time,' said Kennedy. 'They think the place is deserted. Can't think why.' He turned around.

Katie looked at Louise. Then they all heard a clattering at the back of the house.

'It's my mugger,' said Katie. 'He's come up from London, not satisfied with frightening the crap out of me down there.' She was scared out of her wits.

'HELLO!' shouted the Laird.

'KENNEDY,' a voice shouted back. 'I just got the most bollocking fright!'

The girls turned around, as a very pale Iain lurched into the room.

'Good God, you two,' he gasped. Then he leaned on the doorframe and smiled weakly. 'I'm an idiot.'

Katie's heart nearly dribbled out of her feet with relief – and lust. 'That was *you*,' she said.

'God, yeah,' he said. 'Jings. I was just coming up to have a word with Jock about trying to screw Har . . .

never mind. And I thought I saw a woman kind of dancing about.'

'I was *not* dancing about!' said Katie. 'Well, not consciously.'

'And I thought, that can't be right . . . no women around here, so I came for a look, and then a banshee kind of started screaming . . .'

'Did you think we were ghosts?' asked Louise, looking amused.

'No,' said Iain quickly.

'Why are you so white in the face then?'

'Well, look at Katie, she's shaking.'

'I'll go get the tea,' said Kennedy.

'I'll help,' said Louise quickly.

Iain and Katie looked at each other when they were alone.

'Sorry,' said Katie. 'I got . . . I got mugged in London. A while back. I scare easily.'

'I'll say,' said Iain. 'But I'm sorry to hear about that.'

'Hey,' said Katie. 'He didn't hurt me. Just made me susceptible to weirdo stalkers that creep up through the undergrowth.'

'Oh yeah, I meant to mention. Most girls I date like to take out the restraining order pretty much straight away.'

Katie swallowed hard. So were they dating now? 'What are you really doing here, anyway?'

'Jock wants me to take some photographs. He's thinking of advertising in a lonely hearts mag, and thinks photos of his house might go down better than him.'

'He's got a point,' said Katie, as they made their way to the room next door, which was a smaller, but still gigantic, sitting room, and this time shabbily furnished.

A fire was burning in the grate, and Louise was pouring out tea while sitting in a high-backed floral armchair.

'You look quite the lady of the manor,' said Katie, taking a place on a sofa that still had antimacassars.

Laird Kennedy's ears pricked up. 'Are you looking for a husband?' he asked expectantly.

'Quite the opposite,' said Louise. 'I'm just beginning to enjoy the young, free and single life. But I'm sure there are about a million gorgeous girls in London who would jump at the chance.'

Katie nodded enthusiastically.

'They need to be rich though,' said the Laird. 'I need a bunch of money for this place.'

'Oh well, I wouldn't have been any help to you anyway,' said Louise.

The Laird sighed.

'I'm telling you,' said Iain. 'We'll concentrate on the American divorcee market. It's the one to go for.'

The Laird dunked a slightly musty-looking biscuit in his tea. 'So, you're the lassies working with Harry Barr?' he said.

Iain sniffed disapprovingly.

'Just me,' said Katie. 'He seems all right.'

'Oh aye, he's a nice lad,' said the Laird, casting a sideways glance at Iain. 'Lost his mother you know.'

'I know,' said Katie.

'About twenty years ago,' said Iain.

The Laird looked at him again. 'What happened to that girlfriend he had? She was an absolute stoater.'

'He had a girlfriend?' said Louise, eagerly leaning forward. 'What was she like?'

'She was a right beauty,' said the Laird. 'Brought her back from Edinburgh. Gorgeous she was, wasn't she?' he said to Iain.

'Yes,' said Iain grudgingly.

'So, what happened to her?' asked Louise.

'Och, she didnae like it up here, did she?'

Iain shook his head.

'Not a lot for lassies to do.' He eyed them both closely.

'I don't know,' said Katie. 'Sometimes it's nice . . .' she looked closely at Iain. 'Sometimes, it's just nice,' she repeated, smiling at him.

Chapter Nine

'Hello Olivia!' Katie said bouncily, answering the office phone the next day to her boss/chum.

'How goes it?'

Not the grey skies or the falling rain; not the meagre single slice of untoasted bread that appeared for breakfast under a bosom trembling with suppressed tellings off; not the forty-minute traffic jam (traffic jam!) she found was being caused by, of all things, a herd (herd? flock? school?) of Highland coos, funny little stumpy things that looked like dogs done up for fancy dress, could dampen Katie's spirits that morning as she had turned the car up the track that led to the forest office.

The three of them had walked back into town, Iain's fingers gradually entwining with hers, and at the entrance to Water Lane, Louise had gone on ahead and they'd stayed behind, snogging outside like teenagers. She was still walking on air.

'What are you up to?' Olivia asked, sounding suspicious. 'Oww!'

'What's the matter?'

'Oh, it's not you, I've just got this new Thai masseuse

who's very thorough. That or I've been captured by the secret police. Anyway, what are you so cheerful about?'

'Nothing. Uh, I just think it's going really well up here.'

'Really? How come?'

Katie explained Harry's golf-course predicament to Olivia, who made various expostulations throughout, though whether in response to the proposed development or particularly intense kneading, it was difficult to say.

'So, what do you think?'

'I think you have a funny definition of "going really well",' said Olivia. 'It sounds like you're doing nothing at all.'

'I mean about what we should be planning.' Katie didn't think telling her boss was breaking a confidence; she had to do it, surely.

'Darling, of course you're right – ack! I can sue you, you know. This Harry character doesn't know what he's talking about. What does he think will happen – big business goes away if you simply ignore it? That's not very likely, is it?'

Katie admitted it wasn't.

'Of course not. So you have to get out there. You know the drill; the more you annoy them, the quicker you'll drive them out. What do you think for a USP for Fairlish? What's its special charm?'

'Well,' Katie said hesitantly, 'they've got the highest ratio of men to women in Britain.'

For once, Olivia was speechless.

'You're joking,' she eventually spluttered.

'Nope.'

'So I'm here, getting put through torture so I can be nice and bendy for a man who I haven't even met yet . . .'

'And we could eat pies all day here and it wouldn't

matter!' exclaimed Katie excitedly. 'Louise has died and gone to heaven.'

'Arse. But, still, this could be a killer focus, surely? Get all the women of Britain behind the forest, something like that? The Men Preservation Zone.'

'Yes, possibly.' Katie shuddered at what Olivia might come up with.

'Fantastic! Well done darling – and STOP THAT! OK, on to other business. Have you checked your email?'

Katie looked guiltily at the antediluvian computer Derek had provided. It was covered in dust. 'Um, not as such, no.'

'What about your mobile?'

'I can't get a signal.'

For the second time in five minutes, Olivia went silent.

'You're without your mobile phone?' she stuttered finally. 'Darling. I would die . . . I would actually die.'

'You wouldn't *actually* die,' said Katie. 'And it's quite nice when you get used to it. Peaceful.'

Olivia gave an audible shudder. 'Barbarians,' she said. 'Anyway. Uh, check your email.'

Suddenly, the door of the office swung open and Harry barged in, also in an excellent mood by the looks of things.

'Come on, we hae to go,' he said, waving his hand in front of the phone for emphasis.

Katie nodded sharply at him.

'Why?' she said down the phone.

'Can't you just check it?' said Olivia, sounding more unhappy.

'I can just check it if you tell me why.'

'We have to go NOW,' said Harry. 'That's N-O-W – Now.'

Katie looked at him. How on earth did he ever get an utterly gorgeous girlfriend? Very mysterious.

'Look, Katie, it's not work stuff . . . I think your sister's been trying to get in touch.'

'Clara? What the hell does she want now?'

'*Please* just check it,' said Olivia. 'I really have to go.'

'We really have to go,' said Harry, indicating he was going to hang up the phone for her if she wasn't willing to do the job herself.

'OK, OK!' said Katie and banged down the receiver, then instantly felt guilty for doing just that. Clara was her sister after all.

'Come on, come on,' said Harry bossily, jumping up and grabbing her jacket.

'Hang on,' said Katie. 'I have to check my email.'

Caught in mid stride, Harry looked at her as if she'd just spoken to him in Mandarin. 'Your what?'

'Email. You know, tap tap tap then you press send and your message gets rolled up small enough to be sent down a phone line to foreign countries and stuff.'

'I know what it is. What do you have to do with it? You've got much more important things to do right this moment than gassing with your chums,' he said, pointing at the phone.

'For your information, that was my boss. And yours.'

'Ehm, she's not my boss.'

'Oh no, neither she is. Well, mine then. Anyway, it was a business call. But this . . . this can't wait.'

Katie looked at him imploringly. Harry sighed in a way that clearly meant 'women', and went to gossip with Derek.

It took a while to get the computer set up – time spent blowing off dust, mostly. Katie, used to broadband and ISDN, was shocked to find herself under the desk unplugging the phone and listening to the familiar beee . . . bdp bdp bdp prrrrr as the connection very slowly came to life.

She signed into Hotmail thinking with a sigh that it had been four days since she'd checked her mail, so there was going to be a new world record number of people who wanted to sell her prescription drugs to excite her gigantically enlarged penis. But the mail she was actually looking for was about halfway down the page. In typical Clara style it was in bold and festooned with smiley faces and flags.

NOOOOZZZZ!! read the subject line.

Still chill out here in the cross your heart and hope to die, India's fine and so am I state of Goa, an Mark-Clara hav a bit of fun to announce - yes, the stork will be flyin' halfway around the world this year so better hope he's got his Lonely Planet Guide!!!!!! A true gaia event, full of the joy and spirit of the forces of earth are joining these two people into one baby this year, so send your hope and love to the Mother Goddess for all of us!!! Still not sure if comin back, chums - may grant the elf a birth serene and free from western 'medicalisation', no what we mean?!

And that was it. There was no other message; nothing solely from Clara to her sister to explain exactly what the hell was going on, just a group email announcing the imminent arrival of an 'elf'. Katie scanned the cc list automatically. Just as she'd have thought – Clara hadn't even bothered to include their mum. It did, however, include Louise. The selfish witch. Clara assumed her doctrine of 'peace and forgiveness' meant she was free to behave however she liked, and if other people didn't like, it was their problem.

Katie sat down heavily. Well, this really was going to set the cat amongst the pigeons. But they'd been together, what – six months? What on earth was she going to tell Louise? Louise, whose hopes had all been tied up in Max for years; who genuinely thought that when he had babies, they'd be hers?

She thought of her sister, out there where the air was heavy with dust and car fumes; spices and burning incense. How could she even confirm it for sure out there? She doubted it was that easy to find an over-the-counter pregnancy test there. She probably didn't even know exactly how far gone she was. And how was she going to make sure she ate good food and drank safe water? And what about soft cheese and eggs and all those things you weren't supposed to eat, and all those toxic emissions? Katie felt her heart speed up.

Still, she couldn't deny how happy her sister sounded in the email. And then she thought, with sadness, about how happy Louise had seemed recently.

'Don't tell me. Jonny's broken up with Janey and you just wouldn't *believe* what Jemima said to Jessica?'

Katie eyed Harry. After he'd shown a more vulnerable side in the forest, she'd hoped for, maybe even counted on, a cessation of hostilities, but clearly this was not to be. Refusing to deign his stupid remark with a response, she got up and followed him to the door.

'What's the matter then?' he asked, leading her out to the Land-Rover.

'Nothing.'

Harry rubbed the bridge of his nose. 'I'm sorry, but I run a no-sulking office.'

'I'm not sulking, OK? It's personal.'

Just as she'd hoped, the very words 'it's personal' worked on Harry like a charm. He shrank back from her as if she'd said 'it's leprosy', and put the car in gear.

Ten minutes later and Harry's constant sidelong glances

were beginning to drive her crazy, as was his furrowed expression. The road was busy, full of cars all going in the same direction.

'You know where you're going then?' said Harry eventually.

'No I don't,' said Katie. 'I'm toddling along fine in London – well, in post-feminist terms anyway,' she added, almost to herself, 'then my idiot sister runs off with my best friend's man, then I suddenly find myself up here and now my sister is up the stick, and I have to tell my best friend.'

After a ghastly pause, she realised that Harry had been asking if she knew where they were going in the car.

'Sorry,' they both spat out at the same time.

'No, it's my fault,' said Harry, quickly. 'Didn't grow up knowing lots of girls, you know. Don't really understand the rules. Sorry about what I said before too.'

'Sorry, no, it's me,' said Katie, touched. 'I just got a bit of a shock this morning, that's all.'

'From your sister?'

She nodded.

'Is she . . . ahem, happy and everything?'

'Seems to be,' said Katie. 'She's in India. Finding herself. And someone else, as it turns out. She's probably going to have the baby there.'

'That'll be nice,' mused Harry. 'Bit like the *Jungle Book* – the baby can be brought up by bears and things like that.'

Katie cut him a look.

Harry looked uncomfortable. 'Well, I haven't spent that much time around babies either. Or in India, really.'

Katie smiled for the first time that morning. 'What *have* you done?'

'I've done things,' said Harry. 'Once I nursed a sick

badger back to health, even though you're meant to turn them in.'

Katie nodded. 'Anything else?'

Harry squinted. 'Nope. That's pretty much it.'

They were drawing near to a large field that was covered in tents and stands, with as many cars parked there as Katie had seen in the entire time she had been in Scotland.

As they parked in a muddy corner, Katie made her eighteenth mental note to get Olivia to send her up some of those new pretty wellies with the flowers on them; her boots were downright clumpy.

'Where are we anyway?' she asked, getting out of the car. 'Literally.'

'We're at the county show of course,' said Harry. 'They're about to start the judging. That's why I needed you to hurry up.'

'Why?'

'Because everyone's here. We need to speak to as many people as possible.' He attempted to take on a wolfish expression, which failed him utterly. 'Find out – subtly – if anyone's been approached, you know, about selling off a bit of land for anything . . .'

'Anything like a two-thousand-acre golf course, you mean?'

'Subtlety, remember?'

'Harry, are you *absolutely* sure you want to keep this a secret? After all, won't you just start millions of rumours by asking shifty questions like this?'

'Not if you do your job right.'

'Surely it's better if everyone knows what's being proposed, then rises against it, united?'

'*No*,' said Harry. 'For the last time, I don't want a kind of panicky free-for-all, do you understand? Just be subtle, and see what you can pick up. Ah, Laird Kennedy. How are you?'

Kennedy, more eyebrows than face, eyed Harry sternly. 'Fine, Barr. When are you going to come and clear out the backwoods of my damn estate, eh? Every other bugger's got development money pouring out their yazoos, and I want my share, do you hear me?'

'But those trees have a fully integrated eco system . . . they're as old as your family, Laird.'

'And *they* don't pay their way either.' The old man sniffed. 'You tree-huggers. No idea of the financial problems of real life. Don't know if I can get through another winter in this perishing cold.'

Harry looked pained. Katie couldn't quite see how he could continue with the topic of selling land now, without it sounding as though he was making a much appreciated offer.

'Hello young Katie,' said Kennedy, in a distinctly less crusty tone.

'Hello Laird,' said Katie.

Harry looked at her askance and ushered her off. 'You know the Laird?'

'I know lots of people,' said Katie, just to annoy him. 'Getting people on our side for when you give up your daft idea of keeping it all a secret.'

'It's not a daft idea,' said Harry, looking cross. 'It's pragmatic.'

'It's daft,' said Katie quietly, earning herself a warning look.

In the nearest tent they found, to Katie's delight, row upon row of home-baked sponges, lemon tarts, jam tarts and large layered cakes, spread out as far as the eye could see, and for a second she forgot the forest, her sister and Louise completely.

'Wow,' she said to Harry. 'If you ate something like this in London, the Atkins Police would come and chase you.'

'Well, here it'll be the real police,' said Harry gravely. 'Those are for the baking competition. Very competitive event. Michael Craven's won for his black bun three years in a row now and it's all getting very tense around here.'

A tall, rather skinny man wandered across. 'Ah, Barr.'

'Hello Ross,' said Harry gravely.

'What do you think of the teacakes this year?' said the tall man, somewhat mournfully.

'They look lovely, Ross,' said Harry. 'Of course, you know, it's very difficult to tell just by looking at them.'

The man nodded his head. 'Thought as much,' he said. 'That bastard Craven's going to win again, isn't he?'

'You know, Derek and I love your teacakes.'

'Well, that doesn't go for much round here, *apparently*,' said Ross, and stomped off.

Katie looked at him retreating through the flaps of the marquee, then back at Harry.

'They take it seriously, OK?' said Harry. 'Lots of bachelor farmers, by themselves at night . . . baking's just something to do.'

'Why aren't they on the internet, finding fat girlfriends in America?' asked Katie in wonder.

Harry shrugged and led her through and out the other end of the tent.

Immediately the smell changed from warm baking to rich, deep cow smells. Katie wrinkled her nose instinctively, then tried to hide her reaction.

'Animals eh?' said Harry. 'Stinking up the natural human environment of refined sugar and diesel.'

Katie fervently wished he would stop being such a sanctimonious idiot for just ten seconds or so a day, but couldn't remove her fingers from pinching her nostrils together in order to say the words.

The cattle, of all different sizes and colours, were in different pens, and were milling around in the mud, making a lot of noise. Katie hadn't been so close to a large animal since her mother had taken her and Clara on a pony trek when they were small. She'd had hysterics, Clara had smugly taken to it like a duck to water, and believed she had a special affinity with animals ever since.

'Um, what's happening?' she asked Harry, managing not to tug on his shirtsleeve in panic.

'It's a cattle market. They're selling them off.'

A bull gave a particularly grisly-sounding moan, and fixed Katie with his creepily swivelling huge eyeball.

'What for?'

Harry looked at her, screwing up his face. 'Well, do you know where babies come from?'

'Um . . .'

'They're for stud.'

'Oh, OK.' Katie tried not to look at the bull's penis and almost succeeded. 'It's like Boujis in here,' she said, but Harry had already started talking to a man on his right, and they were muttering and nodding and looking at the cattle in a meaningful way.

Meanwhile, Katie had seen something much more to her liking – in a smaller pen, a shepherd was leading a small parade of lambs in, their little coats splattered with ink numbers.

'Oh, look at the lambs!' she squeaked.

Harry and the man stopped their conversation immediately. The older man's face creased in a grin. 'Who would this be now?' he asked Harry, as if Katie were five, or one of the lambs.

Harry looked pink. 'This is our new PR girl. From London.'

'Is she now?' said the old gent, and examined her closely.

Katie felt herself redden too.

'PR? Is that like that Alastair Campbell?'

'No,' said Katie, as Harry said, 'A little bit.'

The man's gentle expression disappeared immediately. 'Those Campbells!' he said. 'Causing trouble from the dawn of time.'

'She's not a Campbell,' said Harry quickly. But the old man had sniffed and walked away.

'Old clan conflict,' said Harry. 'He's a MacKenzie.'

Katie had no idea what he was talking about. But it seemed certain that their policy of softly winning over the locals wasn't going to go as smoothly as they'd hoped.

Wandering off alone through the crowds of animals, she made her way to another tent, this one filled with beautiful, enormous fruits and vegetables; huge leeks, gigantic turnips and shiny spring peas.

'I feel like Alice in Wonderland,' she said out loud to herself, dwarfed by an enormous parsnip.

'Wasn't she always getting herself into trouble?' came a smiling voice.

Katie started in surprise. It was Iain. He was standing, hidden behind a huge tray of super-carrots, with a large camera.

'Oh, you gave me a fright!' she said.

'First rule of journalism,' said Iain. 'Terrify people into submission.'

He started snapping the carrots, and some particularly garish flower arrangements. 'That's Hamish McTrell,' he said, crossly. 'Colour blind, the old sod. Still enters every year. Maybe I should switch to black-and-white film.'

'Are you the official photographer for your paper?'

'No, I do these paparazzi shots freelance, then auction them to the highest West Coast bidder. Pretty lucrative stuff. It's like Posh Spice, only with vegetables.'

'So, you write the entire paper, and take all the photographs.'

'And deliver it, don't forget.'

Katie squinted at him suspiciously. She absentmindedly plucked an early raspberry and ate it. Now he was looking at her, seriously, and all the warm fuzzy feelings from last night came flooding back. She wanted, suddenly, to bury her head in his faded green shirt. But there was a camera in the way. He looked concerned. She realised he must be worried that she was regretting last night in a really major way.

'Sorry, I just . . . got some strange news this morning. Family news.'

'Yeah? Bad or good?'

'Not sure. Strange. It's going to be hard for . . .' Suddenly, she felt strange herself. She wasn't sure she wanted to unburden herself to Iain, a near stranger, especially not in the garden of Eden. 'Nothing,' she said.

Iain nodded his head. 'Uh, OK then.' He looked at her, still concerned. 'Are you going to be all right?'

'Oh, yes, sure.'

'Can I . . . I mean, can we . . . maybe go for a drink some time?'

'Yes,' nodded Katie decisively. 'Yes, I'd like that very much. Look, I'd love to stay here with you . . .'

'. . . taking pictures of vegetables? Are you sure?'

'Yes. Definitely. Plus, it doesn't smell of cow in here. So much. But there's someone I have to go and find.'

'Louise?'

'Yes – how do you know?'

'How many people do you know in town?'
'Good point,' said Katie.
'Well, she's here,' said Iain. 'I've seen her already.'
'Really?' said Katie. 'She *is* going native.'

Everywhere in the windy meadow there were animals: well-behaved black-and-white sheepdogs pretending to show not the slightest bit of interest in the sheep; cattle and their permeating methane smells, which Katie was still having trouble getting used to, the occasional lamb under a farmer's arm. She thought she could hear pigs, but she couldn't see them, and was disinclined to go looking, especially if they were as scary as that bull.

There weren't any children anywhere, and very few women of course, which made it easy to spy Louise, who was prancing down through the fields in a terribly inappropriate pair of shoes, surrounded by eager-looking chaps, one of whom was Craig the Vet.

'Hey,' said Katie, greeting them, and trying to work out a way to get Louise away from the group. She didn't think Louise would appreciate picking up delayed news, and there was always the possibility that any moment a miracle could happen and they would get signals on their mobiles and she'd find out about it from somebody else. It was a possibility that made Katie shiver even more than having to break the news to her.

'Hello there,' said Craig the Vet, smiling his ruddy smile. His arm was very close to Louise's.

'We've all decided Louise should judge the cake show this year. As a special foreign visitor.'

The other men nodded their assent. Louise looked a picture of extraordinary happiness, testosterone and patisserie uniting to form some triumphant trifle for her to tuck into.

'I'm having a terrible day,' said Louise. 'All these horrible men have kidnapped me and are making me eat cakes.'

'Are you telling me,' said Katie, eyeing Craig sharply, 'that amongst all the animals here, there isn't a single sick one?'

Craig looked slightly guilty for a second. 'Oh, they'll be fine. Always complaining, animals. Terrible hypochondriacs. It's a horse whisperer they really want, not a trained doctor.'

Katie looked at him through narrowed eyes.

Suddenly, an absurdly loud intercom system crackled on above their heads and everyone jumped. An elderly voice cleared his throat live on air.

'And noo, the judging for the best home produce of the fair . . .'

He didn't need to say any more. Suddenly there was a stampede of large wellington boots heading in the direction of the baking tent.

'. . . and this year it will be judged by a newcomer to our town, Miss Louise Hodgkins, from London, England, but try not to hold that against her, I'm sure she's a perfectly nice wee lassie and not a thieving conniving Sassenach cheat, but even if she is, I'm sure we'll all extend her our very best Fairlish welcome . . .'

Katie had no excuse but to turn around and follow Princess Louise and her devoted entourage, who were being swept along by the crowd. Clearly Harry hadn't exaggerated when he'd said the baking competition was pretty hot stuff in this part of the world.

Suddenly, out of the corner of her eye, she spied the three town minxes, Kelpie, Thing One and Thing Two. They were clearly absolutely furious at the attention Louise was getting from their menfolk. Katie tried to hurry on past them, but they were having none of it.

Kelpie stepped up. 'Ah see your slut-bucket friend has lost no time in spreading it about,' she spat in Katie's face. She looked as if she was trying to wear her hardest face, but it also wasn't outside the realms of possibility that she was in fact very, very hard. Katie wasn't going to push her luck.

'You don't even know us,' said Katie. 'Just go away.'

'Juhrst go awaaaay,' said Kelpie, keeping up her high level of 'being witty by repeating everything somebody says' technique, which she now had down to a fine art. 'Listen, I don't know who youse are, and I don't care, but the quicker youse FAHK off back to London, the happier wese are going to be.'

'Working in a pie shop in the middle of nowhere? Wow, that does sound happy,' said Katie, who was angry enough to have her mouth/brain overdrive popping into gear. 'Hey, maybe next you could eat all the pies and win *Pop Idol*.'

The girl took a step back, narrowing her eyes. Katie realised straight away she hadn't been to an all-girls' school. Katie was a girl's girl, no doubt about it, but she had spent her formative years in an all-female psychotic bitch fight and had picked up a few tricks along the way. Kelpie, on the other hand, was probably more used to boys laughing and teasing her. Which was good, in that Katie could say lots of mean things to her. But bad, in that Kelpie was entirely capable of turning around and punching her in the face.

Both sides eyed each other warily.

'Do you often pick on people for no good reason?' asked Katie, trying to defuse the situation.

'Just bitches who deserve it,' said Kelpie.

'How incredibly pathetic,' said Katie, and walked off, trying her best to look cool, even though her heart was bursting through her ears.

'Right, that's it – youse are fucked,' said Kelpie, her voice becoming swamped by the people milling around them. Katie was desperately trying to reach Louise before she disappeared into the marquee, but she was just too late; with a flick of her flowery skirt (where had that come from? Katie wondered – at home Louise lived in Earl jeans and high-heeled boots) Louise had vanished.

Inside the tent, it was hot and crowded, the smell of sugar slightly cloying amidst the mass of male bodies in muddy boots. Katie was shorter than everyone else there and couldn't see over the flat caps. But, inching closer to the shortbread miniature castle, she heard Louise's voice.

'Mmm, yes, this is just lovely . . . so tasty and delicious.'

Katie rolled her eyes. For goodness' sake, Louise, these men were already sex-starved – they didn't need flirting with. She could just make them form an orderly queue.

Katie found a gap in the crowd. Behind each pile of baking stood a different man, trying to look humbly proud of his offerings, and blushing formidably as Louise sampled each one. Making a mental plea that there wouldn't be any cream horns on offer, Katie found a space by the side of the tables and tried to slip through.

'Katie!' Louise greeted her joyfully. 'Come and help me sample these lovely treats!'

Katie caught sight of Harry standing at the far end of the tent, eyeing her with consternation. She shot him an apologetic look.

'Louise, I have to talk to you. Also, there's some girls chasing us who want to beat you up.'

Louise stared at her. 'Why?'

Katie looked around, agonised, at Louise's cohort of companions. 'Um . . . for being too pretty to live in the village.'

Louise screwed up one eye. 'Did they call me a slut-bag?'

'No. Um, I believe the word they used was, err, slut-bucket.'

Louise looked disgruntled. 'Oh well. The boys like me.'

Katie grabbed her hard by her floral sleeve. 'Just come over here.'

Louise actually batted her eyelids dramatically at the men waiting with their pinnies on. 'Back soon, boys.'

Katie dragged her to the ladies' bathroom, which she imagined would be completely deserted, until she noticed the man washing the chicken in the sink. 'Nice cock,' said Louise *sotto voce* as Katie bundled her out of the door.

A small Portakabin was standing there, with a little rough wooden staircase leading up to it. Katie headed up it, checking around to make sure nobody could see them enter, then tried the door. It opened into a completely bare room with some technical equipment stacked at the far end.

'It's probably for the best,' Louise said. 'You know, keep 'em mean and all that.'

'*Louise*,' said Katie, trying to intimate by her tone that she was being serious. 'Louise, I've got something to tell you.'

'You're chucking in the job with tightass Barr,' said Louise instantly. 'And you're going to run off with that foxy newspaper man and do a Jennifer Lopez.'

'No! God, no, I can't leave this job. Harry's completely clueless. If I leave, and he continues his "sit on his arse and wait until Tuesday" policy, those guys will buy up his huge precious forest, bulldoze it, stick a golf course there and that'll be it, job done. I can't leave. Plus, yes, Iain is a bit foxy . . . anyway, that's not the point. It's *not*.'

Louise looked up at her.

'Look, Louise, it's Clara. And Max.'

There was a pause. It lengthened into an uncomfortable one as they looked at each other.

Finally Louise spoke. 'See, I think if you were about to say that they'd split up and Max desperately wanted me back, you might have said it by now.'

Katie nodded her head.

Suddenly, the door to the Portakabin burst open.

Harry was standing there, white-faced and trembling with fury. The girls stared at him. Too cross even to speak, he pointed his head at the roof of the trailer. On it were several large black shapes which, if you looked at them closely, resolved themselves to be speakers, whilst, as if in a magic eye picture, the black boxes at the end of the room resolved themselves in front of Katie's eyes to be a microphone and recording equipment for the show's PA system, which was apparently switched on.

'What?' Louise demanded of Katie. 'Tell me! You have to tell me!'

'Is this about your stupid sister being up the duff?' asked Harry. 'Brainlessness really does run in the family.'

Chapter Ten

It wasn't quite warm enough to be sitting outside with your back against an anchor post throwing rocks in the water, but it suited Katie's mood. Oh God, this whole Scotland thing had been a disaster right from the start. Everything that could have possibly gone wrong . . . she thought ruefully for a second of Iain. Well, she could probably knock that one on the head too, now that she was going to be six hundred miles down the road.

There didn't seem much point in going back to the office, because it had a furious Harry in it, and there certainly wasn't any point in going back to Mrs McClockerty's as it had a furious Louise in it, and, as a statistical probability, a mildly hacked off Mrs McClockerty.

So Katie had wandered down to the harbour. The town was quiet – everyone was still at the fair. The swell of agitated conversation that had greeted the girls and Harry when they'd left the Portakabin was frightening. Crowds had parted to make a path as they moved through the field, and behind them the noise would start up again, a worried babble. Kennedy had looked at them, shaking his head, his slow bloodhound eyes looking heartbroken. The Laird had stepped forward, but Harry had shaken him off, saying, 'Can I see you later, Jock?' with his mouth fixed shut.

He'd made them get in his car, perfunctorily patting Louise on the shoulder, and fondling Francis's furry neck with the other. He had not even been able to look at Katie, though, huddled in the back. Louise had been pale and staring at the floor, clutching her hands together. Katie had reached out to touch her knee, but Louise had shrugged her hand off.

Harry had stopped the Land-Rover in the middle of town. He cleared his throat. 'Well, have you any stuff to collect from the office?'

Mutely, Katie had shaken her head.

'Very well then. We'll just say goodbye now.'

He hadn't even stuck out his hand. Francis let out a little whimper. Katie had squeezed her eyes shut. She didn't want to go back. She didn't want to go back to London and her life there. She wanted to taste Kennedy's teacakes, and play with Francis and go fishing with Iain and go walking in the woods and . . .

'Harry,' she had said, her voice coming out high-pitched and squeaky. 'I'm sorry. I didn't know about the microphone.'

'I know,' he said harshly. 'Of course. Who'd have expected a media professional to have the faintest idea about things like that?'

'But Harry, please. You know I'm right. You know you have to . . .'

Harry had slapped the steering wheel in frustration. 'Well, that doesn't matter now, does it? One hundred per cent of everyone in the town and surrounding villages for ninety miles knows all about it. So it's all completely out of my control and you've got your way after all. Are you sure that's not what you meant to do?'

'NO!' Katie had said desperately. 'Of course not. Look, it's been an emotional day.' She gestured to Louise, who wasn't even listening, just staring out of the window, ignoring Francis, who was attempting to lick her hand without having to move himself from his comfortable spot on the front seat.

'It certainly has,' Harry had said grimly. He opened the car door. Katie reluctantly limped out of the back. Louise followed her like a zombie. Harry hadn't looked at either of them, not even Louise.

'Goodbye,' he said gruffly.

And he had got in the car and driven away. Louise had stormed off, and Katie was left alone.

She stared out to sea. She had headed for the harbour, for want of a better idea, and was now watching the little boats returning in the early afternoon, to get the fresh haul in. They'd been out for ten hours already. There were tougher jobs than hers, to be sure.

But did they feel as bad when they messed up the fish? She supposed so. She heaved a sigh, desperately trying to think of someone to blame this on. But there wasn't anyone. She'd been so utterly unprofessional in every way; discussing trade secrets with an outsider would have been bad enough, whether or not they'd been broadcast over the tannoy. And calling her boss an idiot in front of the entire town. Her arms, which were wrapped around her legs, squeezed involuntarily with a rush of shame and embarrassment. Oh God, how could she? How *could* she? She felt like jumping into the bay and drowning, just to stop this infernal mantra going around and around her head.

She tried to think of good advice for when things were going wrong, like considering people worse off than her (but all those people were a long long way from Fairlish, which made her briefly envious and defeated the object of the exercise entirely), people with legs different lengths and peanut allergies and horrible husbands . . .

But it was no use. It wasn't making Katie feel any better, not right now when she was failing so dramatically at every other point of her life. Being sacked made her think of being poor, and being friendless, and being single, and being nearly thirty, and being mugged . . .

Breathing deeply – and realising there was no one else around, just a lonely seagull cawing overhead – she let out a shuddering wail of disappointment, and the tears started to plop sullenly onto the hard stone.

Once she'd started, as is often the way with this kind of thing, she found it very difficult to stop. Feeling alone, useless and helpless, a seriously injured Fiat her only friend left in the world, she let her feelings rip, miserably conscious as she did so that Louise would in all probability be doing exactly the same thing at the other end of town, having found out about her own disappointment in the harshest way possible.

You can't cry for ever, even when you really want to. It's not even that easy to cry yourself to sleep, seeing as the horrible upsetting crying part gets in the way of the nice relaxing dreaming-about-something-else part. So, finally her sobs came to a halt. She rubbed her arm across her nose feverishly, making it bright red in the process and getting traces of snot on her arm. At that particular point in time, she didn't really care. She was going to turn around, pick up her stuff, try and bundle Louise into the car and head for home. Olivia would probably sack her, but she'd find another job, shit, she'd done it before. Just try and chalk it up to life experience.

As she reached up, she realised her legs had gone completely numb. Suddenly, her foot skidded on some seaweed and she watched it, in horrified slow motion, as if it belonged to somebody else, until it was toppling over, and she was falling over with it, and there was nothing else she could do about it and she was heading for the cold grey water . . .

'JESUS!' came a horrified voice, as a hand snatched her jacket. 'It's not that bad!'

Stumbling backwards, she found herself in the arms of a terrified-looking Iain.

'Christ!' he said.

'I fell!' she muttered weakly. She could feel both their hearts beating quickly.

Katie was suddenly very conscious that her eyes had turned into the eyes of a zombie piglet, and her nose was a blood orange. She turned her face away over his sleeve.

'Are you stalking me again?'

With that, he let her out of his arms. 'No, actually. Nobody knew where you went. After . . .'

'Yes, after I ruined everything for everybody,' said Katie miserably.

'No, no,' said Iain diplomatically. 'Everyone thought it was funny, really.'

Katie half opened one swollen eye. 'Really?'

'Well, not funny as such . . . more, incredibly shocking and a bit of a surprise that Harry had been keeping stuff from them, but apart from that, basically, yes, quite amusing.'

Katie let out a deep groan. 'Oh God. I have to leave. Now, actually.'

'Why do you keep looking at the water when you say that?'

'No reason. I have to go now.'

'Here, you're in no fit state to drive. Your face is all red and swollen up.'

Katie gave up trying to hide her face.

'Look, come on. At least come and have a cup of tea before you go,' said Iain. 'I couldn't send you down the road in that state.'

'I'm not going into the teashop,' said Katie fiercely.

'What about the Mermaid then? I'm sure Lachlan will make us something.'

Katie shook her head. 'I don't want to see anyone ever again.'

Iain took her hand and led her behind a large corrugated packing crate. 'OK. Stay here.'

She nodded mutely.

'Do you think you could manage not to leap into the harbour for five seconds?'

'Suppose.'

'OK.'

He was back in five minutes, with two huge steaming polystyrene mugs of builders' tea, full of milk and sugar. It tasted like heaven. Even better, Iain reached into a paper bag and pulled out two square sausage sandwiches, liberally doused in ketchup.

'I don't know if you're hungry . . .' he said.

'Crying for hours always makes me hungry,' said Katie, grabbing one gratefully.

They crouched down out of sight and munched in silence for a few moments. Katie snuck a sideways glance at him. She couldn't give two figs for the rest of it, she thought, defiantly, but she was going to miss this one.

'Thank you,' she whispered.

'Not at all,' he said. 'You've given me the scoop of my career.'

She turned to face him. 'You don't mean that.'

'NO, of course not.'

There was a pause.

'Well, maybe a little bit.'

She slapped him with her napkin.

'Och, I'm only kidding,' said Iain. 'I don't mean it like that. What I mean is, this could work out OK, you know?'

Katie emphatically did not know.

Iain shrugged his shoulders. 'Well, if you like . . . I mean, a golf course. Yeah, it might mean bigger money . . . and more people buying the paper . . . and more women and that.'

'Golf courses don't let women in,' said Katie.

'Oh yeah. Well that's a good reason against it for starters.'

'Yeah.'

'But it really would be awful, you know . . . all these corporate wankers up here, scaring the horses and giving Mrs McClockerty an aneurysm. Nobody wants those tossers around really; we're quite happy as we are, you know?'

She nodded.

'I know you *Sex and the City* girls think we're all bumpkins and that, clinging on to some kind of Amish world . . .'

'I don't think that at all,' said Katie.

'You do a bit.'

'I don't! I wouldn't mind a decent cup of coffee now and again, but apart from that . . .' She swept her arm around, to where the little pastel houses jostled against the headland, as if keeping out of the wind. Above them, sheep were dotted about on the grass, bent at a slight angle in the wind. A little red post Land-Rover was making its way along the cliff. 'You know, this had all the makings of being more than just another stupid job for me. And I've never had that feeling before.'

'Well, I've been thinking, and you know, the paper could go really big on this. Launch a campaign. Go national even.' He fidgeted slightly. '. . . if it would help save the town, I mean. But if we were working together . . . you've got lots of contacts, haven't you? We could really do it. Well, I think so.'

Katie looked into her tea. 'What about Harry?'

'I know, it'll be great!'

'What do you mean?'

'Well, it'll piss him off like nothing on earth, don't you think?'

'What do you mean?'

'If I launch the anti-golf course campaign with you. I mean, what the hell did he think he was doing, keeping quiet about it?'

Katie had a brief flashback to Harry standing alone in the forest glade, completely mesmerised by his surroundings, but said nothing.

'Well, it's a great idea,' said Katie, finishing up her now cold tea. 'But I'm afraid I'm out of a job.'

'Oh,' said Iain.

Katie watched an oil tanker move slowly across the horizon.

'Why do you two hate each other so much anyway?' she asked, on a whim.

Iain drew back a little. 'Of course we don't hate each other.'

'Really?' said Katie. 'Well, your imitation of two men hating each other is certainly pretty impressive.'

Iain sniffed, but clearly didn't want to say any more. 'Och, it's fine.'

Katie found she was suddenly shivering in the breeze. She swallowed hard. She'd been ridiculous to get carried away by this place, and a man she'd just met. There was no point in prolonging the agony.

'You know . . . I think I should probably call it a day. go pack, you know?'

Iain looked at her with his big green eyes. 'You're really going to go?'

'I think so, yes.'

They looked at each other for a bit.

'I'll miss you.'

Katie felt a wrench. 'I'll miss you too. But I don't think I can stay here . . . you know, eating grass and sleeping in a barn.'

He nodded.

'Maybe you could come see me in London some time.'

'Isn't everyone a crook and they charge you a hundred pounds for a pint of heavy and all the cars run you over?'

Katie nodded.

'And all the women are mental for blokes and wear silver bikinis and that?'

'Sure, why not?'

She turned to head back up the quayside, her heart heavy.

'Are there lots of girls like you in London?' came the soft Highland brogue, no longer jokey.

'Millions,' she yelled, from further away.

'Send us a few more, would you?' he shouted over the wind.

She smiled, and waved, then turned and walked away.

Louise was nowhere to be seen back at the lodgings. Katie perched on the side of the bed, slowly folding up her clothes. Outside it was now throwing a gale, launching handfuls of rain against the window like rice. She certainly wasn't going to be driving home this evening.

It had been such a long, dour day. Katie sat on the bed, terrified of going downstairs in case she was confronted by Mrs McClockerty and driven out for humiliating her nephew. She hadn't called Olivia yet – couldn't face it. She would give it until tomorrow for her to have worked through the majority of Harry's rage first.

How could she have let him down like that? Every time she felt sorry for herself, she remembered that it was all her own fault, but that only made it worse somehow. Still, a stubborn little voice in her head insisted that it should have come out; *would* have come out. But it shouldn't have been her to have made it happen.

After three hundred and ninety-two hours of hell – or, at about 11.30 – lying awake under the blankets, failing miserably to fall asleep, she heard the door creak open and Louise sneak in.

'Where have you been?' Katie whispered. 'I was worried.'

'Trying to get pregnant,' said Louise, grimly.

Katie sat up in bed, and held out her arms, and Louise collapsed into them, crying her eyes out.

'Shh,' said Katie. 'You'll wake the dragon.'

Spluttering and heaving, the story of where Louise had been for the past few hours came out. Louise wasn't even aware, hardly, of Katie's terrible faux pas about the golf course. All she had heard was of the final, horrible extent of Max's infidelities, and that had blotted everything else out of her head. She had gone for a long walk, which Katie thought might be healthy, until she discovered that she'd walked for as long as it took to get a mobile signal, then had insisted on the whole grim story from Olivia.

'Thank goodness there isn't an internet café,' she growled. 'He'd have got a mouthful from me. And he still will. I'm going to make him pay. Well, he's already going to pay – saddled for life with that bitch's brats.'

Katie winced, but let it go by. OK, Clara was as daft as a headful of melon, but she wasn't evil . . . just thoughtless, careless . . . and other family traits. She sighed to herself.

'Oh sweetie.' She patted Louise. 'You were doing so well.'

'No I wasn't,' howled Louise. 'How? How can I have a job, and a life, and years under my belt, and a credit card and still let a man make me feel like this? HOW?'

'Because you're human,' said Katie. 'Because you're a person. And a decent person, not a psycho or something.'

'No, just a slut,' said Louise.

'Could we stop using that word? I wish everyone would stop using that word.'

'But . . .'

And it came out. After walking for miles in search of a signal, and feeling incredibly tired, she'd come across a friendly and extremely helpful gamekeeper chappie, and they'd talked for a bit and he'd been very sympathetic and invited her back for a swig of whisky in his office and to cut matters short . . .

'I shagged a complete stranger in a bothy!' howled Louise, dribbling all over the damp nylon sheets. 'And I was on the road back!'

'You still are,' said Katie soothingly. 'I promise, Louise.'

'I didn't even know what a bothy was!'

'There there' said Katie.

Louise put her head in her hands. 'Why? Why would I go back to doing that? Why?'

Katie gave her a huge hug. 'Was he attractive?'

'He was all right,' said Louise in a small voice.

'Yeah?'

'OK, gorgeous. Really muscly and everything.'

'And we're going to forget all about it,' said Katie.

Louise's tears had slightly dried up. 'Well, it wasn't that bad.'

'It was a desperate gesture in a terrible time.'

Louise rubbed her eyes. 'And bothies are very cosy places really. God, I'm so tired. It's amazing, isn't it, how knackered you feel when you've had a good cry?'

She settled herself down onto the sheets. 'Can I sleep here tonight again?'

Katie looked at her warily.

'I've had such a terrible, terrible day . . . well, mostly terrible beyond belief . . .'

She drifted off almost immediately, while Katie lay there, on another lonely vigil, awake in a quiet attic in the middle of nowhere, trying to figure out her own way home.

Chapter Eleven

Katie must have fallen asleep eventually, because the first thing she knew, she was being woken by yelling from downstairs, which sounded oddly masculine, but wasn't. She sat up, rubbing her head. Louise was nowhere to be seen.

There was certainly a commotion occurring. Blearily, she jumped in and out of the shower and threw on some old clothes. She would finish packing after breakfast, she really was absolutely starving, one piece or no pieces. Perhaps if she could distract Mrs McClockerty she could do a quick dive for the Tupperware box of cornflakes and eat them dry.

There would be no avoiding Mrs McClockerty, however, as she was to be found at the bottom of the stairs, the source of all the noise. She was bellowing loudly into an old-fashioned green rotary dial telephone, presumably to someone who was entirely deaf.

'And if they think they can just walk in here with their little caddie wheel things and start demanding ensuite bathrooms thank you very much! There hasnae been an ensuite bathroom in Water Lane in my lifetime and we won't be changing the noo!'

Katie wandered into the dining room, rubbing her ears. In the corner was Louise, who was stuffing her face and at the same time beckoning Katie over furiously.

'Quick, she's out,' whispered Louise, slathering marmalade on toast. 'Eat. EAT!'

'What's going on?' asked Katie, accepting the toast immediately and pouring herself a cup of tea.

'It's all kicked off!' said Louise. 'You're famous! Look!'

She thrust over a slightly becrumbed newspaper. Emblazoned across the front of it in huge type was the headline: SAVE OUR TOWN!

Katie grabbed it. Iain had been as good as his word. Every single thing was in there – the threat to the woods, the need for a campaign, the imminent destruction of the local way of life 'beloved for centuries'. There were lots of references to the idea that almost all the golfers would be English, to a level which Katie privately considered bordered on the racist. But, Katie was touched to see, there was also a reference to how the whole town would stand behind Harry Barr, as he fought to win the campaign. She was mentioned as the girl who had discovered the whole thing, as if she were a secret spy on a top-secret mission. He'd made it all look terribly exciting.

'Mrs McClockerty's been on the phone all morning,' said Louise. 'I think we should store some of this toast in our pockets for later. There's four pieces out.'

'You're very perky,' said Katie suspiciously.

'Can't talk. Eating.'

'Look . . . you know, I was thinking of maybe getting a move on today.'

Louise's face contorted. 'What do you mean?'

'I mean, I've lost my job and I've nothing to do and nothing to show for it and we have to go back to London so we might as well start today seeing as there appears to be a fifteen-minute interval while it isn't pissing it down with rain.'

Louise put down the toast. 'Oh,' she said. 'I didn't . . . I forgot you lost your job.'

'C'mon, Louise, you couldn't have stayed here anyhow! You've got to get back to work and stuff . . . you've got to continue with your life.'

'I wasn't enjoying my life very much,' said Louise thoughtfully.

'Well, at least you still have a job, but I don't, so that's that, OK?'

'Hmm,' said Louise. 'Up until yesterday, it was feeling quite therapeutic up here.'

'Maybe because we're running away from all our problems.'

'Well, maybe "running away from your problems" is the new "facing up to your problems",' said Louise. 'Look at Olivia. She talks everything out with her therapist all day all the time and never gets any better.'

That much was indisputable.

Louise stared down at the table. 'I'm sorry. I'm just . . . I think I might take a bit more leave. I'm not sure . . . I don't really want to go home yet. And I'm amazed you do.'

'I don't!' said Katie. 'Haven't you been listening to me? I've been sacked! I have no job, no money, and a car held together with pieces of string and pies!'

The tears stung at her eyes again.

They had only noticed peripherally that the bellowing noise from the hall had ceased, when the door was flung open. They smelt it first. Louise lifted up her nose like the Bisto kid.

'Is that . . . is that . . . a *sausage*?'

Mrs McClockerty was standing silhouetted in the doorframe, her beefy arms supporting a laden tray. She looked as though she'd had a stroke down one side of her face, until Katie worked out it was her attempt at smiling.

She put two full plates in front of them. There was indeed sausage – and square; fried eggs, something which looked like fried fruit cake, crispy potato scones, bacon, mushrooms, tomatoes and black pudding, which Katie found a bit frightening.

'Full Scottish,' grunted Mrs McClockerty. 'And if you stop those interfering, Rangerover-driving, golfing English bloody bastards, there'll be a lot more where this came from.'

Louise and Katie looked at each other, dumbfounded. Then, not wanting to look a gift horse in the mouth, both piled in.

'This,' said Louise, a muffled ten minutes later, 'is the best bloody breakfast I've ever eaten in my entire bloody life.'

Katie nodded too. God, but she was ravenous. It must be all the fresh air she'd had sitting down on the docks and crying her eyes out.

'See,' said Louise, eventually. 'You can't leave now. Even that old witchbag is coming around. Is it just me or is black pudding absolutely delicious?'

'It's that old witchbag's nephew I'm worried about,' said Katie. 'Well, I don't need to worry about him, because he's sacked me, so I don't really have to worry about a thing.'

'It's this fruit pie thing that's got me,' said Louise. 'I can't believe people don't fry more cakes.'

They piled in. Katie was thinking, ruefully, of all the money she would save at hideous motorway service stations, of which she had approximately nine hundred to pass that very day.

There was a ring at the bell and Mrs McClockerty tore

herself away from brewing them a fresh pot of tea to answer it. Louise craned her neck to hear who it was. Katie tried her best to ignore it.

'It's Craig the Vet,' said Louise excitedly. 'I'm going to see what he wants. And offer him a sausage.'

'Or accept one,' said Katie, but she followed Louise to the door.

'Just wanted to join the fighting fund,' Craig was saying to Mrs McClockerty. He was holding a copy of the paper. 'Do you think we're going to need armed resistance, or will just money be enough?'

'We don't know yet,' said Mrs McClockerty in a grave voice which suggested they might need to stockpile Uzis in the attic. 'Whatever it takes.'

Craig the Vet nodded grimly. 'Aye, whatever it takes.'

'Hello Craig!' said Louise happily.

Craig popped his head around the door.

'I believe you're still in your nightgown,' said Mrs McClockerty disapprovingly to Louise.

'I believe you are too,' said Craig, smiling happily.

'I'm having an emotional crisis,' said Louise.

'Oh,' said Craig. 'I don't know much about those. Kind of womanly things aren't they? With, like, crying and stuff.'

Louise nodded.

'Huh. Do you want to come lambing with me?'

'Absolutely!'

'You *can't*,' said Katie. 'We're going home.'

'You don't even need to get dressed,' said Craig hopefully.

'I'll get dressed,' said Louise.

'You *won't*,' said Katie. But Louise had already gone, pausing only to pick up two pieces of toast, a sausage, a half-fried tomato and a piece of fruit pudding.

'Hello Katie,' said Craig. 'I see you're quite the folk

hero. Well done, by the way. Now we've got a chance to stop the bastards. There's developers trying to move in here every five minutes. Bastards.'

'I hope so,' said Katie. 'But I don't think . . .'

Mrs McClockerty's stroke face suddenly took a turn for the worse. 'Hal!' she said, in a clucking tone Katie had never heard. She craned her neck for a better look through the door.

Harry was coming up the driveway, with an expression on his face that suggested he was en route for a root canal.

'Hello Auntie Senga,' he said, as Katie's eyebrows rose. 'Hello Craig.'

'Hey,' said Craig, patting him hard on the back. 'Lots of work to do, eh? Great to get started early in the morning. Fighting the good fight and all that. Listen, you know the Farmers' Union has already got together and started a fund? They've said if you like they'll park their tractors in front of all the bulldozers. Apparently, it's a pretty even match, but they've got more tractors. And the sewage dispersal unit and that.'

'Yes, I heard,' said Harry. 'And Mr MacKenzie has offered to poison the lot of them for me too. By shepherd's pie, I think.'

'Great,' said Craig. 'I've got some horse drugs that'll work very well.' He turned to Katie. 'Tell your friend I'll see her at the surgery at 9.30. I'm extracting a snake's tonsils, and then we're good to go.'

He vanished down the garden path.

Harry couldn't meet Katie's eyes.

'I'll just go put on the tea for my wee Hal,' said Mrs McClockerty. Then she put out her hand and pinched his cheek.

'Um,' said Harry when they were finally alone. He

stood on the doorstep, unwilling to commit himself to stepping inside.

Katie tried not to look in the least bit interested; to give off vibes of being able to turn around and go back to London, any time she liked. OK, she wouldn't have a job, or a possible new boyfriend, or, for certain, a car, but she would have . . . um . . . well, maybe the satisfaction of being right. That didn't sound brilliant now, but maybe it would keep her warm at night. When she was sleeping under Waterloo Bridge, or being a nanny to Clara's almost inevitably hippy-spoilt child.

'Um,' she ventured in return.

'Can I smell sausages?' he asked incredulously. 'My God, now I know you've done something right.'

'Would Francis like one?' asked Katie.

'Um, no . . . he's off them since an unpleasant . . . butcher . . . never mind. It was very expensive, but I think it worked as aversion therapy.'

'How terribly fascinating,' said Katie. 'You should always come around with any badly-behaved dog stories you happen to have.'

'OK, OK.' He looked terribly unhappy. 'I'm sorry. I'm very very sorry. You were right and I was wrong. How's that?'

'Not bad,' said Katie.

'Except I told you something in confidence and you told the entire Highlands region and some of the Grampians, in which case, you were wrong.'

'Can I direct you back to the previous "you were right and I was wrong" statement?'

Harry said nothing.

'OK,' said Katie finally. 'I'm sorry about that. It was an emotional day. I am really really sorry.'

'I mean, I know you don't know him or anything, but

that bastard Iain . . . this is just the kind of thing he's always looking for. Just to have a go at me.'

'Well,' said Katie, thinking fast. 'If that's the plan, it'll backfire, won't it? Now everybody's behind you and wants to be on your team.'

'There is that,' said Harry, momentarily brightening.

'Exactly,' said Katie. 'It'll all work out for the best . . . if, you know . . .'

'What?'

'Well, you know . . . if I've still got a job or not.'

Harry looked anxious. 'Well, of course you have. I mean, if you'll still do it. Why else would I be here?'

'Jeering?'

He looked at her, hurt.

'Of course, I wouldn't think that,' said Katie. 'Come in and have a sausage.'

'Absolutely not. I need you to come to the office. You got us into this unholy mess, you'd bloody better start getting us out of it. All those things you said before.' His face turned serious. 'You really think you can get us out of this?'

'I don't know,' said Katie. 'But I know how to try.'

Derek was dashing about with coffee and papers everywhere, all of a flutter with excitement.

'The *Mirror* called!' he shouted excitedly as soon as Katie and Harry walked through the door.

'The who?' said Harry, but Katie had already shot forward immediately.

'Really?'

'Aye! They're calling it the Braveheart Barricade. They want to know if we're going to show them our arses and paint our faces blue. Apparently if we do, they'll send a photographer.'

'This is good,' said Katie. 'This is *very* good.'

'Really? Arses and things?'

'I don't mean it like that! No, it's good that we've got a national paper interested already.'

'And the *Herald* and the *Scotsman,*' said Derek. '*Mirror*'s more of a foreign paper really. And the *Scotsman* didn't ask us to take our pants off.'

'Standards aren't slipping as much as I'd thought,' said Katie. 'This is exactly what we need. If we get enough attention, they'll back down.'

'Are you sure about that?'

'It's just one strategy,' said Katie. 'Really, we're fighting to the death.'

She picked up a notepad and a pen.

'OK,' she said. She felt good, at last, she felt in control; that she had a mandate, she had something to do and, best of all, she had a clipboard.

'First, here's a quick plan A. Harry, what do you think the chances are of you just phoning up the guys who want to build this stupid golf course, tell them we're going to spend the next six months giving them hell so they should do it in Surrey instead, and hoping they leave us alone?'

'Absolutely none.'

'Don't be stupid,' said Katie. 'You never know. Tell them about the arses and stuff.'

'No,' said Harry. 'It won't work.'

'Why not? Are you going to be really pig-headed about everything?'

'I'm not the pig-headed one,' said Harry.

'What do you mean?'

'I don't know. You should ask *Iain*.'

'Why?' asked Katie.

'Because it's his dad who wants to build the fucking thing.'

* * *

Katie's horrid instant coffee had gone cold as she digested this bombshell.

Unfortunately Derek noticed right away and dashed off to make her another one. He really was an incredibly good non-secretary.

'His *dad*?'

'Yes,' said Harry.

'Does Iain know?'

'Oh yes,' said Harry. 'I'm sure he does. I think trying to piss off his own father would be quite up Iain's street.'

This was weirder and weirder.

'What's this all about?' asked Katie. She put her pen down.

Harry sighed heavily. 'Well,' he began. 'Once upon a time there were two little boys . . .'

'I KNEW it!' said Katie.

'What?'

'You were at school together and both fell in love with the same beautiful woman?'

'At Dornoch Academy? No. Believe me, our school was not overrun with beautiful women. Or ugly ones. Did you know Fairlish has the lowest number of women in the country?'

'I did, actually, yes.'

'You and that daft friend of yours have doubled it overnight. I'm surprised you're not overrun with offers.'

'Not really,' said Katie, desperate to deflect attention, in case he mentioned Iain. Heck, she was practically sleeping with the enemy.

Harry grinned. 'Why, have you let them get to know your personality?'

'Ha ha. Shut up. Is this story about a woman?'

Harry's face dropped. 'Well, it is in a way.' He paused. 'Look, I'm not sure I should . . .'

'Just tell me,' said Katie softly. 'I promise, I'll keep quiet.'

'Forgive me if I'm not that impressed by that . . .'

'I know. I don't deserve to be trusted.'

He looked at her. 'I think it says something about how few people there are in this town to talk to that I still want to tell you. How depressing is that?'

'It's up to you,' said Katie.

Harry sighed and rubbed the back of his head, as if stimulating his brain to come up with an answer.

'Iain and I were great friends,' he started, softly. 'He practically lived around mine. His mum was – is – a mouse, and I think I could tell his dad was a right prick even then. Iain could always get around his mother, that's why he's such a good flatterer.'

Interesting, thought Katie, filing it away for future reference.

'My mum really liked Iain. He was such an outgoing little boy. Not like me, really. He was always really cheeky to her and made her laugh. Whereas if it wasn't for him, I think I'd just have spent all my time wandering about in the woods.'

Katie nodded.

'And then Mum got sick . . . and, well, Iain didn't come around any more.'

'Why not?'

'His dad wouldn't let him.'

'That doesn't make sense.'

'Iain's dad is kind of the local big shot . . . does a lot of building works. And he'd built the factory where Mum worked. They said quite a lot of people got sick after they'd worked there. Nothing was ever proved or taken to court or anything. But he didn't want our families mixed up. Just in case. Or maybe he thinks thyroid cancer is catching, who knows?'

Katie felt an inexplicable urge to take Harry in her arms and give him a cuddle.

'Anyway, that's why I'm not so fond. Of him. Or his dad.'

'It wasn't Iain's fault, really, was it?' protested Katie. 'I mean, he was a child, he had to do what his dad said.'

'He was twelve,' said Harry. 'And we spent our lives sneaking places. But he never bothered sneaking over to us. So, well, so. Who cares anyway? It's not really important.'

'It is,' said Katie. She leaned out and patted him gently on the hand. Francis rolled a lazy eye towards them from where he was dozing on the floor. They were silent for a moment, whilst Katie searched for something comforting to say without accidentally blurting out 'they'll build that golf course over my dead body' or something equally terrible and tactless.

'So,' said Harry, after a very long pause. 'Still glad you're not fired?'

Katie nodded. Though inside she was feeling very mixed up about Iain. Surely, when you were so young, and had a really aggressive parent . . . of course Harry would hate him, that was beyond question. But it wasn't his fault, not really. Kids didn't even understand dying or stuff like that. Plus, that would explain why Iain didn't get on with his own father.

'Did he ever try to apologise?' she asked quickly.

'Iain? Yes. So what?'

'Nothing,' said Katie, but she felt slightly relieved. There you go. Such an awful misunderstanding when they were children, and Harry had been so cut up about losing his mother he'd never been able to forgive him. Understandable, but it didn't make Iain an evil person. She could even understand Iain's point of view – he was probably really pissed off after all this time that he couldn't even talk to his old friend. Her heart leaped. Maybe, by their work on this, she could bring them back together. Then Harry would be happy and not miserable all the time, and she and Iain could get together and everything would be great and, and, well . . . There she let her fantasy peter out. Um, maybe they could all move to London, or Surrey or something – it had a forest, didn't it? – and she and Iain could rear organic chickens or something.

'Are you still here?' said Harry. 'You look miles away.'

'I was feeling sorry for you,' said Katie stoutly. 'Didn't think you'd want pity.'

''Course I don't,' said Harry gruffly. 'I want plans. And lunch. You?'

'You go,' said Katie. 'I had enough breakfast to fuel a battleship. Let me get some thoughts on paper.'

'Letting children sponsor a woodland creature?'

'Actually, I think most kids would rather shoot the woodland creatures. Plus, nobody ever wants the snakes and beetles and stuff, and all the special interest groups get pissed off.'

'*Special interest* groups for beetles?'

'You have no idea,' said Harry. 'This is one tough job.'

'OK. Road blockades and we build a big wall across the trees.'

'That would be a good idea, Katie, only it's illegal and would result in us being sent to prison.'

Katie glanced at her clipboard. 'So bribing the planning committee should probably go too?'

'I think my aunt's breakfast is addling your brain.'

After phoning Olivia, who had sent them that morning

by Federal Express three packets of Fairtrade coffee and a cafetiere, even though she personally never touched caffeine, wheat or carbohydrates and who was delighted that the whole thing was moving, and pouring lovely coffee for Louise and Craig the Vet who popped in, Louise blabbering on somewhat incoherently about the miracle of lamb birth (though without mentioning the miracle of Clara and Max's imminent birth, thankfully) and Craig making gagging gestures over the coffee until she put six sugars in it, Katie had tried to get down to business. It wasn't as easy as she'd envisaged to come up with a brilliant forest-saving scheme.

In fact, there wasn't – short of confronting Iain's dad, which felt like a terrible idea on about sixteen different levels – one single solution at all. They needed at least three categories – money-raising, media and direct action – and goodness knows how many approaches.

'Getting all the other woodland folk out on a march.'

'When you say "woodland folk", you do mean people working for other forests, and not elves and pixies and what not?'

'Of course,' said Katie. 'Sadly.'

'Well, maybe,' said Harry. 'But a lot of them have already been forced into our position. They might not be that disposed to taking our side, when they haven't saved their own areas and have ended up with holiday parks strewn all over them.'

'One of those naked "Calendar Girls" calendars, except with hot-looking local boys? Louise can do the research.'

'For the fiftieth time, I don't want any arses in this campaign, blue or otherwise.'

'OK,' said Katie. 'Plus, we really need to do a benefit. A big party, to raise money for the fighting fund. Then we can buy advertising, and come up with slogans and do mailshots and proper things. We don't necessarily have to man the barricades, we just need to suggest we might, and that we'll make so much trouble they'd better go somewhere else.'

Harry looked askance at this. 'That doesn't seem very fair, does it? If we win, then they just go off and ruin somebody else's beauty spot.'

'We can't help that,' said Katie. 'Our goal is Fairlish, not declaring golf jihad on the entire world.'

Harry nodded. 'OK. Yes. I see. Right. Well, where shall we have a big party?'

Katie thought about the Laird's house. 'What about asking Kennedy?'

'His house is falling down!'

'Well, we'll just have to have the party on a night it doesn't rain.'

Harry snorted. 'Good luck with that.'

'Think positive! We can hire a marquee and stick it in his garden!'

'What with? We'd be better off getting Willie to build a big bothy.'

'We sell tickets for the party, hire the marquee and use the rest of the money left over.'

'How much were you thinking of charging for tickets? What is this filthy coffee by the way?'

'It's called proper coffee, as opposed to the gravy granules you drink.'

'Well, it tastes weird and bitter and horrible.'

'You'll get used to it.'

'I don't want to get used to it. Why should I want to drink something I have to get used to? Apart from beer, I mean.'

Harry poured away an entire cafetiere full of Katie's precious stockpile down the sink.

'Don't do that!' she screamed, too late.

'Don't be ridiculous, I've got plenty here,' he said, brandishing the catering tub of Nescafé that was all stuck together with sugar grounds and smelled of sawdust and Francis.

'Anyway, I was thinking one hundred pounds,' said Katie.

'To hire a marquee? Christ,' said Harry.

'*No*. Per ticket. Hiring the marquee will cost about a thousand.'

Harry nearly dropped his new coffee. 'You are kidding.'

'No.'

'One hundred pounds *per person*?'

'Yes. Francis can come for free.'

'I don't think people will pay that.'

'Of course they will,' said Katie cheerfully. 'It's for a good cause. And we'll get sponsors in, and auction prizes and try and get celebrities – do you know anyone who lives in the area?'

'The Queen,' said Harry. 'But I don't know if she'd do it.'

'No, probably not. Anyway, we'll think of something, ask all the posh nobs in Scotland. As soon as people find out they're going to be in the newspaper they'll pay anything. We'll get *Hello* magazine to come and things.'

Katie was conscious she was talking faster and faster to try and make it all sound possible, but meanwhile, on top of dealing with Harry's frankly disbelieving expression, her heart was racing, thinking about how she was going to organise everything, pull in a lot of favours, get everything sorted, convince the town, find some bloody attractive women to show up to get the local men to come, and, most of all, how to handle Iain. Without him onside, she would never get this thing off the ground. But if she were friendly with Iain, Harry would have a shit fit of gargantuan proportions. Things were about to get tricky.

Chapter Twelve

Katie slipped up the spiral staircase towards the newspaper office as unobtrusively as she could. It was a wet and windy morning a few days later, and the damp cobbled streets were deserted. She and Louise had been laying low – Katie making plans all day at work, then the two of them whispering into the night in the television lounge which, thankfully, had finally been vacated by the cadaver. Mrs McClockerty had continued her positive campaign of feeding them up to fight the good fight, and as a result of that and no longer being able to go into the bakery for fear of being bullied, the two of them had adopted the Atkins diet and were eating nothing but sausages and eggs. They both felt faintly nauseous all of the time, but oddly thinner.

Katie hadn't heard from Iain at all. She wondered if she should have called him, to thank him for the articles in the newspaper – which was keeping up a daily barrage of vitriol and mustering dissent. No, that would look weird.

She realised as she read the pieces that the name of the person responsible for developing the golf course was never mentioned – it was always a 'corral of shadowy businessmen' or a 'sinister group of faceless suits', never personalised. No doubt this was deliberate, but there seemed to be a real depth of outrage to the writing.

As a result, Katie couldn't walk down the street without people coming up to her and asking what they could do, and whatever it was, they had four pitchforks and an air rifle on standby. At first she'd try to explain about the benefit, which didn't go across quite as well as the blue arse and total war idea had. Finally, she started telling people that they had to give her a hundred quid for the fighting fund, but they'd get invited to a really good party, and that seemed to do the trick.

In London, Olivia had promised faithfully to hike up every single one of her clients with even the tiniest Scottish connection, pester the life out of Sharleen Spiteri, Kevin McKidd and Ewans Bremner and McGregor ('but not Sean, darling, he's the biggest golf fiend you could possibly imagine'), and was anxiously enquiring after Louise.

'She's gone native,' said Katie. 'Honestly, she's like those police officers that go after drug dealers and get addicted to heroin. She's romancing half the town and kind of living out this James Herriot thing.'

'In denial, do you think?' asked Olivia seriously. 'I have some crystals for that.'

'I think you could call it that,' said Katie. 'I prefer "mass hypnotic psychosis". She hasn't mentioned Clara at all.'

Olivia sighed. 'Well, that's not going to help.'

'I don't know why not. If she keeps taking all this leave, Max's kid will be born, grow up, turn eighteen, leave home and all her problems will be over.'

In fact, Katie thought the fresh-air therapy Louise was

getting up here was a pretty good thing, even if she did come in from long walks in the fields rhapsodising and a little manic. What else was she supposed to do, stay at home in NW5 drinking martinis and getting boffed by twats?

'I know I should send her home,' said Katie. 'The problem is, she's really handy up here. She's got to know all the blokes, and is persuading them to come along and sign up for helping out.'

'How?' said Olivia suspiciously. 'I'm not paying her, you know.'

'I know you're not going to pay her, she likes it. And it's good for her. Anyway, she's taking a leave of absence from work. She told her boss the baby news had made her so emotional she was likely to start wailing in front of the clients, and that scared them skinny, so they've given her a month to get over it.'

'Well, that's good. You know, if she's up there helping. For free,' said Olivia, not sounding remotely happy about it at all. 'Meanwhile, what am I supposed to be doing down here by myself? Joining the Rambling Society? Taking an evening class? You know, living this hilarious independent single life with your girlfriends isn't half as much fun without your girlfriends, do you see what I'm saying?'

'Sorry,' said Katie. 'We shouldn't be that long, should we? And you can come up for the big party.'

'My therapist says I should stay away from parties,' said Olivia darkly. 'They stress me out too much.'

'What are you supposed to do for fun?'

'Ashtanga yoga, I think.'

'You know, I am trapped up in the back of beyond with two people who won't work with each other and a depressed nymphomaniac on my hands, and you make squillions and live in Butler's Wharf,' said Katie, 'but sometimes I'm still really glad I'm not you.'

Staying out of anyone's way in Fairlish was never going to be possible for long, plus Katie had to admit that she was dying to see Iain. If only she hadn't been such a prissy drowned rat the last time she'd seen him. Suddenly Katie was conscious she was wearing her best trousers. And anyway, she had to take the artwork in for the advertisement. They were running a large box that said:

> Fairlish FOR US!!! To stop the takeover of our town and the loss of our countryside! Join the fighting fund and come to the party!
>
> C/o Harry Barr & Katie Watson, The Forestry Commission.

This time when she had to stare down Archie at the entrance she didn't care.

Plucking up her courage, Katie flounced into the office. 'I'm going to see Iain,' she announced.

'Oh, OK. Would you like a cup of tea while you're in there?' said previously nasty Archie, in a kind voice that completely belied his thunderous appearance. Katie was getting tired of doing double takes. She hadn't changed, she was still the English witch, but now she was being tolerated, almost revered. Well, dum de dum.

'Dum de dum,' she announced loudly, walking in.

Iain was building a fort on his desk out of Sellotape. He looked up guiltily and quickly covered it with newsprint.

'I'm beginning to think maybe Archie's not worth

the money,' he grumbled, sweeping the tape onto the floor.

They looked at each other.

'Why are you looking so cross with me?' said Iain finally. 'I'm the one who's been slogging his guts out for your cause without so much as a hello from you to tell me you weren't dead in a gully from crashing your rubbish car.'

'My car isn't rubbish,' said Katie, caught off guard.

'No, actually, your driving is rubbish. I was trying to be tactful.'

'I'm sorry,' said Katie, stumbling slightly. 'I meant to say thank you. I've been really busy.'

'Well, I know that,' said Iain. 'I haven't exactly been fishing either. It's no joke when the phone goes every two minutes and it's the *Sun* wanting to know when they can come along and photograph the 5,000 blue arses.'

'That really is coming up a lot,' said Katie. 'Maybe we should do something. In front of a big yellow bulldozer.'

'Well, of course you should,' said Iain. 'It's all in the press, ken.'

'Harry thinks it's a bad idea.'

'Then you should definitely do it.'

Katie gave a half-smile. 'Iain, I . . .' She couldn't quite think how to proceed. 'Iain, I know about your dad.'

'I think we've got a new mouse,' Iain was saying. Then he stopped. 'What?'

'A *new* mouse?'

'What was that about my dad?'

'Harry told me about your dad.'

'He told you *what* about him?'

Katie quickly decided that this was not the time to go into the story of Harry's mother. 'That he was planning the golf course.'

Iain stopped fiddling about on his desk. 'What else did he tell you?'

'Um, just that. I think. Was there anything else?' Katie realised she was being an idiot, panicked and blurted out, 'Oh no. Um, hang on, actually, yes. That you never went to see his mum when she was dying.'

Iain heaved a big sigh. 'God, I wish that man would get over himself.'

'Isn't it true?' asked Katie, eager to hear his side.

'That's not the point. The point is, we were kids, it was a really difficult time and my dad told me to stay away for the good of the family. I was frightened; she looked really terrible and puffy and sick. I didn't know what it was, did I? And what was I supposed to do, climb out of the window in the dead of night?'

'Harry says she really liked you.'

'I liked her too. She was great. We used to have a brilliant time.' He looked nostalgic for a moment. 'Harry and I would disappear at six in the morning and be gone all day – my parents wouldn't care less, but Mrs Barr would make us egg sandwiches to take with us. We'd eat them straight away and come back absolutely starving.'

'What did you do all day?'

'Played in the woods mostly. My mother was trying to bring me up as one of those non-gender-biased children, so I couldn't have any guns or anything in the house. So we basically used to go to the forest, pick up sticks and play stuff with them. Well, we'd start off playing stuff. We'd usually end up hitting each other about. You know it doesn't get dark here until about half eleven at night in the summer?'

'Really?'

He nodded. 'We'd stay out as long as we could stand the midges. We would be so hungry, and his mum would always feed us. I practically lived at their house.' He looked sad. 'You know, I was only wee. You've no idea . . . I mean, she went bald and everything. I was scared too. I was terrified. He's not the only one who misses her, you know. I tried to apologise and tell him I was sorry, but you know what boys are like. I'm sure I didn't get myself across right at all, and after that I just thought, fuck him, if he can't take an apology. Then he got that stupid job with the forestry department and his girlfriend left him and he went right up himself and . . . well, we've kind of fallen out ever since.'

He said the last bit looking shamefaced, and suddenly Katie could imagine what they were like at ten, running out to the woods to play cowboys and Indians or, probably around here, Scotsmen and Englishmen.

'Don't you think it's about time you made it up?' she asked gently.

'What, now my dad's trying to cut down his bleeding precious forest? Not bloody likely.'

'Maybe you could unite against him.'

'Yes, that will help my relationship with my dad.' Iain looked pained. 'You know, I'm caught between . . . between a tree and a hard place here. I'm just trying to do the right thing.'

At this, the doubts that were in Katie's mind evaporated, and she looked at Iain with an open heart. He looked so helpless standing there that she went over to him and put her arms around him.

'It's going to be OK,' she said.

'I know *that*,' said Iain. 'It's just making me crabbit. Pissed off,' he explained when he saw her expression. 'Do you know why I work here? Supposedly for a quiet life. Ha!'

'What are you going to do?' asked Katie.

'I'm just going to keep out of everyone's way and not

answer the phone to my parents. I've thought it through and I think that's the most mature way of handling things.'

'Running away?'

'It's working for your friend Louise.'

'That's true.' Katie thought for a moment. 'But we've got so much to do! For the ball and for the fighting fund, and, you know, the blue-arse thing. You'll all meet then.'

'Well, I don't see why I'll need to see my dad – he's hardly contributing to the fighting fund now, is he? And I see your Mr Barr all the time, can't be off it here. It doesn't come to blows, don't worry. We're what you'd call "icily polite".'

'Icily polite. Hmm. Well, that's a lot to work with,' said Katie.

Iain immediately snapped upright. 'Work! That's what we've got to talk about.'

'What do you mean?'

'You're booked on a radio show tonight. That's why I summonsed you.' He looked slightly guilty.

'You didn't "summons" me – I came to place this ad!'

'I know. Sorry. I should have phoned you before.'

'*I'll* say.'

'No, but listen. You're on the radio tonight. I was just about to ring you.'

'What? What radio?'

'You're in the media aren't you? You must go on the radio all the time.'

'No, I get other people on the radio – you're misunderstanding my entire job,' said Katie, starting to worry.

'Well, anyway. It's at 7.30 tonight. It's in Ullapool – I'll drive you if you like. Pick you up at seven?'

He picked up Katie's ad and studied it with one eye half shut, in a way Katie correctly construed as newsroom showing-off.

'No no no!' she said. 'I've never been on the radio before. What do I have to do?'

'Answer questions from Fergus McBroon. Ach, it'll be easy.'

Katie was feeling panicked. The idea of speaking in front of other people – particularly people she couldn't see but who would be sitting at home, judging her – really troubled her.

'But . . . what about if I accidentally say "fuck"?'

'Well, just don't say it.'

'What about if they say I'm on air and then I panic, I say "cunt bollock wank wank fuck" and I can't help myself?'

'Well, then we'll take you to the doctor's,' said Iain. 'But really, I'm not sure what you're afraid of.'

Katie remembered taking a client promoting a particular form of birth control to a controversial early-morning chat show. 'It'll just be a quick chat,' the perky researcher had said. The client had been eviscerated, once by the host and once by the callers. She shivered.

'I really don't want to do it . . .' she said, biting her tongue.

'So, who's going to do it?' said Iain scornfully. Then he launched into a quite good imitation of Harry. 'Hmm, not sure about this noo . . . what not with the golf and all . . . I say, if I don't mention it at all, do you think it will go away . . .'

'OK, OK,' said Katie. 'Pick me up tonight. But not outside Mrs McClockerty's – if she finds out I've been fraternising with the enemy, she'll cut off our sausage supply.'

The weather could not make its mind up between brief patches of sun, rain, heavy rain and hail, so Katie wore her biggest coat and hoped for the best. Her stomach was feeling heavy and ponderous, and she hadn't even thought about dinner. She just tried to remember the advice they gave their clients – 'be calm, and try to listen to the questions'. She realised now this should be, 'be calm, and try not to vomit for as long as possible'.

Iain pulled up in his nice car. 'Good to see you dressed up,' he said.

'It's *radio*,' said Katie crossly, getting in. 'What happens, they throw me out if I don't look like a model?'

'No, they won't have time after they make you sing the unaccompanied song . . . I'm *joking*. Jings, you really are nervous about this, aren't you? I thought you city girls weren't frightened of anything.'

'We aren't. Just urban foxes and, um, going on the radio,' mumbled Katie.

'Don't mumble like that! They'll never hear you.'

'Oh God.' Katie turned her face and looked out of the window. The hail was bouncing off the wing mirrors.

Iain fiddled with the radio, and tuned in to the right station.

'And you're listening to Radio Ullapool, and tonight we've got a woman who's made a full-sized replica of Michelle McManus out of liquorice allsorts, the mother who's raised eleven children and nineteen baby lambs side by side, and golf lover, Cady Watson. Great, I love a nice wee bit of golf. So, we'll be discussing tee-offs and birdies in a wee bit. But first, here's the latest from Fifty Cent . . .'

Iain turned the volume down hastily.

'Is that supposed to be me?' said Katie. 'I'm the golf lover?'

'You know, they don't have a lot of time to do their research. And Fergus McBroon, well . . .' He made swigging motions with his hand.

'He likes milk?'

'He likes something,' said Iain. 'Allegedly. Anyway, don't worry about it. Now all you have to do is explain you're not a golf lover, in fact, you hate it and what it's doing to our lovely environment . . .'

'What about all the golfers who've heard that trailer and decide to tune in and tell their mates to listen for golf tips?'

'Great,' said Iain, a desperate tone creeping into his voice. 'It just means more listeners, doesn't it? Ah, here we are!'

They swung into the parking lot of a small grey building, with a placard cheerfully proclaiming RADIO ULLAPOOL! on the wall with lots of eighties' graphics.

The reception was completely deserted, although they could hear the station coming over the air.

'And, coming right up, we have Margaret MacNamee, who loved her idol Michelle McManus so much that she started building . . . ah, hang on there just a wee minute. No, folks, I've heard we're just about to play another record. And here's Chingy, with "Right Thurr".'

As he was speaking, an extremely harassed man dressed in black with a clipboard burst out of the plain door ahead, which clearly led to the studios. He was accompanied by a very young teenager following behind him, a gigantic burst of screeching noise and, oddly, a small flock of sheep.

'I KNEW IT!' this man was shouting. 'Didn't I say that eleven children and six million liquorice allsorts were a recipe for disaster?'

'Mm,' said the teenager. As soon as the heavy door shut, all the noise ceased, except for one of the lambs, which was crying.

'And would you get these damn sheep out of the way!'

'Uh, sheep . . . come this way . . .' said the teenager gormlessly, clapping his hands.

'They're not *actually* children,' said the older man scornfully. 'They were *brought up with* children. And as the children in question are actually *feral*, that doesn't really count for much . . . who are you? Are you Cady?' he asked, coming towards Iain. 'I'm Nigel, the producer.'

'Uh, no,' said Iain, who was trying to fend off the sheep, who had circled around him and were bleating furiously at him.

'These sheep really like you. Do you know them?'

'Uh, no,' said Iain again, trying to back away. Katie stared at him in disbelief. He looked at her imploringly.

'Can I throw you my jacket?'

'Why?'

'It's got a banana in the pocket . . . I think that's the problem.'

'Lambs love bananas,' nodded the older man authoritatively.

'Why have you got a banana in your pocket? I thought you were just . . .'

'Yes, yes, pleased to see you, I know. Here.'

He took it out and hurled it at her. The sheep, however, completely ignored the projectile and continued to advance.

'So, where's Cady?' asked the man bossily.

'Actually, I think you mean me,' said Katie, swallowing nervously. 'I'm Katherine Watson. Most people call me Katie.'

The man stared at her rudely. 'Do they? So, you're a female golf expert then?'

'Not really. I'm here to speak out against the new golf course.'

'Help!' shouted Iain, gently collapsing onto a small table, and beginning to sink beneath a wall of sheep. Katie rushed towards him, just as the door to the studio opened again and a cascade of the filthiest children Katie had ever seen thrust through the opening in a torrent. The noise was unbelievable.

They dashed towards the lambs, panicking them instantly, then the entire group of mixed-up, overexcited lambs and small boys with liquorice over their faces cascaded out into the car park on a wave of noise.

There was quiet.

'Are you cowering?' asked Katie finally.

'No,' said Iain, hastily standing up and dusting himself down. 'I'm fine and I wasn't scared a bit.'

'Not a bit?'

'Yes. A bit. Those things nip!'

'I thought you were going to get pawed to death. By softness.'

'Country girl now are we?'

'Come on, come on, we're late,' said the man, hustling them through.

There were two rooms beyond with a huge glass window between them. It was gloomily lit and filled with blinking lights on heavy black equipment. The cheap brown carpet was covered in coffee stains.

'You stay with me here,' he indicated to Iain one side of the glass, where there was a huge mixing desk and lots of twiddly buttons. 'And *you*'re in there,' he gestured to Katie.

In the other room, a man in headphones, presumably Fergus McBroon, was patting a woman on the arm whilst Usher played quietly in the background. The woman appeared to be crying. There were liquorice allsorts all over the floor.

'Put on the headphones, and you can talk to any of the callers coming through. Go, go! And be quiet!'

He pushed Katie into the studio.

The woman got up out of the chair, snivelling and shovelling handfuls of liquorice into the pockets of her capacious cardigan. 'I've never been so . . . so . . . humiliated in all my life,' she sobbed, stumbling out through the door.

Fergus McBroon looked up and gave Katie a tight-lipped grimace of welcome, indicating the rather sticky pair of headphones next to the chair. The music faded out and Fergus leaned into the microphone. An ominous red light came on in the middle of the studio. Katie caught the fumes from Fergus's breath as she sat down.

'And that was Ice-T there with *Motherfumph the police, neegaz*. And we'd just like to say thank you to our guest Margaret there, with the, um, somewhat unscheduled demolition of the world's first ever full-sized liquorice allsorts Michelle McManus. But surely not the last. And now, in our studio we have golf professional Cady Watson . . . a girl and not a boy, which is not what Nigel had down on the card, but hey ho.'

From behind the glass, Katie could see Nigel's face curl up in a snarl.

'So, Cady . . .' Fergus leered at her. 'What would make a pretty young lady like you become a professional golfer?'

Katie felt hypnotised by the big red light, glaring away in front of her. She swallowed down every sweary impulse in herself and steeled herself to speak, but the silence held. Fergus wasn't even looking at her for an answer, he was shuffling pieces of paper about on his desk and pressing buttons. Nigel, behind the glass, was making furious gestures, presumably designed to get her to talk. Her gaze shifted to Iain. He was standing with three thumbs up

. . . how could that be? Belatedly, she realised that one of the thumbs was a banana. She smiled, and relaxed a bit.

'Well, Fergus. Actually, I'm not a golfer. I'm against golfers completely. That's why I'm here. A golfing consortium is trying to buy *Coille Mhòr* forest, and I'm protesting against it. It's a beautiful natural habitat for wildlife, it's been part of the local area for a long time, we're already knee-deep in golf courses and I don't think we should overdevelop the environment.'

'Super,' said Fergus. 'Now, we've got our first caller on line four.'

In fact, the voice could be heard all over the studio, leaving Katie craning her neck around to try to see where it was coming from.

'Uh, hello thair,' said a voice. 'My name's Angus and I'm calling frae Lochinver. And my question is: what is the proper grip for a broomhandle putter?'

Katie tried not to sigh audibly. 'No, what I'm saying is, there's too much golf, and we should protect the trees instead.'

There was a massive 'pffff' on the other end of the line, and then the sound of Angus hanging up.

Fergus took another sip from a polystyrene cup which might have held tea and might have held something else.

'Did they just hang up? Cady, maybe you're not giving the best advice here lassie . . . who says women know about golf! And another caller please.'

'What?' said Katie, but before she could properly respond, another voice was overhead, deep and rumbling.

'Hullllo. This is Gordon, frae Ullapool. And whit ah wanna know is, if you drive the green on a par four and are putting for eagle, is your drive considered in the "fairway" for statistical purposes?'

'Oh for goodness' sake, I can't even *play* golf!' shouted

Katie. 'I don't know! I'm sorry! I'm here to urge everyone to oppose the building of a new golf course in *Coille Mhòr* forest. We want *less* golf, not more.'

'It appears to be hysterical woman night here tonight, listeners!' said Fergus, belatedly realising things weren't quite going according to plan and trying to tackle it by adopting a jaunty tone. He started fiddling with buttons.

'Are they building a golf course in *Coille Mhòr*?' asked Gordon.

'They're trying to,' said Katie.

'Och, it'll be quite nice to play golf in the forest, ken. I used to go there as a young lad.'

'You can't play golf in a forest, Gordon,' said Katie. 'They have to chop it all down.'

'Oh. Och ah see. Och, that would be an awful terrible shame now, wouldn't it?'

'YES!'

'And now, it's Mister Puff D with "Lick her up and down All Over",' said Fergus, fading the music up quickly and making a guillotine gesture to Nigel. Instantly Gordon disappeared. Fergus swivelled his fat arse around in the chair he was sitting in to face her. He had horrid wiry hair coming out of his nose and ears.

'Sorry, who the hell are you and why are you trying to sabotage my programme?'

'I'm Katie Watson and I was booked on your programme to defend bloody nature around here.'

'So how come I've been trailing it as a fucking golf slot all fucking day? Jeez, what's up with you women – all on the blob?'

'You don't know many women, do you?' said Katie.

'Nobody does up here love.' He took another slug from his cup. 'Fucking Nigel, you fucking fucker, you're fucked this time.'

Nigel's voice was suddenly heard in the studio. 'If you think you can find three interesting people a night, five nights a week all by yourself, please do go right ahead.'

The two men glowered at each other.

'Well, what the fuck do you fucking expect me to do now?' growled Fergus. He clearly had absolutely no problem turning on his on-radio swearing radar.

Nigel shrugged.

'Why don't you interview me about our fight to protect our local forests?' said Katie. 'Call me crazy, but you never know, someone might be interested.'

'Well, I've got forty-six callers lined up to ask you questions about golf.'

'Well, they might just learn something,' snapped Katie.

Fergus and Nigel gave each other a look as the music came to a halt.

'And that was the great P-Diddy, a personal friend of mine, and the time's coming up to 7.34. Forecast for tomorrow's weather; there'll be a light scattering of showers followed by heavier showers, with, uh, just snow on the upper slopes, so we know that spring is finally getting here. Now, on the show tonight, we were taking your golf questions, however our guest has informed us that she hates golf . . .'

'I don't *hate* golf,' interjected Katie.

'Do you play golf?'

'No.'

'Do you know what golf is?'

'I know that putting down a golf course in *Coille Mhòr* forest will cause five hundred red squirrels to die out,' said Katie. She didn't, of course, but that sounded quite impressive.

A light blinked on the console.

'And we have another caller . . . line three.'

A man cleared his throat on the line and started to talk in a gruff voice. 'My name is . . . uh, my name is Harry Farm . . . Farmsworth from Braeside, and I just want to say that I was a really keen golfer, but when I found out they were planning on cutting down our beautiful forest I was so angry I broke all my clubs over my knees!'

Fergus looked at Katie, who was doing her best to swallow her grin. Oh, bless Harry's heart. Not a natural actor by any means, but he was certainly trying his best.

'Well, I'm sure you'd like to hear about some of the ways you can help our campaign,' said Katie.

'Yes, I most certainly would.'

'Well, you can write to your local MP protesting, or to the planning department, which is Mr Willie Willson, 25 Cumberland Road, Perth, you can buy a ticket to come to our big protesting party in July, you can join our tractor sit-in or,' Katie was running a little short of ideas. 'Or, erm, you can paint your arse blue and expose it as a sign of protest.'

'No, you can't do that,' said the caller. 'No arse painting.'

'You CANNOT say ARSE on the radio!' shouted Fergus suddenly, his face going puce. 'I mean, *that word*. I'd just like to apologise to all our listeners there for ah, having to put up with that when you were hoping for a nice golf chat, and . . .'

Nigel gestured furiously from behind the glass.

'And no, we are NOT taking another call. We're playing "Suck 'em and See" by Nelly!'

Nigel gestured on regardless. Meanwhile, Fergus started making signs to Katie to get up and leave, and started the music.

The music started quietly, and suddenly a new voice crackled into the studio.

'I'm frae Buchan, and I just wanted to say tae the lassie, that me and all the lads in the rugby team will show our arses painted blue if she'll show us her arse first . . .'

The rugby player from Buchan was cut off as quickly as he began, and the music pushed up louder.

'I have NEVER in my born days!' raged Fergus, standing up and taking a big swig from his cup.

Katie leaped up and fumbled for her bag.

'I hope you're happy, lassie. Now I'm going to have arses on the phone from here until Tuesday.'

'Good,' said Katie. 'Maybe it will teach you to do your research.'

And she skipped out of the door.

Both of them were hysterical and prattling all the way to the car.

'I thought his head was going to burst!' yelped Katie.

'You have no idea what Nigel was saying about him in the booth,' said Iain. 'And you never want to.'

'Oh God. That was exactly as bad as I thought it was going to be.' Katie realised her hands were shaking as she got to the car.

'Oh, I don't know about that,' said Iain, pointing across the road to a bus shelter, where a man was holding a portable radio. He was waving at them, and as they both turned their attention on him, he turned around and started unbuttoning his trousers.

'We've created a monster!'

Katie opened the car window to get a little air. She felt exhilarated. OK, it hadn't been ideal, but she'd managed to say her piece, and cause a little incident – which Iain of course would write up . . . and Harry had called in, and all in all it could just about have been called a success.

'What are you thinking?' asked Iain. 'Are you thinking about how great you are and how well that went?'

'No!'

'A little bit?'

'Little bit.'

'How do you want me to describe you in the paper?'

She eyed him flirtatiously. 'How about "gorgeous ravishing sex goddess"?'

'I was thinking more "arse-obsessed publicity tart".'

'That'll do.'

She went back to staring out of the window and a silence fell, but it was suddenly a silence that crackled with tension. She was very conscious of his presence beside her, his strong hand on the gear stick as they planed down the country lanes. Although it was after eight, it was still broad daylight.

'What do you want to do now?' Iain asked. 'Not that . . . I mean, if you want to do anything.'

'Sure,' said Katie, fighting back a grin and the urge to put her hand on his knee. Hard to get, she told herself sternly. Think poise and grace. On no account think of not having had sex for months or that he's gorgeous or that you're wearing your best knickers, thus proving her a subconscious tart.

'Well, there's the Mermaid or . . . no, hang on, I'm sure they've just opened a really cool cocktail bar.'

'*Really*?'

'*No*. Mermaid or nothing.'

Katie was about to suggest a quiet drink at her place until she remembered she shared a room, and occasionally a bed, with the stuttering banshee of Kentish Town, and lived under the roof of someone who resembled those nuns who looked tough in *The Sound of Music* before suddenly bursting into song and hiding car parts from the Nazis.

She then considered suggesting they go to his place, just to see the look on his face.

'What are you grinning at?' demanded Iain.

'I'm not grinning! I'm just looking forward to my vodka and tonic at the Mermaid.'

'Well, if it isn't the conquering heroes!' said Lachlan, peering over the bar and turning down the radio as they slipped in out of the wind. The rest of the occupants turned to look at them, and waved or raised a glass.

'Would you like to see our arses now, or later, then? Only, I'd have to stand up on the bar, and I just cleaned it.'

'That's bollocks,' said Iain.

'No, no, I'd do it.'

'I mean, you never clean your bar. Two vodka and tonics please. I think I'll leave the car here.'

'On the house,' said Lachlan. 'We're going to stop these outside bastards, and it was good to hear you sticking it to them up in the big town.'

It took a second for Katie to realise that by 'the big town' he meant Ullapool.

'Wouldn't you like lots of new folk in here?' she asked. 'It'd be good for business.'

'I'd shoot them with my gun,' said Lachlan, in the same jolly tone he used for everything else. 'Unless they were lassies of course.' And he gave her a winning smile.

Once they'd settled themselves in the corner furthest away from Dougie Magnusson's accordion playing, it became suddenly awkward between them. After all, Katie was rationalising to herself, it was kind of their third date, and he'd seen her crying in a right state and didn't seem too repulsed, and she still found him more than a bit dreamy. Quite a lot dreamy, in fact. She gulped her vodka and tonic.

Iain wasn't doing much better. He was trying to stop himself sweating by thought power alone, a hard trick to pull off at the best of times, and worse when you're sitting between a roaring fire, an accordionist and forty men, who've known you since you were a child, watching your every move. He wished he'd chosen another pub – there were plenty in Ullapool, although you wouldn't necessarily walk out with all your teeth. He looked at Katie, who was grinning at him, and slurping her drink. Oh God. He hated to think of all those swish city types she'd been with, who'd have wined and dined her and, well, the rest. He was conscious that his hands were clammy. He took another slug of his drink.

Ohmigod, he was knocking it back. That meant he must be thinking what she was thinking, thought Katie. If it was just a casual pint, he wouldn't wipe his hands on his shirt like that, would he? She hoped he wasn't really really nervous. She understood that blokes get nervous, of course, but they were meant not to show it, otherwise it was a bit of a turn-off. Women needed to feel they were completely relaxed and being looked after, which couldn't really happen when somebody was fumbling and knocking their head into your teeth and constantly asking you if everything was all right. What you really needed was to be swept off your feet and not to have to think at all . . . she took a large swallow.

'Another drink?' Iain asked.

'Yes,' said Katie.

He got them large ones.

Two vodka and tonics later, and they were ready. They were relaxed enough not to worry about the consequences, and were chatting away quite normally about childhood pets, if laughing a bit too loudly and deliberately not eating any breath-destroying crisps, even though they were both starving. Iain didn't feel nervous any more, just excited, and very horny. He'd watched a lot of TV through the long winter nights. He wondered if she was one of those girls he'd learned about who'd gone back to pretending they were born-again virgins and you had to buy them jewellery and stuff in exchange for sex, which struck him as incredibly distasteful. On the other hand, girls like that didn't tend to settle for a few drinks in the Mermaid, or at least he wouldn't have thought so, if he'd ever met any like that, which he hadn't.

Katie was thinking that this would be a very good time to get this show on the road, to hit her window of opportunity. It was difficult to judge, so she wanted to get a move on, prompted by finding herself applauding Dougie's rendition of the *Banks and Braes of Bonny Doon.*

As if reading her mind, the conversation suddenly stuttered to a halt.

'Uh, um . . .' started Iain. 'Would you like to take a walk?'

'Why not!' said Katie, in what she hoped was a careless and breezy fashion. She hoped 'a walk' meant 'back to my flat' and not 'let's get down in the dunes'. It was nippy out there.

Actually, at first it was nice and cool outside after the warmth of the pub. They both felt somewhat relieved. As if it was a natural thing to do, Katie slipped her hand through Iain's arm. It felt good there; right. The feel of his warm body this close reminded her of how long it had been since she'd just felt close to someone, unless you counted Louise, which she most certainly didn't.

'Do you think you'll stay here for ever?' she asked softly as they strolled down to the waterfront.

Iain looked around. 'Um, I don't know. I think so . . . I mean, look how beautiful it is. I don't know how I'd cope in Glasgow or Edinburgh . . . I may seem like a pretty relaxed guy . . .'

In fact, he was doing an impression of being anything but relaxed at the moment, but Katie knew what he meant,

'But I get . . . intimidated quite easily.'

He said this staring at the ground, and Katie understood suddenly how hard it must have been for him to stand up to his dad. He was a shy thing really.

'Sorry, that wasn't very rugged, was it? I should say, I'm a crazy sex god scared of nothing and nobody.'

'Well, it's patently obvious you're that too,' said Katie. He smiled. Despite its warmth, Katie was starting to feel the cold.

'Where do you live?' she asked suddenly. It was a reasonable question, wasn't it? And even if it wasn't, didn't men appreciate a bit of directness?

'Well, funny you should ask,' said Iain. 'We're, um, kind of standing in front of it.'

'Oh.'

'Cof . . . ?'

'Yes please.'

Chapter Thirteen

'I'm sorry,' Iain was saying, again.

'It's fine,' Katie was saying, again. The problem was, it *was* fine, until Iain started apologising over and over again, with which it was becoming less fine.

'Honestly, it's flattering, really.'

And it was quite endearing, in a 'here we all are back at university' type of a way. After all, she already knew there weren't a lot of women up here. So. They would wait a little while and try again. She looked around at his tiny house. It was an incredibly sweet little fisherman's cottage, painted blue, with wooden floors and only two small rooms downstairs and a little bedroom and a little bathroom upstairs. It looked out onto the bay and was perfectly charming in every way, although when she'd mentioned it, Iain had thanked her and then said that when families of eight used to live in it, it probably wasn't quite so charming, and she'd agreed. Then they'd sipped (horrible) coffee and skirted around the issue, then he'd moved towards her and she'd looked into those huge green eyes and reciprocated as hard as she could.

But when they'd finally moved it to the bedroom things

had got a little bit sticky, not helped by a long hunt for a condom (eventually found in a dusty pile in the cupboard under the sink, along with Imodium, Preparation H and probably about a million other things Iain wasn't quite delighted with her seeing at this particular stage in their relationship). After this, things had gone downhill, with Iain having problems first one, slightly wobbly way, then, after some anguish, and in a terrible rush, the other.

Katie's response to this in the past had always been to ignore it completely and start again as soon as possible, but Iain was clearly not about to let it lie.

'I mean, it's just been so long . . .'

'Shh,' said Katie. 'Don't worry about it. It's usually crap first time round . . .'

'Was it that crap?' asked Iain, his eyes widening.

'Argh! Shh, OK? We can try again, can't we?' She caressed his lovely face, but it looked petulant.

'Actually, I've got to get up really early.'

'Oh, Iain, you don't want me to go, do you? I'll never sneak into Mrs McClockerty's and it's not like I could get a taxi.'

'Uh, no, of course not.'

They tried to settle down onto the old-fashioned wooden bed, but if there's something more difficult than getting to sleep with a near stranger with whom you've just completed an unsatisfactory sexual experience, it's probably in the Olympics.

'Goodnight then,' said Katie, desperately wishing she'd had the foresight to bring a pair of pyjamas – she hated sleeping naked.

'Goodnight,' said Iain, snuffling down beside her with his head in the opposite direction.

Well, this hadn't gone quite as well as she had hoped, thought Katie. She contemplated going home once more, but she didn't want to make the lad feel even worse, and it was freezing out there. Maybe just put it down to experience that just because someone is nice and charming and takes you out to dinner and makes you laugh, and cheers you up when you're sad . . .

Iain was also lying wide-awake, cursing himself as a fucking useless idiot who couldn't do anything without screwing it up. His dad was right, he thought, ruefully, even if his dad was usually hollering about other things; family businesses and cities and pulling himself together.

Katie lying there was just reminding him what a twat he'd been – he could just imagine her telling her stupid gobby mate tomorrow and them having a good laugh about how crap men were, just like that stupid programme where all the men had been rich useless cocksuckers and the women had just talked about shoes and eaten ice cream for half an hour. He should stop watching it, it was making him more confused than ever. Lying in the dark next to someone who thinks you're useless is perhaps the loneliest place on earth to be. Which is why, when Katie slowly snuck a hand under his arm and around his chest, he took it. And eventually, they both fell into an uneasy slumber.

Katie dashed into the shower the next morning – dashing, she'd decided, was absolutely the best way to forestall any conversation, by pretending they were both so super busy they'd have to have it later. Unfortunately, Iain had adopted the same tactic, which was slightly tricky in the tiny house, as they kept nearly bumping heads with each other.

'Well, we must do this again some time,' said Katie, feet on the stairs. She wished immediately she'd phrased it differently, as it sounded as though she'd said, 'can we meet up again for crappy sex?' whereas, what she'd actually meant was 'can we have another chance, because I really like you and think this is a minor blip'.

'Yeah, really,' said Iain in a carefree tone, which sounded as though he was saying, 'I'd rather eat my table', but by which he actually meant, 'if we could magically erase the night before, honestly I'd really like to see you'.

Neither meaning came across.

'Call me,' said Katie, finally, then she immediately wanted to bite her tongue off. She'd cast the evil spell on men; the two magic words that made it impossible for men ever to call you, even men out here in the wild!

Katie switched on her ansaphone at work; she was madly early. There were three messages. The first was from Harry, completely exultant at his brilliant disguise. She couldn't help but smile; he was telling her it was him in case she hadn't noticed. The second was from Louise, expressing the idea that they maybe should tell each other where they were going in future, because if she was dead in a ditch somewhere, everyone would blame her, Louise, and she'd have to besmirch the dead Katie's name by insinuating that she was out having sex somewhere with some journalist. And the third was from Radio Scotland, asking her to come in for an interview.

Suddenly, she felt perky, rather than disappointed and slightly seedy (and ravenously hungry). This was going to be fine. She could handle anything. And if Iain wasn't interested, he was being an idiot.

'Hey,' said Harry. He didn't seem to have the slightest interest in where she'd been, or why she was wearing the same clothes as yesterday; he just seemed pleased to see her. 'Lots to do!'

'Give me your sandwich,' said Katie.

'What?'

'I can't start work without your sandwich. I missed breakfast.'

'Aunt S getting too much for you?'

'Something like that. Sandwich.'

Harry felt in his briefcase. 'You're going to have to answer to Francis. Do you want some of that weird coffee you like?'

'Yes please.'

Sure enough, as soon as she unwrapped the sandwiches, Francis slinked up from the radiator he was snoozing under and sat at her feet politely until she gave him half.

'What are you doing?' shouted Katie to Harry. 'You're not supposed to spoon the coffee straight into the cups! It'll taste horrible!'

'I thought that was the point,' said Harry, handing over the foil packet. 'And what am I going to have for lunch now?'

'Well, that doesn't matter to me,' said Katie. 'Because I'm going to Inverness to be on the radio.'

'The what?'

'You heard. They want me on BBC Scotland. Which is practically national when you think about it.'

'What do you mean *practically*? That's fantastic!' said Harry delightedly. 'It must have been the phone-in I did that did it.'

'Probably,' said Katie. 'They made me promise not to say "arse".'

'Can I come?'

'I thought you had tons and tons to do.'

'Well, Derek can handle a lot of it, can't you Derek?'

'Yes boss,' said Derek, popping up with a happy smile then disappearing into his cubbyhole again.

'Your secretary has a crush on you,' said Katie severely. She might as well have knocked him on the head.

'What, don't . . . what on earth . . .'

Katie rolled her eyes. 'You are very very easy to tease, do you know that?'

Harry flushed a little bit. 'I didn't want to come to your stupid radio thing anyway.'

'Oh, you can if you like.'

'No, no, you're the PR professional. I'll just stay here and get on with the grunt work, shall I?'

'*Yes*,' said Katie wickedly. '*Now* you're getting it!'

The studio in Inverness was smarter than Radio Ullapool, but not by much. The staff there, though, were a lot friendlier and more efficient, and the presenter was well-briefed and led her through the issues in a nice sharp manner. Katie, although feeling she acquitted herself well (and getting a nice feeling from thinking of everyone listening in at the Mermaid), was a bit disappointed at not being able to stir up much controversy (the ban on the word 'arse' wasn't helping things). A few people called in and offered support, and a few golfers phoned in and complained about being victimised (as victimised as you can feel if you're a fat middle-aged white man with lots of money and a Jaguar, thought Katie privately).

And, too quickly, it was the last question.

'So, Katie – one last sum up of why we should all support Fairlish?'

Katie thought of her unhappy experience the previous night – and suddenly it all came flooding back to her. Someone as gorgeous as Iain should be out spreading his wild oats far and wide, not lying balled up embarrassed in bed. Harry shouldn't be getting bloody flushed if anyone so much as made a little joke about love or sex. Louise shouldn't be being followed around by half the men in the village like greyhounds after a rabbit, however much she appeared to be enjoying it.

'Because there aren't any women in Fairlish,' she said suddenly. 'There are only men – lovely men, really nice blokes – and there's no women for them to um, have relations with, or marry, and the last thing they need right now is another few hundred men descending on them to play golf, which will only make the whole thing worse. So that's why it needs to get sorted out, before all the men there go crazy from sexual frustration, and explode and die.'

There was a silence in the studio. Then the lights of the telephones began to light up in a row, one by one.

Louise was looking at her, concerned.

'I'm a bit worried about what this is going to do for our popularity.'

Katie rolled her eyes. She had dashed to the Mermaid – post the Radio Scotland interview, she had new, very exciting news.

'Well, if they liked you in the first place, I'm sure it wouldn't matter.'

'I mean, what if all these girls start rolling up now?'

'It'll be nice – we'll have someone else to talk to besides those little minxes keeping us away from baked goods.'

'And that's another thing. Think how much it's going to annoy them. They'll probably come around and firebomb the house.'

'Oh yes, that was foremost in my mind. Louise, this is my *job*. And it's working!'

They'd bought pies, hastily, from the bakery, and were

eating them in the Mermaid, early, so they could avoid everyone except Lachlan, who concentrated on giving Katie gigantic winks.

'Is it? Have you got anyone interested?'

Katie smiled in a secretive way, knowing it would drive her friend nuts.

'Who?'

'Well, I wouldn't like to say.'

'Does that mean nobody then?'

Louise turned back to her pie. Katie was bursting. 'Maybe not *quite* nobody.'

'La la la,' said Louise. 'I wonder if I should head back to the bothy tonight? It's quite exciting.'

'OK, OK, I'll tell you. It's just, I've only just heard. I haven't even told Harry yet.'

Inside, Katie was so excited, she could hardly speak. She whispered in Louise's ear.

'Oh my God! Richard and Judy!'

'Yes!'

'The one who keeps falling out of her top!'

'You watch a lot of daytime television.'

'I do not.'

'Anyway,' said Katie, very excited, 'everyone who's anyone goes on it. Bill Clinton. OJ Simpson. Peter Andre.'

'You're not serious.'

'I am!!! They want me! And, um, a local man.'

'You're going to be on telly?' said Louise.

'National telly! Primetime!'

'Five o'clock is primetime?'

'YES,' said Katie. 'Anyway, why stop there . . . I could be on *Good Morning* . . . *Newsnight* . . .'

'That's right,' said Louise, tucking in, '*Newsnight* are going to want you. And *Mastermind*. Do you think they'll fly me down with you?'

'I don't see why not,' said Katie. 'You are involved in saving the men in this parish. One at a time.'

'Wow,' said Louise. 'I wonder if London's changed without us? OOH! Shiny lights! Topshop! Rocket salad!'

'Coffee Republic! Double red lines!'

'Pollution!'

'Congestion Charge!'

'Evening papers!'

'Capital!'

'Yay!' they chimed together.

'Oooh, BUT!' Louise exclaimed dramatically, pointing her knife, 'can you bear to leave the Hibernian vale of lurve?'

'I don't know what on earth you mean,' said Katie sheepishly.

'You dirty stop-out! You know exactly what I mean! I had to tell Mrs McClockerty you were still on the radio when you didn't turn up!'

Katie smiled and tried to look as though she wasn't going to talk about it.

'So, you banged our lovely Iain?'

'Banged is *such* an unattractive word,' said Katie.

'Oh! You did!'

Katie toyed with her food, suddenly having an unhappy memory of Iain rescuing her from the same meal. He'd seemed to like her a lot more then than he had this morning.

'Well . . .'

Louise sat back. 'OK. Size, details, descriptions, the lot. You've got ten seconds to cough.'

Katie felt awkward. 'Well, it was our first time . . .'

'Oh. That bad.'

'No! Yes. Yes. It was terrible. Oh, Louise, I really really like him.'

'Well, jump him again and make it better.'

'I didn't jump him the first time. And I'm not sure it's that simple.'

Louise looked perturbed. 'Man, you like man, man has penis, you lick penis, man like you. Simple.'

'You are such a *Rules* girl.'

'I mean, was it insurmountably terrible, that the thought of having it off with him again fills you with nausea and inexplicable rage?'

'I don't *think* so.'

'And you like him, right?'

'Oh yes. He's cute and he has lovely eyes.'

'Well then. You'll just have to take a deep breath and get stuck in. It's like puppy training.'

Katie nodded. 'It's not that. You know, he hasn't called all day. No call, no flowers, nothing. What if he doesn't want to see me again?'

'Of course he wants to see you again! It's you or a sock in this town! Now, do you think Richard and Judy will fly us down first class?'

'What do you mean, "they need a man"?'

Harry was looking perturbed, but Katie thought she could detect a note of excitement underneath.

'I spoke to the researcher today. She said I have to bring a man to talk about how there aren't any women around, and make an appeal.'

'That doesn't sound like the kind of thing I'd want to do,' said Harry.

'It's for a good cause – loads of women will come to the ball. You'll be famous! It'll be great! Just think about the greater good!'

'Isn't there anyone else?'

Katie had considered this, and thought that while Iain

would be brilliant on telly, it probably didn't give him the right message that she wanted him to advertise for other women, plus she wasn't quite confident about taking him to London – her home. After all, what would it mean if they were travelling down to London together? And, of course, it would make Harry livid, which might have seemed a good idea a week ago, but she didn't want to threaten their rapprochement now. Oh, and he still hadn't called. She was starting to get an unpleasant suspicion over how long it was taking him to get in touch. She was less concerned, now, about teething troubles in the bedroom – all she could think of was his sweetness, how lovely he was to look at. She had a pretty bad case of the Iains in fact. She shook herself back to attention.

'Well, Craig the Vet volunteered, but I don't think he's the kind of person we want – he looks like a farmer, and if you were a girl, you'd think he just wanted a hearty pair of hands to get up at four-thirty in the morning and milk the cows.'

'Nothing wrong with that,' said Harry.

'You think that,' said Katie. 'And Lachlan, but . . . he's a bit old.'

'You mean, he's a midget.'

'He's vertically challenged.'

'Oh, so you're the one using the poncey language, but you're also the one not letting him be on television.'

'I know,' said Katie. 'I feel bad about it. But what can I do? I'm a PR person and thus a bit shallow, you know, and stuff.'

'And I'm shallow enough for you?'

'Oh, come on. And nobody else can leave their animals, except for the technogeeks down at the research plant, and there's plenty of them in London already and every time they get excited they start doing *Lord of the Rings* impersonations.'

'So, by a process of elimination of every man in a seventy-mile radius, you got to me.'

'Yes.'

'Can Francis come?'

'No.'

Harry sighed. 'Oh well. I guess. I've never been to London before.'

Katie's eyes widened. 'Ex*squeeze* me?'

'I mean, I've been through Heathrow before. On my way to other places. Places I actually wanted to go to. But London . . . no, it's just never come up.'

Katie just stared at him.

'I can't believe you've never been to London.'

'Why not? It's not the centre of the universe you know.'

'Actually, it is, as it happens. That's why the GMT line is there.'

'Hmm,' said Harry, sounding unconvinced.

'Oh my God. Well, we can show you London.'

'I've seen *EastEnders*, thanks. I'll probably do without.'

'You big snot!' said Katie. 'You never know, you might love it.'

Chapter Fourteen

It is a completely irreversible law that states that if you are really looking forward to showing off about something – your town, a film you love or a great piece of music – it will undoubtedly appear in its worst possible light. The film suddenly won't seem half so funny, or the person will get distracted halfway through the music and start talking about something else, or they'll come to your town and it will piss down with rain and they'll get mugged immediately.

Harry hadn't been mugged yet (that was more Katie's arena), but, annoyingly, when they'd set off on the Monday morning (after a weekend completely Iain-free, not that Katie was frantically checking for his calls or anything), it had been an uncharacteristically glorious day in Fairlish. The sun had glinted off the hills and onto the shining sea, making the whitewashed buildings look clean and fresh, and the painted fishing boats jolly and homely.

'I'm going to miss this,' said Harry sadly.

'You're going away for *three days*,' said Katie. 'Nothing has changed here for a hundred years!'

'You are joking?'

'Um, why?'

'Well, I mean, look at that tree over there. Notice anything about it?'

Now she looked at it, with some irritation she noticed that whilst the previous week it had been in full pink blossom, now the ground beneath was carpeted with petals, and green shoots were crawling out of the twigs.

'What about it?' said Katie, purely to be annoying.

'It's got a new single out,' said Harry sarcastically. 'You have no soul. The land never stops changing if you bother to look.'

'Ahh, it must be National Pomposity Week,' said Katie.

Then, to make matters worse, as they circled around Heathrow, the rain was coming down in sheets.

'So this is the softy South is it?' said Harry, clearly gearing himself up to a long session of remarks like that. Katie decided the best way to deal with it was to ignore him. Instead, she kept an eye on Louise, who was huddled into the window seat, with some concern. She hadn't said a word during the journey, just stared out of the window, seeming more down with every passing mile. Katie hoped she wasn't regretting coming with them. Although they hadn't packed all of her stuff – Katie could bring it down in the car – there was a sense, unspoken between them, that her time in the Highlands was over. She had a job to get back to, a life to pick up the pieces of. It just wasn't realistic to play at buxom country lass, as Olivia had repeatedly pointed out.

Katie had had several more wittering emails from Clara, but had kept them from Louise. They were hardly going to help. She had sent back a noncommittal congratulations note, and reassured her mother on the phone that everything was just fine, that she knew Max very well (which was of course true) and that the hospitals in India were first-rate (or the one she'd pay to get Clara into would be, of that much she was determined).

But that didn't change the fact that Louise was coming back to a town full of ghosts, and it certainly looked bleak this morning.

So, Katie was especially pleased to see a driver and a very petite blonde girl holding a sign up for them at the airport.

'Hello!' she said, introducing them all.

'Wow, great to meet you!' said the young girl reflexively. Katie guessed that she spent her life, unpaid, as a runner picking up people from airports and was doing her best, but Harry seemed completely charmed and fascinated.

'So, you work in telly then?' he asked. 'Is it terribly exciting?'

'Oh yes,' said the girl, dully, whose name was Hortense, meaning she must be under twenty, as Katie could age the generation of Mauds, Stanleys and Hepzibahs by crazily retro names. 'It's incredibly exciting.' She put a handful of change into the parking machine. 'Sixth floor – the lift's out, I'm afraid.'

'Where are we staying?' asked Katie. She hoped they got somewhere good, like a Marriott. She doubted they stretched to the Savoy.

The girl gave her a bored look. 'Well, he's staying in the Thistle,' she said. 'We thought your PR company was London-based.'

'Well, it is . . .' said Katie. She'd planned on going home, of course, but had still secretly hoped there might be a bit of fluffy bathrobes and room service in between. It had been a while since fluffy bathrobes. Mind you, it had been a while since she'd had her own room, so she supposed she could thank heaven for small mercies.

Louise was still staring out of the window. Katie touched her knee gently, but didn't receive much of a response.

'Ha ha ha,' said Harry. 'I've got a hotel.'

'Yes, you'll need it for all the groupies you get after the show,' Katie retorted, which made him blush and cough immediately.

'So, are you the siblings who want to carry their mother's surrogate baby?' asked Hortense in a bored voice.

Harry and Katie looked at each other.

'*Are* we?' asked Harry.

'No,' said Katie. 'He's the man from the men-only village.'

'You don't look gay,' said Hortense.

Having been stop-starting through the traffic at three miles an hour, they stopped at yet another traffic light. Immediately, a woman carrying a baby started banging on their window asking for money. Hortense, the driver and Katie ignored her reflexively. Harry looked at them in consternation.

'The village where there aren't any women living there,' prodded Katie. 'Where they're trying to save the trees!'

'Oh yes!' said the girl. She looked more closely at Harry. 'Is that true? There are no girls?'

'Not many,' said Harry, going red again. 'Mostly lads work around there.'

'Gosh!' said Hortense. 'Well, there are NO men here. Are they all single and stuff?'

Harry nodded.

'Wow. Are there many TV shows produced there?'

'Not many, no.'

'Shame,' said the girl. Then she looked at him again, with a slightly hungry expression that Katie found annoying for some reason. Eyeing Harry objectively, she supposed girls might go for that fit healthy black-haired sulky look – heck, she might have herself a few months ago. Before she got to know him of course. And met Iain . . .

'So, it's just full of horny farmer types?'

'Actually, we're on the show to talk about stopping a golf course,' said Katie officiously. 'Have you got the brief?' And she handed over a booklet she'd spent some considerable time putting together, full of facts and information on the local wildlife, the environmental damage caused by a flurry of new building, and the superfluity of golfing in the area.

'Yes,' said Hortense, handing over her call sheet. Under 'Heathrow Airport Pick-up' it just said 'The Town With No Totty', and their names.

The flat looked weird, in the way that any place not lived in for any length of time seems peculiar. Mail, all bills and junk, was piled up on the floor. There was one lonely sausage in the fridge. The place smelled a little damp, and hadn't got any bigger whilst they'd been away. In fact, if anything, it was worse. Mrs McClockerty might not exactly run the Ritz, but it was still a huge house, with views all the way to the horizon. Whereas here, from the kitchen window, Katie could practically touch the neighbour's bottle of Fairy. There was no horizon at all. Why had she never noticed that before?

'Come on!' she shouted to Louise. 'We're going out.'

Louise, who was wandering around not doing anything, nodded. They were going to meet Olivia at Chi, a cocktail bar so new and trendy that it was getting them excited about paying twelve quid for two centimetres of liquid with an olive in it, which would then make them cough, and, about two seconds later, fall off their stools. Katie would have secretly preferred a quiet wine bar, but couldn't face missing out on this – Olivia had got them on the guest list, it was meant to be packed full of celebrities and was exactly what a smart girl about town like herself ought to be doing in this day and age, for goodness' sake, not making cow eyes at local newspaper boys.

She pulled on her favourite stretchy D&G sale top and, whilst putting on her make-up in the unflattering bathroom mirror, realised she hadn't put make-up on – at least not *this much* make-up – for absolutely ages. She put some glittery shadow on, just to make up for it. She didn't trust Harry to make it through the wilds of North London by himself, so she was going to meet him at the Tube station and take him to hit London, then, after the show tomorrow, she could show him a few sights. Although she'd asked him what he wanted to see and he'd politely replied Stanfords, the travel bookshop in Covent Garden, she was sure they could do better than that, and he could see how much the capital had to offer. And tonight, of course, he could see how cool and stylish they all were and stop acting so damn superior the whole time.

'Get ready, Louise!' she said, seeing her chum still moping around.

'Is there going to be a big queue for this and is it going to be overpriced and stuffed full of wankers shouting at each other about their bonuses?'

'Yes,' said Katie. 'Everything you love.'

'OK,' said Louise. She pulled on a coat over her tattiest pair of jeans.

'Are you going like that?'

'Why, does it matter? What does any of this matter?'

Exasperated, Katie marched her in to the small bedroom. 'Because, when we're sad, we get dressed and go out and have fun, OK? And that's what we're doing now. So sort yourself out into something pretty or I swear, Olivia's going to kick you from here to next Thursday. And you don't need a coat either. We're back down South, and it's summertime.'

Katie went next door, put on some Donna Summer very loudly and mixed Louise a strong gin (with flat tonic).

'Drink this!' she ordered. 'If you think you're going to avoid London for the rest of your life just because some tosser behaved like a dickhead . . . well, you know, we could all do that, or we could all go out and be fabulous. So drink that, and shut it.'

Louise did as she was told.

'And THINK how much more sex than Olivia you've been having since you've been away.'

Louise momentarily brightened.

They caught up with Harry at Green Park Tube, where there was already a line for the club nearly reaching around the block. He was wearing a thick fisherman's jumper, even though it was much warmer in London, cloudy and muggy and a little unpleasant. He looked entirely out of place.

'I don't want to come across as a rube,' he said, 'but have you the faintest idea what I just paid for a taxi to get here?'

'Complaining about the taxis! Rube error number one!' said Katie. 'We're proud of having the priciest transport on planet earth.'

'Error number one, huh? OK, what's number two?'

They both watched as an entire folded-out newspaper bounced past them on the pavement, filthy pages taking flight, only to be trodden down by somebody else walking through them. Then they looked at each other.

'The litter?' asked Harry.

'The litter,' agreed Katie. 'We're tops at that too.'

'Well, at least I catch on quickly.'

Olivia was standing at the front of the line, looking gorgeous in her usual mix of white and hippy new-age clothes.

'DARLINGS!' she screeched, causing everyone else in the queue – who were much more fashionably dressed – to turn around and eye them coldly as they walked to the front of the queue.

'This isn't nice,' said Harry to Katie. 'They've waited ages.'

'It's very nice,' said Katie as Olivia signed them in at the door. 'It's called VIP.'

'Ah,' said Harry, apologising to everyone behind him, 'I see.'

Inside was mobbed, heaving, with smoke wreathing the air. The bar was six deep and there was nowhere to sit except absurdly low couches that were already stuffed full of teenagers draped over each other in absurdly low trousers. Everyone else was standing or perched on stools, chattering wildly in tiny skirts and brightly coloured shoes. Katie's heart sank. She'd wanted a quiet evening catching up with her friends, and introducing them to Harry, not a clusterfuck where you had to drink to make up for the fact that you couldn't hear anyone's conversation. The walls were made of jagged crystal and white velvet, and there were the most extraordinary spiralled mobiles hanging down from the ceiling that looked as though they could take somebody's eye out.

'Isn't this great!' Olivia was shrieking. 'Damien Hirst made the ceiling.'

Katie wasn't quite sure how great a recommendation

this was, and glanced at Harry. He was staring all around him as if he'd just stepped into Wonderland.

'What do you think?' she said, nodding at Olivia who was indicating four martinis to the barman.

'Wow,' said Harry. 'I can't . . .'

Despite herself, Katie couldn't help feeling a little pleased. Mr Grumpy Boots did see London, after all. Well, she supposed he hadn't seen much like this, if the only pub he'd ever been to was the Mermaid (and she hadn't even seen him in there).

'Great, isn't it?'

'I admit it. I'm a rube,' said Harry, 'but those girls have got *no clothes on*!'

'They'll catch their deaths,' she smiled at him.

'They'll catch something,' he said. 'Sorry, that was completely uncalled for. This place is freaking me out. I mean, they look like they've just stepped out of a fashion magazine . . . not that I ever read fashion magazines of course. They're Derek's.'

'Well, here they all are.'

Sure enough, there were many more women than men in the room, although there was a small complement of men in pinstriped suits looking satisfied with themselves, and a few men whose suits matched the décor. Harry's eyes were wide.

'Follow me!' commanded Olivia, and they disappeared into a quieter side area with a large bouncer standing in front of it. Behind him were little Turkish-style seraglio booths, with embroidered cushions and pink lighting. The women were, if anything, even slimmer, and it was, thankfully, quieter.

'Wow!' said Harry, bouncing onto one of the beds. 'I could get to like this.'

Various women turned around as if preparing themselves

to make supercilious expressions, but when they caught sight of the tall and rugged Harry, they clearly decided not to, and looked interested instead; even more so when Harry pulled off his sweater. Katie winced when she saw he was wearing a green checked shirt, but he certainly looked well-built underneath it.

Olivia raised an eyebrow at Katie. 'How many cocktails has he had?' she asked.

'Sorry,' said Katie. 'It's the big smoke. It's overexciting his little country brain. Harry, this is Olivia.'

'Nice to meet you,' said Olivia. 'Are you olive-intolerant?'

'No.'

'Well, you can have your martini then.'

A uniformed waitress – or possibly a model playing a waitress, so beautiful was she – handed over the drinks.

'Thanks. Nice to meet you. Harry . . . Harry what?'

'Barr.'

'No, *really*?'

'Uh, yes.'

'Like Harry's Bar?'

'Um . . .'

'In Venice. Bellinis, you know.'

'Oh, no. I don't know,' said Harry, looking embarrassed. Suddenly Katie was a bit cross with Olivia for showing him up.

'Huh,' said Olivia. 'So, what do you think of London so far?'

'Well, I haven't really had a chance to . . .'

A skinny elongated blonde girl was sitting with her similarly etiolated friends in the banquette alongside them. Wobbling her drink slightly, she leaned over.

'That's a lovely accent – where are you from?'

Harry flushed. 'Uh, Sutherland.'

The girl stared straight ahead. 'Cool. Is that in France?'

'Scotland.'

Several of the other girls slouching on the Turkish Delight bed were deigning to crane their necks to check out the stranger, who, Katie had to admit, did look like the only straight man in the room.

'Wow, cool! Come and tell us about Scotland! Are you the monarch of the glen?'

'I don't *think* so,' said Harry, looking apologetically at the others. He was clearly torn between trying to do the most polite thing in front of two groups of ladies.

'Oh, go,' said Katie, flapping her hands. 'Fresh meat! Carrion alert!'

And Harry was submerged into a giggling blonde throng. He looked terrified but anthropologically thrilled.

'OK,' said Olivia. 'Full gossip please!'

Louise was already at the bottom of her martini, but a model briskly appeared and replaced it. She started to look a bit happier.

'We got laid!' she announced.

'Hang on,' said Olivia. 'I heard about you. But you're not telling me our Katie here got herself entangled in the fiery wastes of love?'

'Oh boy, did she ever.'

Katie rolled her eyes, although she'd known this would come up at some point.

'Not with?' Olivia indicated Harry.

'God, no,' said Katie immediately.

'Why not? What's wrong with him? He's a bit of a hunk, isn't he?'

'NO,' said Katie. 'He's miserable, rude and totally bossy.'

'He doesn't look that miserable at the moment,' observed Louise. One of the harpies was showing Harry her tattoo and he was trying to look and not look at the same time.

'Well, anyway, no. It's with this other bloke. Who is gorgeous, but a bit fucked up, I think.'

'Ooh, gorgeous *and* fucked up,' said Olivia. 'Nature's sexiest creation.'

'He is gorgeous,' said Louise.

'The problem is,' said Katie, 'because there's no girls up there, they're all a bit screwed up. It's a bit like dating at an all-boys' school.'

'Better and better,' said Olivia.

'No, I mean, like arrested development.'

'I don't mind it,' said Louise stoutly. 'They're all really grateful and loyal. Well, all the ones I've met.'

'Hang on,' said Olivia. 'Are you in a town or at a petting zoo?'

'It feels a little bit of both,' said Katie.

'Hmm,' said Olivia. 'Maybe that's what the men down here think about us. Too many women spreading like topsy, and all going completely insane.'

'Interesting theory,' said Katie. 'So it's been quiet then?'

'Not a sniff!' said Olivia. 'My aromatherapist reckons I'm not opening up my chakras enough.'

'Not opening your wallet enough, more likely,' said Katie.

'Plus, I've just taken on this huge wallpaper consultancy. Wallpaper, I ask you. Have you ever met a straight man in wallpaper . . . and *don't* mention painters and decorators, I've had it up to here.'

Katie looked around. Cigarette smoke was reflecting off the high-set mirrors and chunky glass, giving the whole place a feel of being encased in dreamy smog, as young women floated to and fro, honed, painted and dressed up to the nines, almost entirely for the benefit of other women.

'The situation hasn't got any better then?'

'Yes, Katie, in the three weeks since you've been away, they've declared London a war zone and drafted in lots of American soldiers with chewing gum and nylons. It's been fantastic.'

'Have you heard from Clara?' asked Louise suddenly, out of the blue. She had somehow acquired another full martini in her hand. 'Has she got sick and died and you've forgotten to mention it?'

Both Katie and Olivia looked down at their drinks.

'Louise . . . you've got to put it out of your head,' said Olivia. 'I know you've been away, but you're back now, and you're just going to have to get on with things. Really. For your own good.'

'Do you think?' said Louise suddenly. 'You know, it wasn't until I came back here and back to more stupid bars like this and remembered all these endless, pointless nights out to meet someone new, even before I met bloody Max and you know, I just . . . I just don't want to do it any more.' She put her drink down. 'I mean, am I so awful for being sick of it? Because I just wanted a husband and some children and some chickens. And I know it's really unfashionable to say that and I know we're all supposed to be career women and not give a toss and stand up for our feminist heritage that so many women fought so hard for. But I feel like I'm an idiot for wanting that, and there isn't a single man in this stupid fucking town who feels like that or doesn't just want a quick fuck, or doesn't tell you one thing then do something quite different with someone five years younger than you. Is that fair? How is that fair? And I just . . . I just don't *want* to do it any more.'

She dumped her empty glass on the table and got up and stalked out.

'I didn't realise it was this bad,' said Olivia.

'Me neither,' said Katie. 'Chickens?'

'I'll get her,' said Olivia. 'I think you remind her too much of someone.'

'OK,' said Katie, as Olivia got up.

For a while, she was content to sit, staring around, but worrying about her friend. Coming back to London seemed to have made her sadder than ever. But she'd seemed so different in Scotland. She'd seemed . . . happy. Katie had assumed it was because she was escaping from all her problems and ignoring them. Now she wasn't so sure.

'Hey!' said Harry, sitting down beside her. 'All alone?'

Katie reflected on this for a moment. 'Well, I guess so,' she said.

'Those girls keep squawking at me. They want to go to some party at this place called Bouj . . . Bou something.'

'Oh my God!' said Katie. 'You're here for fifteen seconds and you're eurotrash already!'

'Am I?' said Harry. He didn't sound very pleased.

'Yes, you are,' said Katie, as the blonde girls watched, jealously. One of them gave Harry an ickle baby wave.

'Anyway, no I'm not going out to a party. I'm on national television tomorrow.'

'Ooh yes,' said Harry. 'Me too.'

'I'm sure those girls would be happy to come back to your hotel room. Although your room service bill would be enough to buy your own fucking golf course.'

'No thanks,' said Harry. 'They keep asking if I know Prince William.'

Katie grimaced and shook her head.

Harry looked at her. 'Are you all right?' he asked.

'Yes, I'm fine,' said Katie. 'I just . . . I've just been looking forward to coming home to London for ages, but now I'm here, I . . . suddenly, I can't remember why.'

'Doesn't it feel like home any more?'

'Of course it does,' said Katie, giving it emphasis.

'God, I'm glad you're not like those girls,' he said suddenly.

'Aren't I?' Katie was disappointed. She'd always thought that maybe, at least, she looked as if she belonged in London, even if she didn't always feel it. She could take those girls any time.

'I mean, that London "so cool", don't give a stuff attitude – it's not very nice, really, is it?'

Katie shrugged. 'It's just ambitious people getting what they want, isn't it?'

Harry squinted at her. 'Yes. That's exactly what I mean. That that's supposed to be a good thing nowadays, nobody giving a toss and everyone pretending they don't care and that everything's shit. And it's everyone's right to "do their own thing". Do you know where that gets you?'

'Golf courses?' hazarded Katie.

'Golf . . . uh, yes. Exactly. I mean, I know we don't always have the easiest of working relationships . . .'

Katie clinked glasses with him.

'But I don't think – you know, that you're really that shallow or that you really don't care.'

Suddenly he looked a bit nervous. 'Well, um, when you say what you mean, and so forth. Yes. But, maybe, you know, I've just got more used to it, and . . .'

Suddenly, out of the blue, Katie became conscious of the space between them decreasing. The blonde gaggle seemed to have dematerialised; in fact, it was as if there was no one else in the bar at all. She focused on his broad shoulders and, closer in, at his strong hands and, unmistakably, felt an awkward thrill run up her body. As the music faded to a trance-like haze in the background, she felt them, very slowly, inch towards one another.

'OK,' shouted Olivia. 'I've got her! Just a bit of a crying jag in the toilets; exactly what's needed to cleanse the aura. We're off!'

As if a switch had been flicked, Harry and Katie moved apart rapidly and concerned themselves with making very innocent facial expressions. Which would have been lost on Olivia anyway, because she was concentrating on standing on her spike heels and guiding a floppy Louise out of the door at the same time.

'Anyway, hurry up, Katie, surely you'll want to be calling that green-eyed demon journalist lover of yours, or are you still waiting for him to call?'

Harry, who had stood up on reflex as the women had approached, instantly took a step backwards, as if he'd been pushed.

'Excuse me?' he said, holding Katie's gaze.

Katie found herself in consternation, staring at the floor, trying to process what had just happened. She had been – what, attracted to Harry? Where did that come from, then? She had been – well, what had she been about to do, exactly? And anyway, it was Iain she was interested in, wasn't it? Which clearly wasn't exactly going to please Harry . . . His face was thunderous. Ah. Sticky. Well, she hadn't been *deliberately* keeping anything a secret. He'd never asked, that was all.

'*Iain*?' he said, eyes wide in surprise.

Katie was almost lost for words. 'Don't you listen to village gossip?' she managed, weakly.

'No, I don't,' said Harry. 'I absolutely do not.'

And he turned and walked smartly out of the bar.

Chapter Fifteen

Louise was staying in bed the next day. Katie moved the television into her room with strict exhortations not to miss the show. Katie's good intentions to have an early night had been somewhat thwarted by her lying awake half the night worrying about everything. What on earth did she think she was up to, messing about with her boss? She couldn't even believe that was what she was up to, particularly considering how annoying she found him. Meanwhile, she'd checked her mobile a million times – now it had a signal again, she found she'd forgotten how agonising it was. *Nada*. Nothing from Iain, nothing at all. She was the only girl in the world who could fail to pull in an all-boys' town. It was Louise's fault, really. That outburst about feeling left behind had given her a panic attack, and she'd gone temporarily nuts.

Well, she was just going to have to put a brave face on it and pretend last night had never happened. Ah, the humiliation, though, when Harry found out that although she was sleeping with Iain, he'd never called her. She hated how cheap that made her feel in his eyes. Mind you, it was none of his bollocking business who she slept with, after all, and it wasn't as if she was swapping enemy information. So, they had had a boyhood spat – that wasn't her fault either, for Christ's sake. Why couldn't they all behave like grown-ups about this?

Three strong cups of fantastic coffee later and Katie was in more of a fighting mood by the time the car came to pick her up to take her to the television studios. She certainly didn't fancy stupid Harry Barr, she fancied Iain and she would call him as soon as the programme was over and tell him to stop being such a bloody idiot, then she'd go back to Fairlish and have the kind of historic sex that she'd been thinking about for, well, quite some time.

Delighted to be let loose on her wardrobe again without having to bolster it up with thermal underwear, shapeless sweaters and wellingtons, she went for her absolute favourite wraparound red dress – which was a bit much for five o'clock in the afternoon, but would certainly make her stand out – and a vertiginous pair of heels. London woman indeed. Well, Harry was going to see London woman, and he was going to respect her. Grrr.

Arriving at the studios, she insisted on heading straight for hair and make-up. They plastered it on, of course, so it would look better under the lights, and she felt she could do with a bit of that right about now. The lady also teased her hair into a large sticky-up section at the back, which Katie thought might be a bit eighties' Mrs Thatcher, but the hairdresser assured her was very 'now'. And it certainly added to the height of the shoes. Looking at herself in the mirror, she was practically unrecognisable, and certainly not a Katie Watson who enjoyed herself at county shows, which was precisely the desired effect.

* * *

Harry was sitting in the green room. He looked up when she entered and his face momentarily registered shock at her appearance, which annoyed her all over again.

'Good morning,' she said, cordially.

'You look like a tart's breakfast,' observed Harry, looking up from where he was pretending to be engrossed reading a copy of *The Field*. 'That should please Iain.'

'Ah, sexual harassment,' said Katie. 'Good, I'll be sure to contact my big scary London lawyers.'

Harry went back to ignoring her, but Katie herself felt angry and shaky inside. How dare this pompous git think he had some moral high ground, just because she'd felt sorry for him for one tiny moment in a cocktail bar? It wasn't the law that everyone had to avoid sex was it? Or had she missed a memo? She shot Harry a dirty look, which he pretended not to notice.

Hortense entered, projecting an air of supreme busyness, wearing a headset and carrying an impressive clipboard. A small gaggle of people walked in behind her.

'OK, chums. How're you doing?'

Both of them grunted at her. This discomfited Hortense, who was used to people being delighted to be on television.

'I said – HOW'RE YOU DOING!?' she repeated.

'We're great,' said Harry.

'Great! Fantastic! We're going to have a fantastic show then! Great! Now, let me introduce you –'

She stared at her clipboard, until there could be absolutely no doubt that she had no idea who she was introducing to whom. She indicated an elegantly dressed, very slender woman with an anxious expression and a large mane of put-up hair.

Harry leaped to his feet.

'. . . this is Fennellopy Crystal. She's just written a book on crosstraining dogs and men.'

Harry stared at her. 'You're crossbreeding dogs and men?' he asked, in incredulous tones. 'How does that work?'

'Cross*training*,' she said in an annoyingly patient voice, as if she'd been asked this question a lot before.

Katie snorted.

'You just have to teach them all the same. Talk to men sternly and reward them with praise.'

'To get them to do what? Eat your post?'

The woman laughed an annoying tinkly laugh. 'It's the latest way to get a man, you know.'

'By whistling at them in a very high pitch?'

'It's sold four hundred thousand in paperback.'

'Yes,' said Hortense, nervously. 'And this is Star Mackintosh.'

Star Mackintosh looked about twenty years old and was wearing odd ankle boots that zipped up the middle, pink fishnets, a pale pink leather bomber jacket tightly fitted over enormous boobs, and a tiny fringed denim skirt that only just covered her arse. There didn't seem to be anything underneath the bomber jacket.

'Hello!' she said in broad Mancunian tones. 'I'm the new girl in *Coronation Street*. I always just say what I do, otherwise it's embarrassing for people to come up to me.'

Katie nodded. She'd stood up too, as standing around seemed to be what they were doing at the moment.

'That's why I changed my name to Star. From Tina. It saves time with people having to ask me what I do, ha ha ha!'

'That's great, well done,' said Katie.

Star leaned over conspiratorially. 'You know, I've got nothing on under this bomber jacket.'

Katie nodded.

Star checked out Hortense, who was busy shouting into a walkie-talkie.

'So, I was thinking, the show's live, innit?'

Katie was there ahead of her. 'You're going to get your norks out?'

Star smiled. 'Well, it'll get me the coverage, innit? And Judy's like, already famous for it. I can't believe nobody's done it before.'

'Me too,' said Katie. 'Considering it goes out at teatime in a family slot.'

Star shrugged. 'I've tipped off the tabs, and they're going to try and get one of the cameramen to do a close-up of Richard's face.'

'That's not very sporting.'

Star smiled again. 'Gets me in the papers, dunnit!'

'You should do that too,' said Harry to Katie. 'In case there's anyone out there who hasn't seen them.'

Katie glared at him. 'Jealous?'

Harry sneered. 'God no.'

'You can't do the tit thing,' said Star, sounding agitated. 'It was my agent's . . . I mean, it was my idea first, but I'm the biggest star, so I'm on last. So you *can't* do it first.' She took out her mobile and started texting furiously on it.

'Don't worry Star,' said Katie, putting her hand on the girl's shoulder, 'I won't. I'm afraid we've just ended up on a show with a horrible sexist pig.'

'I thought Richard was meant to be really nice!' said Star, as Katie wandered off to the catering table by herself, to get away from Harry and try to eat a sandwich without getting it covered in lipgloss.

'OK everyone,' said Hortense. 'Richard and Judy will try and pop in to say "hello".'

'Ooh,' said Star.

'Now just remember, be yourselves and have fun – we want to see your natural personalities come through. Although I trust you'll remember this is a teatime show, it's not *Frank Skinner*.'

Star let out a tiny giggle.

Katie sighed. If Harry could stop being a prick for five tiny seconds, she could concentrate on this – their biggest break so far – being a success, get the job done, get the attention levels up, scare the developers off, job done, go home and forget the whole bloody thing. Plus, this was her first time on telly – her mum would be watching and everything. She didn't want to mess it up. She wondered if Iain would be watching. Well, of course he would – the entire town would be out in force. She smiled ruefully. Well, at least her make-up was nice.

The studio was much smaller than Katie had imagined, although she'd been to these things before, on the sidelines, and she always thought that. It was hot, and there were cables everywhere – she heard Harry curse as he hit his foot as they were led along the dark passageways behind the cameramen.

In front of them now, Fennellopy Crystal was talking to Richard in her slow, modulated, somewhat infuriating voice.

'So, if you kept on doing it, I'd simply change the position of the sofa, until you'd learned.'

Richard looked suspicious. 'So, your book is basically just telling women to tell men off until they do what they're told?'

'Of course it isn't,' said Judy.

'See, you're doing it now.'

Fennellopy was wearing a very tight smile on her very tight face. 'It's about rewarding positive behaviour in a positive way.'

'I'm not a dog,' said Richard crossly. 'I'm a tiger.'

'It's not about calling men dogs,' said Fennellopy. 'It's about finding stability in your life.'

'By buying a dog,' said Richard helpfully.

'*No*.'

'It's a lovely book,' said Judy, patting Fennellopy's knee. Fennellopy flinched like a nervous Pomeranian. 'And thank you so much for coming on and telling us all about it.'

She turned towards one of the cameras. 'Now, from one extreme to another – whilst Fennellopy's talking about how to keep your man in London, at the other end of the country they've got the opposite problem. Yes, in the town of Fairlish, in Sutherland, there are fifteen men to every woman!'

As Judy was talking, Fennellopy was briskly whisked away without ceremony, and with much shushing, Katie and Harry were led onto the famous sofa.

'What time does the next bus leave, I hear you ask. Well, here to tell us what it's like, and why they *don't* want a new golf course built, which will mean even *more* men, here's Katie Watson and Harry Barr.'

Tinkly music played, and Katie and Harry tried to arrange their faces into natural-looking rictus grins. Up behind them on screens came large superimposed shots of Fairlish, looking rather lovely.

Judy turned towards them in a smiling fashion as they murmured hellos.

'So, you're Harry, that's right?'

Harry nodded.

'And you live in Fairlish, where there are, how many . . . ?'

'Five hundred and seventy-five men and sixty-six women,' said Richard helpfully.

Harry smiled.

Judy clutched his arm in a motherly fashion. 'Oh, you poor thing.'

'It's not so bad,' said Harry. 'You know, it's an outside kind of life out there . . . you're living close to nature, there's always lots of work to do, seasons changing.'

'But you don't have a girlfriend,' said Richard. 'Tricky.'

'Well, we're quite a quiet community,' said Harry. 'Most of us.'

Katie chose to ignore this.

'Well, you're not quite the quiet community any more, are you, uhn, Katie?' said Judy, reading her notes.

'No,' said Katie. 'Pluto Enterprises want to knock down our local forest and replace it with a golf course, and we're saying "NO".'

'Hmm,' said Judy. 'So, you're actually from London, aren't you?'

'She certainly is,' said Harry.

Katie nodded.

'So, did you find yourself suddenly terribly popular when you arrived there?'

'Well, I don't know about that,' said Katie.

Harry snorted. She shot him a look.

'I mean, compared to London, how did you find it for men?'

'Well, there's a lot of them about,' said Katie. 'But mostly they're really insecure with women and tend to get really jealous.'

'No they don't,' said Harry. 'But the local men tend to

like to stick to the more traditional type of girl. We're not really into the racy city-girl type. Most of us are actually quite old-fashioned in our ways. I don't know how many girls want that kind of thing any more.'

'Well, quite a few, judging by our switchboard!' said Judy, sounding calm, although there was clearly somebody shouting in her earpiece.

'So, I mean, Harry, how do you cope, with the whole, lack of girls thing?' said Richard. He sounded as if he wanted Harry to reply with an intimate rundown of his masturbation timetable.

'It's fine,' said Harry. 'I walk my dog a lot, you know.'

'Ooh, you've got a dog, how lovely,' said Judy.

Katie rolled her eyes.

'And you must be having the time of your life!' said Richard to Katie.

'You'd think,' said Katie. Richard and Judy weren't quite sure how to take this rudeness and Katie felt a pang of embarrassment.

'So, would you recommend any lady viewers watching right now who might be feeling a little bit lonely to get themselves up there right now?'

'If they want to save a forest, then, yes, we could do with them!' said Katie, trying to redeem things with a cheesy grin.

'Or if they're quite loose and just desperate to cop off,' said Harry. 'That seems to work quite well too.'

There was a sudden silence in the studio.

'OK,' said Judy, still in a smiley way, but with a desperate edge to her voice. 'Lovely! Thanks! So nice of you to come in! So that's the town with too many men there . . . and, coming up, just after the break, You Say We Pay and we'll be greeting Star Mackintosh, the youngest hot new star on the block . . .'

They were ushered off the sofa quickly, without time to say goodbye to their hosts.

Hortense was waiting for them outside. 'That was *great*, guys, thank you so much for coming.'

'Great? Did you actually see it?' said Katie. She was shocked and mortified beyond belief at what Harry had just said. I mean, there was banter and then there was . . . well, he'd just called her a slut in front of ten million people.

'No, no, far too busy, but I'm sure you were great.'

There was a car waiting outside to take them back to the airport. Katie slammed her way into the front seat before it slowly drew out into the heavy London traffic. It was a gorgeous, heavy hot day, and the air looked golden and thick as they pulled out alongside the Thames.

Harry could have kicked himself. He was . . . he had to admit it to himself . . . he was jealous. He hadn't thought that this would happen; hadn't recalled that Iain always had to have things absolutely his own way. But it wasn't just that. He definitely . . . the thought was so alien to him . . . it had been such a long time since he'd felt this way . . . that he'd completely overreacted. But the fact was, he thought he liked her. No, he definitely did. She was sparky, and he liked that. Needed it. Harry was conscious, for the first time, of how . . . how steady his life had been. For such a long time. Nothing changed, particularly. And he'd thought he liked it that way. But he didn't. He wasn't happy, not at all, really. Otherwise, why would he be getting himself so worked up by something this stupid? And then blowing it all . . . on television! He should never even have been on television in the first place. What was he thinking? Really, he was only trying to please her. That had been it all along. Christ, he was an idiot.

'Look,' said Harry, who was looking uncomfortably red. How could he have said that? What kind of a man was he? His face went even redder. 'I'm really sorry. I don't know what I was thinking.'

'You were thinking "I'm a really horrible prick and I'm going to say something really disgusting live on television",' said Katie. 'Now, don't talk to me.'

She stared out of the window. There were hordes of people on the South Bank promenade, sitting on benches or wandering around, looking at the second-hand bookstalls or just staring out at the river. Couples walked along hand in hand; gaggles of office girls on their way to the pub; families of all colours with little children running about enjoying the sun and the space.

Harry stared too at the passing cityscape, not really seeing it. Towns weren't really his thing, never had been. It was completely beyond him why people would choose to live crammed one on top of the other and, worse, pay exorbitantly for the privilege. But one thing was clear to him now. He wanted . . . he wanted Katie. He actually did, and he cursed himself for not realising this fact earlier.

'Katie,' he said, leaning forward, softening his voice. This wasn't going to be easy to explain, and he didn't even know if he could explain it or even if she was going to be interested now – maybe her and Iain were loved up, anyway. Maybe it was too late. Maybe he'd just been too wrapped up in himself all along. Bugger bugger bugger.

'Katie,' he said again. She was talking, though, and he couldn't quite hear what she was saying.

'Stop the car,' she was saying to the driver.

She turned to Harry, her hands visibly shaking. 'I think my job's done, don't you? I've changed my mind. I'm not going to the airport any more. I'm going home.'

Chapter Sixteen

Late spring, and the weather was scorching already. London automatically becomes nicer in the sunshine; people almost smile, and eat their lunch outside, or even sit at pavement cafés wearing sunglasses and drinking lattes (cuntinentals, Louise called them, but Katie liked it). This was great, Katie had decided. It was fantastic and wonderful and she wasn't even going to moon for a second about green fields and falling-down houses and mince and tatties and friendly dogs and the way the fresh air smelled of heather, bright and pure and sweet, as the wind swept down the mountains first thing in the morning. She wasn't thinking about that, and horrible men and stupid cobbles.

She was back into the London life and Olivia had taken pity on her, and considered her job – raising the profile of the Forestry Commission – absolutely completed, considering they'd made it to *Richard and Judy*, and subsequently, into various national papers and women's magazines who'd gone in search of this mystical Brigadoon full of hunky men who walked their dogs and wished for nice old-fashioned women. 'Are you absolutely sure we're doing the right thing in telling them?' Louise had said, scandalised. 'You'll ruin it just as surely as that golf course definitely will when they definitely build it now you're not there.' To which Katie had replied 'lala-llalallala' with her fingers in her ears.

She ignored it all. If she even caught the name Scotland in the papers, she quickly turned the page and concentrated on something else, like her new clients, who were trying to market a new range of alcoholic milkshakes and ice creams which were undeniably delicious but, Katie felt, possibly a little unethical. Olivia had said, don't talk nonsense, anyone who ate dairy was already taking their life into their hands, so Katie spent her time on arranging lots of theme nights at bars, then turning up and drinking the milkshakes. It was fun, kind of, and it was uncomplicated, definitely. She got recognised once or twice for being on *Richard and Judy*, and was something of a minor celebrity amongst her workmates, who were constantly threatening to go off and live in the land of endless men, but that didn't last beyond a week or so, particularly as the half-naked Star Mackintosh had garnered the lion's share of the publicity.

Iain – who hadn't even called after the show – began to fade to something of a dull ache in her memory, like a not-quite-healed scab that you forgot about most of the time, until it catches on something. She wondered occasionally what his newspaper was saying, but wouldn't let herself find out.

'I don't miss it, do you?' she'd say to Louise when they were sitting in a nice restaurant or the back of a taxi, and Louise would do her best to shake her head stoically and say no, she didn't miss it either.

As for Harry, well, sod him. A bit of her wondered if maybe he was jealous, but she quickly dismissed the thought. No, he was just a boor, and one she could well do without. Her mother had called to say he looked like a lovely young man, but Louise had been shocked too by his behaviour. Harry might have been grumpy and brusque, but they'd never thought him unkind.

Louise was better now too. She'd calmed down a little, and didn't talk very much about Fairlish either; just a quiet sigh now and again when the weather grew a little too hot and oppressive and there was no breeze coming in off the hills, because there weren't any hills. And life carried on much as before, and the three of them went to smart new clubs and bars and the occasional desultory date that didn't seem to amount to anything much. At least Katie had started walking about the streets again. The spring sank into a muggy, warm summer, and the heat seemed to settle close to the ground, with the car fumes almost visible over the top. People became less cheerful as the sticky nights intensified until it was difficult to breathe. Although, sales of alcoholic ice cream went through the roof.

And then, out of the blue, Clara came home.

It was Sunday, and they were around at Katie's as usual. If you didn't mind stretching through and handing things in and out, you could sit on top of the picture window of the downstairs apartment, which was covered in gravel. Katie wasn't sure it was strictly legal, but it was nice, in the heat, to be outside.

They had the papers, some bacon sandwiches and good coffee and were happily sitting down to explore the tabloids, when, out of the corner of her eye, Katie caught sight of an oddly-shaped, but grimly determined-looking figure, hauling a huge misshapen rucksack up the road. There was something familiar about the walk. Katie put down her sandwich.

'What's the matter?' said Louise. 'Can I have yours? Apparently bacon sarnies are OK on the all-new celebrity bikini diet. It says so right here.'

'You're all going to die,' said Olivia, munching on something brown she'd brought herself in a Tupperware container that smelled of old car tyres.

'I think . . .' Katie was careful not to lean out too far, in case she fell over. 'Hang on here, guys.'

She went downstairs and ran into the street, conscious of the other two watching from above. It was her sister, but not the tanned, slender happy-go-lucky Clara she'd seen last year. This Clara was huge, greasy, brown and sweating from pulling her huge bag behind her.

'What . . . what . . . are you *doing* here?' said Katie.

Clara put her bag down and burst into tears.

Katie led her inside, as the other two came in from the window ledge.

Louise's face was a mask; trying to look cool and unconcerned, she merely looked pale and strange and mildly homicidal. She looked at Clara's face, which was streaked with dirt. She was wearing an old dirty poncho, which didn't really cover her massive, wide bump.

'Hello Clara. You look great,' she said stiffly. 'It really suits you. I'm off out. Anyone want anything?'

Clara's crying redoubled. 'I'm sorry, Louise,' she sobbed.

'I'm amazed you remember my name,' said Louise. 'You didn't before. Excuse me.'

And she walked out, with some dignity, Katie thought.

Olivia brought in a pot of herbal tea, which was disgusting, as usual, but Clara liked it.

'OK,' said Katie. 'Tell me the whole story.'

Except there wasn't much to the story, of course, although it took a while to come out between the choking sobs. Turns out being unmarried and pregnant in India wasn't quite the barrel of laughs she'd thought it was going to be, with the added stress of Max suddenly getting an acute attack of the middle-class boys and wanting to go home and get a job, and realising that actually he'd always wanted a family but in fact really would have preferred it with someone a bit more down to earth, like, say, Louise, instead of a flighty free spirit, like, say, Clara.

'He just got so *cold*,' she sobbed. 'Like, it wasn't fun any more. So he didn't bother.'

'How pregnant *are* you?' said Katie. 'I thought you were only a few months along.'

'No, we got pregnant really early, but I didn't notice for ages. I was throwing up all the time anyway, and my periods have always been all over the place, what with being so thin and stuff . . .'

Katie was internally rolling her eyes but tried not to show it. 'So?'

Clara looked down. 'I think, about seven and a half.'

'*Months*? Good God!'

Katie was pleased Louise wasn't around to hear that; she'd have flown at her. Obviously, despite years of cautioning Louise to patience, Max had forgotten all about contraception within about fifteen seconds of meeting Clara.

'I know,' said Clara miserably. 'Then the monsoon rains came, and we were staying in a little hut, because we're nearly out of money, and Max starts kicking everything about, and swearing, and saying this is all shit and how can we bring a baby into this, and that he must have gone completely crazy when he met me, and he wished it had never bloody happened.'

'I'm sorry, sweetie,' said Katie, putting her arm around

Clara's neck. And she was, too. It doesn't matter how much you might be annoyed with someone, if they truly get their comeuppance, it doesn't make you feel good in the slightest; especially if they're family.

Clara sniffed. 'So, I got a rickshaw into town then caught a train, which took ages, then I caught a plane – I used your credit card number by the way.'

Katie let this go for the moment.

'And here I am. And I don't know what I'm going to do, and I'm going to have a baby with a complete pig, and I don't know where to go or how I'm going to look after it and I'm going to turn into one of those benefits mothers and end up having to go on *Trisha* . . .'

Her sobs began to take on a hysterical quality.

'You're just very tired,' said Katie. 'We are going to do bath, then bed, then figure out what we're going to do later. It's going to be all right, I promise.'

Clara looked at her with an expression that betrayed how much she really really needed this to be true.

'Thanks, sis. I knew I could count on you.'

Once Clara was safely despatched to Katie's bed, they felt it safe to call Louise back.

'Guess I'd better start packing,' Louise said when she returned, refusing Olivia's tea with some disdain.

'Don't be stupid,' said Katie, shocked. 'Give her two days and I'll pack her straight off to Mum's.'

'Your mum won't want the fuss.'

'Nobody wants the fuss! And Mum started it.'

'Don't be daft,' said Louise. 'You know, it looks like friends aren't the new family after all.'

Katie looked at her with huge fondness. 'Don't move out. Please.'

'Honestly,' said Louise. 'I couldn't . . . after what she

did to me. I couldn't spend one night under the same roof as her.'

'I understand,' said Katie sadly. 'But where are you going to go?'

Louise made a funny noise at the back of her throat. 'You know a funny thing? I bet Max would take me back.'

'I bet he would too,' said Katie. 'You wouldn't go though, would you?'

Louise's eyes were shining with tears. 'I'd rather eat kittens.'

Katie crossed the room and gave her a huge hug. Which didn't quite solve the immediate problem.

Louise's parents had retired to Wales. Both Katie and Louise were suddenly very conscious of continuously hugging, and not looking at Olivia. Olivia hated having anyone to stay. Olivia wasn't entirely keen on having people around at all, for any length of time. Olivia's house was a Feng-Shuied shrine in white, cream and taupe, with candles burning everywhere and expensive, fragile pieces of pottery. There was a gigantic Buddha at one end of the sitting room, and lots of expensively-covered cushions scattered around to create a 'womb space'. Personally Katie would hate to live somewhere you couldn't spill tea on the floor, but it was Olivia's temple.

There was a very long silence, followed by a very long sigh from Olivia's direction.

'Well, I *suppose* you could stay at mine,' she said. 'For a little bit.'

'Are you sure?' said Louise. 'I could always go live under Waterloo Bridge. Katie, pass me that newspaper. I'll need it for insulation.'

'No, no. Please. Come and stay . . . until you find somewhere of your own.'

'That will be very, *very* soon,' said Louise. 'Thank you.'
'Thank you,' said Katie, fervently.

Looking after Clara, Katie felt she was getting a sense of what it would be like to have a baby of her own. She cried all day, hated getting bathed and slept at peculiar times. It was fascinating to spend time so close up with a huge pregnant belly. Great big blue veins pulsed from her breasts (now huge) to the top of her stomach. You could actually see it move, kicked from the inside out.

'That is the weirdest thing,' said Katie one day, resting her hand on it as they were watching *EastEnders*.

'I feel like I'm in *Alien*,' Clara grumbled. 'That I only exist to ensure the survival of this . . . parasite.'

'You do,' said Katie. 'That's how the survival of the species works. That's why women always used to die in childbirth.'

Clara sighed again and eyed her big belly with some distaste. Max had phoned, but really just to check she was all right ('how can I be all right?' Clara had screamed, 'I'm carrying the spawn of Satan!'), and to work out how much money she wanted. When Katie spoke to him, he seemed more interested in getting Louise's new telephone number than he did in having any access to his baby.

Katie told Clara he'd feel differently when the baby came, but she wasn't sure about that. Max sounded wretched. He was having terrible trouble getting back in the job market, and now he was carrying the mortgage all by himself, having given his tenants notice. He was, thought Katie, someone who deep down did just want to settle with someone like Louise and have a family. Then he'd seen the men around him swan about with a different gorgeous girl on their arm every night of the week and felt he was badly missing out on something all the other lads were enjoying. So he'd panicked. It wasn't really him. She'd feel sorry for him, if he hadn't cheated on her best friend, then got her sister up the duff, then ditched her. So, as it was, she was icy cold on the rare occasions he got in contact.

Katie had put off phoning their mother, who would get awkward and antsy and not know what to do, but she really had to. If there were two of them around who didn't know what to do, surely that would make things a little easier. At least her mother had been through childbirth, though you wouldn't necessarily think to look at her that she'd approve of something that messy.

It went without saying that Clara's hippy, on-the-road friends had vanished completely. Presumably someone in Clara's circumstances who was not overjoyed and planning on calling the baby Rainbow Sugardrop was just too much of a bummer, man.

So it was just the two of them, and, oddly, although it was much more work, and the future looked vaguely threatening, as sisters, they were getting on better than they ever had before.

The heat rolled on into July. London was suffocating now. Old people were dying in their homes. Dogs were getting trapped in cars. People, suffering from the lack of sleep at nights, were becoming snappish, fraught. The roads were melting, cars were overheating. Clara, lugging about another person, was finding it very difficult, and spent most of the day drinking frappucinos underneath the electric fan, a habit Katie was finding a little expensive. It occurred to her that Clara had never had a job more complicated than massage or making rubbish little pieces of jewellery to sell at music festivals, but she didn't feel able to bring that up – after all, she could hardly ask her to get her feet on the career ladder now. She couldn't even see her feet.

At a deeper level, though, she couldn't stop fretting. Was this it now? Would they stay together, sharing this flat, and she'd help bring up her sister's child? She'd feel responsible – she couldn't just bring some chap home when she felt like it, or stay up playing music all night, or disappear for the weekend if there was babysitting to be done. Clara seemed perfectly wedded to the fact that Katie was going to be the provider for this baby, and there didn't seem to be anything Katie could do about it. And of course, she didn't want to, did she? – this baby was family. She was going to love it to distraction. Of course she was.

It was in this anxious frame of mind that she picked the phone up early one Saturday morning. She'd been out late at some promotion and wasn't really with it. Clara wasn't stirring that she could hear. She'd better get up and fix breakfast for them.

'Hello?'

'Yeah, hi?' said Katie, trying to pull on her pyjama bottoms, which had somehow come off in the heat of the night.

'Katie?'

'Who is this?'

'Oh, come on . . . please, please. Hasn't this gone on long enough?'

Katie recognised Harry's Highland burr and found herself running her fingers through her tangled hair. She'd planned this for ages; how she would be icy, and self-contained and pretend it didn't matter that he had made a complete idiot out of her, but look what he'd lost, and they'd be absolutely desperate of course, and Iain had been crying himself to sleep and would she please reconsider . . .

But under the circumstances, she realised it really didn't matter. That, compared to family, it genuinely wasn't that important.

'Oh, Harry, right?'

But it didn't mean a part of her wasn't immediately pleased to hear his voice.

'Well, of course it's me. Are you still in a massive snit with me?'

Katie's voice softened. 'God, no, of course not. I'd forgotten all about it. Especially after that girl's tits were everywhere, you know . . .'

Star Mackintosh, Katie couldn't help noticing, had gone from strength to strength since accidentally exposing herself on the show. At particularly bad moments, Katie wondered if she should have done it herself.

There was a pause.

'Hello?' said Katie.

'Well, as long as it's forgotten,' said Harry, coughing slightly. 'I have a shocking temper. As, er, you may have noticed.'

'It was a stupid thing to do and I was really insulted,' said Katie. 'But in the wider scheme of things, it really doesn't matter, does it?'

Again, Harry paused. He'd been prepared for fights, tears, faked disdain . . . anything but this, in fact. She genuinely sounded not bothered. His pre-prepared speech sounded a bit rubbish now. 'Well, here's the thing,' he said. 'I know I seem to spend my life saying this, but we need you back.'

'No, you don't,' said Katie. 'I've finished. We've done our bit – started your campaign, got you local and national coverage. I'd be very surprised if they go ahead after the ball; we've made far too much fuss for it to be worth their while. You should be pleased. I heard from Olivia that Pluto Enterprises are absolutely spitting.'

'Yes, but . . . we still need you back.'

'Well, you should have thought of that before you insulted me on national television.' Katie started giving the conversation her full attention. 'Don't you think?'

'Yes,' said Harry contritely. 'I panicked under the stage lighting.'

'That is bullshit!'

'Plus, Francis really misses you.'

'That's just emotional blackmail. Francis is anyone's for half a sandwich. Why are you calling, really?'

'Well, this ball thing you thought of . . . we're going ahead with it, but it's getting a bit out of hand.'

'Out of hand, how?'

'Well, there seem to be a lot of people coming.'

'How many?'

Harry said something which sounded like it might have been 'five hundred' but couldn't have been.

'*How many*?'

'Five hundred.'

'Five HUNDRED?'

'It all went a bit nuts after the telly thing,' Harry mumbled.

'Looks like it! Who the hell is organising that?'

'Well, me, obviously, and Aunt Senga's taken over the catering . . .'

'Christ.'

'Then it all started getting a bit crazy with all these women coming, so all the chaps in the Mermaid started adding things and now we're doing, like, competitions, and slave auctions and things . . .'

'*Slave* auctions and things . . .' repeated Katie.

'Huh, yes.'

'Oh Christ,' said Katie. 'If I could get the time off, I'd almost want to come. I imagine that would be worth seeing.'

Then she wondered how much Iain would make in a slave auction, and that made her sad and a little bit nostalgic, so she tried to think about something else.

'Well, that's why we need you to come.'

'Oh no you don't. You just want someone to put the blame on. Then you'll probably contrive to call me a whore again and it will *not* end happily.'

'That's not true,' protested Harry. 'People are always asking after you. And there's been some . . . ehm, some nice pieces in the paper.'

Katie's heart, despite herself, leaped a little. 'Well, that's . . . but no, definitely not. What else are you up to, anyway?'

'I'm just about to walk Francis.'

'What's the weather like?'

'Um, bit of a fresh wind blowing. Quite stiff. We're going to head out for the cliffs, just as soon as I can wake him up.'

Katie thought how nice it would be to feel a fresh wind blowing right at that moment. Even just standing up to answer the phone had made her sweat.

'Well, good luck with it and let me know how it goes. You remember I told you about my sister?'

'Yes.'

'Well, she's going to have the baby a lot sooner than we thought. And she's come back from India to have it. And she's staying here. And, um, there's no one to look after her but me.' This came out in a bit of a rush.

'What about your mum?' asked Harry.

'We don't want to upset her,' said Katie. 'She's . . . she's a little nervous.'

'Nonsense!' said Harry. 'That's what mums are for. Honestly, you should really use her. Get her in to babysit and come and see us. Soon.'

'Thanks,' said Katie. 'But it's not really practical. Nice to hear from you, though.'

And she meant it. It felt like a little bit of fresh air in her world. And whenever she thought about it over the next few days, she felt a little fresher inside too.

Alcoholic milkshakes came to an abrupt end a week later, after the fifth schoolchild collapsed in the street and the papers started going for their guts, and the pressure really came off at the office. That meant early days and heavy, sleepless nights spent hanging around the flat.

Katie had called their mother, who sounded so nervous and put off by the whole thing that she'd almost washed her hands of her – her mum kept asking stupid questions, like whether Clara was getting married, and where was she going to have the baby, in a way that made it quite clear that, whilst mildly interested, she had absolutely no intention of getting involved more than she absolutely had to. Harry might complain about not having a mother, thought Katie uncharitably, but having one that was more interested in the price of carrots in Blackburn than her first grandchild was no picnic either.

Clara, meanwhile, had become fretful and clingy, constantly asking Katie where her maternity bag was and whether or not all this was going to hurt. Neither of them, though, touched on where the baby was going to live when it was born. At the moment, Katie's money was on her sock drawer.

Katie couldn't be bothered going out either. It was too hot, buses and Tubes had become instruments of torturous death by stinkification, and every bit of outside space was taken up with really young people drinking Smirnoff Ice, shrieking and having millions and millions of chums. Half of Katie's chums had had babies and moved to Brighton, which was almost the same as if they'd all just died. The rest couldn't be rounded up at the same time and required three weeks' notice to plan a social event in the diary, something Katie simply couldn't be arsed with at the moment. How people simply managed to drift together for a night out was completely beyond her. So, she and Clara stayed in, the two of them watching television and drinking iced water, and both, secretly, fretting.

'RIGHT,' said Louise, crashing through the door with her own key. She looked around the front room. It was covered in pizza boxes, empty ice-cube trays and grass, a craving Clara was pretending to have to annoy Katie.

'You,' she pointed at Katie. 'You're coming with me. For a drink. Somewhere nice, that doesn't smell of cardboard and pepperoni.'

'What about me?' asked Clara who, eight months gone, now looked like one of the M&M men.

'*You* can stay in and look after yourself for a change. What, you need Katie to babysit?'

'She likes keeping me company.'

'Katie, you need your eyebrows waxed,' ordered Louise. 'Olivia would have a shit fit. In fact, she will, because we're meeting her in twenty-five minutes. Come on. We're out of here.'

Leaving Clara protesting on the sofa, Louise bundled Katie into the only decent clean top she had left in her wardrobe and out of the door, into a cab and straight off to YYY, a gorgeous new bar which had opened up on the river, just underneath the big wheel, where you could drink overpriced cocktails and stare at tourists as they looked inquisitively at the one-way mirrored glass that made up the walls. It was noisy and air-conditioned on the inside; the terrace, however, was quiet, and they could watch a heavy and beautifully sallow pollution sunset sink behind the Houses of Parliament.

'What's this?' asked Katie. 'An intervention?'

'Yes,' said Olivia, as soon as she'd put gigantic vodka and tonics in front of the three of them. 'You have been useless since you came home and chucked that job in.'

'I did not "chuck" the job in. The client was impossibly rude to us, and I'd finished the work anyway. Pretty much. Kind of. Well, nothing they can't handle.'

'They can't handle it,' said Olivia.

'NO,' said Katie. 'No no no no no. I'm not going up there again. I can't handle the humiliation. Plus, I can't, anyway. In case you hadn't noticed, Clara's having a baby.'

'And you're the father?'

'Don't be stupid.'

'Well, you're certainly behaving like it.'

'The Forestry Commission have been in touch,' said Louise. 'They want you back up there.'

'Well, you seem to know a lot about my business,' said Katie.

'She snoops,' said Olivia. The two girls looked at each other. It didn't seem like the last few weeks had been a particular bundle of laughs for them either.

'They want someone to help out on their big party night.'

'Have they thought about hiring some waitresses?'

Olivia ignored her and went on regardless. 'So, anyway, you're going. You need to write up the final report so we can bill them for it.'

'I can't! The ball's next month, which is exactly when the baby's due.'

'The ball's in two weeks, which is three weeks before her due date,' said Louise. 'You'll have plenty of time.

Get your mum in to look after her. Or she could look after herself. Plenty of people do.'

Katie considered this. Inside, she couldn't help it, there was a part of her that wanted to go back again, just to see what was happening. And, God, she really really needed to get her car. It hadn't mattered much at first, and she'd put it to the back of her mind, but now she needed to pick up cribs and get car seats, and what not . . . yes, all the fuss of having a baby without actually having one.

'It's not up for consideration,' said Olivia. 'Go finish the job.'

'And I'll come too!' said Louise. 'To help you drive the car home.'

Katie looked at Olivia.

'I found the money in the budget to authorise that,' said Olivia, her face a mask. 'Of course, she'll have to help out . . . maybe stay a few days.'

Katie wasn't entirely convinced about using company funds just to get a few days of peace and quiet, but from the look on Louise's face, it was entirely worth it.

'Now – let's have a few drinks and verbally emasculate any remaining men in the room!'

'Yay!' they all chinked glasses.

Clara wasn't pleased. This was an understatement. Clara acted as though she'd never been betrayed in this way before, despite the obvious evidence to the contrary. But Katie reassured her constantly that everything was going to be fine, she was no distance away (a total lie, but Clara had only ever been to Third World countries and the sites of ancient druidic ruins, so didn't know anything about where rural Scotland was likely to be).

Katie also plucked up the courage to phone her mother

to give her an ultimatum, then, just at the last minute, as she was about to go into her pre-prepared spiel, something stopped her. Clara was looking at her bump in the mirror, and self-pityingly complaining how she was never going to get back into her size six hipsters (although at least she'd stopped trying to squeeze into Katie's 'fat day' jeans). When her mother answered, and started complaining about how her ears really hurt when she was too close to the phone when it rang, Katie took a deep breath. Then she handed the phone to her sister.

'You talk to her.'

'*Me*?' Clara looked outraged.

'If you want her, you talk to her,' said Katie, hands held over the speaking end.

Clara huffed her breath out and gestured with her hands for Katie to talk to her.

Katie put the phone down and walked out of the room.

In her bedroom, heart pounding, she waited, for what seemed like an agonisingly long time. Then, finally, she heard Clara tentatively start to speak. Feeling suddenly as if a weight had been lifted off her, she opened her suitcase and started to pack.

Chapter Seventeen

The little trundling train was just as she remembered it from before, except this time someone was carrying a piglet instead of a lamb, and talking to it in a low guttural croon. Watching the little pink body reminded Katie of Clara's baby, and made her squirm a bit, and she turned to talk to Louise. Louise, however, was elsewhere, staring out of the window dreamily, pausing only occasionally to mention another outrageous habit of Olivia's, often to do with the 'it's yoga, you must fart at will' programme.

'Have you ever seen . . . you know, a sky that big?' asked Louise. 'How come we never noticed it before?'

'Because you were moaning about the cappuccino.'

'Not this time!' said Louise, patting her rucksack, where she had stowed six packets of Starbucks' finest. 'What do you think would happen if I opened up a Starbucks?'

'Kelpie would burn it down.'

'Oh, yeah.'

She went back to regarding the flowering hills – there were still daffodils blooming here, even though all signs of spring were long gone in the sweltering South. There were even tiny patches of snow still visible on top of the mountains. Louise was sighing with happiness.

'So, what happens now?' she asked Katie.

'Hmm,' said Katie. 'Well, we put this ball on, I guess. I don't think . . .' her voice trailed off as she stared out of the window.

'I don't know how long we can stay on after that. This should get a lot of coverage, and really bring matters to a head if it's well attended, and if, even better, we get some celebs involved, they're going to have to face us across the board table sooner or later.'

'Are you sure you can't just get Iain to go and talk to his father?'

Katie smiled ruefully. She thought of Iain, too scared to go and visit a dying woman. His father was probably even more frightening. She'd done a bit of research into his company, and 'ruthless businessman' didn't even begin to cut it.

'Well, probably not, for two reasons: one, I think he's probably a bit . . . he probably doesn't think it will help. And two, I am certainly not going to phone him up and ask him.'

'Is that still getting to you? It was ages ago.'

'Is what still getting to me? The fact that the only man I've slept with in a year went completely AWOL the second I left his bed and never contacted me once?'

'Och, nonsense, he's probably scared stiff of you. Give the boy a chance. After all, who's the competition?'

'Louise,' said Katie sternly.

'Uh-huh?'

'Did you just say "och"?'

'Of course not.'

'You sure?'

'Aye.'

The station halt was bathed in late afternoon sunshine, with a fresh sharp wind that felt good all the way through Katie's bones.

'Oh God . . . it's just so nice to be able to *breathe* again. Although I'm sure we'll be moaning about the weather in no time, blah blah blah.'

Louise nodded. Then she pointed across the long moor. 'Hurray! Is that Harry in his Land-Rover?'

It was. He bumped up to meet them, and stepped out, looking a little bit shamefacedly in Katie's direction.

'Hi,' he said shyly.

'Hello!' said Louise, giving him a big bear hug. 'You look great!'

He did look good – he'd caught a touch of the sun on his cheekbones, and his hair had grown longer. He still looked like a young Gordon Brown. But now, Katie, for the life of her couldn't remember why she had ever thought this was a bad thing.

'Well, I see I'm not in the kennel with everyone,' he smiled.

'Oh, I forgot. You were a pig on *Richard and Judy*,' said Louise sternly. 'Then that actress got her baps out and I forgot all about it.'

Harry looked shamefaced again. 'Can I heartily apologise?'

'For sure.' Louise threw her backpack into the back of the Land-Rover. 'Hello, Francis.'

'Hi,' said Harry to Katie.

Katie gave him a half-smile. She was remembering the first time they'd met there. It seemed a long time ago now.

'Hey,' she said. Francis padded over to her, which for

him was just about running. 'Hello there,' she said, as he licked her hand.

'Uh, thanks for coming,' said Harry, looking a little pink.

'No problem,' said Katie. 'Once they'd stuck the bag over my head and bundled me into the back of the van, the rest was a breeze.'

'So, what's new?' said Louise, holding on to Francis in the back seat.

'Actually, ehm, quite a lot,' said Harry. They stopped in the queue at the lights.

'What's that?' asked Louise suspiciously.

'It's a new traffic light. They had to put it in because of all the traffic.'

Sure enough, there were cars all over the road.

'Who are these people?' said Louise, a testy note creeping into her voice.

'Uh, well, we seem to have become . . .' Harry's voice was suddenly drowned out by a pink convertible car screeching past them, playing 'Holding Out for a Hero' at full volume. Leaning out of the car and shrieking were at least five women in varying states of undress, waving bottles and with L plates on their backs. Louise and Katie stared at it in disbelief.

'Um, something of a magnet for, uh, hen nights.'

'You are joking,' said Louise.

'I think maybe we're better off with the golfers,' said Katie.

The pinkmobile stopped short at the lights, then whisked onwards. Coming the other way, a large black limo with six women inside it wearing cheap veils honked their horns.

'Oh God,' said Katie, 'we've created a monster.'

'That's why we need you,' said Harry. 'We're completely

overrun. They're frightening the life out of the techies. And the sheep.'

'Well, this is good, isn't it?' said Katie. 'Lots of people around, lots of money coming in, and lots of the types of girls that frighten the types of men who like to play golf.'

'Not everyone sees it as a good thing,' said Harry. 'Aunt Senga, for example, is beside herself. She thinks western civilisation is coming to an end.'

'I'd have thought she'd like nice girls getting married,' said Katie. Ahead, the pink convertible was stopping. One of the girls got out to be sick.

'Ah,' said Katie.

'Kennedy is very excited,' said Harry. 'The ball is going to be huge. We promised him a cut, so he can fix his roof.'

'I guess that's fair,' said Katie. 'What about his cut for when marauding hordes of girls vomit all over the priceless antiques?'

'It's not the girls so much,' said Harry as they drove through town. Everywhere, there were women, of every shape and size, pretending to look in shop windows or be admiring the view, but all the time their eyes were searching everywhere. Every lone male walking past was under intense scrutiny. It was entirely peculiar. 'It's more the older ladies who come on their own. They stand in the town square and dart after men, like bairns chasing chickens.'

'Bloody hell,' said Louise, endearingly blind to her own romantic history. 'Blooming mad slappers.'

'Has your aunt kept a room for us?' asked Katie.

Harry nodded. 'It's the same one, I'm afraid. Just because she disapproves of our new visitors doesn't mean she doesn't want to make money out of them.'

'I was afraid of that,' said Katie. 'Do you know what would be a good way to keep out a golf course? Build a luxury hotel.'

Harry smiled at her. 'I'm sorry, but I'm afraid your coming up with ideas part of the job is over. Now, you're just helping us with crowd control. Come on anyway, we need to get to the office. Louise, we'll drop you off.'

'Show us your arse!' shouted three girls at Harry from the street. 'Is it blue?'

'Crowd control and damage control.'

'Oh my God, we have *so much* to do,' said Katie, looking around the familiar office. Paper seemed to have piled up everywhere since she'd been away.

'Hello Derek,' she said. 'It's good to be back. How are you enjoying the influx then? Found a nice girl?'

Derek didn't look happy at all. 'I suppose,' he said. 'They're making a bit of a mess up at the caravan park.'

'Good,' said Katie. 'Hopefully all those retired golfers will think it's an encampment of travellers and run a mile. Gosh, I should have got some of my sister's old cronies up here, to do naked dances around the trees in the moonlight. How could I not have thought of that?'

'Because you were busy thinking up all the other naked things people could be doing?' said Harry. He had a pencil in his mouth and was carrying huge sheaves of paper. 'OK,' he said. He took a slug of the coffee Katie had brought him. 'You know, this stuff isn't actually that bad when you get used to it.'

'Horse piss,' said Derek. The other two looked up, surprised. 'Sorry,' he said, hanging his head. 'Haven't been myself lately.'

'OK,' said Harry. 'Here's the to-do list. Number one:

“have a ball”. Number two: “stop the golf course”. Number three: “save the forest”.’

‘You’ve never written a to-do list before, have you?’ asked Katie gently.

‘Uh, why?’ asked Harry, looking defensive.

‘No reason. OK, have you got a sub-list for the ball?’

‘A what?’

‘A list of all the things you need to sort out for the ball. Tickets and things like that.’

‘We’ve sold all the tickets!’ said Harry. ‘In fact, the town shop ran out.’

‘Ran out of what?’ said Katie.

‘Raffle tickets. That’s what I was using for tickets.’

Katie took a deep breath. ‘So, for the most exclusive and exciting ball in Scotland . . . you were using tickets identical to those that can be bought for twenty pence in the local shop?’

Harry thought about that for a second. ‘But people wouldn’t . . . they wouldn’t cheat like that, would they? *Would* they?’

‘You wouldn’t,’ said Katie. ‘The rest of them, we’ll just have to see. At least you’ll have the stubs of the tickets, so we can compare serial numbers if we have to.’

Harry looked at Derek in some consternation. Derek ducked out of the room.

‘Uh, yes. Of course we have. No probs. They’re just over . . . um . . .’

‘OK, what about the food?’

‘Yes,’ said Harry, looking anxious. ‘Aunt Senga is a bit worried. About the sausages and so on.’

‘What do you mean, the *sausages* and so on?’

‘Well, making food for five hundred people . . . that’s going to be a bit of a challenge, don’t you think? Even though Kennedy’s kitchen is gigantic . . .’

'Hang on – Mrs McClockerty thinks she's making breakfast for five hundred people?'

'Well, she was going to rope in some of the local boys to help . . .'

'Oh God,' said Katie. 'I think maybe we should call this off right now. Did you know Ewan McGregor's coming?'

Harry looked confused. 'Is he local?'

'Maybe we should just cut our losses and cancel this right now,' said Katie in despair. 'How are we going to get by on serving one thousand pieces of toast? Oh God. And I don't even want to think about what you're going to do for a bar.'

'Oh yes, the bar,' said Harry. 'Yes, well, Kennedy has said we can put up the stalls from the fair.'

'And serve what – squash?'

'Actually, no, hang on . . . it's here somewhere . . .' Harry scrabbled amongst his pieces of paper.

Katie sighed. This was going to be an absolute nightmare. She should have known coming back was a terrible idea. She couldn't work with this man at the best of times, and these were emphatically not the best of times.

'Ah, here it is.'

He handed her a sheet of expensive paper, with an elegant-looking letterhead.

'Dear Mr Barr,' it said. 'After watching your appearance on the *Richard and Judy* show, we at Tennent's Brewery wanted to offer you our every support . . .'

'Oh my God!' said Katie. 'Do you know what this is? They're offering to sponsor us and give us loads of free booze!'

'Why would they do that?' asked Harry, looking mystified.

'So they can get in the papers of course! It's a great opportunity for them.'

'Really? There's one here from some whisky people too.'

Katie fell on it with alacrity. 'This is brilliant! You, Harry Barr, could not organise a ball in a game of cricket, but at this rate, they'll be so drunk, nobody will notice that their four-course meal is actually a slice of bacon that's only cooked on one side.'

'Well, good,' said Harry.

'This is fantastic,' said Katie. 'Now, seriously, what on earth are we going to do about the food?'

Harry looked at her with slightly puppyish eyes. 'Well, of course, there's always the bakery.'

'Absolutely not,' said Katie, once she realised what he was thinking.

'Well, there's nobody else with, you know, big ovens and things.'

'You ask them then! You know them!'

'I know them enough to be very very frightened. Anyway, they hate you already. Whereas I've always managed to avoid getting my tyres slashed. This has never been a very tyre-slashy type of town. *Please* Katie. You know it's our only hope.'

And without realising how he'd managed to finesse her into it, Katie found herself agreeing to go the next day and speak to Kelpie about the food.

'It's like we've never been away,' said Louise, staring around at the glum attic room as Katie arrived back at the house. Even with the sun out it still got no light. Mrs McClockerty had sent down Katie's stuff, but had charged her for every night it had taken her to get around to it. Unpacking it back into the huge oversized wardrobe was a slightly chastening experience.

'I'd forgotten there was so much entertainment potential in this one room alone,' said Louise. 'Let's go out.'

Katie felt nervous as they headed out towards the Mermaid. What if she saw Iain? I mean, it wasn't like he had broken her heart or anything. Getting your heart broken implied love, and romance, and grand passion and all the other things she and Louise had somehow neglected to tick on their 'Things I'd Like Out Of My Life' questionnaire.

But it was as if she'd been granted a glimpse; a crack through the door into what that kind of life *could* be like. And then, just as she was tantalisingly reaching out a hand, it had been slammed shut.

Well, they couldn't stay out of each other's way indefinitely in this town. And, her nagging heart couldn't stop reminding her, maybe – just maybe – it wasn't too late.

The streets were full of people; it was extraordinary. There were women simply everywhere; the air was heady with the scent of hairspray and fake tan. As they passed by, they raised eyebrows and shot knowing looks at Katie and Louise, as if to include them in the club.

'This sucks!' said Louise hotly. 'We should get T-shirts made saying, "we were here first you rancid old slutbags".'

'Catchy,' said Katie. She couldn't believe the change in the place. Oh my God, if Harry had been selling tickets to everyone willy-nilly – well, they only had a week to the ball. How on earth were they ever going to sort it out?

'Look!' shrieked Louise. 'They *do* have T-shirts.'

Sure enough, opposite them were two women who could have been anywhere between thirty-five and fifty, caked in make-up, favouring the bright red and pink style of Christine Hamilton. Over the top of their button-up shirts they were both wearing T-shirts that read, 'Going like a blue-arsed fly to the men of Fairlish'.

'Oh Christ,' said Louise.

Katie covered her eyes with her hand. No wonder Harry had called her; he really *had* been desperate.

They paused briefly at the door of the Mermaid.

'Come on then,' said Louise. 'If they've turned it into a theme pub we'll just turn tail and go home.'

It wasn't quite that bad. In fact, as the evening light shone through into the bar, Katie realised that someone had washed the windows.

'Hello Lachlan,' she said.

Lachlan's little head was popping over the bar as usual, but there was something different about him.

'Lachlan – are you wearing a Von Dutch cap?' asked Louise, moving forward.

The bar was absolutely spilling over with women. The men were lined up against the windows and the fireplace, with an expression of hunted animals on their faces.

'Why, I'm sure I don't know,' said Lachlan. His little pink face was even pinker than usual. Two blondes of uncertain vintage were leaning against the bar, drinking the yellow wine and looking at him in an adoring way.

'Hullo lassies.'

Louise and Katie looked around nervously. Katie in particular wasn't exactly sure how popular she'd be with the locals, now she'd brought hermageddon down on them. After all, everything had been just fine before they'd arrived, give or take a forest or two.

Lachlan's face, however, had broken into a large grin and he was already reaching up for the vodka bottles. As they moved forward, several of the chaps nodded at them and waved.

'Louise!' said a booming voice, someone leaped in front

of them from the dartboard. Katie thought it might have been Iain, and took a nervous step back, but it was just Craig the Vet.

'Craig!' squealed Louise. 'What's going on? Have you turned half the men into women as some sort of grisly experiment?'

'No,' said Craig. 'They all just kind of turned up one day. It's a bit like that movie.'

'What . . . *if you build it they will come*?' asked Katie.

'No . . . *Dawn of the Dead*,' said Craig the Vet. 'Can I buy you two a drink?'

'Aren't you getting me a drink?' cooed a highly-pitched, instantly grating voice from the corner. There sat a pudgy-faced woman, whose more than ample form was poured into a milkmaid top which laced up at the bodice.

'Um, in a minute,' said Craig nervously.

'Ah. The new Mrs The-Vet?' asked Louise brightly.

'No . . . no, just some woman.'

'I'll have a double please, Craig dear,' yelped the newcomer.

'Well, Craig, dear . . . what on earth has been happening?' asked Louise.

Katie, having ascertained that there was no sign of Iain in the bar (almost certainly off in the sand dunes having it away with one of the new residents, she thought immediately), had relaxed a little, and was looking around with interest. Who *were* these people?

'It was after you were on television – you were very good, by the way,' said Craig, even though Katie knew this was clearly a lie. 'Suddenly all the caravans over at Lochmanagruich were booked, just like that. Then they just started arriving. They're all mad.'

'Craig,' said Katie. 'You don't have a sniff of a woman for years and years, then you turn into every other man on the planet and insist we're all crazy and you'd never commit to one. Next thing you'll be saying you like curves on women, then only go out with sticks with grapefruits stapled onto their chests.'

Craig looked at her. 'Has being famous gone to her head?' he said to Louise. 'I didn't understand a word of that.'

'She's ranting,' said Louise. 'Now, tell me, how are all the animals?'

'What, *all* of them? Well, I've got this crocodile with dysentery . . .'

Katie kept half listening in to the conversation, but wasn't really that interested. Instead, she took a leisurely look around. There weren't half the men she remembered from last time.

'It's great, you know, really,' said Lachlan to her in a quiet voice. 'Thanks for all the muff you've sent our way.'

'Lachlan!' said Katie.

'Sorry, sorry. Young ladies, that's what I mean. Young and not so young ladies of course . . . yes,' he said, serving two largish women pints of cider and black.

'But, where is . . . everyone?'

She meant Iain, but Lachlan didn't know that of course.

'Well, mostly they're at home, up to their nuts in guts . . . sorry, I mean, entertaining some of our new guests. Particularly the techies. It's been a godsend to them. Although probably a terrible drawback to medical science.'

'I bet,' said Katie.

Lachlan mistook her glumness for being offended. 'I'm sorry about the way I speak . . . not really used to lassies, you ken what I mean?'

''Course,' said Katie, watching him beam with pleasure as a curly-haired girl patted him on the head and declared he was just the cutest thing she'd ever seen.

'I think I'm going to bed,' she said to Louise. 'I'm knackered. Plus I need to phone Mum and Clara, make sure there's the bare minimum of psychodrama and knife-fighting going on.'

'Sure,' said Louise, who was looking genuinely interested in Craig's story of a deer that had been run over, much to the obvious annoyance of the pudgy blonde in the corner.

'So, you think post-traumatic stress disorder . . . how fascinating.'

Outside the pub, it was still sunny, even though it was past nine-thirty in the evening. It felt very peculiar. It wasn't warm, but it wasn't freezing either, and Katie pulled her cardigan around her and decided. Two women passed by, asking if she knew where there was a nightclub. She shook her head.

As if by magic, her feet took her straight down to the dockside, near Iain's house. She wasn't going to . . . she definitely wasn't going to knock on the door or anything, or, heaven forbid, look through the windows. No. Not at all. It didn't matter if she maybe ran into him on the street, that would be entirely normal, but she certainly wasn't snooping. And if she saw him, it would be perfectly normal. A normal thing to do in a normal part of town.

So, given she'd planned it all out so well in her head, it was quite surprising what a terrible shock she got when Iain swung around down the stairs of the narrow little alleyway with his arm around the shoulder of a blonde.

Immediately Katie backed into the shadows, until she was actually hiding behind another house. She could feel her heart race, as if it had just had a bad shock. Oh, she had to stop being so ridiculous. What did she think, that Iain, a man with whom she had had unbelievably bad sex once, ages ago, was going to be mooching around, dreaming only of her, calling her name at night, waiting for the moment he could saddle up his big white steed and ride off to scoop her up? Life wasn't like that. Life wasn't anything like that. Not in Katie's life. In Katie's life you couldn't find a boyfriend, and you got mugged, and your family was completely dysfunctional and you kept losing your job. That was your life. She remembered, horribly, the last time she was upset down by the docks, and who had cheered her up, then she turned around and ran all the way back to Water Lane.

She couldn't have wanted to face Kelpie less the next day. She felt terrible, far worse than – she tried to rationalise – their brief flingette deserved. This was pain out of proportion, and it stung, and the last thing she wanted to do now was face down some Valkyrie.

She'd have liked to have roped Louise in, but she was absolutely nowhere to be seen. Probably off fixing crows' broken wings or something stupid like that. Well, it wasn't like she wasn't getting used to being on her own. The morning's headline had been, 'HUGE TOURIST BOOST FOR FAIRLISH MAKES GOLF COURSE UNNECESSARY'. She bet he'd had a huge boost, she thought. Probably more than one. At the same time. She shook her head to try to get rid of the mental images, and steeled herself for the pie shop.

The smell of fresh warm bread, and pies, made Katie breathe deeply in pleasure. Life couldn't be all bad, she supposed, when you could smell good, fresh bread on a sharp summer morning. How could somebody who made such beautiful bread be evil? It wasn't possible, surely. She pushed open the door.

The shop was full, for starters. Full of women, who

were pointing at cakes and doughnuts and Mr MacKenzie, and giggling amongst themselves. Suddenly, oddly, Katie felt very protective of *her* town, and wished they would all go away. She shook herself out of it: next, she'd be reading the *Daily Mail*.

Kelpie was standing next to Mr MacKenzie, who was serving as usual; she had a face like thunder, and constantly muttered under her breath as she doled out scones and pancakes to the customers, replying with absolute scorn if anyone asked for flapjacks, foccacia or anything invented after the First World War.

'Look at her,' said one woman, who had harshly dyed red hair. 'Bet she's a bit annoyed there's a bit of competition around now, huh?'

'God, she's probably been banged more times than a barn door,' said a small woman, her voice a mixture of spitefulness and envy. Kelpie flushed to the top of her pinned-on white paper hat and slammed down the paper bag in front of them, muttering something.

'Aww, what's she saying?' said the red-haired woman. 'Do they speak English up here?'

'Well, I've not come up to *talk* to the locals,' said the short woman, to general laughter.

Katie gritted her teeth. 'Excuse me,' she said, making her way through the crowd. Quite a few of them recognised her and started whispering amongst themselves, a peculiar but strangely gratifying feeling, Katie found. She went right up to the front of the counter, conscious that other people would expect her to be known in the area, and thus popular.

'Um, Kelpie. Uh, can I have a word?'

Kelpie eyed her suspiciously for a long moment. 'Why? Hiv you got another coachload of useless fucking London tarts you need to offload on us?'

The shop went completely quiet.

'No,' said Katie. 'It's worse than that.'

It wasn't anything to do with Katie that Kelpie put down her spatula and followed her out into the little square, where they shared two slices of raisin cake. It was because, she explained, she was about to punch several people in the mouth and she didn't really want to lose her job in the bakery.

'Were you really going to punch them?' asked Katie.

'Och aye. I'd have stuck them in the industrial oven if I could have arranged it properly.'

'Ah,' said Katie. She'd hoped Kelpie hating all their guts might just be a hilarious affectation, but apparently not.

'So, what's this money thing you mentioned, then?'

Katie explained the situation.

'You want me and Tilda and Lorna to cook for five hundred scrawny-arsed colonial bitch bags?'

Katie nodded quietly.

'Without poisoning them or putting anything in the stew or anything?'

'That's right.'

'What about pee and spit?'

'No! I'll report you to the Association of Master Bakers.'

'Master *whats*?'

'Never mind. No spit and no pee.'

Kelpie blew air out of her mouth. 'I just dinnae like the sound of this.'

'Well, what about this,' said Katie. 'If this ball's a success and we make enough money, we can launch a legal bid against this golf course, then the golf course will go away. If the golf course goes away, I go away. And when I go away, all the other women go away too, because there'll be no publicity and everyone will forget about it, and once again you will rule the town in peace.'

Kelpie's mouth twitched. 'I dinnae rule the town.'

''Course you do,' said Katie. 'You're the best-looking here by far. All the men worship you.'

Kelpie tried to look bashful, but failed. 'You're really going to go?'

Katie thought ruefully of Iain. 'Oh yes.'

'OK. We'll do it for free.'

'So, not everything's a disaster!' she confided to Louise, as they met up over the traditional shepherd's pie, now without the side helping of mortal fear and terror. 'And Shuggie and Margaret from the posh place are coming in to oversee it!'

'Great!' said Louise, who seemed to have got a little colour back in her pale city cheeks. 'It'll be great.' She paused for a second. 'What about the auction?'

'What auction?'

'The slave auction of course. That's all the women are talking about. You can hear them, all whispering on the street corners.'

'Are you being a misogynist?'

'No!' Louise played with her peas. 'Just feeling a bit . . . you know, like our thunder's been stolen? Although I know that's stupid.'

'No, it's not,' said Katie. 'Now we know how Kelpie felt.'

'No, not being a paranoid psychopath, I don't know quite how Kelpie felt.' Louise wasn't entirely convinced of the veracity of Kelpie's 'no poisoning' pledge.

'Anyway. What's this auction?'

'Well, it was mentioned in the paper.'

'Oh. Great. So, putting two and two together, I'm guessing this is some great plot of Iain's to bag himself some more nooky. Well, he certainly needs the practice.'

'Don't get old and bitter,' said Louise. 'You'll get wrinkles.'

'Hmm,' said Katie.

'So, yes, it's just what you're thinking. Various men of the town are going to dress in togas, and the women are going to bid for a date with them.'

'Yikes, that is so humiliating on so many levels, I can't even . . . oh, God. Really. Togas?'

'It's just a bit of fun,' said Louise.

'Selling sex for mercenary gain in public,' said Katie. 'Well, it does *sound* fun.'

'And the bidding starts at £100.'

'You are joking. Who's going to pay that?'

'Actually, the women are already offering pre-emptive bids. I heard them.'

'Who for?'

'By the looks of some of them, I don't think they're that fussy. Craig's doing it.'

'Craig who? Craig the Vet?'

Louise nodded.

'Well, you have been having some cosy little chats. Is this turning mushy?'

Louise rolled her eyes. 'I was advising him on whether or not he should put himself up for auction for a date with another woman. What do you think?'

'Clever reverse psychology?'

'No,' said Louise. 'We're just chums. Mind you, it will be interesting to see them all in togas . . .'

'Yeah,' said Katie.

'What about you and the newspaper boy . . .'

'Don't. Don't start me.'

'What happened?'

'Oh, bollocks, I just saw him with some other girl.'

'See,' said Louise. 'We've ruined this place. I'm sorry petal.'

'I'm used to it,' said Katie. 'Stupid blokes.'

'Stupid blokes.' They clinked their cups of tea together.

'That's the problem with the pretty ones,' said Louise. 'Flighty.'

'Whadya mean?'

Louise shrugged. 'They just don't try that hard. What you need is a real man, not a pretty boy. Someone like Harry.'

'Don't be stupid. He's a stuffed shirt.'

'A *beef*-stuffed shirt,' said Louise.

'Who else is doing this stupid auction thing?' asked Katie, changing the subject. She didn't want to discuss Iain any more. Too painful. Or Harry for that matter. Too confusing.

'Well, Laird Kennedy said he was up for it, but I pointed out that as he owned the castle they were eating in, that should probably do it for the ladies. He said no, he needs the money to fix the roof, and he's going to open the bidding at ten thousand pounds.'

'OK,' said Katie. 'Who else?'

'Willie, of course.'

'They're tempting him out of his bothy? Wow.'

'I know,' said Louise, looking dreamy for a second. 'Lucky girl who gets him.'

'OK, OK. I thought we were pretending you were just going on long country walks those times.'

'Were we?' Louise blinked. 'OK then. Lachlan too. A bunch of techies – I think they're doing it as a group prize.'

'Don't tell me – if you win them you get to play Dungeons and Dragons with them for a whole night?'

'They also said they're going to order pizza from Inverness. It costs £100 apparently.'

'To order a pizza?'

'Newsflash: "we're not in North London shocker".'

'It will be if we can't get rid of all these women and this bloody golf course.'

Having lost their bakery pariah status, they felt confident in ordering the apple pie, which was slightly better than the shepherd's pie, though somewhat similar in consistency.

'Iain of course,' said Louise, after a period of time.

'Of course,' said Katie. 'Cocky idiot.'

'I take it you won't be bidding?'

'I might, to save another woman from having to go through what I went through,' said Katie.

'And Harry, I suppose.'

Katie sniggered. 'You wish.'

'Why not? He'll have to. It's his party.'

'Getting Harry in a toga? I think not.'

'Well, don't forget a lot of women came because they saw him on telly. I think he'll make a lot of money.'

Katie shook her head. 'Well, if that happens, it'll be something of a miracle.' She scooped up the last of her apple pie. 'You know, I'm almost starting to look forward to this.'

'What do you mean, *almost*?' asked Louise.

Chapter Eighteen

'So, I thought we could get the Cubs in to clean it,' Laird Kennedy was saying.

Katie was following him around the house. It had certainly been a lot better in her memory than it was in watery daylight. There were cobwebs and missing windowpanes everywhere.

'The Cubs?' she said.

'Yeah, you know, bob a job.'

Katie kicked at some bird poop, which had come through the rickety ceiling and encrusted itself on the floor-boards. Her head felt dusty just walking through the door.

'So, you think the Cubs will overhaul this place in time for Saturday for five pence?' she said wearily. This was a stupid idea. Stupid stupid stupid. OK, she'd managed to find a marquee, but it was only useful for dinner and dancing. Drinks and general meanderings were meant to take part in the main house. And the main house at the moment looked slightly more fit for playing the film set of a condemned haunted mental institution. 'Maybe there's a big contract cleaners in Inverness,' she said. 'There must be, surely.'

She thought worriedly about their finances. They'd sold a lot of tickets, but she wanted to preserve as much money as she could, so Harry could fund lawyers and anything else he might need after she'd gone.

'Naw, it'll be fine,' said Kennedy, clearly oblivious to the huge hole in the elbow of his hacking jacket. 'In fact, they're on their way over.'

For a split second, she had the image in her mind's eye of a thousand tiny wee boys running over the house like rats. 'Really?'

The Laird steered her out to the sadly overgrown lawn. 'Of course,' he said, 'it's really their dads we're after.'

As he spoke, in the distance, Katie suddenly caught sight of a line of men and boys walking towards them, silhouetted against the trees. They were carrying brooms and mops.

The Laird watched them happily. 'Fishermen,' he said. 'Best cleaners in the world.'

Katie thought of the times she'd seen them washing out their boats and fixing their nets down at the port, and was inclined to agree.

'There's not enough work for them any more,' said Kennedy sadly. 'It's all going. And if the golfers come here and price them out of their homes, they're done for. They know that.'

Katie felt suddenly overwhelmed with melancholy watching these strong men, who'd farmed the same oceans for so many generations, get in line to fight for their village and their forest. She felt a lump in her throat.

'Thank you,' she found herself saying.

'Hmph,' said the Laird gruffly. 'Now, if you don't have time to get stuck in with a duster, I'd get out of here, sharpish.'

* * *

Katie's heart was considerably lighter by the time she got to the office. Food *and* somewhere to go! They might just pull this off after all.

'No,' Harry was saying down the phone in his strongest possible tone of voice. 'Absolutely not. NO. I mean it!'

'Who was that?' asked Katie. 'Toga measuring service?'

'Trying to stop Dougie from playing the accordion,' said Harry, covering the speaker with his hand. 'It's a bit of a full-time job.'

'Music!' cried Katie. 'God, I forgot all about the music!'

Harry finished his call and stared at her. 'What do you mean?'

'Well, we need a band, and a DJ and things.'

'Why?' Harry looked puzzled.

'For music. Or do you think we should do everything in complete silence?'

'Uh, no, I think you'll find,' Harry went back to shuffling papers, 'it will be harder to get people to stop playing music than otherwise.'

'How come?'

'Well, everyone plays something. Or sings or something.'

'*Really*? What do you play?'

Harry looked embarrassed. He was feeling embarrassed. Having finally come to terms with the fact that he did actually fancy Katie and wasn't having a mild allergic reaction every time she walked past him, he was doing his best to put it out of his mind and let it wash over him, like pretty much every crush he'd had since he was fourteen. It was the best way, he'd found. 'Um . . .'

'What? The tuba? The bongos? What?'

'The bagpipes, actually.'

Katie stared at him. 'NO!'

'What's wrong with that?'

'Really? People play those things?'

'Yes,' said Harry. He was actually a very good piper. Bloody English thought it was hilarious to sneer at everything.

'I always got them confused with cats,' said Katie. 'Someone once told me that you just put a cat's tail in your mouth and squeezed its tummy, and I believed it for years.'

'You got confused between bagpipes and cats?'

'Maybe I'll stroke yours on the head.'

'Well anyway,' said Harry. 'The lads have a good ceilidh band, so there'll be no trouble with the dancing, and those techie ponces have apparently formed a brass ensemble that can play the entire music from *Star Wars*, so we might have them while we're eating . . . *if* we're eating that is?'

'Ooh, we're eating!' said Katie excitedly. 'It'll be food of the pie extraction. But that's still better than square sausage.'

'The only type of sausage worth eating,' said Harry grinning.

'Hang on,' said Katie. 'So, we're not getting a DJ . . . but we are having dancing?'

'Uh-huh.'

Katie's dancing was entirely limited to a fairly controlled club style (after the rather troubling wave-your-hands-in-the-air-like-you-just-don't-care stage she'd discarded post-university, along with the tie-dyed T-shirt, the dungarees and the whistle), and the occasional unpleasant tussle when she met one of those young men prevalent on the London scene who have been to three salsa classes and therefore think it is quite acceptable to throw you about the room like a sack of potatoes then get upset with you for failing to follow their psychic dancing instructions.

‘What kind of dancing?’ she asked, very suspiciously.

‘Ceilidh dancing,’ said Harry, as though he was explaining it to an unattentive four-year-old. ‘You know – the kind of dancing you do at parties.’

‘Not the parties I go to,’ said Katie.

‘Oh, come on. You must know a few dances. The Canadian Barn Dance? Eightsome Reel? Gay Gordons?’

‘Gay who now?’

Harry tutted. ‘What did they teach you at school?’

‘How to put a condom on a banana.’

Harry rubbed the back of his neck. ‘So, we’re going to have this dance band . . . and all these chaps . . . and all these women . . . and nobody is going to be able to dance with each other?’

‘Oh, I’m sure we’ll pick it up as we go along,’ said Katie.

‘Hmm,’ said Harry, not convinced. ‘Derek! Have you got a minute?’

‘Sure,’ said Derek, appearing from the back.

‘Could you give us a bit of *puirt-a-beul*?’

‘What, now?’ asked Derek.

‘What, what?’ said Katie.

‘Someone needs to learn a bit of dancing,’ said Harry.

‘You can’t do that in here,’ said Derek, looking around in dismay at the papers piled everywhere.

‘No,’ said Harry. ‘Come on everyone! Outside!’

He threw open both the glass doors and they stepped out into the summer sunlight. The dew was still glinting on the grass, and the clearing had turned into a carpet of daisies. Green light came down through the trees.

‘OK!’ said Harry, and Derek sat himself down on the step at the door and started to beat a rhythm on the ground with two pencils. Then he opened his mouth and started to – well, Katie wasn’t quite sure what he was doing.

He was kind of singing, in a high-pitched tone of voice, but it wasn't quite singing; it sounded more like a musical instrument, making fast rhythmic music. There were words, of a kind, but they didn't sound like English, or anything else, more like a fast gabbling to fit the tune. Derek looked completely unselfconscious. It sounded eerie, ancient and wonderful out in the wooded morning.

'What's he doing?' she whispered to Harry.

'*Puirt-a-beul*,' he whispered back. 'Mouth music. It's kind of traditional music around here – if you don't have an instrument and want to dance.'

'It's beautiful,' said Katie. And it was; unearthly, weirdly melodic and yet without any tune Katie could discern.

'Well then,' said Harry, and put out his arm.

'You are joking,' said Katie.

'Of course I'm not joking,' said Harry. 'We'll start with a very simple Gay Gordons. They you can teach some other people. It's an absolute nonsense to have a party if nobody can dance. Come here.'

Katie giggled nervously.

'Here! I mean it!' He'd put his arms up, oddly, to the right. 'OK. I have one arm around your shoulders, and one in your nearest hand.'

Katie stood under his arm obediently.

'OK, now we're going to go forwards for four, backwards for four then do the same thing again. Does that make sense?'

'Absolutely none at all.'

'Derek!'

Derek subtly changed rhythm and counted them in with a one, two, three four.

Katie was still giggling as Harry led her forward, then,

deftly, flipped, so his arm was still around her, but suddenly they were travelling backwards.

'How did that just happen?' she asked.

'Shh. And – KICK!' and they both kicked their feet out in front. 'Good! And again, one, two, three, flip . . .'

This time she managed it.

'And, now, twirl under my arm.'

'*Twirl?*'

'Yes. Four times. Go!'

Hopelessly, Katie spiralled under his arm, as Derek slowed down to accommodate her.

'And . . .'

Then Harry swept her into his arms and, leading strongly, galloped around with her in a speedy waltz. Her new fifties' Topshop skirt floated out behind her in the summer morning and she felt as if she was flying.

'And again!' said Harry, and they started over, and by the fourth or fifth time, she'd got the dance figured out, with all her turns in the right place, keeping time to Derek's mouth music; but neither of them wanted to stop dancing, so they kept it up, under the morning sun, and then he taught her another one, and Derek kept singing and they danced until they were exhausted, and forgot about the mounds of paperwork, and the work they had to do and the threats hanging over their heads, for as long as the sun shone.

At eleven, Iain came past to try and catch Katie, who he'd heard was back in town, but he saw them dancing, and reckoned she didn't really want to be disturbed.

The weather had broken just as they were dancing – as Harry was trying to show Katie a Dashing White Sergeant, without the benefit of the four other dancers tactically required. Katie didn't care, however, and was so proud of the fact that she'd mastered the little twiddly step she'd always associated with Hogmanay girls in sashes who could hop over swords, she refused to stop. Soaking, they'd continued, with Derek retreating inside, until, laughing and entirely out of breath, they'd finally admitted defeat and fallen inside, drenched and giggly.

Rain still seemed absolutely committed to dogging their every move. Despite not being over the moon about how it looked in the budget, Katie had gone ahead and approved for internal heaters. It might be a midsummer night's ball, but they really didn't want people getting hypothermia on their watch. *Hello* magazine was coming, as were many of the newspapers, so they'd decided to keep the death rate as low as possible. She'd never worked so hard in her life, chivvying, begging, making fifteen million phone calls an hour. Her clipboard was working overtime. Actually, she was loving it. Working so hard kept her mind off everything, and she didn't think there was a single person in town she didn't know now. And she was *good* at it. She juggled the newspaper access with one hand, the napkin orders in another and the techies' amazing MIDGE-AWAY invention, a terrifying fan-like contraption designed to blow away insects, with a third.

Kelpie, with Margaret's help, had been amazing, popping in and out of the office with different menus for them to try. They'd settled on Scotch broth, lobster and smoked salmon paella and Eton Mess, which wasn't particularly Scottish but was particularly easy for Kelpie to make with the vast pile of broken meringue cases she stored out at the back of the bakery. She was using them, she explained, to relieve her tension at all the English women crabbing about her shop and demanding cappuccinos and carrot cake, because if she hit another one, they were going to put that stupid ankle tag back on her, and that wasnae going to happen for anyone.

And Mrs McClockerty was baking a large cake with printed on it, which would be available at auction for anyone who didn't want one of the local men wrapped in a sheet. Even Katie's to-do lists were being exhausted.

Olivia was flying up to Inverness and taking a helicopter to Fairlish. Katie and Louise had not the slightest idea of where to put her up, but Katie was thinking of seeing if Margaret had any rooms in her lovely place. Thinking of that made her think of Iain, which made her feel sad, but defiant. The local paper had been great, but the media buzz around the whole thing had been building by the day and she'd spent all day and half the night on the telephone to the national papers – cameras and journalists (all female) were flooding in by the day, from as far away as Canada and Japan, where they seemed to find the idea of the village without any women terribly hilarious. Katie did try to get them to mention the golf course, but that didn't seem to have quite the appeal, and by the day before, they had already arrived in town, extremely grumpy at, a) the lack of suitable accommodation, and b) the sheer numbers of women thronging the streets every day, making it hard to get a decent shot of men looking glum and lonely, particularly as the techies had enormous grins plastered all over their faces, and all the farmers had vanished.

But the whole town had definitely developed a carnival atmosphere. Ceilidh music could be heard everywhere, as people spilled out onto the streets to practise dance steps. Some of the small shops in the high street had put up signs welcoming the visitors and saying 'NO TO GOLF', and within about five minutes, it seemed, there were many signs in people's windows too.

Couple this with the news that, yes, Ewan McGregor *would* be coming, as well as Hamish Clark and at least one hobbit, and the whole town had turned into one heaving hormonal mass of excitement, and shops as far away as Edinburgh were reporting their ball dresses completely sold out. Even Clara and Mum, at home, sounded envious, although Clara said she was simply envious of anyone at the moment who could walk more than two paces without collapsing in a heap and needing to go to the toilet, and warned Katie against getting involved with any of the men, even if there were any left after the locust girls had been at them. Katie assured her this was very unlikely to be the case.

Louise threw her little black dress on the bed. 'I wish I'd brought something fancier now,' she said.

Olivia looked up from where she was attempting to apply Touche Eclat at the wall-mounted sink unit. Being Olivia, of course, she had known about a divine little hippy spa only open to muesli-munching yoga freaks, in a castle down the road – 'It's a gorgeous place, you should see it. Only you can't, non-believers mess up the chi lines, you see' – and was ensconced in some splendour, after choking and spluttering at Louise and Katie's attic.

'I'm so sorry,' she'd said. 'I didn't realise it was this bad. But surely, you could have a total life detox in here?'

'Yes,' Katie said, who had actually got used to the house by now, and rather liked its Presbyterian ambience, stability and deep deep quiet. 'Total detox of everything except spiders.'

'And dust bunnies,' said Louise. 'That's a very friendly name for a very nasty thing.'

It was the day of the party. Still raining outside. Katie had done, she thought, as much as she could possibly do, and indeed, their phones had gone eerily quiet, at least for now. Harry was at the site all day, making sure marquee pegs were put in place and collecting umbrellas to help transport people from their cars across the muddy grounds. Kennedy had offered his main hall as a mingling area, which they'd accepted with relief – it looked like their fantasies of people swanning about the lawn, champers in hand, were going to have to be put on hold. Derek had got hold of a list with guests' names on it, which should hopefully keep out the worst of the gatecrashers. Kelpie had done a forced march around the farms and the institute and recruited forty young men as waiters with a mixture of threats of sex and/or violence.

Louise was staring sadly at her dress. Katie turned back to the paper. Still no sign of Iain. She assumed he was up at the caravan park, where most of the women were staying, and she certainly wasn't going to stalk him. She was going to anti-stalk him, in fact, and avoided the high street unless absolutely necessary.

In fact, Iain had also been avoiding town and doing a lot of walking across the moors, and a lot of thinking. If this party was a success, he could see his dad losing this one. Which would be interesting. And Katie would go. He still couldn't believe how much he'd messed it up, what an idiot he'd been. He remembered back to college; he'd been great then. No probs, girls all over the place in a big city. But coming back to a small town . . . he'd lost his confidence somewhere along the way. And he had to be brave, and go for it. But, deep down, he didn't think he was a very brave person. In fact, from the age of eleven, he'd known for a fact he wasn't.

* * *

Katie turned to the editorial. All week it had been wonderful, bigging up the night, and the town, and never stopping from hammering home the anti-golf message. The second page today was taken over by 'A Message from This Paper'.

> Don't mistake it for a moment. Every hundred years or so, an event comes along that defines a town, for ever. And this is ours. Reading between the lines, this is not just a party for us. Kind of, more the start of a whole new age. Attracting a new profile for the town. Today, Fairlish – tomorrow, the world? It's certainly a chance to put ourselves on the map. Even if we're not all sure we want so much change.
>
> I say, yes we do. Maybe some people will see change as difficult, as new to this town. I think we should embrace it with all our hearts. Some people say our little home is all right as it is. Sod them, say I! Yes, Fairlish is changing, but it's still our place in the world, and letting other people in to share it can only be a good thing. Often in this life, people don't act in time, or act at all, to do the right thing. Until now – and our time is now.

It was a little floral, thought Katie. Not Iain's style at all. Oh well, maybe he'd just got a bit overemotional – nothing wrong with that.

'The thing is,' Louise was saying, 'I never really thought you'd pull it off.'

'You are joking,' said Katie. 'We've got the cream of Scottish society coming. Plus five hundred sex-crazed maniacs from around the world.'

'I know,' said Louise sadly. 'OK, put it this way – I never thought I'd have to work that hard to stand out.'

Katie thought of her own outfit – she hadn't, subconsciously, really thought about it either, and was going to have to wear a white sheer top with her fifties' skirt. She was slightly concerned that she'd be mistaken for one of the waitresses.

'Fear not!' trilled Olivia, who was still angrily twiddling with the useless little shaving light above the basin mirror. She turned around. 'I'm far too young to be your fairy godmother, but look over there.' She fluttered her hands towards her large Louis Vuitton travelling case. Olivia saw no conflict between wanting to bring peace to the world and rapaciously stripping it of its resources to supply herself with luxury goods.

Louise leaped to it. Inside, beautifully folded and wrapped in tissue paper, were several slinky, diaphanous dresses, in delicate, pastel jewel colours.

'What's this?' asked Louise, breathlessly pulling out a twenties-influenced pale mauve creation, all layers of different coloured chiffon.

'Oh, I'm repping London Fashion Week,' said Olivia, carelessly. 'So, suddenly I'm everyone's best friend, blah blah blah, yes Stella, I'll call you back once you take that miserable look off your face, etc etc.'

'NO!' said Louise, pulling out another one. It was a soft gold colour, with a high waist covered in sequins, and a stiff skirt with petticoats underneath it.

'Yes,' said Olivia. 'Thank God you two have been eating nothing else but those greasy sausages. You're going to die at forty-five, but, on the bright side, you are going to fit into these dresses.'

'Eeek.' Louise couldn't help it, she was squeaking with happiness. 'Thanks Olivia!'

'Thank Gharani Strok,' said Olivia. 'And you're going to have to be very VERY careful. No eating, drinking, moving about, sitting down, dancing, that kind of thing. I know what you're both paid, and, to be honest, you shouldn't even be allowed to be standing in the same room as these dresses.'

Katie moved towards the bed. There, underneath the first two, was a deep cherry-red satin dress. She pulled it out of its tissue wrapping. It had a deep sloping boat neck, a tight waist and a full skirt. She looked at Olivia mutely, who waved her hands at her.

'Oh yes, I thought that might go with your dark hair. Try it on.'

It fitted as though it had been made for her. Katie nearly went crazy trying to see it in sections in the tiny basin mirror.

'That is definitely yours,' said Louise admiringly. 'It is absolutely gorgeous.'

Katie swirled around a little more, then did a couple of her new Scottish dance steps.

'Ooh, fancy,' said Louise, who was struggling into the gold dress, which set off her new London blonde highlights expertly.

'There's going to be proper dancing,' said Katie. 'It's pronounced kayleigh, like that Marillion song, but it's spelt differently.'

'Fantastic!' said Olivia.

'What – you can dance it?' said Louise suspiciously.

Katie felt a little jealous.

''Course,' said Olivia. 'You keep forgetting I'm posh really. We did it at school.'

So, between them, Katie and Olivia taught Louise some steps, causing Mrs McClockerty to bang several times on the floor with a broom handle, until the phone in Katie's room started ringing off the hook again and she was sidelined, double answering questions about champagne, napkins, paparazzi, fairy lights and sheeting.

'Well?' said Louise.

At 7.30, they were all set to go, planning to dump the Punto on site and hope it didn't sink into the muddy quicksand.

'I think we're fine,' said Katie. 'Although I wouldn't stand too close to the fairy lights. They sent a fire officer around, but then they gave him a bottle of whisky, so, you know, better safe than sorry.'

'Oh God,' said Olivia. 'OK. Do your best with your frocks,' she looked at them both. 'But, you both look gorgeous. Proper city knock-outs. We'd get into Pangea without a second glance with these on.'

'If we wanted to whore for dubious gentlemen,' said Louise. 'Thanks, Ol.'

'Not at all. I can probably even figure out some kind of a tax write-off when you get trifle all down them. So, country-bound Cinders – enjoy yourselves.'

The Punto didn't quite turn into a pumpkin, though Katie feared for it for a second or two on particularly muddy patches, and driving with heels didn't help matters much either. Even Olivia was impressed as they drove down Kennedy's drive towards the hall. In the twilight, with the dark clouds, it looked stern and imposing, the crenellated roof outlined starkly against the sky, and the countless mullioned windows. Katie was straining to see how it had turned out. All of the windows were lit up, even though nobody was allowed upstairs, because the walls were damp. Kennedy had got someone to put candles in every one ('it's too wet for anything to start a fire, for sure'), so even this early in the evening, the huge house was blazing with light.

'Ooh!' said Louise. 'A proper castle! It's so romantic!'

'Until we get to the bunfight that's the auction,' said Katie. 'Then it's all going to get really tacky and depressing.'

But even she couldn't quite hide her excitement as they swept around the side of the building. Behind the house was a long line of cars disgorging glamorous-looking occupants. There were a fair number of dinner suits, but on the whole, the men were in kilts; a myriad of different colours. She'd been expecting them, of course, she supposed, but she'd also thought they might look a bit stupid. They didn't look stupid at all, they looked wonderful, and it was fantastic to see the men moving around so unselfconsciously.

She stared at the house. She couldn't believe it. Someone had raked the gravel. All the windows were polished; the stones by the door straight and even. It looked . . . it looked like Katie's dream. Her dream, attained with ludicrous amounts of work and commitment from every single person in the town. She shook her head in amazement. How could this dream come true for her when absolutely nothing else went her way? Well, thank heaven for small mercies.

'Men in skirts!' said Louise. 'I'm in heaven.'

They came to a halt just to the right of a long red carpet that led to the house. There was a canopy over the top that was doing its best to keep the rain off, and it was punctuated by huge raging torches that seemed to be withstanding the whipping rain.

'Park your car fir you?' said a young boy to Katie. He looked about twelve, and scared as a whippet. Kelpie had obviously been at him.

'Thanks,' she said, sounding more confident than she felt about ever seeing the Punto again. Then she made her best effort to step out of the car gracefully, sure all the while that her shoes were going to sink into the mud up to her neck, and the beautiful dress would be ruined.

But then a strong arm reached into the car.

'May I help you?' enquired a familiar voice.

Chapter Nineteen

Katie looked up into Harry's friendly face.

'Thanks!' She smiled gratefully and took his arm. He raised her out of the car. He was looking terribly smart, wearing a formal black jacket and a dark red cravat that went with the predominant dark reds in his kilt.

'You look swish!' she said.

Harry looked at Katie. She looked amazing, far better than he'd thought she could. The red of her dress exactly matched his kilt. He thought for a moment of his family sash – in the same tartan, used by the women in his family, then shook his head suddenly. This was a working relationship and, after a bloody eternity, it finally looked like it might shape up into a good one. He wasn't going to fuck with it now – no matter how much he wished things could be different.

'You don't look so bad yourself,' he said. 'For a Sassenach.'

She did a twirl for him. 'For a sausage what?'

'Never mind,' he said. 'Plus, you're needed backstage. Kelpie's gone Gordon Ramsay on the wine waiters, and a donkey broke in and started eating the thistle centrepieces.'

'Can't we call donkey Special Branch?' asked Katie, as Harry helped out Louise and Olivia, who were experiencing some difficulty with Katie's two-door car.

Katie realised she'd been hoping for a little more than 'not bad' as a compliment, but told herself to stop being stupid as she started to walk up the red carpet. Harry himself looked . . . OK, he looked fairly tasty, she'd admit. She smiled ruefully to herself. OK, she'd never have had a choice in the matter, and it certainly wasn't as if she was ever going to go out with her almost-boss – but still. Mentally kicking herself, she wondered if she'd backed the wrong horse. Watching him compliment Olivia, she knew that if she were thinking straight, then she probably had.

Oh, well. He had obviously entered an endless bachelor grumpfest after that girl had left him, and it's not as if he'd ever been anything other than her extremely rude boss . . . but then she remembered them dancing in the rain, and that drunken night in London. Quickly she put the images out of her mind. They both had far too much work to do tonight.

And, as the paparazzi took her photograph in case she was someone and they didn't find out until later, she felt better. By the time she reached the end of the carpet and turned around for the other girls (Louise was waving and making Marilyn Monroe kisses to the photographers), something else wonderful happened – the rain, finally, after six days, stopped. It was peculiar; like getting used to a noise that wasn't there. The battering against the tents ceased, and whilst the ground remained as squelchy as ever, an odd, evening sunshine finally burst behind the huge expanse of dissipating black cloud.

'Hurrah!' said Katie as she passed into the building.

Then, she lost her breath completely. The ballroom

where she'd scared Iain so long ago was exactly as she'd dared to imagine it could be. The wooden floors were gleaming with dark walnut oil. The two great chandeliers sparkled like diamonds. Now, the ancestral portraits lining the panelled walls looked fresh and clean, an absolutely enormous fire was roaring at the far end, and a huge polished mirror reflected the scenes of people having a wonderful time, in smart suits and kilts and beautiful dresses, back into the room.

In the corner was a pretty young man playing the harp, accompanied by someone Katie recognised as the local fireman, on the fiddle. They didn't seem to be playing any one tune, more improvising up and in and out of traditional airs; it sounded beautiful.

Scared-looking black-tied waiters were darting here and there with drinks (banners proclaiming the kind donors of the aforementioned drinks hung down from the ceiling) and, amazingly, tiny hors d'oeuvres – the most perfect miniature baked meat pies, with ketchup to dip them into. Katie couldn't help smiling to herself; she was so amazed at how it had all come together.

The room was absolutely crammed with people everywhere, talking, laughing and drinking champagne in the slightly nervy over-the-top way people do when they find themselves all dolled up for something. There were almost more women than men there, in the most startling interpretations of the instructions 'evening wear', ranging from matronly black and silver embroidered box jackets over magisterial bosoms, to split pink feathery fandangles more suited to Nancy Dell'Olio at a Cher concert. But there were plenty of men too, Katie was overwhelmingly relieved to note, including two obvious circles that had celebrities in them.

'Wow,' came a voice beside her. 'Roight fancy, innit?'

Katie turned around to find Star Mackintosh at her elbow. Star was wearing a spangly yellow Kyri dress that completely ignored the 'either bust or legs, but not both' rule.

'Hello,' said Katie. 'What on earth are you doing here?'

'Great publicity, innit?' said Star. She leaned up to Katie's ear and whispered confidentially, 'I made it look for the photographers as if my boob fell out of my dress accidentally. But, actually, I did it on purpose!'

'Clever old you!' said Katie.

'Thanks!' said Star. 'I'm aiming for the front of the *Daily Record*. I like your dress too. It looks handy for cold weather.'

Katie wasn't quite sure how to respond to this.

'Do you think I could get a crack at Dougray Scott?' said Star, frowning and patting her gigantically over-lipsticked mouth.

'I don't know,' said Katie. 'Put your best tit forward.'

'I will!' said Star, and sashayed merrily into the throng.

Katie wished she could help this reflexive scanning of the crowd for Iain, but she just couldn't. This was ridiculous. Stop it, stop it, stop it, she told herself. Only a minute ago she'd been mooning about Harry, and anyway he was, a) in hiding, and b) she was giving up Scottish men for ever. Cold turkey. Cold haggis. Whatever. They were done for.

Louise entered the room in her gorgeous gold dress, stood outlined in the double doors, stretched out her arms and yelled 'ta dah!' Instantly, several of the men who'd been hovering around the walls made a beeline for her.

'Ah, my insecure, sad, troubled little friend,' said Katie, grabbing two glasses of champagne and taking her one.

'Isn't this *amazing*?' said Louise. 'Olivia's outside

answering questions about fashion designers to *Hiya* magazine.'

'Ladies!' said Craig the Vet, looking redfaced and bluff in a pair of dark blue tartan trews and a waistcoat. He ought to have looked ridiculous, but in fact they rather suited him.

'Are you no by far the most beautiful things in here?'

Louise sniffed the air. 'Craig the Vet,' she said accusingly. 'You don't smell of cow.'

'Not unless *Paul Smith for Men* is made frae cows,' he said, sniffing his shoulder dubiously.

'You look nice,' decided Louise, after looking him up and down for a few more seconds. He bowed. 'Are you going to chat up all the ladies?'

Craig looked a bit nonplussed. 'Um, why, yes, I suppose so.'

'Good for you,' said Louise, patting him on the shoulder. 'You need a good woman.'

'Actually,' said Craig the Vet, 'I was wondering if you'd dance with me later.'

'For sure!' said Louise. 'I know all the dances brilliantly. Katie and Olivia taught me this afternoon. Didn't take long. I can dance with everyone!'

'OK,' said Craig.

'There's loads of totty here,' said Louise. 'You're going to have a great night.'

'Uh, yes,' said Craig. 'Well, I suppose I'd better . . .' He headed back into the crowd.

'*What* does that man have to do?' said Katie.

'What on earth are you talking about?'

'He's obviously nuts about you.'

'Nonsense,' said Louise. 'He hasn't tried to get into my knickers once.'

'Perhaps, Grasshopper, asking you to dance and to

come to look at his lambs is a different way of trying to get into your knickers.'

'Nah,' said Louise, considering it. She looked at Katie again. 'Do you really think so?'

Katie rolled her eyes. 'Durr.'

Louise flushed then. 'I thought . . . I mean, you know, it's fun up here and stuff.'

'Hmm,' said Katie dubiously.

'But . . . well, Craig . . . he's a vet.'

'I had noticed.'

'I mean . . . he couldn't live in London, could he? What's he going to treat, rats?'

'There are vets in London,' said Katie.

'Not real ones.'

'Yes, I'm sure they're quite real.'

'Oh, you know what I mean . . . it's just . . . I mean, do you think he really wants me for a *proper girlfriend*?'

Katie looked across at Craig the Vet, who had been cornered by a woman wearing an enormous pink corsage popping out of her considerable cleavage. He looked miserable, and kept sending glances towards Louise.

'Hello Lachlan,' said Katie, looking down. He was wearing a blue velvet frock coat and matching bow tie and sniffing a glass of wine nervously. 'You look lovely.'

'I know,' said Lachlan. 'I'm fighting them off with a shitty stick. Sorry – a, ehm, smeared stick.'

'You know, you never have to use that special ladies' language with me,' said Katie. 'It's only me.'

'Oh, yeah.' He leaned closer. 'Thank you again for bringing in all the chicks,' he confided.

'Not at all,' said Katie, resisting the urge to pat him on the head.

Katie passed through the room – Olivia appeared and dragged them around her various London friends too, and they did get to meet Ewan McGregor, who was a delight, plus numerous slightly batty women who wanted to share with Katie their joy at finding Fairlish, as if they'd turned up to Battersea Dogs' Home. The conversation levels were rising, punctuated by squeals of girlish laughter. It began to grate on Katie and so she followed Olivia and Louise outside onto the lawn.

Underfoot was still a morass, but the sun setting into the sea behind the hills was breathtaking. Katie stood for a while, enjoying the relative quiet after the noise and heat of the ballroom. Suddenly, she saw a strange, yet oddly familiar sight at the far end of the lawn. Seconds later she heard it – the mournful sound of bagpipes came floating up through the gloaming.

'Oh my God!' said Louise. 'That's Harry!'

Katie screwed up her eyes. Sure enough, looking very serious, there was Harry advancing towards the house, blowing a plaintive lament.

'It *does* sound like a cat,' she insisted.

'LADIES AND GENTLEMEN,' shouted Lachlan at the door in a surprisingly loud voice, 'WE WILL NOW BE PIPED IN TO DINNER. PLEASE TAKE YOUR PARTNERS!'

Harry took the head of the queue at the door.

'I can't believe he can blow that and walk at the same time,' said Louise. 'Makes you wonder how talented he is in other areas.'

Behind them they could hear an anxious shuffling.

'What did he mean, *partners*?' asked Louise, but it became increasingly obvious, as couples, most notably the larger-breasted women with the scrawnier of the techies, started lining up behind Harry and following him in through the entrance to the tent.

'Ah,' said Olivia. She grabbed onto a very camp PR

acquaintance of hers who'd come up from down South. 'You'll do.'

'Darling, with all these gorgeous hunks here, do you really have to limpet yourself onto me?' smiled the London chap.

'For five seconds I do. Be quiet, it's bad for your karma to be impolite.'

Craig the Vet materialised at Louise's elbow. 'Um, would you like to, er, go in to dinner?'

Louise swallowed suddenly and sought Katie's eye. Katie nodded furiously. Heck, the two of them could sort out geography later.

Louise, blushing, nodded her head, and Craig offered her his strong arm. She took it.

That left Katie on her own. She watched everyone else filing in two by two and tried not to mind. After all, she was working here, goddamit. Suddenly, she wished she had a clipboard. That would make her feel less awkward.

The sound of the pipes grew further and further away as the procession started to leave her behind. Smoothing down her skirts, she prepared to slip in at the back, when she became aware of somebody watching her from the other side of the line. She looked up through the pink and hazy sunlight. The person was wearing a plain grey kilt without a pattern and a plain white shirt and grey tie, and had a camera around his neck. He lifted his right hand very slowly and made a waving gesture.

'Hello, Iain,' murmured Katie.

Chapter Twenty

They waited, looking at each other until the line had gone in, and there was no one left outside the tent except a few of Kelpie's scurrying army.

Iain came towards her, and Katie found herself instinctively taking a step or two back.

'You look . . . ravishing,' he said, as if he'd searched through all the words in the world and this was the only one that would do her justice.

'Uh-huh,' said Katie. She wanted to look calm and collected and dignified, but inside she was shaking, and all she could think of was to holler, Where did you go? You left me! You vanished! Why??? But she kept a grip on herself in an attempt to be rational. Her good intentions to give up Scottish men for ever had evaporated at seeing Iain in his gorgeous grey kilt, faster than 8Ace finding £1.49 behind a hedge.

'How've you been?' he asked.

'GREAT,' said Katie. She bit her lip.

'You know, I missed you when you went away . . . I thought . . .' Suddenly Iain looked quite hot in the face.

Classic avoidance technique, thought Katie.

'I mean, after . . .'

After what? Katie thought viciously. After you tried to fuck me, failed and never contacted me again?

'After the time we spent together . . . I didn't . . . I mean, when you didn't want to see me, I quite understood . . .'

Katie swallowed hard. 'What do you mean, *I didn't want to see you?*'

'Well, I figured . . . you know, after the time . . . and then you fucked off back to London, I guessed that was that . . . I mean, I know what you girls are like.'

Katie folded her arms. '*What?* What are we like, Iain?'

'Well, you all sit around in coffee shops and tell each other how rubbish men are in bed, then you don't see them any more, and that's it.' Iain hung his head.

Katie stared at him. Surely he couldn't be so dumb. 'Iain . . . Iain, did you get *everything* you know about women from watching television?'

Iain shrugged. 'No.'

'Iain.'

'Yes?'

Katie put a hand up over her eyes. 'I went to London because I fell out with my boss, and because I felt the job was done, that was all. And you didn't call, or get in touch, or anything.'

'I . . . I kind of thought, after everything that had happened, you wouldn't be interested.' Iain's left eye had developed a nervous twitch.

'And you never bothered to find out?' asked Katie, full of indignation. 'Oh, then I come back and you're all over town, squiring blonde bits and pieces up at the caravan park.'

'Well, yes,' said Iain. 'I think we can both agree I needed the practice.'

They were both silent for a second after that.

'Anyway, you didn't tell me you were back in town.'

'You PHONE girls you sleep with!' said Katie. 'That is absolutely obvious rule number one! EVERYONE knows that! You could ask Francis that and he'd dial a number with his paws!'

'Yes, well, if you'd bothered to let me know you were coming back EVER, I might have done something about it. Anyway, I did leave you a message.'

'I can assure you you didn't,' said Katie.

Iain unfastened his sporran and pulled out a piece of paper. 'Here,' he said, looking disgruntled. 'I thought you'd get it.'

She took the crumpled sheet from him.

'Come *on*,' came a voice suddenly. Katie looked down. It was Lachlan, looking crossly at them. 'It's about to start. If you want your dinner, you have to get in here right away . . .'

The marquee looked awesome. Tables stretched away as far as the eye could see, twinkling with little candles and thistle centrepieces. Of the errant donkey, there was no sign. At every turn, Katie was amazed. OK, she happened to know that the tablecloths were mostly paper, and several young techies had ended up requiring first aid after deciding that the middle of the night, after a long session at the Mermaid, was the ideal time to go thistle-gathering, and about sixty of the candles were slowly melting Santa Clauses she'd finally found in one of the gift shops at the last minute, rather than the plain whites . . . but, with the lights turned down, it was a fairyland.

Everyone was already seated, with an artillery of waiters standing ready to go. Lachlan led them right into the middle, and everyone fell silent, as if they were about to start dancing or something. Katie felt terribly uncomfortable.

'You're over there,' said Lachlan to Iain. 'Table seventy-nine.'

Iain looked at Katie and headed off to the left. She couldn't read his expression.

'And you're here,' said Lachlan, as he led Katie to the biggest table, right at the top of the marquee. There was an empty space at Harry's right hand.

He was looking at his drink when she approached, then, just at the last minute, lifted his face to meet her eyes.

It was like a lightbulb going off in her head. From completely out of left field, she knew straight away. His normally brooding, guarded expression had dropped completely. She'd thought the scene in the nightclub was just a drunken aberration; she was so focused on her own loneliness, she'd never even considered his. She just . . . she was so unused to any kind of male attention, she'd bypassed it altogether.

And now of course he thought it was all up, all done for, the moment she and Iain had walked in through the entrance together. She blinked, still staring at him. But he'd dropped his eyes again and was staring at his empty dinner plate.

She had. She'd backed the wrong bloody horse. She'd been blind to what was right under her nose. The crack in the door she'd seen . . . the glimpse of the desired life. Maybe it hadn't been Iain at all. Maybe it had been Harry all along.

Lachlan cleared his throat behind her and, conscious of five hundred pairs of hungry eyes staring at her, she slipped into the seat beside him.

'Busy?' asked Harry, pain evident in his voice as the

chatter around the room started up again and Kelpie's army leaped into motion, rushing forward to start serving soup.

'Look, Harry . . .' Katie started, and then didn't know how to go on. She could hardly say, 'If you're in love with me . . .' Plus, what if she were wrong? Plus, what was the end of that sentence anyway? She swallowed and looked up at him. He had turned to his left, where a very grand woman Katie didn't know was sitting looking snooty. He was trying to chat to her whilst looking completely unperturbed. The back of his neck was giving him away though. On Katie's right was Kennedy, who was talking about the number of his bedrooms to a wide-eyed busty blonde on his other side. Katie concentrated on her broth when it came, and took a few gulps of wine, her mind racing furiously. Louise was on the other side of the room, where she seemed to be engrossed in a very deep conversation with Craig the Vet. Olivia was already up and going around the room, chatting to one and all in what looked like harsh anti-golf course tones. She certainly wasn't touching any food that might have been made with anything other than soya.

There was no help at hand. Katie winced at herself. How could she have been so naive? OK, so she wasn't Beyoncé Knowles, but things were different up here. She could probably have looked like Harry Knowles, and courted a bit of attention. And Harry must have thought she was taunting him all this time. She closed her eyes.

The posh woman had turned around to talk to someone else, and Katie was suddenly very aware of Harry's bulk at her elbow.

He cleared his throat. 'Well, who'd have thought it, eh?' he said, in a growly tone of voice.

Katie sneaked a peek at him. He looked as though he was trying incredibly hard to be Very Brave. Her heart went out to him immediately.

'All this?' she said. 'It's . . . just great, isn't it?'

He nodded.

'And everyone seems to be having a good time.'

Everyone, reflected Katie, except for the two of them.

Dinner was excruciating, as Katie was completely unable to make any kind of conversation, and it became increasingly clear to Harry that he'd given himself away. She was clearly mortified and desperate to get out of his sight as fast as she reasonably could.

It was just, he'd kind of thought that Iain nonsense was over with once and for all; he'd seen Iain out and about with the cavalcade of ladies who'd arrived, and he knew what Iain was like. Weak. No match really for a bolshy character like Katie. God, why had he been such a stupid prick in London? It hadn't even hit home, until he realised just how much he missed her when she went back. It wasn't the same around the office, with just Derek and Francis on hand. He missed her habit of asking awkward questions all the time, and dashing off to do things, and, well, he just missed her and that was all there was to it.

So they talked about the food, which was surprisingly good and almost completely poison free, as far as Katie could tell; the fact that the weather had cleared up; that wasn't it amazing so many people had come so far, blah blah.

Katie was sure her heart was pounding so loudly he would be able to see it through her chest. For some reason she felt her eyes constantly returning to his hands. He was wearing cufflinks on his shirt, and she could see how strong his forearms looked underneath it. He had such big hands, more suited to working on the land than sitting in an office, she thought. She wondered what it would be like to feel them on her.

'Oh God,' said Harry finally.

Katie's heart leaped. What was he going to say? Was he going to make a declaration? Bring it up? Oh God, what was she going to say? How could she respond?

'I hate speeches,' said Harry.

Katie thought maybe she'd misheard. 'Pardon?' she said, her throat dry.

'Speeches. I hate giving speeches.' He drew a small pile of index cards out of his pocket.

'You're giving a speech?' said Katie stupidly.

'Well, yes . . . got to thank everyone for coming and stuff, remind them why they're here and all that. Then I think Ewan McGregor's going to say a few words, and I think Shirley Manson's going to sing a song later.'

'Oh,' said Katie, mildly wondering why nobody had asked her to say anything. 'Great.'

'We would have got you to do it, but somebody said you might encourage inappropriate arse-showing.'

Katie nodded. 'I don't mean to.'

Harry smiled wryly. 'You never do.'

Harry rapped his fingers on the table as the puddings came around. 'I guess I'd better do it after pudding. Or maybe when they get coffee Or maybe just now.'

In fact, they did have to wait for coffee, by which time Harry looked so uncomfortable Katie wanted to ask him if he needed to be taken to the toilet. 'Don't worry,' she said. 'I'm sure it will be great.'

'I wouldn't be too sure,' said Harry ominously, fingering his index cards.

Derek came bounding up, wearing a dinner jacket that made him look like a waiter. 'I've got the PA fixed up!'

he whispered, indicating a large amplifier with a mike behind them.

'Great,' said Harry, looking like a condemned man. Over the clatter of coffee cups, he stood up with the mike, which brushed his jacket and gave an instant wail of feedback.

'Ah,' he said. 'Good start.'

The room gradually quietened down and he stepped to the side. Once he started to speak, thought Katie, he didn't sound nervous at all.

'Hello everyone,' he said. 'I'm Harry Barr, and I'm the person who runs the forest you're all helping by coming here tonight, so I'd just like to thank you.'

There was a little cheer, and a round of applause went around the room. Harry grinned and went pink.

'Every year, we lose twenty million acres of forest in the UK. Organised lines of replantings can't even begin to replicate the complexity of original woodlands that have developed over centuries; the different species interdependent on one another the way they were always meant to be.

'Golf courses are the opposite of the wild woods. They're manicured and organised. They are an attempt to impose order on the world, to bend it to man's will. To smooth its rough surfaces and expose its secrets.

'I'm glad you're all here tonight, because I'm glad to be part of a group of people which doesn't want all the mystery and adventure gone from their lives. Which believes that our great forests deserve to flourish in peace, which believes that a little bit of Scotland can always remain wild, just as a little bit of our hearts can never be tamed.'

There was a huge nationalistic roar at this, and much thumping of feet on floors, and glasses on tables. Katie couldn't understand why Harry had been so bothered about giving a speech; he wasn't bad at it at all.

'Anyway, we're about to commence the slave auction . . .'

There was massed girly screeching.

'So, I would ask everyone to give generously, as we all make massive tits of ourselves, just like Mother Nature intended.' Harry squinted at the index card he was holding, as if he didn't want to read out the next bit. 'Very quickly, there's a few people I have to thank for putting tonight together. Kelpie MacGuire, who has run the kitchen like . . . well, like one of Stalin's gulags, I think, but I'm sure you'll agree, she's done a fine job . . .'

There was a massed roar of applause, and Kelpie, looking pretty, pink and exhausted in her chef's whites, stepped in and made a bow. She winked at Katie, who suspected that she was having a fantastic time.

'. . . Margaret Senga McClockerty, who has been a *powerhouse* of organisational ability.'

Katie looked around, but she couldn't see her. She must be here, surely.

'Olivia Li from LiWebber Associates in London, who've been handling the PR, and . . .' At this point Harry swallowed and really did go red. He stared at the index card, as if forcing himself to read it out. '. . . our most special thanks go to Katie Watson, who turned up out of the blue one day, and, well, it hasn't always been plain sailing, but Katie, you've worked so hard for all of this to come together . . . stand up Katie . . . and, doesn't she look beautiful?'

Katie was completely blindsided. She hadn't realised . . . people started clapping. Slowly she stood up and found they were whooping and cheering. It was the most amazing feeling. For someone whose life was falling apart at the seams, right now, she thought she was making a pretty good show of it. She felt tears well up suddenly.

'Thank you,' she mouthed to Harry.

He shrugged. This wasn't the way it was meant to be at all. He realised that in his head when he'd written this bit of the speech, she dashed up, flung her arms around him and kissed him in front of everyone. That was a bit stupid when he thought about it now. He looked at her. Very stupid.

'Ehm, no, thank *you*,' he said back. Then they both sat down, awkwardly, together.

Ewan McGregor's speech was short and sweet, along the lines of give Harry all their fucking money or he wouldn't get his cock out. Then the central tables were cleared back and everyone started to move around the room, murmuring excitedly as a small stage was erected in the middle.

Harry was leaving the table. Katie realised she desperately had to say something to him, but she wasn't sure what.

'Where are you going?' she asked.

He paused, as if he really wished she hadn't asked him that question. 'Toga,' he mumbled finally, feeling like the biggest loser of all time.

And he left.

Katie squished up with Olivia and Louise over two chairs right in the middle of the front row, where they had already bagsed the best view of the action. All the men had disappeared, and there was a huge buzz of perfume, smoke, coffee, wine and giggling in the air, as the women hurried back from the toilets and checked their wallets for cash.

'How's it going?' asked Olivia. '*Everyone* is here. Did you spot Richard and Judy?'

'Is he going to be in a toga?' asked Katie.

'Sadly not,' said Olivia. 'But I expect Judy will be bidding. What are you grinning about?' This was directed at Louise, who was sitting with a huge smile plastered over her face.

'Nothing,' said Louise. She tried to stop smiling, but failed, the corners of her mouth twitching.

'And what about YOU?' said Olivia, turning on Katie. 'We saw you waltzing in here with your fancy man! Get caught making out behind the tent did you?'

'No,' said Katie. 'It wasn't like that at all.'

She wondered whether to tell her friends about dinner, but decided against it.

'Well,' said Louise. 'Here's a quick test. "Iain's a prick – true or false?"'

Katie half-smiled. 'I think perhaps he's a bit misunderstood.'

'Ooohhh,' said Olivia and Louise together, but there wasn't time to discuss more, as the lights went down and a drum roll came from the back of the marquee.

'AND NOW,' a hugely loud female voice, that Katie thought she recognised from somewhere, came over the PA. 'WELCOME TO THE FIRST FAIRLISH SLAVE AUCTION!' boomed out, as the lights came up to reveal, perched on top of the viewing platform, Mrs McClockerty, absolutely resplendent in a sparkling huge sequinned corset, which amply demonstrated her magnificent bosom, and a long velvet skirt. She looked amazing. Katie and Louise nearly fell off their chairs, and the cheering around the room was the loudest heard so far.

Mrs McClockerty was grinning broadly and bellowing

into the microphone stand as if she was doing her last comeback on Broadway. 'RIGHT! SHUT UP YOUSE! YOU'LL FIND A CARD UNDERNEATH YOUR CHAIRS WI' A NUMBER ON IT. IF YOU WANT TO BID, HOLD UP THE NUMBER, AND YOU WILL BE HELD TO IT. DO YOUSE UNDERSTAND?'

Everyone bawled lustily.

'AH CAN'T HEAR YOU!'

'WAAAAH!' screamed the crowd.

'Winning bidders will be entitled to twenty-four hours of *full* service from the slave on a date of their choosing, including at least one skill! All right!' said Mrs McClockerty. 'Now, lot number one . . .'

There was a noisy drum roll from the back, and the first of the techies bounced on stage, waving his arms in the air. He was wearing a sheet that didn't quite conceal a pair of tartan boxer shorts.

'Hello!' he bellowed into the microphone, 'my name is Seamus Hannigan, I'm twenty-eight years old, five feet nine inches tall and can provide many special services around the home, including computer mending, web design, technical drawing and erotic foot massage!'

Seamus wiggled his bum provocatively to mass screams from the audience, and the numbers started going up almost immediately.

'And I have fifty . . . sixty . . . seventy . . . one HUNDRED pounds . . . one hundred and twenty . . . fifty . . . one seven-five . . . one ninety . . . TWO HUNDRED pounds . . . two hundred and twenty . . . thirty . . . going for thirty . . . great foot massage . . . going once, going twice . . .' Mrs McClockerty smashed a mallet onto a stool. 'SOLD for two hundred and thirty pounds to number 119.'

Number 119 squealed with delight, revealing herself to

be a tiny porcine brunette. In piggy hooves, she ran up to the stage, where Seamus attempted to pick her up and carry her off, failed, dropped his toga and finally grabbed her podgy fingers and ran out of the marquee, both of them giggling hysterically all the while.

Next was Willie the ghillie, at whom Louise wolf-whistled approvingly. Wisely, after promising to catch a pheasant as a skill, which didn't rouse too much interest amongst the provincial ladies, he let his toga drop from his shoulders and revealed a set of pecs of which Justin Timberlake would have been proud. Bids multiplied accordingly.

'Not bidding, Louise?' said Katie slyly.

'I, uh, no . . . ha, no . . . I mean, I'm nearly skint and, let's face it,' Louise swallowed hard, 'probably fired.'

'Hmm,' said Katie. She'd forgotten about Louise's job, though not, it seemed, as readily as Louise had.

A line of farmers were despatched into the baying crowd of women, who were getting increasingly worked up, screeching themselves into a frenzy, when little Lachlan turned up, wearing a pillowcase and promising a place to rest their pint glasses. The money was heading well north of five hundred quid, and Katie was almost allowing herself to think of the next thing they'd do with the money: lawyers' fees and advertisements in newspapers. Not that she'd be here, of course, she told herself sternly. She'd be far away.

Laird Kennedy did not look at his best, even wearing two sheets in the manner of a Roman Emperor. It ill behoved his ancient lineage to be marching up and down in his bedclothes in front of hundreds of, by now, near hysterical women. He cleared his throat in front of the mike and didn't seem quite his normal bombastic self.

'Uh . . . Well . . . um, this is my house.'

'TWO GRAND!' screamed a high-pitched female voice from the crowd, unable even to wait to put her number up. Chaos kicked off.

'It's not getting a bit *dangerous* back there do you think?' said Olivia, twisting her head around as the bidding went up at a ferocious rate.

'It's all good,' said Katie. 'All cash for us. I tell you what, though, I wouldn't particularly want to be following this.'

Kennedy went, eventually, for an absolutely eye-popping amount of cash. The room craned to watch the tall, imperious-looking woman in the expensive jewellery come forward to claim her prize. Katie was close enough to the podium to hear her hiss, 'What's your title?' to him, then she turned around and smiled bountifully to the cheering crowd when he answered, 'Laird'.

The woman waved royally.

'Can you have children?' Kennedy asked her *sotto voce*.

The room seemed to take a huge breather after this. There was a very definite sense that nobody was going to make more than ten grand, and that they'd just seen the peak of the boys being auctioned off. There was much flouncing off to the toilet and the bar, and the chatter of women just talking amongst themselves rose commensurately.

'AHEM!' said Mrs McClockerty, but nobody paid much notice as she welcomed the next toga-clad victim on stage. It was Harry.

'Harry Barr!' yelled Mrs McClockerty, face beaming with maternal pride. 'No need for him to introduce himself, I can tell you he's the best of the lot here, and if you take him and don't treat him right, ah can tell you right now, you're going to have ME to answer to.' She gestured at herself fiercely. Harry's face burned even hotter. 'I'm telling you, he's the best one here, so get betting you ENGLISH BITCHES!'

Like a curtain, a complete silence dropped over the room.

Katie, Louise and Olivia covered their faces with their hands.

Mrs McClockerty just stood, glowering, as an agitated murmuring started up in the corner of the marquee. Several people got up and strode out, the rest discussed the insult in shocked tones, which was fair enough, Katie thought, given that they'd come up here and given good money of their own accord, and really didn't need to be called bitches for the privilege.

Harry stood there, stock still on the podium, looking as though he was about to be hanged by the neck until dead, and as if he would actually rather welcome the experience.

Mrs McClockerty still didn't seem to realise anything was the least bit the matter. She stared around the room crossly. 'WELL??? ANYONE???'

Katie sneaked a look over her shoulder. Row after row of women was sitting sullenly, arms crossed, completely different from the baying masses only a few seconds before. She looked at Harry again. Oh, this was just awful. Harry couldn't take his eyes off the floor. Only the tips of his ears were showing, glowing bright pink. A terrible silence was hanging in the air.

Katie closed her eyes, took a deep breath, and stood up out of her seat. In her clearest voice, she shouted, 'One hundred pounds!'

Harry's head shot up, and he looked at her as if he couldn't believe what he'd just heard.

'ONE HUNDRED POUNDS!' Mrs McClockerty was shrieking, but Katie hardly heard her. She and Harry were staring straight at each other, and, oddly, it felt as if there was nobody else in the room. Almost unwittingly, she found herself moving a step towards him. Likewise, almost in slow motion, Harry stretched out his hand towards her.

'Going ONCE!' screeched Mrs McClockerty. She looked down. Lachlan was tugging at her skirt. She bent down as he whispered in her ear.

Katie and Harry were still staring at each other, completely oblivious to the rest of the room. Katie was just reaching up her hand to take his. She wasn't quite sure what she was doing, but it felt terribly natural to be doing so.

'AHEM,' said Mrs McClockerty, her beetle brows coming very low as she hollered into the mike. 'It has come to my attention that I may, in fact, have been a wee bittie hasty before and insulted a lot of youse.'

'Ya big fat bitch!' came a heckle from the back of the tent, to widespread laughter.

'So, I've been ordered to say "sorry".' She looked as though this was an extremely difficult thing for her to get out. 'And, to add to that, if you bid for the lovely Harry Barr, you will also, ahem, get the opportunity to . . . *what* was that, Lachlan?' Lachlan whispered into her ear again. 'Cake? Really?' She looked furious. 'OK. Whoever bids for Harry also gets to pelt me with cake.'

At this, there was a renewed outburst of cheering. Mrs McClockerty stroked her sequinned top with a sigh.

'ONE HUNDRED AND FIFTY!' yelled a voice from the back.

'TWO HUNDRED!' came another.

Immediately, the spell was broken. Harry stood up, looked around, shuffling awkwardly on the spot. The bidding increased; people knew who he was and he was the reason some of them had come there in the first place. The figure went up and up, and he stayed, looking miserably at Katie, with Mrs McClockerty's hand firmly clamped on his arm, as the sums mounted. Women were on their feet, clustering around the podium, and Katie suddenly felt very claustrophobic. She had to leave. She got up and headed for the bathroom, closely followed by Louise.

'What's up?' asked Louise, as Katie leaned her forehead against the cold white tiles. They'd left the Portaloos to their own devices and slipped into the downstairs cloakroom of the main house, which felt cold and quiet. There were a few people strolling around, couples talking quietly in corners; assignations being arranged. But there was nobody in the large bathroom, for which Katie was profoundly grateful.

Katie rubbed her hand over her eyes.

'OK,' she said. 'Here's the thing.'

Louise nodded expectantly.

'How long have you known me?'

'Eight years?' said Louise.

'And during that time, we've talked a lot about boys, right?'

Louise nodded heartily.

'About boys we've liked and about boys who've been nasty to us?'

Louise nodded.

'And boys we've chased and boys we thought were rubbish?'

'What's your point?'

'Have we ever been liked by two boys at once?'

Louise squealed. '*Really?*'

'Hmm,' said Katie.

Louise tried to get her head around it. 'Two men really fancy you?'

'I know! I feel like Jennifer Aniston!'

'Wow,' said Louise. 'I don't even know what kind of advice you'd give for something like that.'

'I know,' said Katie. 'We're in uncharted waters.'

She reapplied a dark red lipstick she'd found that went exactly with the dress.

Louise looked at her, shaking her head. 'You seem awfully cool about this.'

'No, I don't,' said Katie. 'One is a dickhead and one's . . .'

'Your boss,' said Louise. 'Oh, for goodness' sake,' she said when she saw Katie's shocked face. 'What, you think I'm an idiot? He's a complete hunk and, oh, by the way – you just tried to buy him.'

Katie heaved a sigh. 'Well then. So, you know, it's probably best to ignore this whole thing and, you know, just go home, and . . .' Her eyes dropped to the floor. 'It's just so complicated.'

'What? Arse bollocks!' said Louise. 'This will NEVER happen again! You'll probably not even have one person in love with you again. You're completely wearing out your quota right now. This is your last ever chance for love!'

'Could you stop saying things like that?'

'No, I mean it. We're not getting any younger, and you get two blokes. I mean, what are the odds? This must be the end! You're going to have to choose!'

'Of course I'm not,' said Katie, trying to sound convincing. 'I've given up Scottish men for good.'

'OK,' said Louise. 'Hypothetically, if you hadn't just said something completely crazy . . . if you had to choose one, which one would you want?'

Katie thought about it. 'I . . . I don't . . . you know, Iain hurt me really badly.'

Louise nodded.

'I thought . . . I mean, I really liked him. But then he just left me flapping about in the wind, and Harry . . . Harry's been so . . . I mean, he drives me crazy half the time, and he's really moralistic and annoying.'

'Uh-huh.'

'But . . . but, there's something about him . . . I'd just . . . I'd just love to know what it'd be like to be with him. Do you know what I mean?'

Louise nodded. 'God, yes.'

'I don't just mean that I want to go to bed with him.'

'Although you do.'

Katie looked annoyed. 'Well. Yes. I suppose. Yes.'

'So, you fancy him?'

'Yes. But I fancy Iain too. And now, he's saying he wants . . . well I don't know quite what he's saying. I think I need to talk to him.'

'He hasn't turned up to be auctioned yet.'

'Well, maybe I need to find him.'

By the time they got back to the marquee, it had changed completely. The auction was over, and all the tables had now been moved to the side, and the band had started playing in the corner. There were people everywhere, drinking, talking, reapplying lipstick. A haze of perfume and smoke hung in the air, and the noise was deafening.

'Blimey,' said Louise. 'I guess your party's a success then.'

'Hmm,' said Katie.

There was no sign of either Iain or Harry in the throng. Every so often a giggly woman would be walking along, arm in arm with her toga, looking pleased but proud.

Mrs McClockerty could be seen talking intently to Lachlan, whilst keeping a firm eye on the cake.

Katie wandered through the crowds in a dream, scarcely knowing who she was looking for. Louise was hard by her elbow. Suddenly, like the parting of the Red Sea, the ocean of people disappeared all around them. They looked around, twitching, only to find the band were all standing, ready to play, and the band leader was looking at them crossly, isolated in the middle of the dance floor. All around the marquee, couples were lined up like Siamese twin soldiers on parade.

'Now, we'll be starting with a Gay Gordons . . .' announced the band leader. 'And a one . . . two . . . three . . . four . . .'

'Oh bollocks,' said Katie. 'This is the one I know, but I don't know it on my own.'

'Quick, scram,' said Louise, and they made a dive for the side of the floor, fighting their way through a tightly-packed circle that was already huffing into the steps.

'Aha!' said two techies, who were standing on the other side, just as they stumbled out.

'It's you two! Come dance with us, all these women are nuts.'

'No they're not,' scolded Katie.

'Aye they are!' said the shorter of the two. 'Three of them just held me down and put their hands up my kilt!'

'Well, that shouldn't be happening,' said Katie, disapprovingly.

'Oh, no, I liked it, ken. It just might be a bit trickier on the dance floor.'

So Katie and Louise let themselves be swept away onto the huge floor, the sound of Dougie's accordion ringing in their ears.

*   *   *

In some ways, Katie thought, dancing was incredibly good for taking your mind off things, and there was something intensely satisfying about the whole room moving as one. In another way, of course, it was completely strange, as she found herself pressed up against millions of backs, trying to avoid rogue stilettos. The music changed, and she was suddenly in a completely new dance, which involved facing your partner, moving to the side, then moving out to the wall to clap . . . and when she came back, her partner was no longer there, and she found herself face to face with one of the farm labourers, whose face she recognised.

'What's going on?' she asked.

'Travelling dance, aye?' he said, enlightening her no further. He was looking very red in the face, as if he was having a completely great time, and he waltzed her around with some energy. 'You just keep changing partners.'

As, indeed, she did, with every whirl and spin of the music. The men on the inside track moved around with every repeat of the dance. There was barely time to say much more than hello to her partners, attempt to keep up, and try to catch her breath before she was twirled off once more. Many of the men thanked her or wanted a quick word about whichever girl they particularly liked, which was touching, she felt, feeling more a part of this community than she could ever have dreamed, standing on that little railway halt, what felt like a very long time ago.

She found herself nodding as she flew along, the crowd seeming to get hotter and heavier all the time, and the music getting louder and more emphatic; so absorbed that it took a while, when she came back from clapping at the wall, to find herself hand in hand with Iain, who was wearing, oddly, a toga.

'Hey,' said Katie, gulping. He looked at her as they took their two steps to the right. 'Didn't you go up for auction?'

Iain shrugged. His hair was flopping over his left eye. 'I thought . . . I thought about what you said, and I thought, well, maybe I shouldn't be seeing any other women . . . you know . . .'

'They don't make you a real slave,' said Katie, her heart pounding, as they kicked their legs out to either side. The woman next to her caught her ankle. 'They can't order you to perform cunnilingus or anything like that.'

Iain looked pale. 'Please . . . look, Katie, I'm really sorry I didn't call you.'

Katie twirled lightly. 'You should have.'

'I know.'

They twirled the other way.

'Katie, if I can make this up to you, any way I can . . . I'd really love to.' He looked at her imploringly, with those big green eyes.

This was the point at which Katie was supposed to head away and clap at the wall. But somehow she stayed firmly rooted to the spot.

'Please,' he said.

He looked so handsome, and so sad, it was all Katie could do not to fall into his arms there and then.

Suddenly she found herself the eye in the storm, standing completely still, as the first of the women behind her in the circle came cascading into her.

'What the hell!' shouted the woman, an abnormally tall, brassy blonde, tripping over her. 'He's mine next.' She pointed at Iain.

'Yeah, bloody move around,' said the man next in line for Katie, whom she'd never seen before. He had a scaly beard and glasses, like the dad in *The Modern Parents*.

Iain wasn't moving either, just staring at her.

'HEY!' came another voice down the line, as they found the dance coming to an abrupt halt, spiked heels bumping painfully into ankles all the way down the tent.

'Yeah, wot the fuck,' came a London squeal. There were several tuts and grumbles in the air as couples collided and came to a pushing, shoving halt down the room.

'Excuse me!' said the blonde rudely, trying to push Katie out of the way. Katie still didn't – couldn't – move, and the blonde fell over, exposing the fact that it wasn't only the men in kilts who were going without underwear that evening. She screamed and grabbed hold of the nearest man – the one with the beard – who promptly tripped over her ankle and pitched headfirst into the crowd.

There was mass screeching, then, as yards of expensive tulle and satin collapsed like a row of dominos, the band stopped playing and it became apparent that two of the women on the floor had started slapping each other.

'Is that your woman fighting?' demanded one of the men of another. 'I'm meant to be dancing with her and she's fighting?'

'Whit?' said the first man. Then he launched a punch.

Within seconds the whole place was in tumult. Too much free drink and hormones in the air had revved everyone up to a dangerously high pitch. The sound of dresses being ripped and glasses being broken resounded through the tent. Mrs McClockerty was being spared her cake-related punishment, as pieces of it were flying willy-nilly all over the place. A line of techies decided this was the great time to unleash their super surprise, as they all bent over and stuck their specially painted blue arses in the air, wiggling them as the paparazzi went crazy.

Still, Katie was staring at Iain, as, out of the corner of her eye, she caught sight of a figure struggling to get through the crowds to see what was causing the ruckus. It was Harry. As soon as he saw the two of them, standing quietly on the edge of absolute chaos, seemingly completely unaware, he drew up short in front of them.

'Katie,' he said hoarsely. 'Iain.'

He knew it would end like this, he supposed. Iain was going to get her. Maybe not for very long, but this time was probably different. Certainly looked that way from where he was standing.

'Harry,' said Katie. Her face was impossible to read. The three of them stood, motionless, as pandemonium reigned behind them.

'WHAT THE FUCKING HELL IS ALL THIS!!!???'

Amazingly, a super-deep, almost unbelievably loud voice suddenly cut across the dance floor and right through the tent. And, even more startlingly, people shut up and turned to see who was shouting.

A tall, powerfully-built man, in a very expensive-looking suit, was standing in the middle of the dance floor, looking absolutely furious. He had heavy brows that were pulled down over his eyes – very green eyes, Katie noticed. Behind him was a cluster of men, similarly dressed. The room was silent.

'Dad,' said Iain, finally.

All eyes focused on the two men. The family resemblance was very noticeable thought Katie, as he drew closer. Same height, same brown hair (although Iain's father's was fiercely combed back and cut very short), and definitely the same eyes. She found herself thinking of what Iain would look like when he got older, then shook her head to clear the image.

She looked at Harry. He was staring at Iain's dad with an expression she'd never seen on him before; he looked furious, but at the same time, lost and a little vulnerable. She wondered if Iain's dad had been something of a formidable presence when they were younger.

Iain's dad let off a stream of Gaelic suddenly at Iain, who looked sullen and stared at the floor. Then he turned around to face the room.

'I came here,' he shouted, 'to see if I could talk to you people. Explain how a golf course could only benefit this bloody place.'

There were instantly boos at this around the hall.

'OH, BE QUIET,' he boomed. 'How many of you lot have come up from Glasgow or Edinburgh? Or London? You all say you love the Highlands, but not enough to move up here and build communities and raise your damn families here.'

His voice dropped as he realised people were listening to him. 'The population's dropping year on year. Look at you, advertising for women on the television. It's a disgrace.'

There was a general muttering at this.

'I'm just trying to put something back into the community, sheesh, ensure it *stays* a community. I'm just trying to stop you being outnumbered by the bloody sheep, for God's sake.'

Katie watched him. He seemed genuinely to believe what he was saying. And he seemed to have a point. She looked around the room. People were letting him have his say. Some were even nodding sympathetically.

He looked around the room. The group of men behind his back were looking terribly disapproving.

'But now I've brought some investors to see you . . . apparently,' he glanced at the group of men behind him, 'respectable golf-loving people aren't going to want to come up here and play, surrounded by rabble like you lot. So, I guess you've won. And you can go back to drinking and fighting your way to oblivion on your own. I hope you're happy.'

There was silence. Katie and Harry looked at each other, aghast and delighted.

Iain's dad turned round to walk out.

'Mr Kinross,' shouted out Harry, his voice ringing loud and clear. Iain's dad stopped and turned back around. 'Are you saying you know what's best for all of us?'

Iain's dad looked at him closely. 'Harry Barr? Well,' he said, almost to himself. 'Well done you. At least you got yourself a proper job, unlike my feckless son over there.'

'For goodness' sake, Dad,' said Iain, looking more like a teenager than a fully grown man.

'I do have a job,' said Harry. 'And that job's protecting our environment the way we like it. Where do you live, by the way?'

'That's not the point,' said Iain's dad.

'I know that's not the point,' said Harry. 'That's why you've been talking complete bullshit. Your only point is money, and I for one could not be more delighted you're going to take it somewhere else.'

There was a huge cheer at this.

'Up the arse would be preferable to me, but it's up to you.'

The investors hurried out of the marquee.

Iain's dad walked straight up to Harry. They spoke quietly, but Katie was close enough to hear. 'I cannot believe the six tons of shit you unloaded on us for this,' said Mr Kinross. 'I certainly underestimated you.'

'I had help,' said Harry. 'And, actually, I think you overestimated your fucking stupid idea.'

Iain's dad coughed. 'Your mother would have been proud,' he said, quietly.

Harry started, unable to speak.

'She would have been too,' came another voice. Iain's.

'THREE CHEERS FOR NO GOLF COURSE!' shouted somebody from the back of the tent, and the place erupted behind them.

Katie watched as the three men gradually came closer together as the band picked up their instruments again. Her heart was beating wildly, and she couldn't help but join in with the cheering and clapping.

Suddenly, a figure darted the length of the dance floor and grabbed Katie around the middle.

'Katie,' screeched Olivia.

The men turned to look at them.

'What? What is it?' asked Katie, who'd nearly been knocked off her feet.

'I got a mobile signal!!!'

'Ehm . . .' Katie was conscious of being overheard. 'Well, that's great, Olivia. Well done.'

'No, no, you don't understand . . .'

Katie noticed Olivia was holding out the telephone.

'It's for you. It's your sister.'

Chapter Twenty-One

The next hour was absolute chaos. It wasn't Katie's sister speaking on the phone; it was her mother. Clara had gone into labour, and was asking for her. She was hysterical, apparently.

'But I can't get down there in less than twelve hours!' said Katie. 'Tell her to cross her legs or something.'

'I think this is a pretty impatient baby,' said her mother. 'Just try and get here as soon as you can, will you sweetheart? She's really crying for you. The hospital aren't happy with her at all. Her blood pressure's all over the place.'

'But it's midnight!' said Katie. 'Nothing's even running. I'm completely stuck up here!' She found herself choking back tears.

The three men were listening hard.

'Shh,' Olivia was patting her arm, as was Louise, who'd just arrived. 'We'll just have to drive through the night, that's all.'

'Who's sober enough to drive?' sobbed Katie, extending her arm. 'Everyone's pissed as farts!'

Iain's father gave a small cough suddenly. 'Excuse me miss . . .'

'Katie,' said Katie, sniffing.

'Hmm, yes. Well, I don't know if I can be of assistance, but I understand it's something of an emergency . . .'

Katie nodded.

'Well, I do have a helicopter standing by for Inverness.'

'Oh,' said Katie, looking up at him, feeling a spark of hope.

'Is it a big chopper?' came a voice. They all turned around.

'Hi, I'm Ewan McGregor,' came the famous voice. 'I hear from Olivia here you've got a bit of a problem, and, well, I've got a plane on standby at Inverness, so, please – be my guest.'

Katie's eyes opened wide. 'You don't mean it?'

'Consider it my donation. Or, at least, the production studio's. It can come back and get me later; I just want the bloody dancing to start up again.'

'Oh, thanks . . .' said Katie, unable to express her gratitude to the men. 'Thank you so, *so* much.'

'Not at all,' said the film star. 'Thanks for an excellent party. Usually these things are complete crap.' And he disappeared back into the throng.

'Well, we'd better be going,' said Iain's dad. 'These babies . . .' he glanced at Iain. 'They don't wait around.'

Katie held on to Olivia and Louise as they left, sweeping past Iain, Harry and the rest of the room.

'Shall we pick your stuff up?' asked Olivia.

'No time,' said Katie.

'Well, I mean, who knows . . . you might never come back here again.'

Katie allowed herself one smile through her terrible anxiety.

'Oh. You never know.'

* * *

Louise and Katie had never been in a helicopter before, and couldn't help being excited, as they took off into the even now not quite pitch-dark night; the castle and the marquee becoming a more faded point of light below them, surrounded by the huge and ongoing woods that engulfed the rest of the countryside.

'It's so beautiful here,' said Louise sadly.

Iain's dad, who was sitting in the row behind them, sniffed thoughtfully. Katie reckoned she ought to say something to him, but couldn't imagine what.

'Thanks,' she said again. 'Thank you so much.'

'No trouble,' he said. Then he looked at her. 'Were you the girl my son talked about?'

'Um, I don't know,' said Katie, swallowing hard.

'Works for that Barr chap.'

'Yes,' said Katie.

'It was a bad business that,' said Iain's dad. 'When Harry's mum was so ill, you know . . . I didn't think Iain needed to see another boy go through life without a mother, after his own mum left . . . kept them apart. Then, when I saw how stupid an idea it was, he was just too scared to go. Thought he might catch something, or whatever. He's just . . . a wee bit weak. That's all.'

Katie nodded.

'Well,' said Iain's dad, heaving a sigh. 'It was nothing to do with my company you know. It was just a sad thing that happened. Publicity and rumours can be a pernicious thing. Though I guess you'd know a bit about that.'

Katie nodded again.

Mr Kinross sighed. 'He's a good lad, you know.'

Katie stared out of the window at the stars. They were nearing the town.

'Good luck with your sister,' said Iain's dad, gruffly patting her on the shoulder.

* * *

The private plane was something else. Although they were concerned about Clara, they couldn't help exclaiming as they were whisked through a side door at the airport and straight onto the runway. Louise even stopped and posed at the top of the stairs, waving to imagined crowds of fans.

'Oh, this is the life,' said Louise, when she saw the huge upholstered seats and carpeted cabin.

'Have you never been on a private plane before?' said Olivia.

'SHUT UP OLIVIA!' the two girls shouted.

They ordered cocoas from the stunningly beautiful hostess, who was managing to conceal extremely well her disappointment at the fact that they were just three girls and not, say, an international movie star.

Katie took her drink and stared blankly out of the window. From her reflection she could see she had mascara all down her face; from all that exertion while she was dancing, no doubt. She felt in her handbag for a tissue. Her hand came across a crumpled piece of paper. As she drew it out, she realised it was a sheet from today's paper, that Iain had given her. It was the leader page. As she spread it out, she stared at it, trying to work out why. Her tired eyes itched, and then, suddenly, she got it.

> **D**on't mistake it for a moment. **E**very hundred years or so, an event comes along that defines a town, for ever. **A**nd this is ours. **R**eading between the lines, this is not just a party for us. **K**ind of, more the start of a whole new age. **A**ttracting a new profile for the town. **T**oday, Fairlish – tomorrow, the world? **I**t's certainly a chance to put ourselves on the map. **E**ven if we're not all sure we want so much change.

It was her name she spotted first, all those capital letters, beginning with K. Grabbing a pen from out of her bag, she scribbled down the first letter of each sentence.

> **I** say, yes we do. **M**aybe some people will see change as difficult, as new to this town. **I** think we should embrace it with all our hearts. **S**ome people say our little home is all right as it is. **S**od them, say I! **Y**es, Fairlish is changing, but it's still our place in the world, and letting other people in to share it can only be a good thing. **O**ften in this life, people don't act in time, or act at all, to do the right thing. **U**ntil now – and our time is now.

As the plane soared over the dark world she clutched the piece of paper to her tightly.

Although it was stupid o'clock in the morning, the maternity wing of St Thomas's Hospital was buzzing; however, they were definitely the only girls in ball dresses. Katie and the girls ran down the halls searching for the labour wing. A friendly nurse directed them the right way, and Katie burst into the suite, her heart in her throat.

Clara was lying in bed, looking sweaty and wide-eyed. Their mother was sitting calmly right beside her.

'WHAT! WHAT'S GOING ON! ARE YOU ALL RIGHT?' yelled Katie, her fear and exhaustion pouring out of her.

Clara's eyebrows lifted. 'Oh, wow, Katie,' she said in a dreamy voice. 'How did you get here so fast?'

'My goodness,' said their mother, getting up. 'Thanks for coming.'

'THANKS FOR COMING!?' shouted Katie. 'I heard there were death-defying nightmares going on down here.'

Clara thought for a moment. 'Oh yes. Well, I was a bit frightened when it all kicked off, you know.'

'Maybe we called you too soon,' said their mum.

'I'm only having a baby, I'm not dying,' said Clara. 'Aaah.'

'Oh, for God's sake,' said Katie. 'Where is it? Where's your baby?'

'Still inside,' said Clara. 'But I've had the epidural now. It was great. Lovely in fact. Contraction due any second now . . .'

A midwife bundled in. 'Come on with you there,' she said, peering up between Clara's legs.

'That was a lovely epidural,' said Clara, dreamily.

'We had to stop you screaming somehow, love, it was waking the other patients.'

She felt around. 'OK, now, you're going to push really hard.'

Clara shut her eyes. Katie took one hand and her mother took the other.

'Come on, now, just push . . . that's right . . . OK, I can see the head now.'

The other two girls immediately ran down to the other end for a look.

'Oh my God!' said Louise.

'Is it gross?' said Clara.

Katie desperately wanted to head down there too, but Clara was holding her hand so tightly she wouldn't get away without amputation.

'Oh my God, it's coming out!' said Louise. She turned to Olivia. 'I can't *believe* I'm watching Max's baby being born.'

'You're brilliant,' said Olivia.

‘I *know*,’ said Louise.

The door flew open.

‘Am I missing it? I can’t believe you’ve stopped screaming.’

It was Max.

Louise took a step back.

‘Hello Max.’

He looked slim, tanned and very very drawn, and as if he’d just seen a ghost.

‘Louise,’ he said.

‘You’re missing it!’ yelled Clara.

Louise stood aside as the midwife ushered him to where the baby was coming out. It landed in his arms, making something of a slithery sound, covered in red goo. Olivia jumped back, in case it splashed on her outfit. The baby opened its tiny scrunched-up mouth and started to scream.

‘Oh my God,’ Max kept saying. ‘Oh my God.’

‘Would you like to cut the cord?’ the midwife asked him.

‘God, no,’ he said, handing the baby over. ‘I’d faint. Oh God – it’s a little girl.’

‘Just what we need,’ said Olivia, until Louise nudged her.

Katie couldn’t speak at all, she couldn’t stop crying.

‘Oh goodness,’ said Clara, like a big sigh. The midwife took the baby, still bawling, and wiped her down, then handed her to her mother and went back down to the business end to poke around some more.

‘Oh my goodness,’ said Clara again, as they all crowded around. ‘Oh my goodness.’

‘She looks just like you as a baby,’ said their mother, who was absolutely tearful.

‘She looks just like a baby,’ said Louise. ‘A perfect baby.’

Katie was too busy admiring the exquisite little fingers and toes. 'I can't believe . . . there's one more person in this room. How did that just happen?' she asked.

Clara looked at her with an exhausted smile. 'Thanks, sis.'

'You looked like you were doing all right,' said Katie, taking her hand again.

'I mean, thanks for looking after me.'

Katie thought of the small flat again. Well, look, their mother was here, and she would share in it, wouldn't she? It wouldn't be so bad. She needed to get back to real life, away from Brigadoon, with its complications, and . . . she looked at the baby, who looked as exhausted as her mother. She yawned, a tiny little cub yawn, and Katie's heart melted. Well, there would be love.

'That's no problem,' she said, squeezing Clara's shoulder. 'That will never be a problem.'

'Oh, no,' said Clara, unable to take her eyes off her tiny daughter. 'No, I don't mean that. Um, we're going home with Max.'

Max moved up and put his arms around her shoulders. 'Uh, yes,' he said, deliberately not looking at Louise. 'I think it's time to face up to my responsibilities.'

'Well, that sounds romantic,' said Louise. Then she stopped herself. Fortunately Clara hadn't heard her anyway, being completely caught up in every first flicker of her daughter's face. 'Sorry,' Louise said. 'I mean, congratulations.'

Max looked at Louise then. It was a long look. 'I'm sorry,' he said. 'It just . . . life . . . I didn't know what I wanted, and . . .'

Louise moved forward and stood in front of him. 'It's all right,' she said, although by the look on Max's face, he wasn't sure if it was all right at all. 'Honestly,' she continued. 'I don't think we were right. Not really. It couldn't have been.'

Max looked taken aback by this new calm Louise, who was no longer phoning him drunk at three o'clock in the morning to enunciate to ten decimal places exactly how much of a wanker he was.

'Anyway,' she went on, 'I'm moving.'

'You're what?' said Katie, starting.

Louise smiled. 'I . . . well, last night Craig the Vet and I got to talking.'

'I *knew* it!' said Katie.

'And, erm,' Louise was actually blushing. 'I think I'm going to, er, maybe give up my job.'

'You did that ages ago,' said Olivia. 'Trust me.'

'And, maybe go help him out for a bit.'

'Help him out *how*?' asked Katie.

'You know, receptionist, assistant, that kind of thing.'

'Sexual plaything?'

Louise smiled. 'I wouldn't want to talk about any of that in the presence of a baby, thanks.'

Max looked gobsmacked. '*You're* moving to the country?'

Louise nodded.

'I always wanted to move to the country,' said Max.

'Ahem!' said Clara, loudly. 'I've decided on a name.'

Clara had made a huge point of not knowing what to call her baby until she saw its face.

They crowded around.

'Please, not after a fruit,' begged Katie. 'Anything but that.'

Clara shook her head imperiously. 'This baby's name is . . . Glastonbury Romany Watson Evans.'

Max's face dropped, until he could muster a forced smile.

* * *

It was seven a.m. Time for home. Katie said goodbye to everyone, with promises to meet up at Clara and Max's the next day – their mother was staying there to help with feeding (Max, not the baby).

Louise, full of nervous excitement, was going home to pack. Olivia was going to work; she had a big story on her hands.

Katie walked across Waterloo Bridge alone. At that time in the morning, the city was just waking up. It was going to be another beautiful day. The great river was already shivering with early morning sunshine, and she didn't even care that early commuters were staring at her in her dress. To imagine, this was the first ever day in history with Glastonbury – oh God, Katie wondered if she'd settle for Toni – in it. She opened a bottle of Perrier water she'd picked up in the hospital and stared dreamily out onto the water.

She didn't want to go home. To her empty, silent home. Even having Clara still in it would feel a bit better than nothing at all, she thought. She wondered if there was anything in the fridge. All her summer clothes were still in drawers she supposed. A coal barge passed underneath the bridge, and the man on the deck waved to her. She waved back. She was home. It was stupid to think she could choose between two men. This wasn't the kind of thing that happened to her. And what was she going to do? Do a Louise and kick it in and move? It was dumb. The whole thing was dumb. That damn place had cast a spell on her that, in the bright light of the morning, just didn't stack up.

If she took it in little steps, she supposed, it would be all right. First, the clothes. Get changed. Maybe have a long bath. Yes, a bath would definitely be a good plan right about now. And a nap. A long nap, on clean sheets, in a flat with nobody else in it. Then she would go and see her sister, and her niece – wow, she was an auntie. One thing at a time. Being an aunt felt like a terribly old thing to be. And then the day after that, she would go back to work, just as she had done before, and she would pick up another account and work hard and hope to meet a nice stockbroker and everything would be absolutely fine, and eventually time would go on and she would think about Scotland as if it were only a dream, a silly interlude in her life, when all the boys liked her and she had . . . well, it had had its ups and downs, but she had had fun. And she could go up and visit. She'd need to get her car at some point, and of course she'd have to visit Louise. And maybe while she was there she could see the others . . . and remember one evening when anything could have happened. And try never to think about what she could have done.

A car screeched to a halt right behind her, but she ignored it. The traffic had been building up steadily since she'd been walking. There wasn't a rush hour in London any more; it was all the same. She didn't bother turning around. She knew once she turned around, the spell would be broken and she'd have to go home and start the rest of her life.

'Katie,' yelled a voice.

Katie blinked and turned around, gradually.

There, on the other side of the road, was a man doing his best to dodge through the traffic towards her.

'What . . . what are you doing here?' Katie asked.

Mind you, she said this only after she had literally thrown herself from the side of the bridge into his arms, and he'd held her for a long time, and she'd said, over and over again, 'It was always you, and I didn't even know, and then I did, but . . .' then she'd burst into huge racking sobs that went on for ages.

'Shh,' he'd said, stroking her hair at last. He wanted to bury his whole face in it.

'I thought I'd really pissed on my chips, with Iain and everything . . . and then just disappearing . . .'

'No,' said Harry. 'No, it was really just me being a jealous idiot. I couldn't have pissed more on my chips. I realised . . . I'm not grumpy because of my mum, or because it's just the kind of person I am . . . it's because I'm,' he cleared his throat, 'a bit lonely. I drove a girl away once, and bloody hell, if it doesn't seem to be becoming something of a habit.'

Katie clung on to him very hard.

'I sorted it out with Iain, by the way.'

She looked up at him, tears still streaking her face. 'Good.'

'I probably shouldn't tell you this, but I will, because I want you for myself.'

'What?'

'He was chatting up somebody else when I left.'

'Good for him,' said Katie, almost ready to smile at the sweet, weak man she'd got to know. She'd have to keep the paper, she thought.

He nodded quickly. 'Plus, the women are heading out too. Somebody told them there's forty men to every woman in Alaska.'

'Cool,' Katie nodded.

'Katie, look. I've wasted so much time by not saying anything. And being a bit of a prick.'

Katie nodded again. 'You were.'

'I know. Love means, turning into a complete prick. Apparently,' said Harry.

Katie gulped painfully when she heard him mention the L word.

'But I won't stop any longer. Please, please please please come back with me. For ever. Live with me, my house is much nicer than Aunt Senga's. Although you can stay there if you like. I don't want to rush you. Or, you know, we could come to London a lot, I promise. I could even look for a job here if you want, that's how much I want to be with you.'

Katie half-laughed. 'There are NO forests in London.'

'No? Well, I'm sure we could plant one.'

She clung on to him even tighter. 'You know, I think you probably could. But, you know, let's go home first.'

'Where do you mean?'

'Scotland,' she said.

And then he kissed her for the first time, and she realised that actually, it didn't matter in the slightest. Wherever they were, home would always feel like exactly wherever he was.

'So, why . . . why are you here?' she asked eventually, as he led her back across the road to the waiting Land-Rover, which already had six traffic wardens standing around it, looking at their watches for the second they ticked into penalty time.

He looked at her as if this was the stupidest question in the world. 'Well . . .' he said, opening the door to reveal a sleeping dog on the front seat. 'Francis wanted a run.'

Francis opened half an eye. On seeing Katie, he leaped up immediately, delighted to see her.

'I always said my dog liked you,' Harry said, unwilling to take his hand away from hers to get around to the other side of the car.

Francis, after greeting Katie hysterically, then did a most peculiar thing. He jumped down from the front seat, circled around the car and jumped in the back, without prompting.

Harry shook his head in amazement. 'Shall we go and pick some things up for you?'

'Some proper coffee would be good. You must be knackered!' said Katie. 'Did you drive all night?'

'No,' said Harry, 'this car can fly.' He got in the car and took her hand. 'I just didn't want to invite myself to lie down on your bed.'

Katie shook her head, unable to believe how happy she felt. 'In the future, can you just *tell* me stuff you want to do? It'll make everything a lot less complicated.'

Harry looked at her, and grinned wickedly.

'OK, maybe not *everything*.'

Harry pulled out into the busy traffic. 'Which way?'

'Not this way!'

'We're going to be one of those couples that bicker a lot, aren't we?'

'Yes,' said Katie. 'I think so. Then we'll make it up and it'll be lovely.'

'OK,' he said, smiling. 'By the way, much as I am dying to hold you for ever and never ever let you go, I've already had nine speeding tickets in the last seven hours, and I suspect you should probably take your hand away from under my seat belt.'

'All right,' said Katie. 'Can I keep it on your leg?'

'Yes please,' said Harry. 'By the way, is this a good time to tell you I'm actually the love child of the Laird and heir to ninety thousand a year?'

'But you were keeping it quiet so you could find a woman who only loved you for yourself?'

'Yes.'

There was a pause.

'Well, are you?'

'No,' said Harry. 'Iain is though.'

'Oh shut *up*.'

And they turned around, and then the car crossed the bridge into North London, up the road where there were millions, then thousands, then hundreds, then, a long way beyond, just a scattering of cars, the end of the line of a great chain heading north, onwards and upwards for hundreds of miles, until they reached the sea, and the big clean sky.